COLLECTED WORKS OF ALFRED JARRY

Atlas Anti-Classic 9

COLLECTED WORKS OF ALFRED JARRY

EDITED BY ALASTAIR BROTCHIE & PAUL EDWARDS

VOLUME II

Three Early Novels

DAYS AND NIGHTS

EXPLOITS AND OPINIONS OF DOCTOR FAUSTROLL, PATAPHYSICIAN

ABSOLUTE LOVE

TRANSLATIONS BY ALEXIS LYKIARD, SIMON WATSON TAYLOR, & PAUL EDWARDS

Atlas Press, London

Published by Atlas Press,
27 Old Gloucester st., London WC1N 3XX

(third, revised edition)
The translation by Simon Watson Taylor of
Exploits and Opinions of Doctor Faustroll, Pataphysician
originally appeared in *Selected Works of Alfred Jarry*,
published by Methuen & Co. ltd.

Printed by C & C Offset Printing Co. Ltd.
A CIP record for this book is available from
The British Library
ISBN 1 900565 36 6
ISBN-13 978-1-900565-36-3
This book is supported by the French Ministry of Foreign Affairs,
as part of the Burgess programme run by the
Cultural Department of the French Embassy in London.
www.frenchbooknews.com and by the
ARTS COUNCIL OF ENGLAND

Liberté • Égalité • Fraternité
RÉPUBLIQUE FRANÇAISE

ARTS COUNCIL ENGLAND

CONTENTS

Exploits and Opinions of Doctor Faustroll, Pataphysician (1898/9)

BOOK EIGHT: ETHERNITY

ABSOLUTE LOVE (1899)

EDITORS' NOTE

Our edition of Alfred Jarry's *Collected Works* has turned into something of an on-going project, and is changing as we progress. In this second volume we have decided to gather together three of his six (finished) novels, and the next volume will now contain the remaining three. Volume I contains Jarry's two first books (*Black Minutes of Memorial Sand* and *Caesar-Antichrist*) along with a selection from his later essays and journalism. Jarry's *Ubu Plays* have long been available from Methuen.

As noted in the first volume, Jarry's works benefit from annotation, but in these first three volumes we have limited ourselves to notes that directly illuminate the text; they are indicated by a ● in the margin and can be found at the end of each respective volume. More interpretative notes are planned for a future volume of the *Collected Works*, the *Commentary*, and are indicated here by the symbol O. The *Commentary* will also contain illustrative matter and essays related to the texts in the first three volumes; it will only be available for purchase directly from the publisher, with details and ordering information at the back of the present volume. Plans for its publication have yet to be settled, though information will appear on our website (www.atlaspress.co.uk) and will be sent automatically to anyone signing on to the email list to be found there.

We would like to thank the following for their help: Milie Von Bariter (Outrapo), Michel Décaudin, Anne Feillet (Outrapo), Thieri Foulc, Paul Gayot, Terry Hale, Brigitte Loret, Gersan Moguérou, Robert Poulter, Félix Pruvost (Outrapo), Dirk Reimers and Jürgen Schiedeck, and above all, Chris Allen, for his extensive editorial contributions to all volumes of these *Collected Works*.

Alastair Brotchie and Paul Edwards

Days and Nights

Novel of a Deserter

Translated by Alexis Lykiard
Introduced and annotated by Alastair Brotchie

INTRODUCTION

Alfred Jarry had already published three books when *Days and Nights* appeared in 1897, though he was still only 23 years old, and this was his first novel. Like many first novels it has a strong autobiographical content, which here primarily concerns his short and entirely pointless military career. However, this narrative forms only one layer of a highly intricate, not to say arcane work.

Jarry had been conscripted into the army in November 1894. As a single man with no dependents he should have had the privilege of serving his country for three years, followed by further years as a reservist. In fact he contrived to be invalided out after only thirteen months. The novel describes some of the means Sengle (the hero, who is certainly Jarry himself) employed to achieve this (book 3, chapters II and III, for example). We can be thankful Jarry succeeded in escaping the army, despite the permanent harm done to his health, for the two years following his release were highly creative.

Before being conscripted into the army Jarry was already a prominent figure in Parisian literary circles, more notorious than celebrated, perhaps. Three years spent blacking whiting and whiting blacking (which suggests another meaning of the book's title) were unlikely to further his career. By the end of 1897 he had written the majority of his important works: *Days and Nights*, most of *Faustroll*, numerous shorter texts and — most important of all — he had unleashed Ubu on stage before a world that recognised itself in him all too clearly. The resulting scandal, and the biggest theatrical riot since *Hernani*, made Jarry famous.

Jarry advertised *Days and Nights* in his magazine *L'Ymagier* as exposing "the atrocious crimes of military medicine," and the scenes of incompetence he describes in the novel are undoubtedly based on incidents he had witnessed. The case of Max Lebaudy, given the name of Philippe here (4, IX & XI), caused quite a stir at the time because of the social position of his family. Jarry was indeed in the next bed, in the hospital of Val-de-Grâce. Nearly all the characters in the novel are based on actual people, most of whom are identified in the notes. The most important in Jarry's real life were Léon-Paul Fargue (Valens) and Maurice Dide (Nosocome).

It was Maurice Dide, a fellow conscript and hospital intern, who showed Jarry the various methods he used to deceive the military doctors. They remained friends in Paris after their release and the hashish scene in bk. 4, ch. IV is a direct transcription of a social gathering *chez* Dide. He later became an authority on various mental illnesses and the author of several books in that field, and died in 1944 while being deported to Buchenwald.

The identification of Valens with the poet Léon-Paul Fargue is more problematical. Jarry had met Fargue in 1892 at the Lycée Henri IV, and they had had some sort of homosexual affair, which may or may not have been physically consummated. Jarry's obscure evocation of it, *Haldernablou*, can be found in the previous volume of these *Collected Works*. Valens shares many of Fargue's characteristics, and it is obviously his ex-lover whom Jarry describes in bk. 2, ch. I:

> *Before Valens, he had had several friendships which came to nothing; he had put up with these second-bests, he later realised, because they looked vaguely like Valens... One such friendship lasted two years, until Sengle perceived that his companion had the build of a stable-boy and splayed feet, and no literary ability apart from his affectation of Sengle's own...*

Before Jarry's army service Fargue and he had separated on very bad terms; they never spoke to each other again. Jarry was famously unforgiving in arguments and it is surprising therefore that Valens, the "ideal", should bear such a strong resemblance to Fargue. Jarry had a few later attachments, but none as intense as this first, and it would seem that certain aspects of later "friends" are also embodied in Valens.

Apart from his long stays in the military hospital, arranged by various ruses suggested by Dide, Jarry survived the army by strictly, and literally, obeying the rules to the point of absurdity. One of his officers, Gaston Roig, his immediate superior, reported this exchange with the regimental sergeant-major at Jarry's induction:

> *"Name?"*
> *"My name is Alfred Jarry, Monsieur, originally from Laval, now a man of letters in Paris."*
> *"Fine, my friend. But from now on you must call me* 'mon capitaine' *not 'Monsieur'."*
> *"Very well, Monsieur, henceforth I will call you* 'mon capitaine'*."*

He was a ludicrous figure on the parade-ground, too short to hold his rifle properly or to march in step, with a uniform and boots which were far too large. He used his stature, and the risible literary pretensions of his sergeant and officers, to escape drill whenever possible.

Consequently he was invalided out for chronic biliary lithiasis on 14 December 1895, though with an excellent record. Both the army and medical practitioners remained favourite satirical targets throughout his writing career.

This inglorious military interlude, and its accurate description in the novel, hardly seem to justify the novel's sub-title since neither Jarry nor Sengle actually desert. Desertion is indeed the connecting thread in *Days and Nights*, but in a wider sense. Two other types are meant, both of which with their reflection in Jarry's life — his desertion of homosexuality, at least in its physical aspects; and his desertion of reality itself, for "artificial paradises".

Arnaud (*Alfred Jarry, d'*Ubu roi *au docteur Faustroll*) described *Days and Nights* as "*L'histoire des amours singulières de Sengle et de son frère, son Double, Valens*" which admirably sums up one of the novel's major themes. Sengle "deserts" love by pursuing it to a bizarre contradiction where he discovers not the envisaged "double" but (for Sengle = "single") himself. However, even this is not extreme enough: in order for his entirely narcissistic and egoistic love to exist it needs a witness, even if that witness is of doubtful reality and so idealised as only to be, yet again, his own self. The chapter which describes this strange erotic doctrine, "Adelphism and Nostalgia" (2, I), associates it with time and the past. Love is here a sort of intense nostalgia, rather in the manner of Proust, and the past becomes one of the methods Sengle employs for that other desertion — from external reality.

That the book's title (and sub-title) is not meant literally is made explicit in bk. 4, ch. II:

And he believed above all that there are only hallucinations, or perceptions, and that there are neither nights nor days (despite this book's title, which is why it has been chosen) …

This is underlined from the novel's beginning. The first three chapters have titles, either day or night, which are the opposite of when they occur. Day and night also stand in for various apparent contradictions which Sengle either ignores, reverses or resolves: dream/reality, perception/hallucination, present/past, memory/anticipation. These opposites are further reflections of the theme of the "Double", and are not only described by Jarry in the more theoretical chapters (e.g. 4, I & II), but are actually embodied in the style of writing in the more poetic ones. Some of these are highly dense pieces of writing, more prose poetry than narrative — not light reading...

From the very outset Sengle is at odds with the world, believing himself "above the herd," which is several times contemptuously dismissed. The army is, of course, a threat to his "superiority" for the aim of its discipline is the deliberate reduction of its conscripts to will-less imbeciles (as in bk.1, ch. IX):

There are two such instincts of self-preservation, the noble and the ignoble. The noble instinct is the instinct to preserve one's self and maintain one's individuality impervious to outside forces.

How is Sengle to escape, to desert from this existence, which is in fact a sort of illusion created by mass auto-hypnosis (1, IX, last paragraph)? Actual desertion is thwarted by circumstances, and so it is (apparent) reality itself that must be evaded. Sengle's dreams become more real than the nightmare of army life, which is described like a bad dream, or as if by someone in a trance, in a jerky, telegraphic style. Descriptions of army routine are suddenly, without any warning to the reader, interrupted by memories of his childhood, of Valens. Memories of the past are set down more precisely than perceptions of the present, the past is more real than the present (e.g. 1, VI & VIII). Valens, moreover, is what for Sengle "distinguished day from night" (1, I), yet they are separated, and so day and night merge together.

The days are filled with stupidity, the nights an illumination which Sengle soon seeks in drug-induced states and eventual madness. For Sengle only a deliberate confusion of these states can make his present bearable. A central chapter (1, III), in which the legend of the "flying heads" is recounted, indicates the dangers of his project — the link between the real world and Sengle has become tenuous and may easily break. The last line of the book implies it has.

Sengle's relationship with reality is ambiguous; references to the "external" recur throughout the novel, but especially in bk. 4, ch. II, "Pataphysics". He is able to influence events directly, he can control the fall of dice, and later: "The world was simply a huge ship, with Sengle at the helm;" yet the world is also a great windmill whose sails he can move, a notion that is "a bit quixotic". Sengle's omnipotence, therefore, is perhaps only an illusion or a hallucination. This contradiction has its pataphysical reconciliation in Jarry's misattributed reference (from Taine not Leibniz): "Perception is a hallucination which is true". Sengle can, to some extent, control his hallucinations, his dreams. It is a dream which proves him in charge of the external, by waking him at the hour he had desired (4, X, the final line). The two authors cited by Jarry in the novel are relevant to this theme. De Quincey's "Consul Romanus" is a method of calling up a specific hallucination by clapping hands; and Hervey de Saint-Denys, translator of the book containing the "flying heads", also wrote a work on the directing of dreams.

From the first, contrary chapter title, reality is out of joint, or rather it is shown to be relative to Sengle's consciousness. Reversals of meaning and context abound and the novel is cut up, again without warning, with dreams (2,VI), nightmares (4, I), or with dream-like digressions of logic (4, III), and parables (5, II), whilst bk. 3, ch. IV even describes a collective hallucination. Certain other chapters are evocations or direct transcripts of drug states (caffeine, 3, III; hashish, 5, IV) and some include self-parodies of Jarry's own style. The longest of these, "Amber" in 3, V, includes one of Jarry's favourite words, "obeliscolychny", which allows one to think that this piece is a parody of his own earlier writings — while *Days and Nights* is not easy, its style is far simpler than the baroque symbolism of *Black Minutes*.

Arnaud, however, suggests another purpose for the apparently arbitrary inclusion of these texts, that Jarry may have been discarding past works written in collaboration with the now-despised Fargue. In another narrative which suddenly intrudes into the novel the past again assists Sengle in his desertion. The story of his childhood pilgrimage to St. Anne (4, IV) seems an interruption, until St. Anne, as nostalgia concretised, is revealed as his intercessor with the external.

These themes of the Double, Past and Present, Reality and Dream are intertwined in a remarkable interior "plot" of incredible complexity, only the outlines of which may be sketched out here. These preoccupations had an authentic basis in Jarry's everyday life, and describe a sort of occult autobiography.

Jarry's own desertion of reality began around the same time he was writing *Days and Nights*. *Ubu Roi* had made him famous, and the lead actor's characterisation of Ubu had been based on certain of Jarry's own eccentricities and mannerisms, particularly his speech. Jarry gradually assumed the role of Ubu in real life and was addressed as such even by his closest friends (at least in public), whilst himself employing the royal "we" of Ubu-speak.

His initial indulgence in hashish and opium, following the literary tradition of de Quincey, Nerval and Baudelaire, soon gave way to a prodigious consumption of alcohol, absinthe in particular. Rachilde described his daily routine:

Jarry began the day by consuming two litres of white wine, then three absinthes between ten o'clock and midday, at lunch he washed down his fish, or his steak, with red or white wine alternating with further absinthes. In the afternoon, a few cups of coffee laced with brandy or other spirits whose names I've forgotten, then, with dinner — after, of course, more aperitifs — he would still be able to take at least two bottles of any vintage, good or bad. Now I never saw him really drunk...

In this state of permanent inebriation Jarry's mental processes worked at full speed. Ubu held forth with a torrent of preposterous anecdotes and inventions. Many of his friends found his bizarre unstoppable eloquence extremely disquieting, yet he was one of the sights of literary Paris, never lacking an audience. Later, poverty meant that food was usually omitted from his daily intake, and later still ether had to be occasionally substituted for absinthe. He had deserted everyday life in any usual meaning of the phrase, and quite soon it deserted him. He died in October 1907, aged 34.

Days and Nights is a novel that bridges the gap between the literature of the 1890s and that of the modern movement. One of the last significant works to employ the language of the Symbolists, it also contains passages which look forward to many of the devices of "modern literature": interior monologues, fusions and descriptions of subjective and interior states — dream, hallucination, recollection — *in their own terms.* (Joyce was certainly familiar with Jarry's work, and the Surrealists' debt to him is immense and acknowledged.) A novel forever on the verge of formal chaos, it is held together by the prodigious personality of its youthful author, and demonstrates once again why Jarry is so vital a source for so much of the challenging writing of this century.

Atlas Press would like to thank Alexis Lykiard for his excellent rendering of a novel so spectacularly difficult to translate; also Paul Gayot of the *Cymbalum Pataphysicum* for shedding light on various obscurities; and, from the same organisation, both Thieri Foulc, for his detailed inspection of the finished translation, and Stanley Chapman, for his verse translations.

DAYS AND NIGHTS

NOVEL OF A DESERTER

BOOK ONE

ON THE TRAIN

"In France as in Prussia the soldier is no more than a man enslaved; the first chance of freedom and he is a fugitive, whenever the opportunity arises."

The Good Serviceman, by M. de Boussanelle, corporal in the King's forces, Paris, 1770.

I

FIRST DAY

"Do shut up, you nasty carrot-top," said Ilane, shaking her fist at the bird in its invisible cage. "Koo!" came the top-string cello response, swelling in intensity with the noise of the girl's convulsions in the big bed flush with the floor, white right up to the wall and door and beneath the great oak cupboard whose door-leaf baritoned each time she struck it. The other couple, Margot and Valens, shifted, somewhat startled, amused, and one of Ilane's outflung claws scuffed Margot, marking Valens across the stomach. Sengle, finding comical even these ups-and-downs of monotonous toil, scarcely stirred while breathing soundlessly, glad to be out of reach, his arms laterally outspread and approximating the motion of oars, in the same way as the male tarantula is said most often to avoid that stiff poisoned limb.

There were many childish things in the room. A tiny blue lamp was moving around, fastened to the shell of a tortoise that was scratching and scraping about. There was an alarm-clock in the form of a skull scumbled with calcium phosphide, whose mandible muttered and cracked, and which was never allowed to wake anyone, its action requiring too ugly a grimace. There was also a slate on which Ilane, for a bet which Sengle said was more childish than all the others, inscribed a number from time to time, wiping off its predecessor. And it was midnight only when slate and clock agreed.

The room, those in the room and their actions were the same at other hours of the night, Sengle and Valens unresponsive to the girls, since they could talk more intelligently to one another, but not talking to one another because by being together they understood each other well enough. Day was delivered via the vans of market-gardeners, like the rolling rush of sea curled in a cowrie shell; and after a discussion between the foursome to ascertain whether 17 or 18 was written on his slate, with Sengle proposing to efface it and begin all over again, the two couples set out on two tandems, since in the light of what follows Sengle needed his tiredness to be pronounced, and his brother accompanied him everywhere because this dear head before him and not a yellower or whiter star was what distinguished day from night, so that he should not be too unhappy.

II
FIRST NIGHT

The Champs-Élysées, fog, some cyclists, like them a few minutes before. Sengle, correctly clad, differs from the expectant crowd outside the Palais de l'Industrie in that his hat does not sport the triangular card illuminated with a number, writ large. Street-vendors are selling this souvenir and others even costlier for framing, protesting to those who refuse them that a number is indispensable so that when in there, already part of the herd, one's clothes will not be stolen.

Still none too disciplined one waits on the benches, more like schoolboys in this huge class, with the clowning of soldier prefects.

Then naked in another hall, anthropometry commences; always soldiers, under their blue guillotine-blade, and striped-uniformed pedlars. One is about to be measured on the scale of this gibbet called a weighing-machine; let's hope Sengle is not heavy enough. But meanwhile there is the warm odour of shorn sheep; it is quite immaterial whether one mounts the stairs and surfaces from amid the rabble like a young god, the visual and tactile atoms of the other bodies are too close really. Why is this gibbet not haloed with the rainy circlet of a shower! They are there crucifying a small, very ugly man, and one of the braided uniforms inches thumbs into his gingery groin. Non-combatant services, someone announces. Caught up in single file, Sengle has climbed the stairs, has no time to recognise himself. A tap at his muscles, fit for military service, the voice and pressure simultaneous, on towards his clothes.

"That'll all have to come off," says one soldier, for his hair is long.

III
ANOTHER DAY

Sengle the free is condemned to death and he knows the date. And here drifting along is his gondola-shaped white-iron bed. Sengle like the oriental king has his body cinched up to the waist-line in black marble, which will swathe him higher still, and he recollects a stroll he took in the woods with his brother, feeling as if he had taken hashish. His body walked under the trees, material and well-articulated; and he knew not what fluid plasm floated above, like a cloud made of ice, and which must have been his astral body; and something more tenuous was moving heavenward three hundred metres higher up — his soul perhaps — and a visible thread linked the two kites.

"Brother, do not touch me," he told Valens, "or the thread will tangle in the trees, like running with a kite between telegraph poles; and if that happened I've a feeling I would die."

Once he had read in a Chinese book this ethnology of a people foreign to China, whose heads could fly up to the trees to seize their prey, connected to their bodies by an unravelling red thread, and were then able to return and fit back on to their bleeding necklaces. But a certain wind must not blow, for should the thread break, the head would fly away over the sea.

Like his brother Valens, whom he knows will be far away for ten months, Sengle the free distances himself from the soldier and relives his own past as Valens' present, as impressions pleasing to himself and hence the only ones true to his spirit. And suddenly the memory of that other inspection-room through which he had passed previously floats back towards the white gondola-shaped bed.

In a vast red and grey studio below the oasis of a great lamp. Severus Altmensch, the Jewish eunuch; their host, the painter Raphael Roissoy; Freiherr Suszflasche, the famous German aesthete; the publicist Bondroit; a young girl, a professional model, known as Huppe; and Sengle himself.

Huppe had been explaining to Sengle that she would enjoy viewing and having his body as she had done with Raphael Roissoy's and, prior to him, Bondroit's, but she held no hope of such an outcome with the German aesthete. Sengle answered that it would be more amusing to see, even if it were impossible for Huppe to make use of it, the body of the Jewish eunuch Severus Altmensch, for in fact no one knew whether he lacked so much as to be a eunuch or merely enough to prove him a Jew. So they dreamed up a ruse. The game proposed, quite natural in an artist's studio, was to draw lots to decide who should pose nude on the model's dais; and without cheating, although Sengle might have predicted the result, the lot fell upon Severus Altmensch. Who refused to comply. Sengle held him by the shoulders — with his fingertips — and Huppe stripped him...

Severus Altmensch was naked, but for his feet, which seemed more deformed for being only guessed at, encased in their built-up boots. Hollow-chested, belly jutting as the tip of a tetrahedron, arms like two laths, legs of a faun — a faun in an etching, castrated out of decency — and every limb protruding as if disjointed. A vicuña's or llama's curly astrakhan luxuriated everywhere, a wool evoking suint; and with his claw-sharp nails he combed his enormous belly's triangular pubis towards his chest, point upward.

Huppe willingly did her best to oblige him; Severus uttered little cries, simpering and biting at her breast. Her efforts came to nothing since he was a masochist, a fetishist and a clerk of court, and he writhed on the carpet while sucking the beak of a stuffed peacock.

By the luck of the draw, Freiherr Suszflasche then undressed and cut almost as ignoble a dash: though twenty-four years old, as stunted as a twelve-year-old, as Schopenhauer demanded of his peers. Belly and bones alone were alive.

Raphael Roissoy, handsome and sulky of face, with the effeminate body of Da Vinci's St. John the Baptist.

Bondroit passed muster. Sengle was last, and they agreed that his body was the most chaste and best-proportioned, despite the overly studied look of his burgeoning moustache.

And since there were only six naked bodies, there was no offence against public decency. Suddenly the doorbell rang — and Bondroit, stark naked, went and opened the door — to Moncrif, whose gingery ugliness almost matched that of the shrivelled Severus Altmensch. The newcomer, taken aback and fearing a paradoxical rape, sat down still caparisoned in several Inverness capes. And everyone regarded him with profound horror, for he was the seventh and, although clothed, constituted the OFFENCE.

And the six disappeared in the smoke of the great lamp, whose glass had cracked. And scandalised by the present Seventh, they rushed to their clothes, barefoot over the cracks.

IV
CANDLE-SNUFFER

Sengle, who would have preferred to have been rejected before anyone cut his hair, was anxiously wondering whether or not he would be, before plunging into that sordid livery. He had only once seen a soldier in close proximity: by chance, in a third-class carriage near Brest, repatriated, naked under his greatcoat and breeches. Dirty skin was visible through the holes in his pockets. He smelt of shit, fever, sperm, boot-polish and rifle grease. The clothes thrown at Sengle had evidently wiped down the bodies of several Tonkinese. Sengle understood the usefulness to the regiment of long johns, to counteract the contact of these linings. Physically disinfected, all well and good, but the stench lingered in the mind. Aggravating detail: the boots. He searched for whatever was the smallest size. And was swallowed up into twenty-three-centimetre leather boxes that left room for roll, pitch and toss, blistering the heel with their perpetual flux and forcing the instep into unwonted gymnastics so as to keep them on, with the hypocrisy of padding, black and viscous.

Symmetrically, a similar slime kept the képi's leather supple. Buttons with badges fit for some arsonist lackey wafted verdigris to his nostrils. And the jacket sleeves were long — regimental sizes envisaging a differentiation less distinct, with respect to the shorter arms, than that between anthropoids whose feet were hands but whose hands were also feet, comparable to the jellyfish which has but one hole for anus and mouth.

The corporal felt more at ease for not addressing him as Monsieur.

The theory studied in the dormitories — with the new recruits dressed and lined up "in military posture" around the NCO, mostly peasants, proudly inspecting their martial costumes — pleased Sengle, for he thereby learned what the stripes denoted and how to distinguish rank. As he had never been bothered with these tin gongs and the like, owing to laziness and instinctive repugnance, this science was tirelessly forced down his throat and dinned into him.

"There's no more Sir here. You call me Corporal and not Corp. Nor Corporal Sir, neither; you only call officers Sir..."

V
ITINERARY

After a veteran had made Sengle's bed, whose sheets seemed to him terribly grimy under their grey and brown prison blankets, the colour of shrews and field-mice, he fell asleep amid the noise and the draught from the two big doors.

He who was scared of mirrors saw himself, through these openings, reflected in other soldiers.

The dark wood partition between the bunks towered above him, like stable mangers or the *portières* of third-class carriages. Dimly-glimpsed hands were shaking out of windows stinking bits of equipment whose names he did not know. The train rolled onward to places like Amiens and Lille...

The houses turn redder as the train pushes further north: smoking in their terra cotta, their mouths sport the letters: BAR. The road is powdered and pumiced with the ashes of ancient faded "redcoats". Beneath the carriages' ironwork an abominable cobbled surface. The northern region of today has this much in common with ancient Ecbatana: the towns, like primordial man, are still formed of earth baked red by the sun.

The train rolled onward to places like Amiens and Lille; it passed through Halluin and Menin.

Then come fields of sodden rye, and trees that are only clearly discernible at sunset, because at that hour they are exactly what Memling made them, just huge curled feathers. After this, all is grey and no horizon is visible at all. An embankment runs parallel to the train, under the telegraph wires. And matching its parallelism to these surveyor's lines, the sea clashes and foams its three or four fathoms of water. Beyond, there is nothing but sandy-coloured sky. We have left behind places like Bruges where trains halt inside cathedrals, and where the houses in the narrow streets are painted in hues of dying monkey or thigh of nymph on heat; where in the beer-drinking square a little old woman sells candlesticks of unbaked clay. Night has risen fully from the sea, and the waves light up the shoreline with great sawblades of emerald-green phosphorus. The train runs alongside beaches where the only trees are the poles set up by Sunday archers...

Sengle passed through Halluin and Menin and only woke at the first Belgian soldier.

It was the quartermaster tugging at his feet: "Up you get! The sarge wants you!"

Barely awake, he went downstairs in his blood-red trousers and his page-boy's jacket with the sharp-edged buttons. The sergeant-major wished to pick his literary brain in order to solve a newspaper logogriph, which he could not understand anyway.

After various other staircases, he emerged into the courtyard, an immense chamber-pot formed by the four military buildings, and illumined diffusely by the snow, made sulphurous at one corner by the yellow glare from the guardroom window, and its smoking chimney.

A very beautiful song with indistinct words ascended from a gleaming air-vent, a mouth letting out the hallelujah of a whole Breton crowd on pilgrimage, or an interpretation of the sounds Samuel Taylor Coleridge heard amid the celestial spirits upon the slimy sea:

... Sweet sounds rose slowly through their mouths,
And from their bodies pass'd.

Around, around, flew each sweet sound,
Then darted to the Sun;
Slowly the sounds came back again,
Now mix'd, now one by one.

Sometimes a-dropping from the sky
I heard the skylark sing;
Sometimes all little birds that are,
How they seem'd to fill the sea and air
With their sweet jargoning!

And now 'twas like all instruments,
Now like a lonely flute;
And now it is an angel's song,
That makes the heavens be mute.

And Sengle remained a long time listening to the cook filtering the morning coffee through an obscene song.

In the moonlight the dial wrote with a silent grimace: four o'clock.

Sengle climbed back towards his unit's quarters, or to some approximation among the multitude of identical doors and landings, and in several such rooms, occupying the place he had left, he saw bodies just like his own, scarcely even in relief upon the flatness of the beds. Just when he had found his actual bed, a loud sound came reverberating along the raised equipment-rack as an old bandsman-drummer skidded barefoot the length of the racks, shunted heavily into his stacked-up kit, and promptly deluged the sleepers with piles of packs and kit-bags.

A measure of silence was restored and, in anticipation of the terrible bugle-call, the day began to flatten its frosted snout against the window-panes.

VI
PRESENTATIONS

Whistle blast. Last halt. A whole load of people has arrived, doubtless the general's shown up with them, all soldiers military, hauling along with them a gilded contraption, the standard, proudly erect from a lieutenant's belly (the despatch-holster, the Aristophanic herald would say). And then there's a whole pile of stones and it's more comfortable not to dismount from the machine and to remain seated, at a halt, left foot on a cobble. The slightest movement of the right foot is all it takes to set off again. All the same, thinks Sengle, it would be more militarily correct to alight and simply lean an elbow against the bicycle, for here is the general opposite us presenting his sabre, the drummers beating the salute, all those poor devils still with packs on their backs and presenting arms...

Another whistle blast. By the right, quick march.

Sengle drowsy and deafened pedals along monotonously behind the band, like a squirrel in a rotating cage turning a bird-organ, ahead of the music dogging his tracks, wiping mud from the drummers' bums in front.

That evening, the sergeant:

"You've got a cheek, my lad, failing to salute the flag."

"The flag?" said Sengle. "I didn't do it out of bravado. Saluting the flag would never have entered my mind. Besides, I was too busy watching the others saluting."

"The general included. Let's hope he doesn't chuck you inside for a month."

Next day, defaulters' parade:

"Fifteen days' detention privates Mathurin, Kerlevezou and Gautier. Remaining inside barracks, at windows, without removing headgear during trooping of the colour on the parade-ground."

That was all.

VII
PRESENTATIONS CONTINUED

Since the sergeant-major had summoned him on the first evening, Sengle had been invited by his officers to come and play the decadent poet at the Colonel's Wife's *soirée*. He had put his foot in it by not showing up, anyhow, and Lieutenant Vensuet, who was in charge of a literary course for quartermasters, read them some of Sengle's work.

And after summoning Sengle to his quarters, the lieutenant read him his own verse (he had produced some), with this bizarre epigraph:

> "The miller of nuptials had lost his grandson. He climbs the ladder. He knocks a nail into the door. Says to the spider: 'As for you, Nail-in-the-Cross, spin your wall'."

PASTORAL

On fields of hope the sky's calm survey scans
The trellis-patterned lawns its smile admires.
A lovesick sea-green elm's fringed foliage fans
The parched horizon's sun whose brow perspires.

The clustered wind swirls ribbons from a hat,
Laughing, red-cheeked; the spider — widowed maid —
Corkscrews down napes of necks its swagged webs that
Cloak Harlequin on threshold's tabbed parade.

A fiddler's lightning shriek splits wide the grange
Where — trailing through the sawdust puppets breathe
Then jerk to life — these dancing heels make strange
Designs. The craft's bow braves rough seas that seethe.

Below the Sunday bells, whose jangling jaws
Wring wrought-gold tones from gemmed caparisons,
Green crystal mandolins of troubadours
Lick twin-horned cries from mumbled orisons.

The crimson sun rolls dry across the moor
As, two by two, pairs shelter from the dark;
Their clattering clogs approach the rain-safe door.
Will humming-birds soon glisten in the ark?

All's scourged by sleet. The arrowed palms of poles
Clap-splash and bubble-burst the forest's seat.
Black thunder bolts and clangs steel's rugged holes
In rip-torn shell-shot damask's stiff-necked pleat.

My double pupils overlap, then close;
Upon my cross's wall leaves made their beds.
Eternity's sharp talons plunge, grip, pose,
Twist, screw tiaras on king's croziered heads.

When russet dawn turned rose-gold day, ghosts died
And clumsy feet crushed flat the hedgerow rose.
Time's plectrum's swing — now left, now right — spreads wide
Like soaring flights of clouds a planter sows.

From seaweed's grotto cricket-springs arise —
(A cobalt volute swirls from ingled chants) —
Each palpitating drop in flute-stops dies.
The streamlet's drumbeat wake led furrows' dance.

From carnal expectation turned to ice
Shrugging off vertebrae in tombs' cold nights
From him who shames our cupola of rights

In full gold sunshine shall the grey teal stun
Ivoried thrusts of flat-browed bulls' paired horn.

"Officer's verse," said Sengle respectfully, like a brothel-girl professionally flattering some poor private.

Vensuet, who was pretty intelligent, blushed.

He declared that his two stripes were only a means of making a living, that he was an anarchist, even in art, and he tried to show how well informed he was.

"I keep in touch with all the youthful experiments. I'm not content just reading our great *contemporary* poets, Victor Hugo and Alfred de Musset. I know Maupassant, Zola and Loti by heart; I admire the *unfathomable abyss* of *The Book of Pity and of Death*. I've been to see a production of *Trimardot*. It captures the peasants' way of life so faithfully! The farmer-type, everyone dying on him, and all he thinks of is his cattle. The lyricism of Trimardot's speeches does *jar* a little, compared to this accurate study, but they're so forceful and the poetry's so wonderful! Did you see *Trimardot*?"

"Somewhere else," Sengle said, "I experienced ecstasies just like yours. At the Music-Hall in the Boulevard Jovial, where for me the mime artists expressed the most realistic passions, without exaggeration, exactly as they work in all of *us*.

"It was an Italian pantomime, which started off like every Italian pantomime, until Pierrot and Cassandra killed Harlequin, and the Doctor, after running on tiptoe thrice round the corpse, stopped in his tracks at the thought of cash, and dragged it off for dissection in his laboratory.

"When Pierrot picked up the dead man and stuck him to the wall by spitting behind the corpse's head, since *rigor mortis* had not yet set in; then when he turned away from the body, wanting to load it on to his back, and it slipped off three times buckling at the knees, which invariably happens when one attempts to carry off one's murder, and is left grasping air; and it sat bolt upright again, mockingly, when Pierrot went and peered closely at it; and since it had now stiffened, the only possible means of transportation was to hold it by the hips and bump it along to the laboratory door, where Columbine, having lifted the curtain, swooned away and had to be carted off in the same jerky manner; then it was evident that the Mime's author knew all about life and death, and *we* recognised every scene we had lived through, and passions orientated like our own... The King uses We.

"But where the impression was frighteningly lifelike, with *nature* itself revealed before us, was right here, and it was especially fine.

"Pierrot sat down to calculate on a piece of paper the dead man's estate and the dead man, or rather Death, appeared behind the chair naked to the bones (the mime was invisible in his red tights which were indistinguishable from the wine-red back-cloth and had bones artfully painted on to them; when green spotlights played across the bones, the flesh dissolved into blackness, as when one looks at one's arm in two mirrors held inexactly at forty-five degrees and two images are imperfectly superimposed, leaving a slight radius between their fluid forms) and extinguished the candle resembling his finger which lit Pierrot's left side, and then the right-hand candle when the left had been relit. He walked in time to a phrase from the trombones. And when Pierrot turned round and saw his own dread Remorse, Cassandra ran to pick him up from the floor where he had fainted clean away, and proved to him that there was no one there. Then they re-opened the laboratory cupboard inside which Harlequin was becoming, ever more calmly, an as yet undissected *corpse*. And after this verification of their senses, the dead man returned dressed in his tracery of bones; this was repeated four times, with inextinguishable fear on the two old crones' faces as they vainly checked, to the reprise of a jig, the flesh of that grinning corpse clad in its carnival mask and multicoloured lozenges.

"And at the end the skeleton mingled with everyone in the grand ballet finale. Isn't that the best of *realism*, and the subtlest observation of our everyday lives?"

"Clearly," said Vensuet, so as to seem to understand, "it's the *profound conception* of Holbein and the Dance of Death, *Memento, homo...*"

Sengle, after a military about-turn, accentuated the first two steps of his retreat, distressed that anyone should know — like an old woman — about art history, Latin tags and generalisations.

VIII

FOLLOWING A TRAJECTORY

In the morning they had orders to remove the fatigues which covered their red breeches and to polish the buttons on their no. 3 greatcoats, worn tucked in, and whose left flap held the bayonet. They fastened to their straps two cartridge-belts and a pouch, and the sergeants, after pairing them off to draw pull-throughs down the Lebel barrels, checked the double-spiralled lustre. Then a cry of: "Down!" The adjutant lined them up in a row, bayonets fixed, facing the wall, and "at will" they lined up the small black and white targets in their sights. Corporals with rifle-rests were reciting to each man, one by one, the theory of corrections to the aim. A bayonet pinned a white card to the wall and the gunlayer was in charge of shifting a mobile bull's-eye. From a window, a corporal raised and lowered a target which the men aimed at in turn, their weapons loaded with blanks, and with the weaving-loom noise of their repeating action. The whole row, shivering and slithering on the icy surface, kept an eye on the time. Gloves were forbidden. Now and then somebody would come down the last couple of steps from the sleeping-quarters, set foot in the courtyard, and stagger towards the bayonets.

The order was given: fall in, dress by the right, eyes front. They awaited the orderlies and all those who, to avoid target practice, were maintaining no one had informed them of the setting-off time. Roll-call again, then by the right, quick march. The gunlayers had left two hours earlier. Preceded by the bugle, that instrument of regulation. Hampered by rifles slung from their shoulders, two puny, out-of-breath fellows hurried along in the rear, struggling with the enormous weight of the ammunition case.

The iron grille of the barracks, the tree-lined avenue, the town, the relief of walking without packs, the clogging mud where cattle flounder, after the barracks' ice. Then the near-vertical slope where the blunt cobbles end. To left and right, leading towards convents and boarding-houses, alleys with ancient names, and these names lost amid the trees. Breathing becomes wheezy and Sengle involuntarily speeds up to get it over with. Flat terrain where gasping persists until permission is given to "march at ease." Sengle can hold his rifle in less regulation manner: his arms are not long enough to reach the butt-swivel and grip the middle of the sling. And he can step out of line as far as the footpath to avoid the macadam which jolts his frozen feet and the boots he imagines almost as puncturable as a rubber tyre.

The embankments with russet hedges and blue moss, where he used to pursue crickets with a knife for blocking up their holes behind them, when he was free. The river over which a free skater glides. Beyond the poplars, an ancient cross for which he had long searched, as if in dream, knowing it to be there before he discovered it, where instead of Christ objects associated with his Passion are crucified, and a wooden pyx resembling an egg-cup is concealed close to the upright like nocturnal birds, looking out for prey. The hammerless rifle one carries under one's arm, as soldiers do only after a uniform is dead, and which unerringly hits its mark, because aimed in freedom. That sound of wash-houses along the riverside, the drum school, "teetum, titum," behind the hedges as one is pissing. The bridge and the symmetrical rails heading for Paris, and the sea.

The descent on to the rocks that are a road on which a bicycle's forks would shudder, for fear of a cart forming an obstruction further down, and the route like a race-track leading to villages and riverbanks. The farm with an extraordinary weather-vane, a pale athwart a pierced heart and the Chinese dragon pursuing its tail. The squamous pond full of duckweed, wherein gurgle bubbles of fringed water-beetles and big pitch-coloured hydrophili.

A whistle blast, signifying: shoulder arms, quick march. Present — arms. The salute for a returning company.

The dew-laden valley and running stream, with jagged white sheets of ice and a glimmer of sun on its banks. The gamekeepered copses on the hillsides where Sengle would go ferreting, where he chased with a switch a long undulant russet snake that escaped by swimming away. The brook's ditch is huge and cold, the military raiment paralysing. He goes looking for a narrow section to leap across. What with these rags, no worry about getting dirty. He has swollen hands, melting calves, leaden feet, head peeling under his képi, back hunched in recollection or anticipation of pack. The rifle laid to rest on the ground is muddy up to the trigger-guard, rain trickles into the barrel, which around its muzzle has syphilitic patches of rust. There'll be another weapons inspection, his boot-boy will be busy.

A jump from the slope into grass and boggy ooze, piss against the hedgerow. Then half a packet of cartridges each and line up in single file to await your turn. Strictly forbidden to take aim, on penalty of prison; there is no need for practice, the line of sight has been reviewed enough previously. At least there is no fear of accident, the cattle think. What's more, one must progress to the stage of firing from an upright position, ordering arms and then readopting the prone stance of marksman facing the target. There is a sergeant close by each man to keep him busy with advice and supposedly to correct his aim; above all, to insist upon a regulation posture, probably grabbing him should he not be properly aligned with the target. And no officer passes in front of the rifles, it is lowly privates who are sent to check for ricochets and bullet-holes. The officers have nothing to fear, however, for the regiment is miraculously domesticated and "butterfingers or madmen" would be torn apart by their comrades, no order even required.

IX
OF MILITARY BRUTISHNESS

This word is not an insult to the army.

"Discipline, the principal strength of armies," according to the training-manual, demands from the soldier an unthinking obedience and allegiance at all times. It must first suppress the intelligence, and then substitute just a few animal instincts based upon that of self-preservation, lesser wills subsumed into the will of the leader.

There are two such instincts of self-preservation, the noble and the ignoble. The noble instinct is the instinct to preserve one's self and maintain one's individuality impervious to outside forces. Minds cannot fight each other to the death, since they are by no means precisely opposed to one another; they are intellect, and this they hold in common. For another reason, bodies do not eat each other, fearing that to strike others teaches them to return the injury. And, by the way, it is none too certain that the perception of "others" is very clear cut where they are concerned. A bourgeois, a peasant and a soldier will recognise that all bodies have one identical instinct, that of the herd, and they will be outraged by anyone who does not act "like everyone else". Bodies (or the herd) are discontinuity. Bodies are separated in space and feel interdependent, because discontinuity would be destroyed if it did not strive for continuity. But the continuum is perfection, the absolute, infinity, since these qualities are equipollent; so, just as there cannot be two infinities, which would limit each other, there can only be one continuum. Matter, bodies or the herd, which are discontinuity, can replace the continuum that is the Spirit only after annihilating it. This annihilation is achieved by known procedures, and by machinery with more or less fixed gears, depending on the strength or weakness of the instinct of self-preservation.

Hermits would mortify their flesh through physical exhaustion, through fasting and prayer, which redirected their spirit towards God. Soldiers are subjected to ceaseless toil, to the mess-tin (water is the soldier's usual drink) and spit-and-polish. Apart from exercise, one's occupations are what occupations should be: they can occupy one indefinitely. Boots by pivoting upon heels dig suction-holes in the mud of the parade-ground and should be curiously greased. Never wax them, they say: polishing wears out the leather. Yet they have to be black. What then? I don't give a f..., a corporal would say. And black indeed they are. Now the inner linings of the trouser legs are of white linen which must remain immaculate despite the contact with polishes and dubbing. Thus one must always blacken boots which always turn white and constantly whiten strips of trouser invariably stained black. It is, moreover, of vital importance that army boots be polished to a brilliant shine on their soles.

The soldier's proper position is cataleptic rigidity, auto-hypnosis via the black line of the rifle against the wall to which he presents arms. An intelligent general *might* be a great magus, but he would need to resist being overcome by a more rigorous *ascesis*, submitting to the influence of mesmerism turned back upon him.

X

AS YOU WERE

At first they marched very rapidly, in extended order, rifles at the level, across the big meadow near the parade-ground, the slope so steep towards the top and with its hedgerows that there seemed only green sky. A spindly steeple hovered in the shape of an outspread kestrel immobile as the shadow of its prey. The tone of the commands was pitched high too, in the cross-wind. Firing commenced.

"Target at twelve hundred metres!" from the corporal.

There was certainly a quaver at the end of this phrase, whistling in the wind, following a trajectory. They tried firing blanks at the large immaculate target where there was also a black cross, like two lines drawn to hypnotise a cockerel. And there came the noise of a shoot, nothing ever bagged, as dreamed of, in the lonely meadow:

Let's shoot, let's shoot, shoot off,
Our fore and aft shit-shots.
Arse'ole, arse'ole, arse-
'oldier I would be
To save the old cunt, save the old cunt,
Save the old cunt-ree!

And then the whole company marched in line, very flexible, convex and concave, feet in holes or hitting bumps in the ground, peacefully, between the sergeants and the sergeant-major doubling from van to rear, and without any thought whatever, which was by no means disagreeable. Sengle slept perfectly and was strolling across the meadow alone and in time only with himself. He was watching insects in the grass and wrens in the hedges.

Suddenly he had to watch out. After the break — hillside urinals and knapsack refectories — there would be manœuvres, with the lieutenant explaining new drills.

Lieutenant Vensuet, vacuous in plumage of blond moustache, his hackles up, fluffed out in red and black.

"I shall give the order: COLUMN AGAINST CAVALRY. The four platoons then form a square in the way you'll be shown. But on the word CAVALRY, fix bayonets without further order or explanation or having to be told. That's the drill. Don't go imagining that in war you bayonet-charge so as to rip up likely-looking horses. That was all very well in Frederick II's day. Perhaps there's a deterrent effect, like broken glass stuck on top of a wall, to scare off riders so you yourselves dare stay put. But when you're out of ammunition, when your range of fire has decreased from two thousand down to a hundred metres, it's more practical to abandon rifle, bayonet and all and clear off... Got that, sergeants? Let's start: COLUMN..."

Having been completely asleep, Sengle was dreaming lucidly. That afternoon he would read some book or other while his boot-boy polished away; he would offer the corporal a drink and leave at five o'clock, a twenty-four-hour pass in his pocket. His suitcase in town was packed, at six p.m. the train for Paris would pass by again, alongside the parade-ground and the drum-school. In Paris, a civilian once more, he would send his military belongings back to the regiment for fear of being prosecuted for misappropriation, and be in Bruges with time to get well settled before legally becoming a deserter. And his father would agree to send him a monthly allowance. He revelled in his last day of military service, in the beauty of the grass, the resonant dust, and for the first time the fun of playing soldier... It was the final break, before the third phase of the exercise.

Pile... psalms!

His neighbour is very funny too, he bungles the pile arms every time. The lieutenant arrives:

"Corporal, you will get this squad to pile and unpile arms throughout the rest-break. And when the drill is completed, the company will return to barracks at the double. And I shall be tearing up all the company's passes this weekend... Fall in!"

Yet another half-hour of extended order, the return journey one of running interspersed with halts on the knee and shooting-drills among the herds of cattle and the Saturday markets.

Sengle, his pass torn up like the others, could only go out the next day at eight o'clock. There was no hope of catching a train right in front of the station-master without a pass, while in mufti he would be recognised. That whole day he wrote and for the most part slept beside the fire in his room with the shutters closed, by lamplight, and his suitcase did not remain packed since he was not brave enough to wait for next Sunday, and he had to have freedom — not even that, just to read and sleep in peace, without a uniform — sooner still.

BOOK TWO

THE BOOK OF MY BROTHER

My loved one departed,
Left me broken-hearted.
Charles Cros

I
ADELPHISM AND NOSTALGIA

Sengle was not quite sure whether his brother Valens had ever existed. He well remembered a shared student orgy, and the day before his army medical a bicycle ride through air so balmy and solar that it was fluid, amid a perpetuity of insect- and bird-song like the hum of atoms overheard, and the tiny explosions of those shells trees shed, which it pleased them to crack beneath their resilient wheels. It was exactly how he imagined the music of the spheres. Then he learned that Valens had left France and was vegetating in fever-ridden India, about the same time as Sengle was cloistered inside the convict-hulk of the military snail. A letter took two months to get there, and its echo slept a span of four months.

That was why he dared not write to Valens at all and thought he must have been dreaming. Sengle had absolutely no memory for faces and could not recollect his mother's features even by imagining himself tracing them in the air, two days after her death. And he could not remember Valens' face at all. Despite three or four photographs, one taken on his departure. The eyes avoided him and the dumb mouth was as monstrous as the taxidermy of a bird.

In my immense grief-stricken solitude
I sense my brother has forgotten me.
His dear face pales, his features all elude
My grasp — and falsehood clouds my memory.

His portrait lies before me as I write.
It's handsome maybe ugly — who can tell?
This Double vain and empty like a shell.
His voice, once loved, no more rings clear and bright,

Its awkwardness which seemed as if designed,
Belated riches he may not have known.
Beyond the letter it now calls to mind,
The stroking pen quite suddenly breaks down.

He rediscovered a less elusive look and a mouth that for want of words breathed a little life into an older picture of Valens taken five years earlier, almost a child still, in a black sailor-suit, amid some foliage. And then he saw that he was perhaps mistaken and was looking at himself seven and a half years ago, and that he must have murmured these verses before a mirror which must have held his face without its ageing.

Sengle was discovering the true metaphysical cause of the happiness of loving: not the communion of two beings become one, like the two halves of man's heart which, in the foetus, is both double and separate; but more that enjoyment of anachronism and of communing with his own past (Valens was doubtless in love with his own future, and perhaps that was why he loved with a more tentative violence, not yet having lived his future nor being able to understand it fully). It is admirable to live two different moments of time simultaneously; this is all that is required to live out authentically one moment of eternity, or rather, all eternity, since it has no moments. It is as enormous a shock as would be Shakespeare's, returned to some Stratford-on-Avon museum where they were still exhibiting his "skull at the age of five". It is the jubilation of God the Father, one with yet twofold in his Son, and that perception which the first term has of its relationship towards the second could only result in the Holy Ghost. The present, possessing its past in the heart of another, at the same time lives out its Self and its Self plus something. But, if a moment of the past or present existed separately at one point in time, it would be unable to perceive this Plus Something, which is quite simply the Act of Perception. This act is, for the creature that thinks, the most supreme enjoyment conceivable: there is a difference between that and the sexual act of brutes like you and me. — Not me, Sengle corrected himself.

The word Adelphism would be more precise and look less medical than Uranism, despite the latter's exact sidereal etymology. Not sensual, Sengle was capable only of friendship. Yet to find himself again in his Double predecessor it was essential for him to reconnoitre, as a soul, a body beautiful enough to bear comparison with his own.

And Sengle, in love with the Memory of Self, was in need of a living, visible friend, since he had no recollection of his Self, being wholly devoid of memory.

He had attempted to create within himself this memory of Self by shaving his sparse moustache and subjecting his body to a meticulous Greek depilation; but then he realised he was more in danger of looking like a fairy than a little boy. And above all it was vital for him to remain what Valens was to become, until that ill-starred day when, their two-and-a-half-year age difference being no longer evident, they would be mistaken for one another, being too like twins.

Before Valens, he had had several friendships which came to nothing; he had put up with these second-bests, he later realised, because they looked vaguely like Valens: it takes a very long time to see into souls. One such friendship lasted two years, until Sengle perceived that his companion had the build of a stable-boy and splayed feet, and no literary ability apart from his affectation of Sengle's own; these endeavours made the rounds for months afterwards, alongside various reminiscences cobbled together in his ex-friend's brain. An ardent fencer, Sengle was equally displeased by those who were wary of sharpness as he was by those who were not good enough cyclists to relish speed.

Sengle was horrified by such types, who considered themselves poets and so would slow down while riding along to contemplate "the vista". One must have little faith indeed in the subconscious and creative mind to need to explain to it what is beautiful. And it is stupid to take *written* notes.

If man has been inspired enough (having learnt that geometric figures whose lines are lengthened externally produce other figures with similar characteristics yet greater dimensions) to perceive that his muscles can move, by pressure rather than traction, a skeleton exterior to himself — a preferable locomotor indeed since it does not need centuries of evolution to convert itself according to the line of maximum functional force — being the mineral prolongation of his bone structure, and almost infinitely perfectible because based on geometric principles; he should use this machine with gears to whisk up forms and colours as fast as possible with a rapid suction as he whirls along roads and bicycle tracks; for by serving the mind pulverised and scrambled scraps of food one is spared working through memory's destructive oubliettes, and after this assimilation the mind can far more easily recreate its own new forms and colours. We do not know how to create out of nothingness, yet we could do so out of chaos. And it seemed obvious to Sengle, though he was too lazy ever to go and see it in action, that the cinematograph was superior to the stereoscope...

It was perhaps due to this comprehension that he no longer remembered Valens' face at all.

Whatever point in time he explored, he could nowhere see a break in that continuing parallelism shown by Valens in everything for the space of two and a half years. Even in the old book of heraldry he skimmed through in the library, their coats of arms were superimposed like major and minor suits, just a few pages apart since their initials were neighbours in the alphabet:

Sengle (1086).
On the escutcheon's sable field the lilies sow
Their crosses argent, flowery sobs that grow
Across the mourning cloak for kings laid low.
The jagged lion, or, scatters terror to and fro.

Valens (1301).
A lion sejant, or; rose collar lets him know
His roars and leaps are held at bay. To show
Allegiance: raising dexter paw that he bestow
A flower, or, but one of three that blow
On sky azure, plucked royal emblems given so.

For the moment, Sengle particularly missed the past when he had been free... to tub every day, to have wearable clothes, not to be forced to do drill twice daily, and to come back indoors without trembling in front of clock-faces.

II
FALLING

The men are in fatigues, fatigue jackets tucked into their breeches, belts over that, with batons on their right shoulders, doubling towards the new barracks. Sengle is delighted at escaping arms drill: he imagines himself back at the school gym, tarted up for the annual prize-giving, streamers shrouding his horizontal bar of polished ash with its steel core, the rings rattling against each other, the trapeze with brass ends, the sawdust into which one sank after vaulting off floorboards steaming with French chalk.

He was conducted along with half his section to one side of the bars at the end, between which a sergeant leaned, delivering various prolegomena upon falls and disablements — none too worrying since they would lead to hospitalisation. The sergeant-major interrupted and the session began. After the parallel bars, where, as on the ladder and horizontal bar, Sengle was quite at home, there was the round, horizontal beam two metres off the ground; this had to be reached via a tall step-ladder and then walked across. Sengle's boot-boy and all the little bumpkins swarmed across as though on tree branches, and there was amazement when Sengle looked down at his feet, went weak at the knees and, nauseated by this exercise, jumped off before taking two steps. The corporal did not jeer though, despite a comment from Sengle which went over his head:

"Inferiority in military drill is a form of superiority, since it takes brains and nerves to have phobic shakes."

However, at the sergeant-major's whistle they changed apparatus and approached the cross-beam in order to execute various routines on the trapeze and rings. Sengle noticed that the exercises he was familiar with and which required particular strength were not called out by the corporals, who either did not know or could not do them; he later learned that the training-manual did not run to these.

Next came rope-climbing. From the top of the smooth rope Sengle very plainly distinguished the corporal's voice as he whispered to another man:

"After he panicked on the horizontal beam, how's he going to manage when he's told to walk the cross-beam?"

He feigned exhaustion, uncontracted his grip and tumbled down the rope. There were already several soldiers astride the high beam.

Members of the 2nd platoon were wrenching limbs tackling the preceding apparatus.

The sergeant-major whistled Fall In and the four sections of the 1st platoon went to the foot of the cross-beam. Sengle, aware he could not possibly get across without *wanting* to jump off the narrow madrier on to the mud floor, trusted he would not have to cross. A sergeant traversed, arms cruciform, then some corporals and several privates, all dark against the skyline, whose feelings he learnt later. The beam, five metres off the ground and five metres long, was not wide enough to walk on except with one foot in front of the other. The men from the first group, the first section, went across; then those of Sengle's squad...

Some way off in the courtyard there was a cry, some noise, a crowd, the sergeant-major departed... One of the bumpkin climbers who had been doubling across the small round beam had fallen on to one of the upturned gallows which buttressed the ends of the poles like a set square. His foot was swelling up, there was talk of a broken leg, and someone rushed off for the absent adjutants. Not having been ordered to do so, Sengle refrained from starting up the ladder to the cross-beam; and trusting in aid from the External, less external to himself than the military thing — for the military thing did not obey him *directly* — he took up the position, one foot on the lower rung, of somebody who very much wants to climb aloft but, like a good soldier, waits for the word of command. And the sergeant-major blew the whistle for a break.

The sergeant-major blew the whistle for a break, but there was still A QUARTER OF AN HOUR of gym.

The break period was lengthy because of the injured man and the officers' consultations. And afterwards *it poured with rain and hail* and they took shelter in sheds by the courtyard.

Sengle said to the captain who was addressing him:

"I still would not have gone over that beam, because I would have refused; and you would have read me the Penal Code; but others after me would have refused too."

The next day, read out at daily parade:

"Due to yesterday's rain having rendered the apparata slippery, and wind increasing the likelihood of falls, all soldiers are forbidden on penalty of detention from mounting the cross-beam, until further orders."

"That's all very well," said Sengle, "bowing to external circumstances, but you'd need to make sure it became permanent."

And the following Tuesday, gymnastics day, he reported sick. The others went over the cross-beam since the weather was fine and then on to the assault-courses without, however, any incident except for one man with a double hernia who claimed to the sergeant that he dared not jump down into the ditch three and a half metres deep, and who was forced to jump in, climb out, and jump back in again throughout the breaks.

Sengle had less and less time in which to desert, because there was gymnastics again on the Friday before Sunday leave, and he would not have a pass since he had reported sick. And he tried something else.

III
CRUTCH'S CRIPPLE

Sengle had been to see the medical officer, ingenuously thus: knowing himself to be constitutionally quite incapable of obeying *certain* army orders, he hoped they would start to realise he was unsuited for service. Especially since he had not recovered from influenza, which he thought he had significantly exacerbated with the double fatigue, sexual as well as muscular, of his last days of freedom; now he really did have lung trouble. And he envisaged this legal liberation as being the ultimate deliverance, far preferable to desertion by rail.

He was forgetting his contempt for doctors, civilian ones included, although he had atavistic experience of them: when still a child his uncle had fallen off his horse and broken his arm. On the third day the doctor (a celebrated physician) removed the fracture dressing in order to investigate his handiwork, gangrene up to the shoulder, which had to be disarticulated, and he was then flung through the window by the father of the torture victim. His mother, prey to the dismal diagnoses she overheard pronounced by this famous dunce — as famous as Mr. Deibler — died at a fixed date from a benign illness, following this prophetic idiot's instructions. This science is, in any case, senseless, treating diverse and variable beings, when a science can only consider like units, mathematical points or systems of points; it cannot be applied to intelligent beings, the internal structure of whose bodies, like their minds, most probably differs, and whose hearts are placed on the right, if not hanging from an earlobe; if hearts are worn dressed to the left it is only from modesty.

... Dr. Busnagoz, blond and breezy just like Sengle's sixth-form teacher, was not so stupid that he didn't practise "one law for the rich," but only so as not to seem too blimpish; he would slap four days on moribund creatures who risked a consultation with him, while habitually letting loose upon the town the newly arrived Parisian intake. Incapable of believing that a Parisian could be ill, he would treat them paternally as likeable leadswingers.

The first in line showed him his right hand, whence protruded an immobile, withered middle finger. Busnagoz said briskly:

"Did you mention that to the medical board? Right, do you want it cut off? Well then, keep it and do your service."

The second man:

"Doctor, sir, it's me, my name's Boudaire; one of my legs is seven centimetres shorter than the other..."

"I know," said Busnagoz. "Are you going to come and bother me every morning? Give him an emetic."

With Sengle he was charming, but murmured:

"Let's have your story... My friend, I have here in this regiment one soldier who's not the requisite height, far from it; a hunchback you can see at the rear of his company, dragging his pack around on his hump; this limping cripple I'm obliged to ignore because the medical board passed him fit; a man with a squint in his right eye, whom I simply tell to aim with his left; a deaf man, an imbecile... all of them doing their service. How can I let you out? I'm going to find some pretext to get you a one-day pass; so go out on the town, and come back and see me — not straight away! — when you feel too debilitated..."

Sengle found himself back in the Court of Miracles: the imbecile, the deaf, the half-blind, the paralytic, the lame, the hunchback and the dwarf — caryatids under their packs bulging with the entire army, wracked and tormented by the punishment detail's bayonet drill. The NCO squad facing them, even more grotesque than their opposition, spat imitations of orders out of their hydrocephalic gobs, spraying the remnants of their intelligence on to their crippled limbs, bandaged in an orthopaedic harness, like cart-horses.

It was all the same to Sengle whether the masses died in the army and whether the larvae that served them for souls passed from the bodies of the possessed slaves into those of swine; but like the elderly barber amid the nine thieves condemned to be beheaded, he wished to be included neither in the ablation of brains nor the disfigurement of bodies.

CONSUL ROMANUS! enthused de Quincey; the brains, purples and laticlaves! Valens remains handsome as the upright of the imperatorial toga; his curls uncoil their springy ringlets like nocturnal serpents; and, with képi flung down into the mud, his face glows with the pale gold from an electric sun or a ball of lightning.

Sengle and Valens arm-wrestled as though fingering a statue of Antinous; and Sengle, for having withstood the onslaught of the hero's shade, obscurely made ready, slipping the lock of Valens' hair as enough of a lever under the boulder of their cave, to the discomfiture of marauders.

IV
THE BULLET HOLE

Here's one who's beginning the rout: Boudaire has undone one of his packets of cartridges and breathed new life into the classic military suicide, his game foot unbooted. Exultant, Sengle goes to look.

One of his squad companions, Nosocome, a medical student, carries the stricken man; Busnagoz holds forth:

"Nothing to be done. Impossible to extract the bullet. Perforated abdomen. Part of the liver extruding. Just a case of letting him die."

Nosocome, better qualified than Busnagoz, was ordered to make out a report:

"Autopsy performed by us confirms diagnosis of MO (2nd class) Dr. Busnagoz, with the following differences:

"The bullet did not remain in the wound but lodged in a ceiling beam in which it made only a shallow hole and where it is clearly visible.

"The bullet did not enter the abdomen but above the diaphragm, level with the sixth left intercostal cavity, and exited perforating the right omoplate.

"No damage to the heart or even the pericardium, merely brushing the tip and passing through the right lung.

"The tip of the reddish-brown organ protruding from the wound was not part of the liver (the latter, as is common knowledge, not being situated above the diaphragm) but hepatised pulmonary tissue.

"The injury was not severe and the subject could have recovered given a normal dressing."

NOSOCOME *Hospital intern, currently Private, 2nd class, Qth Regt. of the line.*

V
UNDER SPITTLE

"Sergeant, why have you left your men in fatigues? The captain said greatcoats."

"But sir, the other companies..."

"F... that! You're not a sergeant in the other companies, are you? Get them into greatcoats."

"So much the better," Nosocome said, "no spit and polish."

"It's infuriating," said Sengle to Nosocome, "undressing thirty-six times, what with the cold from these doors."

"Yes, you're lucky to be off sick and not coming."

Roll-call.

"Anyone absent?" said Papille.

"Sengle's absent, sir, off sick."

"Tell him to get down here."

"He's excused drill."

"Baths aren't drill. Have him properly dressed and reporting here."

They waited exactly one hour, on the ice of the barrack square in front of the infirmary where the showers were, until the other companies had finished; and the sergeant-major, so as to make use of this delay, ordered them to undress in advance, at least down to their shirts.

Then they had water thrown over their heads, their feet in tubs viscous with sediment from previous bathers ill- or rarely washed, especially corporals, in view of their rank.

Shivering on the square, Sengle had glimpsed the sick men behind their windows, playing draughts and cards and reading a variety of books, assorted novels or panegyrics upon Monsignor the Archbishop of Tours. One of them came to the door and told how he had been there almost continuously since his induction into the army, chronically clap-ridden, getting confined for a month every time, as was the custom after each separate containment. He preferred the isolated infirmary to the stupid town and kept returning to seek the MO's *severest* treatment, fiery needles, for his malady. From his window every Saturday he would delight in the companies marching past in the snow.

Blackened by the dirty water and reddened by the icy wind, Sengle went downstairs again towards the Corneilles Barracks, taking advantage of the fact that he had been made to go out on exercise under orders although ill, to go out again in his own time — although confined to barracks like all those reporting sick — and primarily to cleanse himself in some bathtub, in town.

VI
CONSUL ROMANUS

Sengle's prisoner's bed was borne away on the current down the irrigation ditch and swallowed by the little arch of the field's bridge, and he walked along the gilded road with Valens.

For a long while it unwound from the spool of the nearby mill; then the gorse, like green charcoal on which wide-open mussels were cooking, was consumed and there was smoke, and the dark buildings of the silver mine.

One had only the memory of yellow things: the flowers and the sun, like zoophytes when touched, must have carried life off into the caverns of the earth.

They descended as if toppling down a ladder or like a waterfall become bifid and walking humanly, so as to stride over stones; and these were subterranean thermal springs of fresh water, so close to the sea that their floor bristled with crabs and rock-pool insects. And they bathed.

The swimming-pool, scooped out by the parish priest of the little market-town, called to mind a rounded font of granite, or a sea-shell, since it extended rushes like parasitic antennae on one lip; or a covered pond, serving as a sepulchre, beneath a church.

Valens swam, then stood smooth and golden as a statuette in the middle of the shallow water, his hair like a hole in the warm steamy vapour, which the ore tried to imitate. If one could plane black diamond, the shavings would have been his hair.

And, as when a silver skeleton is brought in at the conclusion of feasts, he stooped down, and amid his dense-packed muscles his back smiled with nine delicate vertebrae. His tawny gold chest clicked gently against the flat water and for a brief glimpse his hips had a bronzer tinge about them on the sides, like a faun not midway between man and beast, an athletic ephebe rather, worthy of casting in metal. Then two narrow feet spread apart, divergent flight of two nacreous fish, and Sengle saw the water through his fingernails.

The fossorial ecclesiastic and water-sprite of the bountiful cistern plunged in with them. And he dived under for a very long time as if he wished to excavate his undertaking still further. The old boy puffed at the bottom of the water, blowing bubbles. His mouth exhaled air in time with various gestures, he addressed the silt, the words climbed up in oscillations and made tiny explosions like the boreal words *azure* and *gules* that Pantagruel unfroze. He panted out abstract words through contractions of his Breton cheeks:

"*Barailherez*," he yawned, producing no bubbles but encircling himself with little ripples. "*Streffiadur... huanad... halan*."

He sneezed, sighed and wheezed, playing underwater. Sengle and Valens had dressed and were seated on the edge of the cistern, hands clasped about their knees and feet stirring the rushes, following his undulating course by the guideline of the words made visible.

"*Dominous vobiscoum...*" boomed one big bubble which burst joyously in front of the children.

And the clergyman reappeared fully clothed, at the other end of the cistern, put on his black hat behind the rocks and swooned away, slipping through the steam's incense, like the silver swan of the mine, tarnished until burnt by the sulphurous vapours.

VII
COCK-CROW

Rise and shine, soldier,
Rise and shine, soldier
Quick as you can.
If you won't rise and shine,
Off and report sick...
Rise and shine, soldier...

The last trump pursued Sengle from the cistern of Lethe. Who can say whether the dead don't pass their time — or *Time* — in remembering, retrogressing into organic dissolution back to their primordial soul of stone; and whether it is not highly disagreeable for them to be reawoken (nocturnal oblivion being above all yet *another* memory) when the day of Eternity dawns? Especially if the latter requires them to perform the diverse drudgeries of hell.

Valens' memory remained in the thermal baths of the mine. If a man who is separated by a break of continuity from his past were to roll over, cut in two longitudinally by a train's rolling iron, one would be terror-stricken before the great red wound. He had best stay lying on his back: at least his death makes of the snow a purple robe; and he can die naked, free from the liveries of the day.

If you won't rise and shine...

But Sengle has not gone to bed at all, coming off sentry duty, seated in the guardroom. It is two a.m.

He must get up, at least from his chair. There is an *Alarm* and a night exercise. He has orders to wake the sergeants and dispatch orderlies to knock on the officers' doors.

He runs through the rooms, chin-strap in place, weighed down with cartridge belts and webbing, exaggeratedly military: "Sergeant so-and-so, stand to!" and he hustles them, orchestrating their fumbling, through the grumbling rooms towards the drill square.

A sonorous and glossy mass, fantastically churlish and bristling, with a singsong staccato voice, dragged along its cattle-hooves and neck-bells; one might have thought a bison with a saucepan tied to its tail was clanking it majestically behind.

And all this headed down towards the town, passing the iron portals, as through a toll-gate.

The whole regiment had departed: it was the most decorative undress.

Book Three

THE CYANIC DREAM

And if they drink any deadly thing,
it shall not hurt them.
The Gospel.

I

O JUST, SUBTLE

Sengle had once been to see a friend in hospital. There were billows of white dunes — and the same effect miniaturised, as through field-glasses reversed, were one to inspect a jar full of non-absorbent wadding on a central table. There was no demarcation between this whiteness and the white faces, and the only vivid colour was the founder's bust in tarnished bronze.

Knees turning over churned the sea.

And it seemed that the vault of white mushrooms had been abandoned for a very long time judging by the quietness of billets dangling from their strings.

One could tell that the patients were very dirty, bathed only in their own sweat, but iodoform devoured the stench as the moon does the clouds.

This was the amputees' ward. It is extraordinary how all invalids resemble amputees, all their blood draining from faces down towards legs, real or phantom, under sheets which are dressings to them but concealment to others.

And then it was ONE O'CLOCK. At roughly this time those operated on during the morning came round from the chloroform, and a nagging groan began, increasingly loud, a dreadful steamship siren.

Sengle departed, between the frothing mounds, in his wake frenzied men begging him to kill them. But it was not amputees whom Sinbad, in the dungeon undersea, cudgelled with bones from their own limbs.

The military hospital is the most cheerful of military buildings because there are so few uniforms inside.

The male nurses are civilians — when the sanatorium is mixed — and the MOs, some of them, are decent enough to show up as physicians.

The nuns and doctors wear black, with a touch of white, and the patients vegetate in grey.

The hospital opened up to Sengle full of the dappled greyness one rides through in the incense of an opium den.

And the medical corporal about-turned at the reception desk and carried off with him all the army.

II
PYTHAGORAS

Sengle doffed his infirmary strip, which was only a soldier's uniform with yellow chevrons, and staunched the absurdity of his blood-red colours under grey realgar.

And nobody paid any more attention to him than to any other new arrival, until he got into bed.

The civilian medic gave him a thermometer, a fine hospital thermometer, a maximum having a very thick stem with a very thin bulb from which the mercury could not fall back again. And Sengle remembered something Nosocome had shown him. Lying on his back, he put the thermometer upside-down under his left armpit. The warmed stem expanded not, as usually, with the mercury within the bulb, but so that it shot down the capillary well almost to the very end. Aware that it is dangerous to present paradoxes to the layman, Sengle righted the thermometer, and the nurse came when eight minutes were up.

"Forty-three," he said. And Sengle, horrified at divulging his trick by overdoing it to the point of improbability, could not but exclaim that he was mistaken. The man checked it in the daylight by the window.

"It's quite right, forty degrees, three tenths."

Sengle repeated the figure to himself and observed the nuns gathering quickly around him, making mention of prayers; and the nurse enquiring whether wet cups would be needed, to keep the MO happy in the event of death. He gulped down some caffeine he had brought until he almost passed out; his pulse became really rapid; and when Nosocome came to see him he noted that his eyes were glassy.

It seemed to Sengle that the window facing him was a great deal nearer...

III
AZURE UNBUCKLES AZOR

The glazed vision preceded Sengle's eyes by two metres like goggles constructed for the protuberant optics of anoura, or the great flattened shadow that flits ahead of horses drawing public vehicles, pursued by the light of lanterns. Then varying rays thrummed at the four panes and a coloured, clearly defined form materialised. On the white screens of all the beds, on the green grilles of the parallel bedsteads, the face of a prone serviceman, fallen like a wooden toy-soldier, came into focus along with his apparel. Scalped head and bristling boots were undulating too white or too black for the lasting memory of the one hallucinating; and glowing like the green and red lamps to port and starboard, the twin stains of heavy dye, basic and acidic — blue jacket and carnation-red breeches — were delineated on the recumbent body by the now vertical army-belt.

The blue and red being trembled like a horizon at sea under the obliquity of a squall; and he continued cooking on the grill of green beds. And suddenly his torso and abdomen swelled horribly and he convulsed as usually happens on a grill. His blue arms and red legs, arched in the curve of a crescent's horns, became mutually entangled in ramifications of swollen fingers and suddenly bared toes; and the image was far too symmetrical to remain human.

The red and the blue, ill-defined at first like the arms of the town, had the hermetic significance of anatomical engravings. And Sengle studied — one itemises things during fever — the diagram on the huge white sheet of paper, or the specimen solution between the monumental lamellae of two hearts, arterial and venous, sporting the heraldic colours of pathological analysis, and, like two octopi groping one another with their tentacles, mingling the blood and sky of their veinlets and arterioles, at the ends of the symmetrical curve of the visceral foliage.

The two luminous enamels ate up the partition of the black belt, as the teeth of green and yellow corn at the base of a landscape nibble and indent whatever goes before; they intermeshed like a cranial suture, and everything became scrambled into a violet which rapidly turned blue then black.

Sengle's heart beat with resounding intensity and frequency, the caffeine having been fully absorbed, and this roused him from dream like a clock striking the morning hour.

And then he dreamed again of dissected hearts, hearts detached from gastropods, amid elongated vessels like the rubber bulbs of injectors; hearts of Egyptian crocodiles, embalmed in glass vases, while the animal hovered behind the last convulsion of its jaws. He saw a very fine crocodile, glaucous grey like all crocodiles, but with its claws the regulation cyanic blue as dispensed in the preceding dreams, the upper sides of its feet embossed with blue oedema, the upper eyelids also blue, and the sexual organs. And he knew, as one does in that most immediate science of dreaming, that this admirable azure was the apanage of the being with but one ventricle.

Mindful of ontogenies, he saw pickled foetuses squatting on the lobster-pot swell of crystal vases, each heart diagrammatic in its transparent chest; and new-born cadavers not two weeks old, whose hearts like those of embryos had joined auricles because of the persistence of the *foramen ovale*. And despite the alcohol solvent, he recalled the bluish shadow like kohl upon their finger-pads, their sexes and their upper eyelids.

His tongue was white with the caffeine and rustled like a recently snowed-upon road.

His hand placed across his heart could make out its purring tremor; his hand was cold against his damp chest, his feet drained of blood; and he dreamed he was blowing snow off the upper sides of his blue fingers.

He wandered in moonlight over snowy plains; he took refuge at Nosocome's house, at the foot of the great statue of Marsyas, in front of the soot-choked chimney; Nosocome, apparently insane, was cramming silver coins into a glass money-box of philosophic form in which bubbles gurgled and acid vapours gleamed. Amid the red steam greenly glowed a little lamp hanging from a tripod. In a crucible polyhedral wisps of whiteness were cooling; and Sengle desperately walking towards suicide and the crystals of silver nitrate absorbed the lunar caustic as if eating sugar; cyanic blueness radiated from stomach to epidermis as a black sun towards the circumference of the sky; his cold hands and cold feet assumed the heraldic azure; and his blue sex mirrored that internal cosmetic upon his upper eyelid.

The absorption of the mineral ancestor brought him closer to that single-ventricled forebear, at least as far as the symptoms visible to others were concerned;

and since his eyes were glassy as per the thermometer's promise, an apparent corpse in his cyanic garb, he firmly believed he was regressing to his mother's womb, and his twin heart had become a monster because of the communion of the auricles, and the exclusively blue blood began to distend the extremities of his body.

IV
THE HEMERALOPES

Sengle had a fortnight's leave, a "convalescence pass" for Paris. And turned blue and red squaddie once again, he went out across the town towards the station.

He passed several officers whom he neglected to salute but who did not call him back. And anyway, to prove to himself his goodwill regarding military obsequiousness, six paces forward and six paces back, he did raise his hand in regulation manner *for*:

Two postmen;

Seven schoolboys;

One bank messenger;

One omnibus driver, who was walking in full uniform in a park garden. And as some cyclists were hanging around there too, their machines propped against the shrubbery, he naturally asked for the bus station.

He saluted one of the cyclists because he was wearing on his left sleeve a horrible little club badge, all twisted up.

He entered the cathedral, asking for the verger, in order to kneel in homage before him. He then humbled himself at random along the route he was following, before:

The zinc flag on a wash-house;

A Mr. Punch signboard on a shop;

Several commissionaires, because of their insignia;

A cook's errand-boy, on reflecting that he might perhaps be a mess orderly, although concealing the fact by virtue of the similarity between his service uniform and his fatigues.

And with the night, as opportunities for saluting were becoming less honourable, he approached the shifting lights of the railway station.

On the avenue he met a group of soldiers wracked by bizarre gestures. They were not drunks who, swilling away according to the symbols of infinity, are driven from one gutter to another, and trace very precisely in their zigzags the laws of refraction. These soldiers were groping forward, fingering the walls, until they encountered the pain of bumping into the first passer-by, or the jolt of falling off the pavement. And they resembled blind men leading each other towards the ditch, Breughel in uniform.

Sengle caught parts of sentences and pieced together their complaints:

"We'll never find the hospital. That's three times now we've been right round the town. The hospital's collapsed. Like last year, when the MO found only the walls standing on his evening rounds, in his negligence he hadn't warned the engineers. The roofing caved in on the typhoid cases, who were evacuated to the corridors of the maternity hospital. It's the truth, one patient recovered that way. So are the hospitals in this town going to collapse every year because of the MO's slackness?"

And they set off again, fumbling about on a fourth circuit.

Sengle understood their hallucination after he had read their regimental number. In a small, hilltop garrison nearby, cases of night blindness were increasing, owing to the altitude. On his morning rounds the MO would have dispatched them to hospital immediately, but they had to wait for a convoy to form and be sent off without a guide, after the evening meal. On arrival in the hospital town after sunset, their amaurosis making nothing at all of the artificial lights, the poor wretches stumbled about in absolute blackness. People were used to it. That was why the officers had not been at all offended by Sengle's lack of military etiquette.

May this chapter make clear to the mob, that great collective hemeralope which can only see by familiar glimmers of light, that others can consider it a morbid exception and calculate the right ascensions and declinations of what, to it, is a starless night; may it be granted a pardon for what in this book it considers a sacrilege towards its idols, since all things considered we state the following: that not every day do military hospitals collapse because of the carelessness of medical officers; that it is possible that this might even be quite a rare occurrence; that there were several years when such was not the case; that it was perhaps just an isolated event; that, despite its authentication (see certain periodicals from the summer of '89), we have the indulgence to describe it as only a hallucination...

Sengle, mindful of the words of the Gospel, thought first of looking for a ditch or a glass shop-front for the temporarily blind men to topple into; but for fear of missing his train, he contented himself with saying to them:

"I am the General; do try to assume a military posture."

V
... ON MY LITTLE GREY HORSE

Back home, Sengle received from Lieutenant Vensuet this prose piece and a letter asking him to forward it to the *Iodure de Navarre*:

AMBER

"Cymodocea, my sister, since Poseidon does not wish to halt with his tricuspid lance this wandering island whereon I am a prisoner, I am inserting this papyrus for you inside a sealed amphora which the sea-eagle shall carry off when it comes according to its wont to ravish the turtles which lay and hatch their eggs under the sun's sevenfold blaze, and are trapped along with myself in this enclosure of dark-tinted glass.

Sister, have you forgotten the day our father Nereus — having chanced upon us intertwined and asking of each other that which only men can give us, those men who cleave the sea's violet womb with their black vessels (and the wound's twin lips flutter like wings), who hang their milk-swollen sails from rigid masts and sow the waves' furrows with their grain-sifting paddles — first threatened to prise us apart with his trident, like the soul of the lymnaea from its spiral shell, even though we were joined only by the sea's fluid breath? He flung you into the depths and made this new island rise up under me, which has trawled me back like a net over the face of river Ocean, and which is encorbelled with ramparts of glass and on its perennial course engenders a circular swirl more dangerous than Scylla and Charybdis. Shall you ever again go to pluck from the bed of river Ocean after the love-bouts of monstrous physeters those jewels left to the sea as a reward for her intervention: those ingots of amber more precious than gold, since amber floats and is ceaselessly impregnated by daylight's rays, until it resembles a grey cinder; which groans like sulphur when we grasp it in our glaucous hands and on stormy days gleams without burning with ten thousand heron-crested sparks?

I shall see my father Nereus no more — for his wrath is eternal — nor you, Cymodocea;

and if I have borne away the noise of the sea's shapes in a shell that is her motionless mouth, I know that the sea has changed, and no longer addresses me with her grave murmur, for she slithers without unfurling along this island of lubricious glass which turns like a vase between a deft potter's hands, and while turning advances a little, as the sun above us, whose reflection she is, drifts slowly towards the western waves where the Pillars of Heracles are.

The isle drifts slowly towards the western waves with no need of a pilot, for the sea's plasticity keeps it from bruising itself against the reefs and those seeded islands known as the Disseminated Isles.

Last night tricorned Phoebe arose, but I did not see her because of the height of the walls. One long ray plunged straight into the invisible sea, and a faint gleam therefrom resurfaced upon the island shore. And I saw, like a gentle and circular dance around a crater, the naked and draped forms of Hecate's priestesses who thrice turned around the ramparts in the opposite direction to the rotation impressed by the encircling sea. The isle stopped for a moment under the cloud-pocked sky, and a red glow smouldered around its shores. A redder gleam gave echo upon a distant obeliscolychny.

This obeliscolychny has undoubtedly stopped our course, for it has the form of some gesture, some command, and reminds me of the masts of men's ships, as the shell that is the sea's mouth reminds me of the imprint with which the oval quills of vessels sign the violet stomach of Her Who Laughs.

On seeing this, I bayed as a dog will at Phoebe and ran astray throughout the entire island, as far as the tomb of Micromegas.

The giant is laid to rest across the whole length of the island in his iron coffin, his head below Ursa Major. And he goes slowly towards the west, with the whole island, thus forming a cross with the poles; he steers the whole island and me with it towards the twin Pillars of Heracles, and I love the dead giant of whom and upon whom is written in Ionian letters how astonishing is the sight of this great body that remains lying on a tiny island.

I have been unable to bring Micromegas back to life or join the quotinoctial circling of virgins around the enclosure.

Every night I stand naked against the glass wall and gaze at my image glued close to me, standing in the liquid sea.

There is an inscription upon the wall stating that whoever passionately kisses his Double through the glass, for them the glass comes to life at one point and becomes a sex, and person and image make love through the wall, whether by the will of the immortal gods or the artifice of some skilful man who has constructed machines to resemble the living, and which move, oscillating on the waves and to the island's libration, on the other side of the glass.

The clouds have rained all day, and water flows across the isle to rejoin the subterranean sea. The isle has resumed its course towards the western billow and I do not see the sun, drowned behind the twin Pillars of Heracles, but a rainbow with both its ends upheld by the two distant capitals.

Our siren songs used to say that whosoever passes in a boat beneath the rainbow changes sex: I shall return this evening to the glass wall."

....

Cymodocea, hanging like a marine epeirid by her hair of glaucous byssus between the Pillars of Heracles, watches the moving isle of dark crystal advance. A white form glimmers in the depths, and fingernails grate against the terrestrial silvering of the glass on the other side of the sea. Then a white star kindles and an oval crack appears within the wall of glass; the white form becomes visible. Blood, born from the tooth of glass, drapes it from abdomen to empurpled fingernails.

The sea whistles into the wound, filling the vase of the isle which, already clear of the two columns, tilts backwards; and the mingled water and air gush up to the rainbow which sputters out, through the hole similar to the spiracle of a physeter.

And Cymodocea recovers the purple and white body floating on the water like an incense-casket full of whale sperm.

"Officer's prose," said Sengle, flinging the manuscript into the fireplace, along with a match, for this was not winter.

Book Four

THE BOOK OF DRICARPE

"Let us see then what stories you want to tell me."

Don Quixote.

I
SCHOOLBOY GAMES

The court-martial. Sengle, shaven-lipped, brought down from the cell, grips his revolver in a hand still blue-gloved despite scrubbings, inside the top pocket of his regimental greatcoat. The prisoner's right arm is sheathed in a black sleeve. There are many other shaven-lipped prisoners who have the black sleeve, and they resemble old boys of a school in their particoloured uniforms.

The military formalities are enacted, and the defence's pleas, for form's sake, with Africa and hard labour at the end of it, in particular a lengthened term of service with riskier escapes.

Sengle, when free, could hit seven bulls in a row with a target pistol, to order. He is only awkward with the military-issue Lebel rifle. One, two, three, four, five, he has won five strips of badges at Aunt Sally; five of the most gaudily bedizened have jumped out of their car. Six. Despite the tradition of news items, Sengle has kept nothing for himself. Through the preceding incense he hits the crowd in between with a hollow sound.

In the dispersing smoke the night-light still hovers, and Sengle, soiled, wipes his belly and chest with his handkerchief.

II
PATAPHYSICS

Sengle came to believe, on the strength of testing his influence on the behaviour of small objects, that he had the right to assume the probable obedience of the world at large. If it is not true that the vibration of a fly's wing "makes a hump on the other side of the world," since there is nothing at the back of infinity, or perhaps because movements are transmitted Cartesianly, in rings (it is clearly proven that the stars describe ellipses, or at least elliptical spirals on a narrow course, and that a man in a desert who thinks he is walking in a straight line tends to bear left, and that there are not a lot of comets); it is evident that a tiny motion radiates outward with significant displacements and that the reciprocal collapse of the world is incapable of moving a reed in such a way as to make it aware of the fact; for the selfsame reed, swept along in the retreat — which is never a rout — of its surroundings, would remain in its rank and file and confirm that, from all viewpoints, its relationship to its surroundings was permanent.

Nosocome had suspended under glass a horizontal straw by a silken thread, and verified that the approach of a source of animal heat did not displace the enclosed air enough to cause a libration. From several metres away Sengle obtained declinations with a brief glance.

Sengle played dice one day in a bar, against Severus Altmensch, first to fifteen. Three times running he threw five, five and five. And he took pleasure in announcing these incredible sequences to Severus in advance, he could see them whirling before they emerged from the opacity of the dice-cup. And on the second throw, already somewhat drunk on absinthe and cocktails, he rolled five, four... The idiotic bourgeois Severus laughed derisively; and a SIX. No one would play dice with him any more, for he would divest them of considerable sums.

His power, exhaled towards the External, flowed back, drawing into himself an influx of mathematical combinations. Sengle constructed his curiously and precisely equilibrated literary works by sleeping a good fifteen hours after food and drink; he would then ejaculate the result in a paltry half-hour's scribble. Which might be anatomised and atomised indefinitely, each molecule being crystallised according to the law of mass, with rising scales of vitality, like the cells of the body... Philosophy professors are declaiming that this similarity to natural processes smacks of Masterpiece.

And regarding his practicality, he was fully confident, his experiments having always shown — unless the inductive principle were false, but in that case the laws of physics were all false too — that he only needed rely on the benevolent return of Externals, which would jar him and jam him in a series of dead-ends until he emerged, via the inner staircase of salt, at the summit of the Pyramid. And that had never failed him yet.

As a result of these reciprocal relationships with Things, which he would habitually control through his thought processes (but we all of us can, and it is by no means certain that there is a difference, even in time, between thought, volition and act, cf.

the Holy Trinity), which thought processes he did not distinguish at all from his actions, nor his dreaming or his waking; and perfecting Leibniz's definition, that perception is a hallucination which is true, he saw no reason not to say: hallucination is a perception which is false, or more exactly: *faint*, or better still: *foreseen* (*remembered* sometimes, which is the same thing). And he believed above all that there are only hallucinations, or perceptions, and that there are neither nights nor days (despite this book's title, which is why it has been chosen), and that life is continuous; yet that one would never be aware of its continuity, nor even that life exists, without these pendulum movements; and life is primarily verified by the beating of the heart. It is very important that there are heartbeats; but that the diastole is a rest for the systole, and that these little deaths support life, is merely a routine statement not an explanation, and Sengle did not give a damn for it and its formulator, some sciolist or other.

The world was simply a huge ship, with Sengle at the helm; and contrary to the Hindu concept of the huge Tortoise carrying the tiny universe, the least absurd image was that of the Roman scales, where a fabulous weight was reflected (the intermediary fulcrum of the balance-beam being the lens, though this supposition is contrary to all the laws of optics) and balanced by Sengle. More philosophically, and Sengle, not deeming pride a sin, liked to imagine this grandiose scheme, now constructed in observance of theories of image-formation, with the rays crossing at the same point as above — thus it was indeed Sengle who was identified with the enlarged image, and the imaginary figure; and the minuscule world, turned topsy-turvy by the projection of its gigantic replica on the screen of the other scale-pan, toppled, like a wheel revolving, under the traction of the new macrocosm.

A bit quixotic, the concept of this great windmill, but it is only imbeciles who still distinguish mills by their grinding alone.

And Sengle had dulcinified or deified his strength.

III
SOME TRUISMS

Science, say the bourgeois, has dethroned superstition: an illness is no longer caused by the devil, but by microbes that one knows how to destroy according to well-established procedures. Therefore one goes from pure science to applied science worthy of La Palisse: a statement of what is visible to the mortal eye (it is always a matter of mortal eyes, hence vulgar and very flawed, even supposing them reinforced by scientists' microscopes; and the sensory organ being a cause of error, the scientific instrument simply magnifies that sense in the direction of its error).

Ancient doctrine says: illness, physical injury, what you will, is an episode in the eternal struggle of Ahriman against Ormuzd, the principle of evil against the principle of good. The invocation of Ormuzd combats the cause of evil and not that evil itself, which is only an effect, consequently renewable for as long as the cause exists.

Within superior intellects, Ormuzd and Ahriman take pains to do battle personally. There, evil is always overcome by prayer. The same applies to simple souls. It is the scarcely novel theory of Dr. Mises that there is no difference at all between the sphere, the form of a rudimentary body where no protuberances have developed (Ormuzd, let us suppose), where no concavities have been scooped out (Ahriman), and the form of a perfect body — again the sphere, since this body will possess all the protuberances and all the hollows (if it is pure, these aspects at least in the memory-state, which is no different from what is vulgarly termed present reality), and will thus offer a multitude of reliefs and depressions, and be infinitely rough: which as one knows is the definition of a smooth body, its smoothness resulting from the extreme minuteness of the protrusions, in direct ratio to their multiplicity. These superior intellects, who are few, recognise each other by diverse physical details. One can say of them what the Gospel says: "If they drink any deadly thing, it shall not hurt them." In practical life, the bourgeois or the men of science call them mad or sick, since the bourgeois is not learned enough to study the body and the scientist is too learned — in cerebral histology — to study the spirit.

With the scientist and the bourgeois, the same comparison applies as that between the simple mind and the man of genius. The scientist is the man of genius in analysis (we do not forget the synthetical mind, they say, of Claude Bernard, etc., but all science is analysis rather than literature, is it not?) because he knows, even if he does not make it, that a synthesis is possible. He always omits the principle of synthesis, which we call God, a living principle to which, perhaps unknowingly, the theory of *idées forces* leads back. The bourgeois is not capable of grasping the principle of synthesis and looks for it just the same — by analysing. The results are identical.

IV
THE SILVERING ON THE POOLS

The belfry's like a poplar. On its crown
Of darkness gleams the Saint in golden gown —
A melancholy weather-vane — complete
With Daughter. Relics rest beneath their feet.

Sengle when a very small child had been taken on this pilgrimage to St. Anne, and retained a number of memories of it.

Firstly, this was the longest railway journey he had made, all the more so since he had always been sick travelling by rail.

Then one went inside the sacred circles of grey stone, and everybody climbed the painful steps on their knees, right to the summit of the triangle of granite; and he was playing standing up among them, because he was a very small child.

And at the foot of the staircase, along a straight road, there were ditches with pools and blue frogs, and Sengle liked the pools a lot because one never knew what creatures one would find in them, nor even, what with drying up in the sun, whether one would find the pools, or the same pools again, and one always thought one had dreamt them.

Sengle's first impression of love had been of waves fleeing his path.

There was also water, but lacking plants or creatures, in the three stone basins of the fountain. Old women held out and extolled bowlsful of this miraculous water, yet hurled them at your heels and cursed you if you walked past them. One, to whom he had refused alms, said to him:

"God bless you... God bless you, straw up your arse and fire inside."

From one of these old women they bought for Sengle a little silver ring which very gradually wore away upon his finger, until it almost vanished.

He knew the basilica illumined all night like a parvis brazier, Eucharist for the great portal's red mouth.

He was entranced by the costumes and the *Grecian* beauty of the girls, and smiled a little that the richest farmers' sons could be distinguished by breeches riding up under their armpits and their shorter, stiffly-starched smocks.

He imagined St. Anne as a double star, sun and moon, making dry ropes from frothing filaments of squalls, and scraping the sea clean of its shifting viscous verrucae; and icing over burning mills with such cold that she freezes even flame.

He never saw the stones of Carnac; but he did see that the piers of the bridge at Auray were of triangular granite; and he had the female mutes lip-read his words, and although deaf they answered him with one mathematical voice; and a male deaf-mute who neither looked nor answered shook a hanging lantern over thirty skeletons beneath a trapdoor.

Both deaf and dumb, for tips his fingers grope
On pubic menhirs' ericaceous heath;
Like glow-worms round his dangling lantern's rope
The bones of thirty martyrs lie beneath.

The triton's zephyr stirs the wine-dark sea;
Sea-unicorns on barren moorlands float.
From ossified moon-spectres weasels flee;
Their scythes of steel give flight to ermined stoat.

On oak-trunk's scarecrow limbs the Breton owl
Will shuffle off its urchin-feathers' grime,
Crunch mayflies' wings on rocks, then hoot and howl.

The pilgrim's shadow writes inside his cowl.
While tardy midnight's stroke begins to climb
Through plumage-skirmished skies, the great stones chime.

And he was taken back on foot to various railway stations, along an early morning road of gorse ocellated with the crescents of tiny black scorpions.

He never went back to St. Anne but several times on the train passed the blue and white sign indicating the town. By night, from some distance ahead and for some distance after, the town called him through the sound of the sea with a perennial clanking of waggon bells; by day, a multitude of little yuletide yews would lift their fingers towards him, their upswept yardarms exactly like a forest of seven-branched candelabra in the temple at Jerusalem.

And he would remember a host of things he had seen at St. Anne and which had never been there, such as one of the figures of Death amid the Holy Innocents, head shaped like a savage's club, with whom he had lengthy boxing-bouts in a dream, in a non-existent vault inside the basilica.

And St. Anne was all that was pleasant, to the senses and the soul, in Sengle's distant past.

Sengle therefore chose St. Anne as his intercessor with the External and synthesis of all his strength strewn like saxifrage in the interstices of military stones. And he formed this synthesis through a perpetual invocation according to his own lights and rites.

When he reckoned he was prepared, he resolved upon a conclusive trial, to find out whether the weapon was ready.

V

DURING THE LAMPS

At four-thirty, a nun came to say prayers in the wards, and before five o'clock they ate. Sengle went to present the sister with three thick plates, for broth, chicken wing and a baked apple, descended to the canteen to buy a "chocolate whirl", paid the male nurse for the wine he was forbidden, and the last six quarter-hours — when card-playing or reading were allowed — dripped monotonously away in the two carcel lamps, which the double centre and far ends of the long table fought over.

No one dared stay up after seven o'clock since the day a sergeant entered the Infectious Ward on the stroke of seven — Sengle just had time to sheathe himself fully dressed in his sheets — and listed for four days in the Cells, up there in the Prison

Wing, the names of those not bedded down and naïve enough to have left their case-charts on their bedside tables.

At eight o'clock, all whispering between beds having ceased after complaints from the serious cases, there was no precedent for anyone being awoken in the main ward; and Sengle had never been able to re-open his eyes before the chill dawn hours dropped from the fanlight of the ward's high window.

During the night no other rounds were made save by the feathered footfalls of the elderly nun, bringing something to drink for the latest arrivals, whom she adjudged the gravest cases. And Sengle knew of these from hearsay.

He could think of no harder imposition, by way of trial of His Lady, than a rude awakening that night at ten o'clock.

VI
DRICARPE

Dricarpe was a former barman and publican — hmm? said the MO. He boasted that he had only once been arrested, for a fraud that consisted of announcing the headlines of a newspaper, which had never existed; and on Sundays a cousin would come to see him, a former wig-maker for Baldies. His hand movements would cross diagonally, like a playing-card jack, and his face was heart-shaped; his breath was hot and smelt, his eyes constantly closed, their lashes mingling with the blond down on his cheeks. Hands of a blind man or a modeller, fingers of a hunchback or a cutpurse. In the clattering old hospital slippers he walked around like a tawny owl or a nocturnal pimp. He displayed great devoutness in order to ingratiate himself with the nun, and made all the patients' beds each morning so as to get more to eat; contradictorily, he abused and terrified her with unwonted oaths. Smoked frenziedly, as if to rasp away his larynx; spat blood anyway, and vile gobs of mucus that Carlyle referred to when he dubbed the splashy excretions of the fluffy birds that Dricarpe resembled: *owl-droppings*. Seemed dazzled by the size of the wards, and the absurd freedom therein, despite being shut in with bars. All in all, fearful of noises and lights, and impudent towards surveillance like one for whom circumstances had rendered the idea of prison almost innate.

VII
WOODEN HORSES

Just as Don Quixote, riding his hobbled nag in the enchanted forest, escaped the invisible blows of the sledge-hammers by way of Sancho's senseless stories, so Sengle and Dricarpe on their adjacent beds would listen and narrate, and inside their heads were sounds of knocking upon closed coffins, or, through cracks in doors, towards the light. And it seemed natural to them to end up telling prison tales, for we all know how to be *something other* than the fable we are listening to, so in this way, they were comparatively free, their words chasing away the prison bars. Sancho's tales broke off in explosions of burlesque fear; Dricarpe's lungs would crumple and flood with pus while he spoke, and there were grinding halts for replacing spittoons. Thus they rode beneath the well-proportioned plane trees and cypresses of the garden.

VIII
BEGGARS AND PRISONS

Dricarpe said:

"First I'm going to tell you a story about beggars. Two beggars meet, Rue de Rivoli: 'Come on, let's go to that little coal-merchant's for a drink.' It's a blind man saying this to a paralytic who's got the shakes. Two large glasses of wine. The paralytic has the newspaper read to him by the blind man and says to him, 'Good health.' "

He broke off to spit at length in paroxysms and, as though following notes, began another story.

"A card-carrying beggar-woman had taken her child along with her for the day. Got drunk with other beggar-women. Meets a beggar selling flowers. He offers her a drink. She gets him one as well. Several more. In the end, it was nine o'clock in the evening. At nine, no more money left, neither her nor the flower-seller, he says to her:

" 'Lend me your child to go cadging for booze money.'

"So off he goes with the child along the café terraces, and she follows behind. He takes advantage of her being drunk, takes off with the child, and he'd collected up eight or nine francs between the two of them. Takes off with the child to a bar, where there were whores. The girls know him, and seeing this nice-looking little child they buy the kid milk and cakes. He has a few drinks and goes off with the child to sleep in a hotel, Rue Simon-Lefranc, puts the little boy to bed and lies down drunk on the carpet, so he won't be accused of rape. Waking up next morning with not a sou left, goes off with the child down the Champs-Élysées about noon, to beg enough for his lunch. Goes to the Madeleine to pick up some discarded flowers to hustle with. Has some lunch and goes off for a drink at Monsieur Rabus's. They tell him the mother's just been in, he has his drink and leaves the child in a corner. Meanwhile, the mother's making a fuss at the police-station: crying, been robbed, etc. Then she turns up and finds him in the bar."

He hawked up again and said to Sengle:

"I'm going to tell you about the young beggar girls. Parents send them out, and young boys too, from six years old to eighteen, supposedly to sell stuff, pins, pencils, shoelaces in a basket, mainly round about the big stores, Louvre, Bon Marché. They have to bring back a certain amount to their parents, two to six francs; but instead of peddling things, they're on the game. And it's more the parents' fault because they tax the children, do nothing and beat them.

"I'll tell you another day about the beggars who hire out children... about women unhappily married to their husbands, as the lowest sort of prostitution. There are some of them with children go drinking together, even though the husband doesn't bring back enough money. There are some who don't have children and apply to those who have, and to neighbours. Go off with one or two of them to beg, because they've got more cheek than women who really are mothers. The first sort hire out for drink money, afraid their husbands will find out they go begging.

"The cripples: cripples, bandy-legs, etc. Their way of life, getting up at eight o'clock to go off on their rounds till eleven; and their *tools*, which between themselves means downing several drinks, two or three absinthes that is, to *work with*. 'Pass me my tools,' they say in front of the public. Call the pitch they work (beg) a *site*, and when their work's done they arrange to meet up to dine together in the squalid hovels where they generally go and eat. Afterwards, booze till two-thirty. That's the time 'the toffs start coming out,' time to get back on site, because they've no dough left. If the pickings are good, work only till five or six o'clock. If not, off to the bistro for a bit more Dutch courage and catch the seamstresses leaving work, Avenue de l'Opéra or Rue de la Paix or maybe Rue Tronchet, and by the Madeleine. Go and eat after that, and start the serious drinking till ten or eleven. If they're too drunk, off to bed, if not, work the theatre crowds. Occasionally meet some old beggar-women (thirty or forty years old) like themselves, who'll sleep with them for a crust and a doss, because they haven't done a stroke. Or young girls of twenty will take up with a cripple for the money, not being smart enough to live it up...

"There are beggars selling newspapers...

"But the able-bodied beggars are mostly in prison..."

IX
REPORTING

Six in the evening, a new patient in a blue Inverness cape and a male nurse who is carrying his hospital admission order.

"Here's Monsieur Philippe," says Dricarpe to Sengle on seeing him turn over towards the light.

"Good day, Monsieur," says the little man, taking off his jacket and spurred army boots before lying down on the bed to Sengle's left. "Are you awaiting discharge too?"

"In a month."

"Then I'll be free before you... Do I have my temperature taken this evening? I've a touch of fever. It's big here though, dirty and depressing. Can't one go out every day?"

"If you ask the senior surgeon's permission. But I'd sooner get my discharge first and have one last fling afterwards."

"You know that getting out wasn't much use to me at Biarritz?"

"I know, I read about it."

"Because I wasn't in the residence assigned to me. I hid in an inn where the scoundrels sold me out. Otherwise I'd have made a dash for it on horseback to my place, lain low and been uncatchable. But the gendarmes got me first."

He was talking quickly and concisely, with the voice of a confiding child, hurried and breathless. Two male nurses came with a thermometer.

"Have you a temperature?" said the duty nurse.

"I always have a slight one in the evenings."

"38 are we? Oh yes, you're wringing wet and anyhow you mustn't tire yourself."

And the orderly on call put a tick and a dash on his square-ruled case-chart by the light of a candle placed upon the shelf by the bed-head.

"What time is the doctor's round?" asked Philippe.

"Eight o'clock. You get up before, but it's not compulsory."

"Do we stay in bed for the doctor's round?"

"Yes, that's a good idea for the first few days."

"I shall be in bed."

The porter came in.

"Monsieur, here are your letters and newspapers," he said obsequiously.

"Thank you very much... You may go. What a potato-face," he said to Sengle.

"Yes, not bad," replied Sengle, already drowsy. The nurses had considerately left the candlestick in its ovoid glass by the bedside, and the blond head with sensual lips and forceful chin, an almost feminine combination however, wavered over the crackling of unfolding newspapers. The nurses stared in curious and respectful contemplation that was quite comical. One of them brought a white porcelain spittoon.

"Thank you, but I'm not spitting much."

Sengle dropped off completely.

"Very nice isn't he?" Dricarpe said to him as he was closing his eyes, perceiving the last two rays from the candle and the night-light hanging from the ceiling as the lower limbs of a gigantic golden R.

X

MILITARY TIME

"Don't tell me you're not out to get yourself buggered, with your silk hanky round your neck, Miss Fairy Queen!"

"I'll punch your gob in!"

"You don't fool me, I've only got to see you flouncing about and I'll bugger you myself. We're not good-looking, but my we're randy. Just a teeny bit..."

A brawl, a bayonet drawn with the same sound a pistol makes when cocked; a little rookie male nurse who slumps back across Sengle's feet; a fat body on top, blood and vomit.

Sengle wakes up, understands nothing, is disgusted, remembers, and asks Dricarpe, awake since the first thuds and who because he has not seen the implausible murder answers:

"What time is it?"

"It struck ten a minute ago."

XI
TOWARDS ONE DATE

Sengle ceased being active, which for him consisted in keeping watch for whether the supernatural External was busy constructing schemes for him, and he was aware of time through the discontinuity of events, whose only relationship was by succession, and they filed past towards one welcome date. So Sengle, free, like a child with an Épinal print, later watched military parades passing, it being pleasant for him to recall even a horrible *past*.

One day, one evening.

Ravachol was so called because he knew how to read and now and then, in a single phrase, would air some very basic anarchistic idea which was always the same. After very many years' service he contracted syphilis in Tonkin and a fever that left him hemiplegic. He had been hospitalised three years, awaiting his twelve-hundred francs class I pension, for war injuries. The Administration was trying to infer that the hemiplegia was post-syphilitic and to contrive, if nothing else, to confiscate his papers and expel him from the hospital.

This is what happened once: Ravachol with his exterior skeleton of elaborate crutches came to a halt beside a boundary-stone, doffed his képi and begged:

"Alsatian, wounded in Tonkin..."

A deputy had him reinstated.

Philippe gave Ravachol two louis. Neatly kitted out as an old veteran, he sallied forth with an orderly to a soldiers' brothel; he promised the orderly five francs for planting him atop the woman, just as he had laid him on his bed in the Infectious

Ward, and then to military command he vigorously shunted his paralysed loins.

He returned completely drunk and played draughts, at which he was very adept, with a fat aphasic. The aphasic upon losing punched him; Ravachol gripped one corner of the draught-board and lashed out; and, crutchless, he crashed over off-balance amid laughter.

One day, one morning.

The two MOs came to Philippe's bed. The senior officer was the one with the least medical qualifications.

"Are you sure this one's not playing up?" he said, indicating Philippe. "You know that they've thought up some very sophisticated devices for transferring tuberculous sputum. In the bottom of a short, wide test-tube. There's a pipe that goes right down to the base. You breathe through another tube. The whole lot can be hidden in one's hand. It's put up to the mouth and out comes the sputum."

"Chief, sir, have you auscultated him? There's a very distinct and noisy cavity here on the left."

"There is evidently a cavity," said the senior-rank after listening, without, however, seeming to know the signs by which a cavity is recognised. "It's a real nest of bacilli in there. I'm no longer surprised at his sputum. He must most certainly be drained."

"Excuse me, Monsieur... Chief, I mean," Philippe said. "I've had this cavity since the age of twelve and I know the left lung's completely gone; but Dr.– who looks after me told me never to let myself be drained; the cavity is constricted and this operation would enlarge it. I'm resigned to not being invalided out, but I don't want to be killed."

"There, there, calm down, no one's going to do anything to hurt you," said the second MO, giving him a little pat on the head. "Let me have a listen with the stethoscope as well."

"Some soldier he is," said the Chief, seeing Philippe suddenly pass out. "Come now, is your cannula in place?"

"Perfectly, but I must have touched the apex of the heart. Why did he move instead of keeping still?"

"It's doing me in, I'm choking," said Philippe, raised back to a seated position.

"But you're not being drained," said the Chief. "This isn't a syringe, it's a probe. Come now, since the hole's been made, let us relieve you; and the cavity's being explored now as well..."

"I trust my own doctor more than you," Philippe retorted.

"Be careful, you risk worse by not going through with it."

"Go on if you must," said Philippe gritting his teeth, despite Sengle's signals, and his hissing at him:

"You young fool!"

The alternating creak of the tiny pump, trainees form a circle, the red liquid distils in the three-neck bottle held by the nurse.

Philippe no longer says anything, his shirt is pulled up over his head.

"Now then, he didn't need draining," said the Chief.

"Perhaps the cannula was wrongly inserted," said the MO.

"Well, carry on then," he said to the nurse, "let's see what does come out."

"There's only blood coming out and small fleshy fibres."

"No matter, a good bleeding is always worthwhile," said the Chief, rubbing his hands. "It was a mistake giving up that old practice, never did anybody any harm."

They leave, Sengle calls Philippe every name under the sun, and meanwhile the chief nurse applies a bit of collodion to the puncture on the heaving back.

One day, one afternoon.

On a bench they played dice, threw bread to the sparrows and organised races for plane-tree leaves in the wind which gusted past them towards the miniature lake. Then Dricarpe resumed his stories — or rather his own story:

"There are beggars don't mind being arrested because *they've got jobs* in the Seine jails. They don't mind being sentenced to six months or a year. They've started off with a month or two and got a taste for it; they don't want to work outside any more and cadge around when they get out, so they can get a foreman's job making slippers (1 fr. 25 per day), or balloons, or mailbags, etc. Or in the kitchens. They're freer and have hardly anything to do. They're put down there because they (some of them) earn less. There's five tenths for the prisoner and five for the house. The inmate on five tenths gets five for the canteen and five for his fund on release. There are some on only four or three tenths, those doing over one year in prison and those in for more than five years, respectively.

"They're made foreman because they have more influence over the young ones and know the ropes better, and they grass to the screws, and also mainly because they get so many perks with the goods — one sou per so many thousand mailbags, or four francs per month, or two centimes for every five hundred lanterns completed. They have the right to spend this bonus, so that the work gets done better and quicker. If they did real work, they'd earn less. And they're only on three tenths. The bonus goes to the canteen.

"Work for cripples in prisons? There was a time they didn't work, a one-armed fellow didn't work. He'd be made to line up in a crocodile round the courtyard with those not working. Now they're made *to sew mailbags* and make up boxes of kindling for lighting fires. Or else they're orderlies who ring the bell, or at the clerk's office they call people from the workshop up to the office. The old ones, over sixty, or those with bad eyesight, work's always found for them to keep them occupied, or Nanterre. They're put into the *Senate*, where they sort paper off-cuts from the Hachette publishing-house, into coloured and white pieces. They get themselves put there because they're graded there but don't do any work. There's just enough room for four or five, and they're as many as eighty there. They might wait a month before doing any work, and they're out before then.

"The Nanterre Sanatorium is run by the Board of Guardians. They have some very good doctors... there are some there. The patients are half-dead old crocks. When he's on his rounds the doctor mostly doles out Hunyadi-Janos or bismuth, since there's no room for the seriously ill, and the place is full of slackers. The doctor gets through eighty of them in ten minutes. Treatment is ignipuncture or leeches. To a diarrhoea-case: 'Give him a day off, leave him in the refectory so he doesn't catch cold.'

"For bronchitis cases, they hand out a glass of cold herbal tea. When there's a change of baker, the bread's all right, but hardly better than in jail and not up to army bread. They make little men of dough. For the display basket.

"I'll tell you more about the flower-sellers, young girls who pretend every night to sell the flowers they're holding when really they're on the game, near the Olympia, Rue de Sèze, at the roundabout..."

Nosocome's rounds brought regimental news:

"Detail down below. Fire!"

Nosocome had returned after six days' convalescence. He had not been allowed to book in a substitute so as to be able to go out. He sets off with his squad in fatigue-dress, manning the pump.

A fire, like any other fire. There is an iron façade that is not burning, but merely hot, up which a man can climb to carry the hose nozzle higher and save a few possessions. Nosocome is first to ascend and several metres up is felled by a beam. The injuries to his arm and foot, which had required two months' bed-rest, re-open from the strain before his fall. All the same he reascends, the officers watching with some concern.

"There's no more danger," says the first company's lieutenant. "Let's lead them off for a spot of drill, the Fairground's not far. They don't have rifles, they can do some boxing. The other company's in uniform, they'll do weapons drill on the march."

"What about leaving some behind though," says Lieutenant Vensuet, "to keep an eye on the fire, and it'll give them a rest too. They need one. Or rather, send the injured back to barracks and have the others wheel."

"And look at that great oaf over there, about to go off with them. Bloody lead-swinging Savoyard, stay right where you are and wait for your mates, you're going off on drill!"

"That soldier's worked hard," the peasant fire-victim comes and says. "He's injured and he's bleeding everywhere."

"It's Nosocome," says Vensuet, "I recognise him now."

"Ah! Nosocome is it," says the first lieutenant, "that's different then, he doesn't need a rest, he can stay with us. Fall in, dress to the right. Line up behind your file leader, Nosocome, you bloody jackass. Eyes front. By the right..."

One night.

The potato-faced orderly was the victim of a *bit of a wheeze*. He had to hang about for two or three days because of "stiffness" brought about, said the MO paternally, "whilst pissing against a wall?" He would sleep the whole day through or tell jokes, laughing resoundingly next to Philippe, who never got up any more. His tuberculosis having been diagnosed as "typhoidal variety", nurses would grab him every hour and after stripping him naked would thrust him into an icy bathtub beside his bed. Came his night-time screaming-bouts and sick men, colossal blacksmiths or labourers, would toss and turn then go over to his bed and threaten to bust his jaw for him. Finally he was put into a separate room at the end of the main ward, his only neighbour a Norman believed to be shamming because he had remained paralysed in his left arm for two days after a clumsy ether injection from a student. And Philippe's screams could be expected at regular intervals, like clocks or bells. He improved and cheered up when they allowed him to be brought back into the main ward, where the joking orderly was still fast asleep.

On the eve of the wheeze, the diminutive tuberculoid signalled to the padre passing on his rounds. The latter rapidly returned with his reversible vestments, promptly donning them, no one taking any notice. He confessed him by doing the talking himself, folded back the colours of the discreet chasubles and clandestine stoles, administered the sacrament to the sick man. Who, when night had passed, was very well, thanks to forty grammes of alcohol, a gift from the MO puffed up with the prospect of a nice long leave. And then suddenly he turned quite pale, panting with each movement of his ribcage, within a semi-circle of gawping spectators who had dashed over from their card-tables. Potato-face drowsed on, his mouth wide open. And then the one who had been confessed all at once turned yellow, put on a grimace, and spudface jumped up in his night-shirt and ran shrieking through the wards, down the stairs and into the garden. Soldiers came with an all-purpose coffin, and two days afterwards the identical absurd spectacle was repeated before the glass panes of the anatomical lecture-theatre. For the first time Sengle realised he was in a traditional hospital.

XII
THERE IS ONLY ONE JUST MAN IN SODOM

The MO, who was most unusually a scholar, working for himself, not at all military nor overmuch the *doctor*, recommended Sengle for a discharge, having started ward duty when Sengle was no longer *visibly* ill, because he understood Sengle was dying of nostalgia — although such a case is not catered for in MO's handbooks.

He recommended Dricarpe for a discharge, who was "fortunately" ill enough for regulations to authorise it (being invalided out is made harder for those on punishment) and thus saved him from future spells of penal servitude.

He wanted to recommend Philippe and was the only one who realised he was truly ill, his hierarchical superior preferring to send him off to die elsewhere, lest his own hospital be held responsible.

He chatted to Sengle, gave him excellent, intelligent advice about his health in civilian life, and together they discussed army doctors.

"I am shocked," said the MO, "by the ignorance of the trainee doctors and their stupidity. You didn't see properly, but it was a trainee whose trocar touched the apex of Philippe's heart.

"More useless than the most useless of civilian medics, they move on to the provinces and in minutes cut short countless lives. The MO's role could be so good, the only safety-valve in this hellish boiler called the army, which will explode from the revolt of intelligent persons — or of tortured patients — if they are not let out. If militarism continues, the State ought to make millionaires of the two or three great doctors in whom it takes pride, by way of compensating them and their pupils for the incredible task it sets them: deciding upon the life of the intellect — before and during military service. Because it's only the intellectuals who are likely to go under. And they jail you, or turn the real pedants and executioners into bailiff's clerks or cesspool-cleaners. I shudder to think of my son getting in their clutches..."

"Will you have him discharged?" said Sengle.

The MO changed the subject.

XIII
LAST GULES

The eve of discharge.

"Well, Sengle," said the MO, "tomorrow it is. Not too put out by that, are you? Go for a stroll round the garden, try breathing enough sky-blue to keep some on your eyelids and fingertips."

Sengle passed various officers off sick who demanded no salutes, they were going by the notices along their routes: *Please avoid undue exertion*, etc. And he walked around the ornamental lake. No more leaves were falling into it, and all those which had, had sunk. Their settled mass was piled up to just below the surface, and there was only a large swathe shaped like a wreath of rather soggy purple velvet. The goldfish were swimming along the circumference, their bodies half out of the water as though in prints; they made a whole circuit in front of Sengle, a fat one in the lead, and finding in this exploration, already renewed hundreds of times, no water unpoisoned by the leaves' blood, they set off again as if in step, with the gasping one-two of their military gills.

One of the little red-breeches, snout beneath the drizzle of the central fountain, guzzled life — and Sengle the hour — from the solitary clepsydra.

BOOK FIVE

SISYPHUS FAVOURITE

Hélène Suasse, abandoned by doctors and in her death-throes... vomited a two-headed snake.

Ex-voto from the Basilica of St. Anne.

I

A LITTLE SACRILEGE

Sengle was a Catholic and used to confess — now and again — to a young priest whom he had had great difficulty in finding, and who would, almost at a stroke, sanction all his sins — in that they were part of his nature and as such (were it not scandalous thus to judge faults) led towards God. Those whose minds and bodies are elect, barring unforeseen upsets, can go along with the gravitation of their acts around their interior synthesis, without disobeying any of the stipulations in the Decalogue, as they respect in God, themselves. The altruistic commandments: "Thy neighbour's good..." are aristocratic formulae for isolation. "Thou shalt not take the Name of the Lord thy God in vain" is the only valid courtesy; it is absurd to spit upon one's mirror, even if inspecting it through magnifying glasses. Carnal knowledge is not unrepugnant only among equals; and indeed it is only fornication that Moses forbade.

And Sengle, so as to counterbalance in the symmetry of the External the paradox of his own non-conforming freedom, condescended, in one of the panels of the confessional triptych, to kneel, although inside the central sentry-box a military priest kept watch.

And the confession was like any other confession, with the added amusement that the priest believed that he was addressing routine soldiery, interrogating him primarily about drunkenness, brothels and swearing.

"No," Sengle answered simply to these questions; then he accused himself on various grounds he took pains to explain concisely; and at last received the formula of which the ancient sacerdotal zouave was but the transmitter.

The potential assassinations having been accepted, and all else required for the escape towards his self, Sengle had not foreseen that it was more comprehensive, to bring everything tumbling down, if one also, perhaps not too directly, spurned God underfoot. His free existence would be returned to him after the *Consummatum est* like a final military password.

The padre, having partly understood, and feeling honoured in his confused soul for having conversed with an intelligent person who tomorrow would be a somebody and no longer a man; perhaps simply following the ritual farewells upon the successive releases of his imprisoned flock, questioned him about his health, requesting details.

Sengle resolutely and *sincerely* related his nosological sufferings, his anatomically curious heart attested by various doctors, and the whole truth according to the certificates and the inside of the hospital.

Then in the morning he performed the necessary sacrilege.

Dom–, to whom he accused or glorified himself later, pronounced:

"The Commandments would be dreadful if they demanded that a complex self confide in one unworthy of it. Christ in His parables spoke according to people's actual understanding. And one must be of the herd in order to converse with that herd — except in works of art, which do not concern it."

II
MYTHOLOGIES

Sengle took his mirror, and reread therein the story of Sisyphus.

The mountain was constructed with great care:

In the shape of a tetrahedron, or a pyramid formed by three joined staircases, whose steps, according to one fixed law, appeared to become ever steeper in proportion as they narrowed towards the summit.

And between the hands of Mr. Sisyphus the Lord of Hosts replaced the fateful rock, roughened by so much unevenness that it could best be compared to a perfectly polished globe.

And the Eternal instructed him and said:

"Behold, for you alone I have allowed the diamond, by cleaving it along new planes, the capability for being cut in the form of a sphere

"Since, being infinitely hard, it will therefore be of an infinite elasticity

"And when you have climbed two, three or four steps of the pyramid

"With this sphere between your hands, and because of its slipperiness it shall slide through your fingernails, because it is very heavy,

"It shall rebound from the red porphyry steps to a distance increasing according to a two-, four- or eight-fold geometric progression across the plain of turquoise

"And it will be quite impossible for you to carry it to the summit.

"This is why I am giving you the task (on pain of death, and to ensure that you stop for not a single moment there will be one of my angels of increasing rank as you mount higher, and whose power will be like several gilded degrees ranked one atop the other) of bearing the diamond sphere to the terminal cupel of the porphyry pyramid;

"And lest you become vexed and climb at breakneck speed, like a being deprived of sense, exasperated like a man playing cup-and-ball to the death and never putting a head on the pale's shoulders;

"See: I am going to attach a ball and chain to each leg, and hence you will go less quickly and it will be less tiring to watch you;

"And as for you, aim well your will in one single direction, the way to this mountain's peak;

"And this will happen after your head is shaved and you are garbed as a convict; for I have no desire to annihilate intelligence; and to that end I do not wish even to know that you have any.

"And so that my power may be manifest, I shall allow the people to come and see you twice daily, I mean those with common sense — stout and sedate men that is, maidservants and small children.

"And the latter shall find you very handsome, and you shall be very proud, and they shall all desire to be like you, at least until they reach the age of reason.

"And each day I shall give you, on recitation of your *Pater*, one obol and an ort of mildewed bread,

"And I shall also give you rest, when you have finished raising your sphere

"Like a dung-beetle rolling a turd.

"And so that you shall derive pleasure from this work, you are allowed and even enjoined, during this allocated rest,

"To polish your diamond with scruples and a soft brush (it's an old decanter-stopper and needs assiduous attention) and with anything else you consider worth acquiring for that purpose, spending without check upon your monies what you will;

"And in so doing you shall escape both sloth and sleep and you shall say you are a martyr, although really I had rather you complete your task without thinking or speaking at all, but with all the more care

"Like myself, when I constructed this mountain."

And Mr. Sisyphus, who was a very sensible man, was obedient to the very letter.

At the end of one lustrum the Lord of Hosts descended like a ferocious spider, wondering to what use the work done by Mr. Sisyphus over the past five years could be put. Destiny, his father, had told him that this diamond sphere was the symbol of (ball) lightning which might be rolled upon the Giants' heads if they should storm heaven again. But the Eternal knew very well that, were there a resumption of this cataclysm, Mr. Sisyphus would drop his decanter-stopper and spend time watching the angels, caught on the steps like flunkeys on a coach, getting their throats a bit cut. Besides, how does one disembrain a giant with a decanter-stopper? How had he not thought of this earlier? The Lord of Hosts would install all along his porphyry mountain a scenic-railway wagon made from the dried carcass of an enormous wasp, its hard skin having been emptied out, utilising the complaisant and (usefully) underused strength of Mr. Sisyphus, and would thus recoup various monies.

And he made haste, solemn as always however; and the angel-flunkeys sounded their trumpets, and those perched highest sounded their trumpets with most respect, hence louder, and since the perspective of sound was observed, the Eternal heard only one equally intense trumpet-blast, as if but a single tier of flunkeys had sounded trumpets.

And the Danaïdes, immemorial pendant to Mr. Sisyphus on the other end of the mantelpiece, wished to drum on their traditional barrel; but it was too long since it had been holed (this explanation is anyhow absurd, they told themselves; for a trumpet sounds because it is drilled from end to end; and if our drum had no hole in it it would, consequently, be even more impossible to draw a sound from it. And the Lord of Hosts would have nothing to drink.).

When the Lord of Hosts set off to march towards the porphyry mountain, he became ill. For the diamond sphere, which had turned into a real diamond, was shining in the sun cervically upon the mountain, and Mr. Sisyphus was taking a rest upon a considerable sum atop the inaccessible mountain. And the Eternal opened his mouth and so did Mr. Sisyphus, and the Eternal listened, and Mr. Sisyphus spoke thus:

"Dear Master,

"You have created all things, Darwin and that law whereby function forms the organ or develops it if it already exists, physical exercises, training and Choppy Warburton.

"You put back into my hands a diamond sphere so heavy that after a few seconds my weary hands had to let it slip; and I had to run after it, its mass increasing in its fall according to a very beautiful law, and then recommence my labours further down. Which is fine.

"But borne between my hands the weight of this sphere remained invariable, and devoting myself — so as to serve You — to this hygienic sport, the strength in my muscles grew through training and the ball did not become heavier. Like speed squared, so to speak, my aptitude for transferring the ball to the cupel whither You commanded me also necessarily increased.

"It would be extravagant to add that, as I approached the summit, and moved further from the earth, the ball's weight diminished appreciably, for Your mountain is very high.

"Now that my task is done, one attraction is deserting Your hell, and You are no longer Lord of Hosts; but You know that He was created only through a mistranslation of *Sabaoth*; and that will do just as well," said Mr. Sisyphus, departing.

And the mountain still exists: it's on show to tourists, they call it Peter-Botte, in the Ile-de-France, and there is a small version of it at the end of the Pont-des-Arts, with stone lions around it. The Eternal, if Mr. Sisyphus had not at last "potted" his ball, would have created perpetual motion, which is no small matter; since then he has sought other inventions so as to construct a machine involving man that will last a long time, or at least a century; he's made many attempts but to date has come up with nothing presentable. That is why he starts over again the whole time — the only real Sisyphus.

Like modesty closing upon her brow the greater eyelids of her hands, Sengle drew across the mirror the wooden wings of the triptych.

III

DOLLS' ENAMEL

Two and a half years afterwards, Sengle went with Nosocome to the children's hospital. He had donned a long white cotton houseman's jacket akin to a military fatigue-coat, like his companion; and they proceeded first through Nosocome's ward, bothered by nurses at the bends of staircases. In all the beds little girls were staring straight ahead of them, which is the main exercise of the sick; and in one central bed a large doll, rather bigger than the little girls, was the only one to follow the visitors with an intelligent look, like a portrait that is.

In a boys' ward, Sengle picked up a lancet and Nosocome asked the nurse if there was a patient who was *peeling* markedly. She swung down the right-hand side of a four-year-old's bed, drew back the covers and pulled up his night-shirt. When Sengle placed the lancet against his stomach:

"You're going to hurt me, Monsieur," said the little boy, following images elsewhere, within his transparent head.

Nosocome uttered a few well-meaning banalities and Sengle, with a barber's gestures, began shaving the tiny straw-coloured scales, from the right side of the stomach towards the groin, and collected them in an envelope.

The nurse opened the other iron handrail of the mechanised bed and the scales sinister were also collected.

"No need, Nurse," said Nosocome, "to bother telling the Director that an outside doctor collected some scrapings; it's for research which mustn't be disclosed, into the scarlatina bacillus."

Sengle with his fingernails powdered with scales nipped the nurse's throat in a conspicuous gesture of violation; she laughed and was unaware. Then, after washing their hands, they left.

IV
ASSASSINS' TALK

Pyast and Herreb sat cross-legged around Nosocome's study; Sengle lay in a corner, behind a table. On the plinth of Marsyas scrolling up his marble above the mutually violated sexes of his internal organs, like the successive cones of a hair, the burner smoked black, then red, according to the incense — benjamin, styrax, then myrrh — and the perfumes erected a cylinder filling the whole centre of the room, their undulations dying at the entrance to Sengle's angular asylum.

There was a girl with a dog on a divan.

"Here's Hakim," said Nosocome, giving the Polish poet Pyast, the German philosopher Herreb, and Sengle, a Eucharist of hashish pillules.

They waited for one hour, until Nosocome jumped up, shouted that he wanted neither whores nor dogs in his home, least of all whoring bitches, manhandled beast and girl to the door; and then the talk began.

NOSOCOME. In eighteen hundred... eighteen hundred thousand... till... vile billions of pills...

PYAST. Thousands of viblions of pill-boxes.

NOSOCOME. An elephant in a block! you block-head... four elephants in a glass box.

PYAST. "A simpleton always finds another only more so..."

NOSOCOME. This little morsel lives at the corner of the Boulevard Saint-Michel.

PYAST. And the Boulevard Haussmann wants to get off with her, a nice free sampleton.

NOSOCOME. He gets simple like that, in his cups. Here's a free verse in the sample.

PYAST. He's no need of bottle, he cleans himself out with an arse-glass of free wurst.

NOSOCOME. That's crazy, I've not seen it, no...

PYAST. That crazy Jeannot.

NOSOCOME. And Hunyadi-Janos is no wet flannel.

PYAST. Flannel's like corns on your feet, no one wears it any more.

NOSOCOME. As from tomorrow you shall wear flannel.

PYAST. From tomorrow? We'll never get out of today.

NOSOCOME. You're linking cause and effect? You're taking your head in your hands.

PYAST. Let's explain ourselves in the Paris of words.

NOSOCOME. The base is the flame. And you're in the middle of the shadow or the light.

PYAST. I'm in the middle of what? In two or three hundred years perhaps.

NOSOCOME. Your likeness is natural.

PYAST. I really must find it again.

HERREB. Suppose we stick up posters for it?

NOSOCOME. You mentioned flame, I believe? You were in the water.

HERREB. Are you penetrating two things at once?

PYAST. In the middle, with two paper hoops... I think... In the middle, with...

NOSOCOME. Suc-cess-ive-ly.

HERREB. He's found it.

PYAST. I dropped it. It was sitting along the lie of the fields, so it had its back to the road.

NOSOCOME. But if you were in the middle, you couldn't anticipate that.

PYAST. There are schemes which cannot be sinuous.

NOSOCOME. That's fifteen years you've been explaining something to me.

PYAST. Fifteen years...?

NOSOCOME. You trying to prove shomething?

PYAST. Shun nothing.

NOSOCOME. Now then, in your smugglering, could you clip your words?

PYAST. Polish morale...

HERREB. Polish mural...

NOSOCOME. You all but said long live Poland...

PYAST. You're a Russian foot, a foot and a half.

NOSOCOME. Take that back.

PYAST. I'll take half back and you'll be left with three-quarters of a foot. Ha ha! I've lifted three-quarters of his foot. You're a foot, and a corn on a foot, so you're a madrepore, madrechaun, madly coral paw! Conclusion, you can't grasp it, you're a foot-corn.

HERREB. He has five corpses at the end of each foot!

PYAST. You're a brain informer. You've the obelisk in one finger and a corn on your foot. Ebonite in one little finger...

HERREB. What quite?

PYAST. Ebb-at-night. It's not a fish, the Holy Ghost, so it swims in abbot's wine. The Holy Ghost's a goldfish. Grace is an advance. From the back forward.

HERREB. Grace is a pederast?

NOSOCOME. In the front to backside sense.

PYAST. What's its universal suffrage? Universal suffrage is when one spends a sou a day on a daily newspaper. There's *The Times* and the daily *The Day*. That makes two dailies daily.

HERREB. And how much time?

NOSOCOME. How can he perceive a thing so much greater? He scathed himself.

PYAST. If you had a beam in your eye...

NOSOCOME. We all know it depends on the size of the beam.

PYAST. Does that seem obvious to you? You don't trust the evidence of a beam in the eye? One can't change the printed word.

NOSOCOME. He scathed himself.

The talk passed back and forth at an exaggerated speed, cut short by immeasurable silences, haschischins having no notion of time, doubtless due to the abundance of images, and, being rich in years by the milliard, they unaffectedly expend three hundred years for a minute, or a second. They no longer have any notion of distance, optical *accommodation* no longer functioning except as a cinematographic trembling, and need a periplus to land a hand upon the arm of their chair. There was a silence after Nosocome's conclusion, which was on a coined or archaic word, notoriously incomprehensible anyway. The four were still almost lucid; Sengle in his corner more screened from the scents was listening and taking notes, and they resorted to ruses for further hallucination.

The spirit flame under the burner was extinguished, the fire covered, and in the darkness Nosocome began rhythmically running on the spot, the board floor quivering.

A sound exactly like a train was heard, clank of pistons, whoosh of whistles (an imitation familiar in all music-halls) and these words were exchanged:

"Augustine! Augustine...! Where are you going? where are you going?"

"To Paris, to Paris."

A red disc appeared, Nosocome's cigar.

"The smell of smoke doesn't bother you, I trust, Madame?"

"How dreadful, the two trains are going to crash!"

"Paris, all change," said the nigger minstrel raising his cigar in greeting.

Sengle, despite the hint, no longer recalls the first military train, for Halluin and Menin. His train climbs towards lunar lands.

Another willed hallucination: in the next room:

"Hear the requiem mass."

NOSOCOME. Feet first. Enter.

PYAST. His feet arrived before him.

NOSOCOME. There's flesh here that doesn't smell fresh.

They light the lamp again, but the land of hashish is in the room now, *brought back* by the lunar train. The air is pure glycerine, and just as continents are encircled on maps, Sengle and the trio have their entire bodies haloed with a fluid twelve centimetres thick, at first Loie Fullerish, then dark violet. Sengle notices that approaching gestures painfully shock his sensitivities, which are all on the outside.

Herreb, who was advancing alone through the door to represent the funeral cortège, has his face wholly blurred because the dark layer is so thick. He leans on a stick, then raises it horizontally — his hands at either end.

HERREB. Hang yourselves up.

NOSOCOME. The chief of police.

PYAST. Into the ditch. Awkward pitch.

NOSOCOME. D'you do horizontal bar work?

PYAST. He correctifies corns. Corns and carbuncles are walking nails.

NOSOCOME. Fairly like general paralysis.

PYAST. Fairy of general paralysis?

Herreb, brandishing his beam, which is immense, and swathed in his astral aura, walks towards Sengle. Sengle from the pain of contact with his own aura lifts both arms, brings them back towards his head and prods out his spread fingers in the direction of Herreb's eyes.

HERREB. Oh! the nails! the green nails! they're sinking into me...

PYAST. You've a nail in the sole of your foot. It's also the plank of salvation, the last hope. With your stick you're the old man of the woods. If you're the old man of the woods you're the plank man, an orang-outang hubbub, adoobarb.

NOSOCOME. A kiosk where he bar-barks.

PYAST [*gesticulating*]. Tree-man, come and be arborous with me, in the arboury.

NOSOCOME. Four woodsmen and a wood corporal.

PYAST. Ha ha! a wood corporal! More like a garden gnome.

NOSOCOME. *ArcaNA ambo.*

HERREB. Oh dear, Monsieur,
he said as he barked his violet aura, like a world astray.

Sengle no longer listened to the crazed conversation, his attention was riveted like that of the tree-man, who grasped his stick by its middle and was letting it revolve gently, almost vertical, generatrix of two superposed cones meeting at the tip, formed of the non-natural fluid of the bodily auras. A Xipehuz was born, upright and luminous, and the old man of the woods spoke brilliantly in the viscous air, three hundred years between each word, and Sengle listened in eternity.

THE OLD MAN OF THE WOODS. I have seen a fog from hell. Oh! I'm suffocating, oh! how pretty... oh! it holds together so well! O the centre. And there, that's a molecule. The centre, it's marvellous. The centre, oh! it's beautiful. My, the centre! O the centre of God. And its periphery. A periphery with only a centre. There are gardens. Oh how tiring to move. I feel a peripheraesthesia... Oh dear.

Nine hundred years, then he walked towards the others, and, condescending god, simply said:

"I am the old man of the woods."

Nine hundred years.

"Oh! look, it's falling."

Nine hundred years of the slow fall of the stick through the substantial ether.

"I've ice around my cane. Oh! it's turning. You turn around my ideas. But my ideas aren't round. Pentagonal. The pentagon is comprised of straight lines. An idea's not a path, it's not sinuous. It's a join, that, a re-soling..."

Sengle was musing that he had said PERIPHERY and not *surface*, and that the Xipehuz was therefore alive. The man's fluid bumped into Sengle and very painfully the man whined again:

"Oh dear, Monsieur."

And he again disappeared for some years in the opaque mist. Nosocome and Pyast were arguing.

PYAST. A snail sees with its foot. During the day it was disguised as a slug, it was a snail-helix. It's the middle, I always hold on to the middle point.

NOSOCOME. The old man of the woods is chopping us up.

PYAST. But he's not going straight through me, that's a refinement.

NOSOCOME. Three days we've been here.

THE OLD MAN OF THE WOODS. O my baton.

PYAST. Your batumble.

He drew near again, and as before Sengle had to protect himself with mesmeric passes.

THE OLD MAN OF THE WOODS. Oh! I'm lost, these nails... The nails, the ice. Come now, let's see, green nails.

He walked over to Sengle again and said with supreme contempt:

"Are you watching me, Monsieur?... Oh! he's kicked me with his shadow."

Lucid Sengle wanted to make him inhale ether.

THE OLD MAN OF THE WOODS. The vapours have changed.

Three hundred years, and in a voice of breathing one's last:

"Ah! you've demolished my smell."

All night, nonetheless, he came and went through the two doors. Sengle placed an open umbrella on the floor and told him it was a green toll-gate; and thinking himself enclosed for myriads of years he trudged ever more elderly, shrunken over his cane. They bolted the doors, and he knocked:

"Monsieur, open up, he's dead. Scoundrel, what have you done with this intestine?"

PYAST. His intestines are hailing, let them burn.

HERREB. You've reeled out the dead man's intestines off the funeral train and wound them on to a bobbin. Why do you unreel bobbins? He reels out bobbins at the

Bobino.

NOSOCOME. He has small instintestincts.

PYAST. I knew a mobile called Pompoteau. Pompoteau, mobile; auto, mobile.

HERREB [*knocking at the door*]. Present, here's a surface one.

PYAST. Can't he say his name?

NOSOCOME. One should not demonstrate oneself in the street.

HERREB. Open up, Monsieur, here's the dead man.

PYAST. Why knock three times? Four and two make six, and half of six is three.

NOSOCOME. Metaphor.

PYAST. Félix, Félix!

NOSOCOME. What?

PYAST. My dear friend, there are three what, there are three what, there are three...? That's the way a duck speaks French, who's... Canal, what's passing in front of you. You were spilling.

NOSOCOME. I wasn't spilling out.

PYAST. It's a parallel with the canal. You're parallel to the canal. What a wretch, he's fathered your folly.

NOSOCOME. He's fathered me fully on the bicycle of your b..locks.

PYAST. *ERgo nominor leo.*

NOSOCOME. Get on with you, Jules Simon. The condition for two parallels to be parallel is that they are in opposed directions.

PYAST. But speak for the resultant.

NOSOCOME. It's your paralleliresultant.

PYAST. What a bore! no result from it. Do you want a salad of spectacles?

THE MAN [*behind the door*]. O nails, that's not made of glass, pull out the nails, o the little nails, corns, corny clowns, Footit...

NOSOCOME. A hell must be a sort of a rest, since one wouldn't know what to do there.

PYAST. You see how smart he is. Caricature!

NOSOCOME. Hell's not a pain in the a..e.

PYAST. Since it's the only thing possible.

NOSOCOME. So did he want to know this something, the old man of the woods?

PYAST. And why did he come in wanting to find out?

NOSOCOME. Does he want to know something? Hell is ten-dimensional space.

PYAST. Skip your dimensions, at least nine of them are honourable.

NOSOCOME. There are three, then the pit...

PYAST. The tyre...

NOSOCOME. The time...

PYAST. And conversely. The present has spatial dimensions.

NOSOCOME. Logic is the hammer of reasoning.

PYAST. Logic that kills. Hey, word-guzzler: rhizomorhododendron.

NOSOCOME. I expose myself rhizumed in public places.

PYAST. He... nothing.

THE OLD MAN OF THE WOODS [*entering*]. Coffee goes down because it has a few niceties.

Other haschischins who had not spoken at all are stretched out on the floor, amid vomit; the perfumes piled randomly upon the incense-burner are turning foul.

"Are you frying eggs?" Pyast asked Nosocome.

Sengle the most lucid — for the hashish state is the most similar to his normal state, since it is a superior state — by a simple reversal has become almost a normal man, and has taken notes. He wants to open the window so as to evaporate in the air the iridescent bubbles with which Hakim is choking him. The others, in the midst of their Wandering Jews' journeys and their frenzied exclamations, bellow:

"Stop him throwing himself out."

The old man of the woods, his crisis abating, again becomes the German philosopher Herreb. From a corner it decorated he unfurled a French flag, tucked it behind his head and cried:

"Long live Félix Faure! Long live the Republic!"

Nosocome retrieved the flag, rolled up two-thirds of it, wrapped the last third round his waist and shouted:

"The English are here!"

"What if we burned the flag?" said Sengle.

"The flag is eternal because it's the motherland," said Pyast.

"That saves the trouble of burning it," thought Sengle.

A tricolour-striped paper lantern is discovered and lit.

"The lantern," said Pyast, "is a luminous hole with a flag around it."

They hung it from the end of the flagpole, second staff for the old man of the woods, and Herreb resumed his precipitate gait. Sengle lying down again in his corner fixed, as Herreb was fixing the Centre, a moon, the projection, on to the white ceiling of the light demarcated by the lantern's circular crown, greater and whiter than the real moon, at its centre a black being, the brass ornament on the tip of the flagstaff, which is the man with his bundle of firewood or a lunar monument with two cornices, full of countless all-consuming creatures.

The moon, dispenser of death, is in the room, conjured up by Hakim, and Sengle will keep her, flattened like an opera topper, in a round hat-box. Hakim has become very ancient and stunted to below ground level, the window is open on the deserted morning pavement, Nosocome is sitting immobile on a corner of the bed, Sengle drowsing on the floor; and under the gaze of the first passers-by (Nosocome's study is on the ground floor) Herreb, who has flopped down with his lantern which has caught fire, with the flagstaff's brass tip like a helmet's spike, snores blissfully, his Teutonic torso draped in the republican muslin of France.

V
LETTER FROM SENGLE TO VALENS

"My dearest brother, here are the scales of the dragon freedom, which you must put on. They need only be grafted on to one area, and you don't have to take any notice of the lime-tree leaves. This, I think, is the best way of making this graft dependable and invisible.

"On cycling trips we washed our hands of machine-oil with soft soap and handfuls of fine wood-shavings. You must rub your arms hard with one such handful of shavings across the vaccination area, or better still, since here the tissue closest resembles the cells of these scales, both sides of your stomach in the region where we remain hairless. There will be no abrasion yet the blood will still come and carry the scarlatina towards your heart. That's better than having over you an army uniform or, inside you, the dozen bullets you are risking. My affection hopes you will be well and truly ill.

SENGLE."

VI
I HAVE YET OTHER SHEEP
(Continuation of Sengle's letter)

"P.S. — Another envelope to follow containing tiny yellow mushrooms and some other agreeable bits and bobs. You can amuse yourself by rubbing them inside the rim of your corporal's képi and those of your section neighbours: they'll soon get alopecia and ringworm. You can also safely keep some favus on your fingernails, provided you wipe it off in friendly fashion on the brush custom-made for use upon military soldiers' heads. There follows too, inside a special container, a Pravaz syringe filled with diphtheria cultures, which I recommend only if your scarlet-fever loofah hasn't given a sufficiently effective massage; this last operation would prove, after several months of invalided-out freedom, fatal, and you would be better advised to dilute this small clyster with water from the room jug. Nosocome is curious to know if water will pass it on effectively... For the second time, affectionately, keep well.

S."

Nosocome explained to Sengle:

"The only way of transporting our bacilli and cultures by post is by Japanese chafing-dish.

"Because the culture remains live only at a temperature that must be calculated in advance.

"The Japanese chafing-dish, to be found in every Japanese bazaar, is a tin can the size of your hand, pierced by five holes or tubes. It is sold with five scrolls of special onionskin paper, tight-rolled, which burn smokelessly for eight hours.

"Nothing is visible and there is a very steady temperature of forty-five degrees inside the can.

"The culture tubes are attached inside the chafing-dish so as not to vibrate, and the temperature is lowered as far as necessary below the forty-five degrees, by enlarging the five holes.

"In the same way as the cultures are fixed inside the chafing-dish, it is advisable to fix the latter inside a wooden box, with invisible holes, as an air reservoir and insulator against rapid cooling, in case our client is drafted more than eight hours away from Paris."

VII
OPAQUE CARDS

For having wanted to make these alchemies general, in March, their factotum Dricarpe died.

The Champs-Élysées, fog, some cyclists. Street-vendors are offering triangular illuminations for hats. In his espadrilles Dricarpe, eyes narrowed and blond under the tarnished sun, moves like a skater on a grey pond, or like the nocturnal ponces. The cards he is selling have little booklets sewn inside which he proffers with an anoblepic look and a cards-on-the-table transparency of gesture. He spiels behind a urinal:

"Medical discharge, Sir, how to get one. I'm selling it for two sous. A small pamphlet compiled by Dr. Nosocome, based on the lectures of Monsieur Scheffel, professor at the Gnadenthal. All the dodges described in the old-time beggars' manual, a prolapsed rectum using a bit of animal intestine, as instanced by Ambroise Paré...You want," he shook a bunch of bizarre miniature ironmongery, "a *Jew's harp*? With this music behind your teeth, where it's invisible, since it sticks to only one of the jaws and isn't detectable even when the mouth's open, with each inhalation the auscultator, wherever he places his ear, hears subcrepitant rhonchi, third-stage tuberculosis. D'you want...

"Or instead, here are the formulae," and he extracted them from his squalid fly, where they had been concealed in the six chambers of a golden revolver with a diamond-studded grip, "in these minute tomes grey as the weather, of superhuman discoveries that we guarantee none of the asses born into Medical Schools, amid the mud of fumbling science, will glimpse in five hundred years. The first contracts the body by a third of its height for one day; the second, by means of a simple injection as described, paralyses for as long as desired to the point of cadaveric rigidity and the onset of putrefaction. The third, anticipated by Swédiaur, has already come in handy once... A thousand francs each prescription for freedom. The formula is guaranteed limited to a single copy only, and after seventy seconds — the time it takes to read it

— the phosphoric letters, on contact with the air, and the paper, deflagrate and burn up spontaneously..."

A policeman, seeing Dricarpe accosting a young man in the urinal, came running up.

"The sixth..."

Dricarpe's brains crudely bespattered the two interior walls of the dihedral angle of slate slashed on with obscene inscriptions. The young man, who was a poet, held in his hand the golden revolver. He was later acquitted pleading self-defence.

VIII
EN ROUTE *TO DULCINEA*

The lamp burned upon the red table and breathed its cricket's chirp. The walls were papered yellowish-green, and it might just as well have been the song of the moss insects' elytra as the intimate tearing of the trunk of sulphur with its crystalline heart.

Bronzed darkness speckled the white mask looking out from the wall, and beneath the moulding Valens began to appear and take on life. He raised his eyebrows slightly towards the outer corners, kept his eyes lowered and wept a little of his soul, like a wraith of smoke, from his eyelashes through his hairless lips and chin, at Sengle. And his mouth mused.

The mouth alone, like a leaf from a tree, is different on every face, and is the only feature one can draw without knowing how to draw, since one will invariably intimate with lines curved at random, lips and movements of lips that actually exist. And even when their voices are similar, two speakers have different mouths. Because there are moments when they do not talk and when the mouths remain themselves. It was lips militarily tamed for the convention of language that the little deaf-mute girls at Auray would watch closely before answering them with the geometry of a uniform gymnastics.

Valens was silent and this indeed was the voice of the Silence of Valens free.

And it is physically proven that lips cast in plaster are more eloquent than red lips: the latter drink the light and are black really; the mask's mouth returned to Sengle the kiss of all the suns sucked up together and of all the lamps expired on the table where they'd read.

And Sengle believed that at that very moment (without his wondering if the dreamed-of morbid inoculation were possible or whether the tins with the Japanese paper burning inside were enough to conserve life through minute imitations of its loss) his brother was awaking to freedom and escaping, as he himself had done two and a half years before, upon mounts of grey smoke.

And to relive this past he raised himself up towards the mask; and the head was no longer the visit of a body that could not get in through a cat-flap in the wall, but Sengle had upon *their* table and under *their* lamp the brain and soul of his brother.

The white countenance was absolutely the sort found in a hospital ward, embossed with candid beds, the nostrils seemed the rising of drawn-up knees, and the forehead was tugged over the spirit like a white coverlet.

Valens still returned to Sengle's eyes the lamp's kiss; the rustle of elytra persisted still, and this was the reviviscence of the two brothers' last outing, the humming atoms like the tiny yellow crickets which inhabit the polyhedral galleries of sulphur; and again it was absolutely similar to the music of the spheres.

The head was wholly alone and bare, and it was the intellect of Valens that Sengle covered and raised aloft between his hands, out of the red and blue of the disciplinarian chrysalis.

The head was too alone even and too bare; the soul of Valens (Sengle still recognised the life or soul only by movements analogous to heartbeats) was simply leaking, streaming through the lips, like a vase overflowing. When Valens was totally present in the room his soul was a great blue-brown butterfly, its wings raised highest towards the outer corners, which fluttered with the twinned flight of his eyebrows and eyelashes, uncovering and re-covering the miraculous ocellure of his eyes that were two black pools.

Sengle loved pools and the creatures that fly over pools; one never knew, he thought *en route* to St. Anne, whether one would find the pools, or the same pools again.

A curl had remained crimped into the plaster on one side of the forehead; under Sengle's caress, the marvellous butterfly uncoiled towards him its spritespiral which was a dark crinkled feather, like the old trees in the first dreamed-of desertion; and, alive, he crumpled it as one bending an index finger to beckon someone.

The Chinese ethnography of a people foreign to China… a certain wind must not blow...

The lamp elytra stridulated swifter still, and the din became more continuous, like a last trill.

Sengle leaned towards his brother, from this point intuited, across the distance, as free, in order to give him back all the affection of the good kiss of sonorous light.

The plaster mouth became flesh and red to drink the libation of Sengle's soul. The lamp had turned red, then black, the metal died out in the eye and the air poised a mist of tears.

And after the momentary redness, the lips were green and adhered all chill to Sengle's blackened lips. These were too many complementaries.

The table rocked and Sengle was on the ground in the wake of the pile of crumbling snow, this time with a recollection of the caffeine rustling across his tongue, in the bed of the mixed hospital. He buried his face amid the tiny scales, several of which stuck.

"Why did the mouth turn red to drink my soul, which escaped through the occiput when my face entered the flesh of the mask?"

And Sengle was fumbling in the night towards his Self vanished like the heart of a bomb, his mouth upon his murder.

IX

ACCORDING TO MONSIEUR PRUD'HOMME

We asked M. Prud'homme for the end of Sengle's story, his lucid Memoirs having stopped here.

Answer: "Old age is the *leit-motiv* of childhood, contraries are identical, etc."

M. Ribot has already explained the same thing physiologically, and we know that Sengle lived (and would die, by virtue of the fine phrases above) on memory:

The belfry's like a poplar. On its crown
Of darkness gleams the Saint in golden gown...

St. Anne presides over a monument and a blank page.

RÉPUBLIQUE FRANÇAISE
Liberty — Equality — Fraternity

GENERAL ADMINISTRATION
OF THE BOARD OF GUARDIANS, PARIS

Name of
Establishment Dept. of M.

Asylum of
St. Anne

Name			*Age*
Profession	*Temperament*		*Constitution*
Admission date	18	Ward	Bed no.

Date

CASE HISTORY

"The patient Sengle was born of healthy parents, but subsequent upon genesial excesses developed cardiac disorders that must have led to his discharge on medical grounds from military service, to his great regret, for this was an excellent soldier (not one punishment received). He never gave indications of cerebral disturbances. The wild mania with which he is now stricken must be attributed to the fall of a very heavy piece of plaster that detached itself from the wall while he was writing at his table, and caused a violent concussion of the cranium, according to the findings of our investigation..."

Sengle had read in a Chinese book the ethnography of a people... Would fly away over the sea.

Exploits and Opinions of Doctor Faustroll, Pataphysician

A Neo-Scientific Novel

Translated and annotated by Simon Watson Taylor
Introduced by Paul Edwards

INTRODUCTION

FAUSTROLL: PORTRAIT OF THE AUTHOR AS A PATAPHYSICIAN

This book will not be published in full until the author has gained enough experience to appreciate the beauty of all its parts. These fatal words were scrawled at the end of the Lormel manuscript of *Faustroll*. Jarry would never live to see it in print. As part of the story concerns life after death, the suggestion is also that only by opening the portals of death could a critic, or indeed the author, be in any position to testify to the ultimate truth of its contents — a dilemma usually only associated with the Bible. Jarry turns a joke aimed against those who would not publish him into a statement that implicitly refuses to evacuate the unknowable from the heart of literature. His book contains not a few mysteries, but the response of the College of 'Pataphysics was to explain what could be explained by painstaking annotation, and to repeat, after Boris Vian, that "Everything is in *Faustroll*". Being the most emblematic of Jarry's works and a touchstone of his life, *Faustroll* has become the "Bible" of Pataphysicians, and it was to become an inspiration to a number of major writers and artists of the twentieth century.

Gestes et opinions du docteur Faustroll, pataphysicien was written between late-1897 and mid-1898, that is to say after *Les Jours et les nuits*, with which it shares common preoccupations, namely the writing of autobiography and the theory of 'Pataphysics. There is little shared territory, however, with the more commercial *L'Amour en visites*, also written shortly before, or with the first drafts of the comic-opera *Pantagruel* (apart from the Rabelaisian vocabulary and the fact that, in Rabelais, Pantagruel and Panurge travel from island to island just as Faustroll does here). Then, in 1899, "Dr. Faustroll" suddenly reappears… as the signatory of the essay "Commentary and Instructions for the Practical Construction of the Time Machine". Whilst this reads like a chapter from Book 8 of the novel, a more substantial continuation of the *Gestes et opinions* was to be Jarry's speculative journalism, published under the headings "*Spéculations*" and, aptly enough, "*Gestes*".

The novel was completed in the spring of 1898, revised in 1899, and published posthumously (Fasquelle, 1911), as the work was not considered commercially viable by Jarry's closest publisher friends. In his lifetime, coherent extracts were published in two of the leading literary journals of the day, the *Mercure de France* and *La Plume*. All editions are based on the first edition and a combination of two manuscripts — known as the Lormel MS. of spring 1898 and the Fasquelle MS. of 1899 — which reveal small but interesting differences. These will be commented upon in the notes.

The best way to picture the world of *Faustroll* is to imagine the covers opening out to reveal a game-board. On the map are islands, just as in the *Odyssey*, there is a ship for a counter and many strange figurines. There is also a box full of accessories: 27 books and 27 imaginary beings, some letters, a painting machine, films, and ancient Greek scrolls to unravel. It is not so much a treasure hunt, though, as a forcible eviction. Faustroll is confronted by a bailiff who wants three years' unpaid rent, just as Jarry himself was evicted from his flat off the Boulevard du Port Royal before being offered temporary bed-space by the Douanier Rousseau. In the few years that Jarry had left before dying of abject poverty, malnutrition and tubercular meningitis, he transformed his everyday misfortunes into an imaginary world: Faustroll hangs himself and lives; his bailiff discovers that his victim is a genius and becomes his galley-slave; his bed becomes a ship to ride a sea of troubles; his library turns into a series of countries you can journey in. There is, however, a logic that goes beyond wish-fulfilment, in this substitute universe; the world of Faustroll is governed by new scientific principles and the science that describes them is 'Pataphysics.

The first fictional Pataphysician was Père Ubu, a grotesque tyrant modelled on Félix-Frédéric Hébert, a grandiloquent physics teacher who could not keep discipline at the Rennes Lycée. The plays that centre around Ubu were born from schoolboy skits and an oral tradition that Jarry contributed to and then brought before an adult audience. Although it said "doctor of Pataphysics" on Ubu's visiting-card, this new science is only evoked on stage for comic effect; in "The Autoclete", for example, Pataphysics is the science that allows Ubu to guess that the soup will be too salty and summon better dishes from the ground… if he only knew how to go about it. And yet the humour and comic definitions here contain, in embryo, a much more truly scientific endeavour. 'Pataphysics came to represent the *possible*, whatever can be modelled or imagined, whether in physics or in literature. In *Caesar-Antichrist*, "The Pataphysician" is "the Antichrist and God as well", in one person, "axiom and principle of the identity of opposites". Ubu had been but a bloated larva in *Ubu Roi*, but in 1895 he is identified with Caesar-Antichrist. The chrysalis in which the writer's over-subtle art sought form was the difficult play *Caesar-Antichrist*; with *Faustroll*, Jarry's mature work is born: Dr. Faustroll is the imago, the world's first intelligent Pataphysician, modelled on Jarry himself, or, rather, on his way of writing.

The first principle of 'Pataphysics, in practice, is that everything in the real world can be appropriated by literature (because all things are equivalent and there is no hierarchy, only absolutes and singularities): rubber stamps, legal prose, the formulae of the physical sciences, scientific methodology, other people's books, other people, films, the prayer-movements of the Brahmins, mathematics and anything that constitutes a sign or gesture. A fiscal stamp becomes a decorative vignette, legal prose the language of adventure, mathematics can be used to calculate the surface area of God, the literary tradition becomes a map of the world, other writers can put words in your mouth just as you can put words in theirs, enemies become puppets, films become paintings and hands raised in prayer can help you swim. Jarry realised, before the Surrealists, that anything can be decontextualised. As a journalist, Jarry chose to review *anything* that came in book form, whether fact or fiction, and learnt from them the varieties of prose that speak our world. By a return effect, reading Jarry makes the reader realise how *literary* science, religion and the law can be. In *Faustroll*, everything is literature, and all literature is equal — hence the appellation "*Livres Pairs*", "equivalent books", for the 27 volumes that include critically acclaimed masterpieces, the Bible, avant-garde Symbolism, a schoolboy play (*Ubu Roi*) and a particularly naïve children's story (by Desbordes-Valmore).

Faustroll is divided into eight Books and forty-one chapters simultaneously (Book 2 starts at chapter VIII, and so on). The narrative is initially linear and then the structure appears to break down, partly, but only partly, because the novel is a patchwork of pre-existing fragments; publication of "Elements of Pataphysics" (bk. 2) was announced in *Black Minutes*, and chapters XXVII to XLI, for example, read like cast-offs from *Caesar-Antichrist*. But the reader's disorientation is mostly due to the narrative being interrupted by philosophical digressions, and because Faustroll dies in chapter XXXV, leaving us with a series of emissions from beyond time and space. There *is* narrative unity, though the novel's structure bears more resemblance to Dante's *Divine Comedy*, Sterne's *Tristram Shandy*, or Rabelais, than to the popular norms of Naturalism and Best-Sellers, with their closed universes, sympathetic heroes with whom you can identify, and sentimental plots with endings that, like theatre trap-doors, are either open or shut. *Faustroll* is one of the experimental texts upon which Modernism was built.

This book feeds off a shared literary culture, mostly contemporary, and was never intended to be difficult, just *beautiful*. Only the passing of time has made it appear arcane. To specialists of the 1890s (currently the most fashionable decade in literary studies in France) the text presents no real readerly difficulties apart from the obsolete words and sometimes complicated syntax. As for the plot, it can be reduced to a few episodes, memorable enough to allow the reader to keep his or her bearings:

Book 1. The bailiff Panmuphle seizes Faustroll's library and other worldly goods, leaving only his bed/skiff/sieve. Faustroll hurls him into the cellar, which is a lake of wine. Panmuphle emerges drunk and writes up what happens next, starting by copying out for the reader's benefit Faustroll's manuscript:

Book 2. "Elements of Pataphysics", including two practical experiments. First, relativity is absolute: all observations depend on viewpoint and the scale of the scientist (for example: the force of capillary tension exerted on a scientist the size of a mite). Secondly, a word deprived of any meaning can therefore be used to convey any meaning (for example: "Ha ha", to which Faustroll returns in chapter XXIX).

Book 3. Faustroll and Panmuphle are joined by Bosse-de-Nage, the bum-faced baboon (based on the Belgian writer Christian Beck) who only ever says "Ha ha". The three of them sail forth in the skiff on dry land, thanks to suckers on the oars. They visit the imaginary worlds created by writers, painters and musicians Jarry admired, having safely avoided the island that represents Louis Libaude, a former collaborator (editor of *L'Art littéraire*, and eventual owner of the Lormel MS.).

Book 4. They moor in the Rue de Venise and Faustroll goes drinking and whoring with the marine bishop Mendacious (based on Paul Valéry). They engage in pataphysical discussions about nudity and auto-suggestion: the sight of a horse's head, says Faustroll, is enough to make him act like the Horseman of the Apocalypse. Then they go out to unhook shop signs. Seeing the one for a horse-butcher's, Faustroll lists the people he would kill first. In a fit, he strangles Bosse-de-Nage "from behind".

Book 5. Mendacious reads a book by Pierre Loti in the toilet as an aid to defecation. In a not unrelated scene, Faustroll leaves Henri Rousseau to daub over officially recognised art with his "Painting Machine".

Book 6. Faustroll is back at the brothel in bed with Visited. The Painting Machine, meanwhile, is now in the Palace of Machines where it projects thirteen films.

Book 7. Faustroll launches his skiff on the canal behind the Bastille only to commit suicide by sinking it. Panmuphle dies, Faustroll floats off to the "unknown dimension", but Mendacious swims away and (narrating) finishes the chapter.

Book 8. Faustroll continues his "Elements of Pataphysics" by emitting "telepathic letters" to Lord Kelvin.

There is little that is conventional in this "neo-scientific novel" (though the sub-title may have been added by the editors Jean Saltas and Gaston Danville, since it does not figure in the Lormel MS.). The book is not a pedigree genre but a cross-breed of cross-overs, combining art and science, Rabelaisian fun and metaphysics. More precisely, it is a collection of pataphysical exercises — or adventures — and to define Jarry's novel requires attempts to define 'Pataphysics. No catch-all definition exists, since 'Pataphysics is Jarry's writing style and partly also his lifestyle. I do not refer to his sometimes eccentric behaviour (the notorious anecdotes involving firearms, bicycles, put-on accents and comporting himself like a Père Ubu in public before an eager or terrorised crowd), only to his single-minded commitment to literature, at the peril of his health, comfort and survival.

In this book, 'Pataphysics is defined as the science of the particular (chapter VIII), whereas science concerns itself, of course, with general laws and repeatable phenomena. Jarry's apparently perverse interest in epiphenomena and unique occurrences was in the air at the time. Marcel Schwob, in his Preface to *Cœur Double* (1891), had argued that artists should focus on the "contingent". Saint-Pol-Roux, in his Preface to *Pauses in the Procession* (1893), wrote: "Faced with the same problem, everyone can find their own particular solution that will satisfy the general conditions." Scientists such as C.C. Baly were discovering that atoms of the same element were not necessarily exactly the same, and H.G. Wells extrapolated from this a new metaphysics in his essay "The Rediscovery of the Unique", which might as well have been entitled "Elements of Pataphysics", so close is it to Jarry's propositions. Oscar Wilde was particularly enthusiastic about Wells's essay and one can only speculate about whether Jarry and Wilde discussed it when they met in May 1898. The upshot of laboratory experiments was that infinitesimal differences were assuming metaphysical proportions, and metaphysicians were naturally reminded of Lucretius's concept of the Clinamen. Lucretius explains the possibility of Free Will in a material universe by putting chance and indeterminacy at the heart of the universe. Imagine atoms travelling in a straight line in empty space: the Clinamen is the sudden, infinitesimal "swerve" of one atom that leads to a collision with another and the origin and formation of matter. Jarry is not anti-Science, he is, like Wells, applying the latest popular treatises of science to literature and philosophy. More than that, Jarry demonstrates that physics is underpinned by philosophy, in this particular instance, ancient Greek philosophy, and that *all science is pataphysical*, since all scientific models are imaginary and temporary. When one compares the positivism of the nineteenth century with the concept-based science of the twentieth, one can only agree with him.

The non-Euclidean geometries of Nikolai Lobachevsky (1829), János Boylai (1833) and Bernhard Riemann in the mid-nineteenth century defy reason since they describe an apparently impossible mixture of two- and three-dimensional space: Riemannian space is two-dimensional curved space that is not curved in some "enveloping" three-dimensional space, and therefore cannot be "pictured". Jarry must have known of Riemann's works since the "foliated space" of Faustroll's library (ch. VII) is a reference to the parallel universes of Riemann's geometry (1857), also mentioned in Jarry's "Time Machine" essay. Newtonian physics received another blow with the Michelson-Morley experiment of 1881 which, to everyone's surprise, showed that light could not be "pushed"; it was a scientific conundrum only resolved in 1905 when Einstein decided to work on the assumption that the speed of light is the same for all observers: it is thus an absolute, the consequence being that space and time are not, they are relative, everywhere exceptional. The examination of "laws governing exceptions", otherwise known as 'Pataphysics, correctly describes what William Crookes sought to do when the spark from a copper cathode, expected to be white, flashed green. A new entity was discovered: the electron (1891). Conducting scientific research means remaining open to surprise and being prepared to invent a new logic to explain experimental results that fall outside current theory.

It was Crookes, too, who warned of the dangers of anthropocentrism and who first wrote the cautionary tale about the homunculus on the cabbage leaf to teach the relativity of the observer who relies on sense observations. In plagiarising the text, Jarry made its lesson in relativity his own. Relativity stops at nothing. Gaston de Pawlowski's *Voyage to the Land of the Fourth Dimension* contains pages about relativity and what we would today call the space-time continuum. In fact, much of the metaphysics of modern science is to be found in the Decadent literature of the 1890s. Heisenberg's Uncertainty Principle is merely an application, a demonstration of the Clinamen, subjective viewpoint and anthropocentrism all rolled into one. Einstein's General Theory establishes that cause does not necessarily precede effect, as Jarry predicted (ch. VIII). Einstein proved not only that the universe does not conform to the way we *experience* space, time and matter, but that the only accurate way to apprehend the universe is through abstract concepts that make no sense to our senses or to our *bodies*. Not only do imaginary numbers function in quadratics, now the universe is governed by *imaginary laws*. But what is mathematics if not aesthetic?

Putting his theory into practice, Jarry supplied a chapter to describe his main character, not as Dickens would with a statue of cloth to indicate relative wealth and social class, innocence or experience, but by means of atomic dimensions, an age suspended in time, and a made-to-measure body inspired by aesthetic considerations that could only exist in a digital universe or in a book. Faustroll is a book: he bathes in wallpaper, his eyes are ink with "golden spermatozoa" that symbolise the golden seam that lies at the heart of the books that count.

The second pataphysical principle is the identity of opposites, already very much at work in *Caesar-Antichrist* and visible in the name "Faustroll", combining as it does the cerebral Faust and the earthy Troll (Jarry played a Troll in *Peer Gynt*). Jarry neither invented the principle nor lifted it from a single source, for the idea has had an erratic but very long philosophical history, simply because all philosophical principles suggest their opposite, even that of non-contradiction. In the pataphysical universe of his novels, scientific paradox is substituted for the usual plot reversals: the "machine to inspire love" put on Marcueil's head backfires and falls in love with him (*The Supermale*); soldiers surround Erbrand and die when they shoot him according to the most elementary ballistics (*La Dragonne*); and whilst novelists were resorting to the public interest in post-hypnotic suggestion to have their criminals suggest murder to innocent intermediaries, Jarry has Emmanuel hypnotise Varia to inspire her with love (*Absolute Love*) in what is possibly the most metaphysically frightening novel ever written. Jarry had trained himself to turn ideas on their head, which was the future of science.

In 1899, while he was penning his *Monsieur Teste* (1896–1929), Paul Valéry summed up his activity by saying that he was "writing the life of Doctor Faustroll". Stéphane

Mallarmé and Marcel Schwob praised *Faustroll* in private letters to Jarry; Guillaume Apollinaire put it in print: "*Faustroll* and the new French translation of *Wilhelm Meister's Theatrical Mission* are the two literary events of 1911". The Surrealists promoted Jarry wholeheartedly, and Philippe Soupault prefaced the 1923 reprint. "*Faustroll* marks a turning-point in the history of criticism," wrote André Breton. He continued by describing Jarry's use of scientific sources: "It goes beyond analytical criticism and creates a synthesis instead, thus raising itself to the level of art." In 1929, René Daumal had his famous essay "Pataphysics and the Revelation of Laughter" published in the avant-garde magazine *Bifur*, and all the quotations turn out to be from *Faustroll*. "I am Faustroll," wrote Daumal. "In the beginning, Faustroll laughed the world into existence." The novel, one gathers, was infectious.

The College of 'Pataphysics was founded in 1948 in order to promote Jarry among the "happy few". One of its most inspired members, Boris Vian, wrote a continuation of the final chapter of *Faustroll*. But perhaps the most important artist to have lived and worked entirely in the spirit of Jarry and Faustroll was Marcel Duchamp. He is on record for having said that Jarry was his most important influence (along with Rabelais), and it was of the 1911 edition of *Faustroll* that he must have been thinking in particular when he told the art historian Serge Stauffer in 1965 that he found "an encouragement [...] in Jarry's general attitude towards what passed for literature in 1911." The pataphysical method of making *negatives* do the work of *positives* (according to the principle of the "identity of opposites") is clearly visible in Duchamp's life and work. Duchamp wanted an engagement ring with coal instead of diamond, wedding ankle-rings instead of finger-rings, he nailed coat-racks to the floor, used maps for wallpaper and made works of art by buying household goods in department stores and calling them art, readymade.

To trace the underground influence of Jarry through the twentieth century would be a difficult though rewarding study. Though the novel is never out of print in France, *Faustroll* is not quite a "classic", quite simply because it is not taught in class. It is considered difficult and retains something of an aura because it has come to represent — to caricature matters somewhat — that side of Jarry which is not Ubu. Many young readers who study *Ubu Roi* in France are unprepared for the variety of Jarry's *œuvre*, not to mention his radical approach to the novel as a genre. But "underground" classics find their own readers...

EXPLOITS AND OPINIONS OF DOCTOR FAUSTROLL, PATAPHYSICIAN

A NEO-SCIENTIFIC NOVEL

"There are eight abodes, eight places of sight, eight deities, and eight Purushas. Whoever understands those Purushas in their division, and again in their union, has overcome the world. I ask thee about the Purusha in the Upanishads. And thou explain not him to me, thy head will fall off." S'akalya knew him not, so his head fell off. Moreover robbers took away his bones, mistaking them for something else.

The Brihad A'Ranyaka Upanishad.

Book One

PROCEEDINGS

I

SUMMONS PURSUANT TO ARTICLE 819

In this year *Eighteen Hundred and Ninety*-eight, the Eighth day of February, *Pursuant to article 819 of the Code of Civil Procedure and at the request of M.* and Mme. Bonhomme (Jacques), *proprietors of a house situate at* Paris, 100 *bis*, rue Richer, *the aforementioned having address for service at my residence* and further at the Town Hall of Q borough.

I, the undersigned, René-Isidore Panmuphle, *Bailiff attached to the Civil Court of First Instance of the Department of the Seine, in session at Paris, residing in said City*, 37, rue Pavée, *Do hereby summon in the name of the* LAW and of JUSTICE, Monsieur Faustroll, doctor, *tenant of various premises dependent upon the house aforementioned, residing at* Paris, 100 *bis*, rue Richer, *and having proceeded to* the aforementioned house, bearing upon its exterior the number 100, and having rung, knocked, and called the aforementioned variously and successively, no person having opened the door to us, and the next-door neighbours declaring to us that this is indeed the residence of said M. Faustroll, but that they were unwilling to accept a copy of this writ and, inasmuch as I did find at said premises neither relations nor servants, nor any neighbour willing to accept service of this present copy by subscribing to the original thereto, I did proceed forthwith to the Town Hall of Q borough at which place I did personally deliver this present copy to his Worship the Mayor, who did certificate the original thereto; *within the maximum period of twenty-four hours, to pay to the claimant into my hands as tender in full and valid quittance the sum of* Three Hundred and Seventy-two thousand *francs 27 centimes, in respect of* Eleven *quarters rental of the aforementioned premises due on the* First day of January last, *without prejudice to those subsequently falling due and to any and all other rights, actions, interests, costs and distraint, declaring to the aforementioned that failing satisfaction of this present Summons within said period of time, he shall be constrained thereto by all lawful means, and notably by the seizure and impounding of such goods and chattels as may be present on the premises leased. Wherefore I did deposit this present copy of the foregoing at the premises aforesaid. Cost:* eleven *francs 30 centimes, including 1/2 sheet of special stamped paper at 0 fr. 60 centimes.*

PANMUPHLE

To Monsieur Faustroll, Doctor,
c/o the Town Hall of Q borough, Paris.

II
CONCERNING THE HABITS AND BEARING OF DOCTOR FAUSTROLL

Doctor Faustroll was sixty-three years old when he was born in Circassia in 1898 (the 20th century was (-2) years old).

At this age, which he retained all his life, Doctor Faustroll was a man of medium height, or, to be absolutely accurate, of $(8 \times 10^{10} + 10^{9} + 4 \times 10^{8} + 5 \times 10^{6})$ atomic diameters; with a golden-yellow skin, his face clean-shaven, apart from a sea-green mustachios, as worn by king Saleh; the hairs of his head alternately platinum blond and jet black, an auburn ambiguity changing according to the sun's position; his eyes, two capsules of ordinary writing-ink flecked with golden spermatozoa like Danzig schnapps.

He was beardless, apart from his mustachios, through the judicious use of baldness microbes which permeated his skin from the groin to the eyelashes and ate away all the follicles, without any need for Faustroll to fear that his scalp-hair or eyebrows might fall out, since these microbes attack only fresh young hairs. From his groin down to his feet, in contrast, he was sheathed in a satyric black fur, for he was man to an improper degree.

That morning he took his daily sponge-bath of two-tone wallpaper painted by Maurice Denis, with a design of trains climbing up spirals; a long time ago he had given up water in favour of wallpaper — seasonable, fashionable, or according to his whim.

So as not to embarrass the populace, he drew on over this design a shirt made of quartz fibre; baggy trousers of dull black velvet drawn tight at the ankles; tiny little grey boots, with even layers of dust carefully preserved on them, at great expense, for many months past, broken only by the dry geysers of ant-lions; a golden-yellow silk waistcoat, exactly the same colour as his skin, with no more buttons than an undervest, and two rubies as buttons for the breast pockets, very high up; and a greatcoat lined with blue fox fur.

On his right index finger, he piled emerald and topaz rings right up to the fingernail — the only one of the ten which he did not bite — and the line of rings was kept in place by a specially designed linchpin made of molybdenum, screwed into the bone of the ungual phalanx, through the fingernail.

By way of a tie, he passed around his neck the ceremonial ribbon of the Great Strumpot, an Order invented by himself and patented to avoid any vulgarisation.

He hanged himself by this ribbon on a specially constructed gibbet, procrastinating for a few quarter-hours between the choice of the two asphyxiating make-ups called *white hanged man* and *blue hanged man*.

And, after cutting himself down, he put on a sola topee.

III
SERVICE OF WRIT

In this year Eighteen Hundred and Ninety-eight, this tenth day of February, at Eight o'clock in the morning, pursuant to article 819 of the Code of Civil Procedure and at the request of M. and Mme. Bonhomme (Jacques), the husband both in his own name and in support and authorisation of the lady his spouse, proprietors of a house situate at Paris, no. 100 *bis*, rue Richer, the aforementioned having address for service at my residence and further at the Town Hall of Q borough,

I, THE UNDERSIGNED, RENÉ-ISIDORE PANMUPHLE, BAILIFF ATTACHED TO THE CIVIL COURT OF FIRST INSTANCE OF THE DEPARTMENT OF THE SEINE, IN SESSION AT PARIS, RESIDING IN SAID CITY, 37, RUE PAVÉE, do hereby summon in reiteration in the name of the Law and of Justice Monsieur Faustroll, doctor, tenant of various premises dependent upon the house aforementioned, residing therein at the aforementioned rue Richer, No. 100 *bis*, which bears at present the number 100, where having proceeded and having knocked variously and successively without obtaining a reply, we betook ourselves to Paris, to the office of M. Solarcable, commissioner of police, the latter granting us his assistance in our undertaking; to pay to myself as Bailiff and bearer of said summons, the sum of Three Hundred and Seventy-two thousand francs 27 centimes in respect of Eleven quarters rental of the aforementioned premises without prejudice to other claims, the named party having refused payment of these claims.

Wherefore I have seized in distraint and placed under the authority of the Law and of Justice the following objects:

IV
CONCERNING THE EQUIVALENT BOOKS OF DOCTOR FAUSTROLL

In the premises detailed above, entry having been effected by M. Lourdeau, locksmith at Paris, no. 205, rue Nicolas Flamel, with the exception of a bed of polished copper mesh, twelve metres long and without bedding, of an ivory chair and of an onyx and gold table; sequestration made of twenty-seven assorted volumes, some paper-backed and others bound, with the following titles:

1. BAUDELAIRE, a volume of E. A. Poe translations.
2. BERGERAC, *Works*, volume II, containing the *History of the States and Empires of the Sun*, and the *History of Birds*.
3. *The Gospel According to* SAINT LUKE, in Greek.
4. BLOY, *The Ungrateful Beggar*.
5. COLERIDGE, *The Rime of the Ancient Mariner*.
6. DARIEN, *The Thief*.
7. DESBORDES-VALMORE, *The Oath of the Little Men*.
8. ELSKAMP, *Illuminated Designs*.
9. An odd volume of the *Plays* of FLORIAN.
10. An odd volume of the *Thousand and One Nights*, in the GALLAND translation.
11. GRABBE, *Scherz, Satire, Ironie und tiefere Bedeutung*, comedy in three acts.
12. KAHN, *The Tale of Gold and of Silence*.

13. LAUTRÉAMONT, *The Lays of Maldoror.*
14. MAETERLINCK, *Aglavaine and Sélysette.*
15. MALLARMÉ, *Verse and Prose.*
16. MENDÈS, *Gog.*
17. *The Odyssey*, Teubner's edition.
18. PÉLADAN, *Babylon.*
19. RABELAIS.
20. JEAN DE CHILRA, *The Sexual Hour.*
21. HENRI DE RÉGNIER, *The Jasper Cane.*
22. RIMBAUD, *The Illuminations.*
23. SCHWOB, *The Children's Crusade.*
24. *Ubu Roi.*
25. VERLAINE, *Wisdom.*
26. VERHAEREN, *The Hallucinated Landscapes.*
27. VERNE, *Voyage to the Centre of the Earth.*

In addition, three prints hanging on the walls, a poster by TOULOUSE-LAUTREC, *Jane Avril*; one by BONNARD, advertising the *Revue blanche*; a portrait of Doctor Faustroll, by AUBREY BEARDSLEY; and an old picture, which appeared to us to be valueless, *Saint Cado*, issued by the Oberthür printing house of Rennes.

It was impossible to enter the cellar due to the flooding thereof. It appeared to be filled, to a height of two metres, with a mixture of wine and spirits, though no barrels or bottles were to be seen.

I have installed as guardian thereof, in absence of the subject of distraint, M. Delmor de Pionsec, one of my witnesses named hereunder. The sale will take place on whatever day shall ultimately be decided, at the hour of noon, in the Place de l'Opéra.

And from all the aforementioned facts, I have assembled the present official report, the compilation of which occupied me from eight in the morning until a quarter before three in the afternoon, and of which I have left a copy for the subject of distraint, in the hands of his excellency the aforenamed commissioner of police, and with the guardian, and without prejudice to any further actions, the above matter wholly in the presence of and assisted by Messrs. Delmor de Pionsec and Troccon, attorneys-at-law, residing at Paris, 37, rue Pavée, the required witnesses who have with myself signed original and copy. Cost thirty-two francs 40 centimes. For the copies were used two sheets of official paper costing 1 fr. 20 centimes. Signed: Lourdeau, locksmith. Signed: Solarcable, commissioner of police. Signed: Delmor de Pionsec. Signed: Panmuphle, bailiff. Registered at Paris, the 11th day of February 1898. Received five francs. Signed: Liconet. True copy certified. (*Illegible.*)

V
NOTICE OF WARRANT ENABLING IMMEDIATE SALE

In this year *Eighteen Hundred and Ninety*-eight, the Fourth day of June, *at the request of M.* and Mme. Bonhomme (Jacques), the husband *residing at* Paris, rue Pavée, 37, *electing domicile in my office* and further at the Town Hall of Q borough;

I, the undersigned, René-Isidore Panmuphle, BAILIFF *attached to the Civil Court of First Instance of the Department of the Seine, in session at Paris, residing in said City*, 37, rue Pavée, *have signified, declared, and under the above heading deposited copy with M. Faustroll...*

. . . .

Whereas this present half-sheet of special stamped paper at 60 centimes is insufficient to record the diverse marvels which I discovered at the home of the said Doctor Faustroll, having drunk my fill in the cellar into which he had hurled me; the present deponent provisionally does solicit the favour of his honour the President of the Civil Tribunal of the Seine to authorise, in so far as the cost of stamped paper does threaten to exceed largely the amount deposited, the description of the ensuing events on unstamped paper, so that a record may be retained for the Law and for Justice of the said marvels, and that such record may not perish.

VI
CONCERNING THE DOCTOR'S BOAT, WHICH IS A SIEVE

To C.V. Boys

Doctor Faustroll, arising from under the sheets covering the polished copper bed which I was not authorised to seize, and addressing himself to me, speaking to me personally, said:

"It is probable that you have no conception, Panmuphle, writ-carrying bailiff, of capillarity, of surface tension, nor of weightless membranes, equilateral hyperbolae, surfaces without curvature, nor, more generally, of the elastic skin which is water's epidermis.

"Since the days when saints and miracle-workers went sailing in stone troughs or on coats of coarse cloth, and when Christ walked barefoot on the sea, I know of no creature — apart from myself — other than the filiform water-scorpion and the larvae of water gnats, capable of making use of the surface of ponds, either from above or beneath, as a solid floor.

"It is true that it has been possible to construct sacks made from a material which allows air and steam to pass through but is impermeable to water, so that one can blow out a candle through the cloth and yet the same cloth will retain its liquid content indefinitely. My colleague F. de Romilly has succeeded in boiling liquids in a bell jar whose base was made of gauze with a fairly wide mesh...

"But this bed, twelve metres long, is not a bed but a boat, shaped like an elongated sieve. The meshes are wide enough to allow the passage of a large pin; and the whole sieve has been dipped in melted paraffin, then shaken so that this substance (which is never really *touched* by water), while covering the web, leaves the holes empty — the number of which amounts to about fifteen million four hundred thousand. When I place my sieve on the river, the water's skin tautens against the holes, and the liquid flowing beneath cannot penetrate unless the skin breaks. But the convexity of my round keel offers no projecting angle, and the pressure of the water during launching, while jumping rapids, etc., is reduced by an external non-paraffined shell with much larger meshes, sixteen thousand only; this serves additionally to protect the paraffin glaze from being scratched by reeds, just as an interior grill saves it from damage by feet.

"My sieve, then, floats like a boat, and can be laden without sinking to the bottom. Not only that, it possesses this advantage over ordinary boats — as my learned friend C.V. Boys has remarked to me — that one can allow a thin jet of water to fall on it without submerging it. If I should decide to expel my urates, or if a wave should break over the side, the liquid will simply pass through the mesh and rejoin the external waves.

"In this perpetually dry boat (called a skiff, doubtless because it is constructed to carry three people), I shall henceforth take up my residence, since I am forced to leave this house..."

"Doubtless," I said, "because the premises are no longer furnished."

"I also possess an even finer skiff," continued the doctor, "of quartz fibre drawn out by means of a crossbow; but at the present moment I have just deposited thereon, with the aid of a straw, 250,000 drops of castor oil, in imitation of the beads on spiders' webs, alternately large and small beads, the vibrations per second of the latter being to the vibrations per second of the former in the proportion of $\frac{64,000}{1/2,000,000}$ under the sole influence of the pressure of the liquid's elastic skin. This skiff has every appearance of a huge genuine spider's web, and catches flies just as easily. But it is only fitted out for one person.

"And since the present one carries three people, you shall accompany me, and someone else to whom you will shortly be introduced — not to mention some others, for I am bringing along some beings who have managed to escape your Law and your Justice between the lines of my seized volumes.

"And while I enumerate them, and summon the other *person*, here is a book, handwritten by myself, which you can seize as the twenty-eighth volume and read, so that you may not only contain yourself in patience but may also very probably understand me better during the course of this voyage, though I am not asking your opinion about its necessity."

"Yes, but this navigation in a sieve..."

"The skiff is not only propelled by oar blades but also by suction discs at the end of spring levers. And its keel travels on three steel rollers at the same level. I am all the more convinced of the excellence of my calculations and of its insubmersibility in that, as is my invariable habit, we shall not be navigating on water but on dry land."

VII
CONCERNING THE CHOSEN FEW

Across the foliated space of the twenty-seven equivalents, Faustroll conjured up into the third dimension:

From Baudelaire, E.A. Poe's Silence, taking care to retranslate Baudelaire's translation into Greek.

From Bergerac, the precious tree into which the nightingale-king and his subjects were metamorphosed, in the land of the sun.

From Luke, the Calumniator who carried Christ on to a high place.

From Bloy, the black pigs of Death, retinue of the Betrothed.

From Coleridge, the ancient mariner's crossbow and the ship's floating skeleton, which, when placed in the skiff, was sieve upon sieve.

From Darien, the diamond crowns of the Saint-Gothard rock-drillers.

From Desbordes-Valmore, the duck placed by the woodcutter at the children's feet, and the fifty-three trees with scored barks.

From Elskamp, the hares, running over the sheets, which became cupped hands and carried the spherical universe like a fruit.

From Florian, Scapin's lottery ticket.

From *The Thousand and One Nights*, the eye of the third Kalender, who was the son of a king: the eye poked out by the tail of the flying horse.

From Grabbe, the thirteen journeymen tailors massacred at dawn by Baron Mordax on the order of the knight of the papal order of Civil Merit, and the table napkin which he tied round his neck beforehand.

From Kahn, one of the golden peals from the celestial goldsmiths' shops.

From Lautréamont, the scarab, beautiful as the trembling of hands in alcoholism, which vanished over the horizon.

From Maeterlinck, the lights heard by the first blind sister.

From Mallarmé, the virgin, the bright, and the beautiful today.

From Mendès, the north wind which blew upon the green sea and blended with its salt the sweat of the galley-slave who rowed until he was a hundred and twenty years old.

From the *Odyssey*, the joyful walk of the irreproachable son of Peleus in the meadow of asphodels.

From Péladan, the reflection, in the mirror of the shield silvered with ancestral ashes, of the sacrilegious massacre of the seven planets.

From Rabelais, the little bells to which the devils danced during the tempest.

From Rachilde, Cleopatra.

From Régnier, the sorrel plain where the modern centaur snorted.

From Rimbaud, the icicles hurled by the wind of God into the waters.

From Schwob, the scaly animals imitated by the whiteness of the leper's hands.

From *Ubu Roi*, the fifth letter of the first word of the first act.

From Verhaeren, the cross made by the spade in the horizon's four brows.

From Verlaine, voices asymptotic toward death.

From Verne, the two and a half leagues of the earth's crust.

Meanwhile, René-Isidore Panmuphle, bailiff, began to read Faustroll's manuscript in deep darkness, substantiating the invisible ink of sulphate of quinine by means of the invisible infra-red rays of a spectrum whose other colours were locked in an opaque box; until he was interrupted by the introduction of the third traveller.

BOOK TWO

ELEMENTS OF PATAPHYSICS

To Thadée Natanson

VIII
DEFINITION

An epiphenomenon is that which is superinduced upon a phenomenon.

Pataphysics, whose etymological spelling should be ἔπι (μετὰ τὰ φυσικά) and actual orthography *'pataphysics*, preceded by an apostrophe so as to avoid a simple pun, is the science of that which is superinduced upon metaphysics, whether within or beyond the latter's limitations, extending as far beyond metaphysics as the latter extends beyond physics. And an epiphenomenon being often accidental, pataphysics will be, above all, the science of the particular, despite the common opinion that the only science is that of the general. Pataphysics will examine the laws governing exceptions, and will explain the universe supplementary to this one; or, less ambitiously, will describe a universe which can be — and perhaps should be — envisaged in the place of the traditional one, since the laws that are supposed to have been discovered in the traditional universe are also correlations of exceptions, albeit more frequent ones, but in any case accidental data which, reduced to the status of unexceptional exceptions, possess no longer even the virtue of originality.

DEFINITION. *Pataphysics is the science of imaginary solutions, which symbolically attributes the properties of objects, described by their virtuality, to their lineaments.*

Contemporary science is founded upon the principle of induction: most people have seen a certain phenomenon precede or follow some other phenomenon most often, and conclude therefrom that it will ever be thus. Apart from other considerations, this is true only in the majority of cases, depends upon the point of view, and is codified only for convenience — if that! Instead of formulating the law of the fall of a body towards a centre, how far more apposite would be the law of the ascension of a vacuum towards a periphery, a vacuum being considered a unit of non-density, a hypothesis far less arbitrary than the choice of a concrete unit of positive density such as *water*?

For even this body is a postulate and an average man's point of view, and in order that its qualities, if not its nature, should remain fairly constant, it would be necessary to postulate that the height of human beings should remain more or less constant and mutually equivalent. Universal assent is already a quite miraculous and incomprehensible prejudice. Why should anyone claim that the shape of a watch is round — a manifestly false proposition — since it appears in profile as a narrow rectangular construction, elliptic on three sides; and why the devil should one only have noticed its shape at the moment of looking at the time? Perhaps under the pretext of utility. But a child who draws a watch as a circle will also draw a house as a square, as a façade, without any justification, of course; because, except perhaps in the country, he will rarely see an isolated building, and even in a street the façades have the appearance of very oblique trapezoids.

We must, in fact, inevitably admit that the common herd (including small children and women) is too dimwitted to comprehend elliptic equations, and that its members are at one in a so-called universal assent because they are capable of perceiving only those curves having a single focal point, since it is easier to coincide with one point rather than with two. These people communicate and achieve equilibrium by the outer edge of their bellies, tangentially. But even the common herd has learned that the *real* universe is composed of ellipses, and tradesmen keep their wine in barrels rather than cylinders.

So that we may not abandon, through digression, our usual example of water, let us reflect, in this connection, upon the irreverence of the common herd whose instinct sums up the adepts of the science of pataphysics in the following phrase:

IX
FAUSTROLL SMALLER THAN FAUSTROLL

To William Crookes

> Other madmen cried ceaselessly that the figure one was at the same time bigger and smaller than itself, and proclaimed a number of similar absurdities as if they were useful discoveries.
>
> *The Talisman of Oromane*

Doctor Faustroll (if one may be permitted to speak from personal experience) desired one day to be smaller than himself and resolved to explore one of the elements, in order to examine any disturbances which this change in size might involve in their mutual relationship.

For this purpose he chose that substance which is normally liquid, colourless, incompressible and horizontal in small quantities; having a curved surface, blue in depth and with edges that tend to ebb and flow when it is stretched; which Aristotle terms heavy, like earth; the enemy of fire and renascent from it when decomposed explosively; which vaporises at a hundred degrees, a temperature determined by this fact, and in a solid state floats upon itself — water, of course! And having shrunk to the classic size of a mite, as a paradigm of smallness, he travelled along the length of a cabbage leaf, paying no attention to his fellow mites or to the magnified aspect of his surroundings, until he encountered the Water.

This was a globe, twice his size, through whose transparency the outlines of the universe appeared to him gigantically enlarged, whilst his own image, reflected dimly by the leaves' foil, was magnified to his original size. He gave the orb a light tap, as if knocking on a door: the deracinated eye of malleable glass "adapted itself" like a living eye, became presbyopic, lengthened itself along its horizontal diameter into an ovoid myopia, repulsed Faustroll by means of this elastic inertia and became spherical once more.

The doctor, taking small steps, rolled the crystal globe, with some considerable difficulty, towards a neighbouring globe, slipping on the rails of the cabbage leaf's veins; coming together, the two spheres sucked each other in, tapering in the process, until suddenly a new globe of twice the size rocked placidly in front of Faustroll.

With the tip of his boot the doctor kicked out at this unexpected development of the elements: an explosion, formidable in its fragmentation and noise, rang out following the projection all around of new and minute spheres, dry and hard as diamonds, that rolled to and fro all along the green arena, each one drawing along beneath it the image of the tangential point of the universe, distorting it according to the sphere's projection and magnifying its fabulous centre.

Beneath everything, the chlorophyll, like a shoal of green fishes, followed its charted currents in the cabbage's subterranean canals...

X
CONCERNING THE DOGFACED BABOON BOSSE-DE-NAGE, WHO KNEW NO HUMAN WORDS BUT "HA HA"

To Christian Beck

> Hey, you, said Giromon gravely; as for you, I'll take your robe for a storm-sail; your legs for masts, your arms for yardarms; your body for the hull, and I'll f...... well pitch you into the water with six inches of steel in your stomach for ballast... And since, when you are a ship, it's your fat head which will serve as a figurehead, then I shall baptise you: *the dirty b.......*
>
> Eugène Sue, *The Salamander*
>
> (*le pichon joueic deis diables*)

Bosse-de-Nage was a dogfaced baboon less cyno- than hydrocephalous, and, as a result of this blemish, less intelligent than his fellows. The red and blue callosity which they sport on their buttocks was, in his case, displaced by Faustroll, by means of some strange medication, and grafted on to his cheeks, azurine on one, scarlet on the other, so that his flat face was a tricolour.

Not content with this, the good doctor wanted to teach him to speak; and if Bosse-de-Nage (so named because of the double protuberance of the cheeks described above) was not completely familiar with the French language, he could pronounce fairly correctly a few words of Belgian, calling the lifebelt hanging at the stern of Faustroll's skiff "swimming-bladder with inscription thereon", but more often he enunciated a tautological monosyllable:

"Ha ha," he said in French; and he added nothing more.

This character will prove very useful during the course of this book, to punctuate some of its overlong speeches: in the manner of Victor Hugo (*The Burgraves*, part I, sc. 2):

And is that all?

Nay, listen yet:

And Plato, in various passages:

— Ἀληθῆ λέγεις, ἔφη.
— Ἀληθῆ.
— Ἀληθέστατα.
— Δῆλα γαρ, ἔφη, καὶ τυφλῷ.
— Δῆλα δή.
— Δῆλον δή.
— Δίκαιον γοῦν.
— Εἰκός.
— Ἔμοιγε.
— Ἔοικε γάρ.
— Ἔστιν, ἔφη.
— Καὶ γὰρ ἐφω.
— Καὶ μάλ', ἔφη.
— Κάλλιστα λέγεις.
— Καλῶς.
— Κομιδῇ μὲν οὖν.
— Μέμνημαι.
— Ναί.
— Ξυμβαίνει γάρ οὕτως.
— Οἶμαι μὲν, καὶ πολύ.
— Ὁμολογῶ.
— Ὀρθότατα.
— Ὀρθῶς γ', ἔφη.
— Ὀρθῶς ἔφη.
— Ὀρθῶς μοι δοκεῖς λέγειν.
— Οὐκοῦν χρή.
— Παντάπασι.
— Παντάπασι μὲν οὐν.
— Πάντων μάλιστα.
— Πάνυ μὲν οὖν.
— Πεισόμεθα μὲν οὖν.
— Πολλὴ ἀνάγκη.

— Πολύ γε.
— Πολὺ μὲν οὖν μάγιστα.
— Πρέπει γάρ.
— Πῶς· γὰρ ἄν;
— Πῶς γὰρ οὔ;
— Πῶς δ' οὔ;
— Τί δαί;
— Τὶ μὴν.
— Τοῦτο μὲν ἄληθὲς λέγεις.
— Ὧς δοκεὶ.

Here follows the narrative of René-Isidore Panmuphle.

BOOK THREE

FROM PARIS TO PARIS BY SEA OR, THE BELGIAN FAMILY ROBINSON

To Alfred Vallette

Inquiring what men of learning there were then in the city, and what wine they drank there.

Gargantua, Ch. XVI.

XI
CONCERNING THE EMBARKATION IN THE ARK

Bosse-de-Nage descended with tiny steps, making sure of the flat adhesion of his feet as one unrolls a glued poster, carrying the skiff on his shoulder by the ears, in imitation of the ancient Egyptians teaching their disciples. The red metal surface, like that of the boat-fly, began to shine in the sun as the long boat ventured its xyphoid twelve-metre long prow from out of the passageway. The curved blades of the oars made a clangorous sound as they scraped along the sides of the old stone walls.

"Ha ha!" said Bosse-de-Nage as he deposited the skiff upon the pavement; but on this occasion he added nothing to his statement.

Faustroll rubbed the rubicund cheeks of the cabin-boy against the grooves of the sliding seat to lubricate the mechanism; the scorched face glowed more luminously still, swelling up in the bows as a lantern to light our way. The doctor sat aft on his ivory chair: between his legs was the onyx table covered with his compasses, maps, sextants and various other scientific instruments; he threw at his feet, in place of ballast, the curious beings retained from his twenty-seven equivalent books and the manuscript seized by myself; then he passed around his elbows the tiller's two guide-ropes, and motioning me to sit down, facing him, on the felt sliding seat (which I could not help obeying, drunk as I was and ready to believe anything), he shackled my feet to two leather fetters at the bottom of the skiff, and thrust into my hands the handles of the ash-wood oars, whose blades moved apart with the surging symmetry of two peacock's feathers preening.

I pulled at the oars, moving in my backward position I knew not whither, squinting between two lanes of moist lines in a grey horizontality, overtaking forms looming up from behind me which the sharp-edged oars chopped off at the legs; other distant forms followed the direction we were taking. We ploughed through the masses of people as through a dense fog, and the acoustical sign of our progress was the screech of tearing silk.

Between the distant figures which followed us and those near us which crossed our path, one could distinguish other figures, vertical and more or less stationary. Faustroll consented to explain to me that the function of navigators was to make land and to drink, while the role of Bosse-de-Nage was to draw the skiff up on to the bank at each halt on our errant way, as also to interrupt our conversation, where a pause might be convenient, with his interjections; thus, I gazed at the beings hoving into view from behind me, in the same way as did the watchers in the Platonic den, and I consulted on successive occasions the teaching of the vessel's master, Faustroll the doctor.

XII
CONCERNING THE SQUITTY SEA, THE OLFACTORY LIGHTHOUSE, AND THE ISLE OF CACK, WHERE WE DRANK NOT

To Louis L…

"This dead body," said the doctor, "from whose carcass you can see old fogies trembling in senility and young men with red hair, equally cretinous in their speech and their silence, giving beaks full of flesh to speckled, handwriting-coloured birds, like ichneumon flies boring into flesh to lay their eggs — this dead body is not only an island but a man: he is pleased to call himself Baron Hildebrand of the Squitty Sea.

"And since the island is sterile and desolate, he can grow no kind of beard. He suffered from impetigo in childhood, and his nurse, who was so old that her lore was sufficient to encourage unusually copious stool, predicted to him that this was a sign that he would be unable to dissimulate from anyone

the infamous nudity of his calf's muzzle.

"Only his brain — and the anterior motor centres of the medulla — are dead. And because of this inertia he is, on our navigatory route, not a man but an island, and this is why (if you both behave, I will show you the map)…"

"Ha ha!" said Bosse-de-Nage, waking up suddenly; then he relapsed into an obstinate silence.

"…This is why," continued Faustroll, "I find him mentioned on my fluvial map as isle of Cack."

"Yes," I said, "but how is it that this crowd of people and birds which has come to scatter obituaries on the corpse can raven upon him with such confidence, in the middle of this vast plain, while all these greybeards and young men, if I am not isobic to them, are blind and without sticks?"

"See here," said Faustroll, opening his seized manuscript, the ELEMENTS OF PATAPHYSICS, book N, ch. ζ: *Concerning Obelischolychnies for dogs, while they are still baying at the moon.*

"A lighthouse raises its pr... in a storm, says Corbière; a lighthouse lifts its finger to point out from afar the place of safety, of truth and beauty. But for moles and for you too, Panmuphle, a lighthouse is as invisible as the ten-thousand-and-first sonic interval is imperceptible, or the infra-red rays by whose light I have written this book. The lighthouse of the isle of Cack is dark, subterranean, and cloacal, as if it had looked at the sun too long. No waves break against it, and thus no sound guides one to it. And your cerumen, Panmuphle, would close your ears even to its subterranean rumblings.

"This lighthouse nourishes itself upon the pure matter which is the substance of the isle of Cack; that is to say, the Baron's soul, exhaled from his mouth by a leaden blowpipe. From all the places where I refuse to drink, flights of pages, guided by his scent, come like magpies to suck life (their own, *exclusive*) from the syrupy and smoking jet emanating from the saturnine blowpipe. And so that it shall not be stolen from them, the greybeards, organised into a monastery, have built upon the Baron's carcass a little chapel that they have christened CATHOLIC MAXIMUM. The speckled birds have their dovecotes there. The people call them young wild duck. We pataphysicians call them simply and honestly shit-diggers."

XIII
CONCERNING THE LAND OF LACE

To Aubrey Beardsley

After leaving this displeasing island behind, our map was refolded and I rowed for another six hours, my toes held by fetters, my tongue hanging out from thirst — we would have been mortally ill had we taken a drink in that island — and Faustroll kept me drawn so upright with the parallel jerks of the two cords of his tiller that, in my backward motion, I could just see straight astern the island's smoke still rising until it was hidden by the doctor's shoulders. Bosse-de-Nage, so exhausted from thirst that he was quite livid, gave out only a dim light.

Suddenly a purer light than this emerged from the shadows, but in no way similar to the brutal genesis of the world.

The king of Lace drew out the light as a rope-maker plaits his retrograde line, and the threads trembled slightly in the dim light, like cobwebs. They wove themselves into forests, like the leaves which hoar-frost engraves on window-panes; then they fashioned themselves into a Madonna and her Child in the Christmas snow; and then into jewels, peacocks, and gowns, intermingling like the swimming dance of the Rhine maidens. The Beaux and the Belles strutted and preened in imitation of fans, until their patient gathering broke up with a cry. Just as the white junonians, roosting in a park, complain raucously when the lying intrusion of a lamp apes prematurely the dawn's reflection of their ocelli, so an artless shape burgeoned in the forest of raked-over pine-pitch; and as Pierrot serenades the confusion of the moon's entwined ball, the paradox of day burrowing underground arose from Ali Baba screaming in the pitiless oil and the jar's darkness.

Bosse-de-Nage, as far as I could judge, understood these prodigies very little.

"Ha ha," he said succinctly; and he did not lose himself in further considerations.

XIV
CONCERNING THE FOREST OF LOVE

To Émile Bernard

Like a tree frog out of water, the skiff edged forward, drawn by its suction discs along a smooth descending road.

In this district of Paris no omnibus had ever passed, nor railway, nor tramway, nor bicycle, nor probably any openwork boat with a copper skin, moving upon three rollers set at the same level, manned by a doctor pataphysician, who has at his feet the twenty-seven most excellent quintessences of works brought back by inquisitive men from their travels, manned also by a bailiff named Panmuphle (I, René-Isidore, the undersigned) and by a hydrocephalous baboon knowing no words of human language except *ha ha*. Here, instead of street lamps we could see ancient monuments of carved stone, green statues crouching down in robes folded in the shape of hearts; heterosexual ring-dancers blowing into unmentionable flageolets; finally, a seaweed-green calvary in which the eyes of the women were like nuts cloven horizontally by the suture line of their shells.

The incline opened out suddenly into the triangle of an open space. The sky opened out too, and a sun burst open in it like the yolk of a prairie oyster bursting in the throat, and the azure became reddish blue; the sea was so warm that it steamed; the re-dyed costumes of the passers-by were splashes of colour more brilliant than opaque precious stones.

"Are you Christians?" asked a bronzed man, dressed in a gaudy smock, standing in the centre of the little triangular town.

"Like M. Arouet, M. Renan, and M. Charbonnel," I answered after some reflection.

"I am God," said Faustroll.

"Ha ha!" said Bosse-de-Nage, without further commentary.

Thus I remained in charge of the skiff with the baboon cabin-boy, who passed the time by jumping on my shoulders and pissing down my back; but I beat him off with blows from a bundle of writs, and observed with curiosity from far off the demeanour of the gaily dressed man who had approved of Faustroll's answer.

They were seated beneath a great archway, behind which was a second, and behind these there blazed the greenness and fatness of an historiated field of cabbages. Between the arches were tables and pitchers and benches set out in a barn and on a threshing floor, crowded with people dressed in sapphire-blue velvet, with diamond-shaped faces and down-coloured hair, the furry surface of the earth and of the people's necks being both like cows' hair. Men were wrestling in a blue and yellow meadow, disturbing sand-grey toads whose frightened croaks reached me in the boat; couples danced gavottes; and the bagpipes, from on top of the freshly drained barrels, droned out the flight of ribbons of white tinsel and violet silk.

Each of the two thousand dancers in the barn offered to Faustroll a girdlecake, hard cube-shaped milk, and different liqueurs in glasses as thick as a bishop's amethyst is wide and holding less than a thimbleful. The doctor drank from them all. Each person present threw a pebble into the sea, stinging the blisters on my hands, novice oarsman that I was, as I held them up to protect myself, and stinging the multicoloured cheeks of Bosse-de-Nage.

"Ha ha!" he growled, to express his fury, but he remembered his solemn oath.

The doctor returned to the sound of bells, with two big maps of the country, which his guide had given him absolutely free; one represented realistically, worked in tapestry, the forest surrounding the triangular space: the rose-red foliage rising above the blue mass of the grass, and the groups of women, the wave of each group with its crest of white bonnets breaking gently against the ground, in an eccentric circle of dawn shadow.

And on it was written: *The Forest of Love*. On the second map were enumerated all the products of this happy land, men at the market with their plump yellow pigs, themselves plump and blue, stuffed into their clothes like sausages. They were all as blown up as the cheeks of a bagpiper, as full of wind as a bagpipe or a stomach.

The Christian host took leave of Faustroll courteously and sailed away in his own boat towards a more distant land. And we could see the red line of the sea's horizon cut the beam of his rose-coloured sail.

We rubbed the adipose cheeks of the hydrocephalous baboon against the slide rails of the felt seat; and when I had taken up the oars once more, and Faustroll had taken the tiller's silken guide-ropes, I crouched and stretched out once again in the alternating movements of the oarsman, over the conjoined waves of the dry land.

XV
CONCERNING THE GREAT STAIRCASE OF BLACK MARBLE

To Léon Bloy

At the valley's mouth, we skirted one final calvary, whose frightening height might have led one to take it, at first sight, for a gigantic, black, mass altar. At the blunt point of this improbable marble pyramid, between two acolytes strongly resembling cynocephali of Tanit, the huge king's head carbonised itself in the moon's furnace. He was grasping a tiger by the scruff of its neck, and was forcing the people of the Squitty Sea to climb up on hands and knees. After their bones had first been slashed by the blades of the successive steps, he let the monstrous hunter gorge itself with their flesh from butchers' hooks gripped in his fist.

He welcomed Faustroll with honour, and, raising his arm from the summit of the calvary, he deposited in our skiff a viaticum of twenty-four Squitty sea-ears skewered on a unicorn's horn.

XVI
CONCERNING THE AMORPHOUS ISLE

To Franc-Nohain

This island is like soft coral, amoeboid and protoplasmic: its trees closely resemble the gesture of snails making horns at us. Its government is oligarchic. One of its kings, as the height of his pschent indicated to us, lived upon the devotion of his seraglio; to escape the judgement of his Parliaments, which was motivated by envy, he has crawled through the drains right down to below the monolith in the main square and has gnawed it away so as to leave a crust only two inches thick. And thus he is two fingers' breadth away from the gallows. Like Simon Stylites, he hides away in this hollow column, since it is fashionable today to place nothing on the platforms of the capitals but statues, which are the best caryatids in bad weather. He works, sleeps, loves and drinks on the verticality of a long ladder, and has no other lamp in his waking hours than the pallor of his nuptials. One of his minor achievements is the invention of the tandem, which extends to quadrupeds the benefits of the pedal.

Another king, versed in halieutics, decorates with his fishing-lines the tracks of circular railways resembling the beds of rivers. But the trains, with the cruelty of youth, chase fish before them or crush embryonic bites in their bellies.

A third king has rediscovered the language of paradise, intelligible even to animals, and has brought some of these animals to perfection. He has manufactured electric dragonflies and has counted the innumerable ants by use of the figure 3.

Another, remarkable for his hairless face, instructed us in useful wiles, so that we became competent to make full use of our free evenings, consolidate our dead-drunk credits and gain, without wasting our talent, the rewards of the French Academy.

Another mimes the thoughts of mankind, using personages of whom he has kept only the top half of their bodies, so that there may be nothing inside but what is pure.

Yet another is elaborating a huge tome, with the aim of computing the qualities of the French, who, he claims, will be as brave as they are gay, as gay as they are witty; in order to devote himself entirely to this labour, he has contrived to lose his young progeny in the forest during a country walk, profiting from a moment of inattention on their part. And while we were banqueting in his company and that of the other kings, on different rungs of the great ladder, Bosse-de-Nage having the job of keeping its foot steady, the shouts of the news-hawks in the magical square informed us that his nephews were that day, as on previous days, searching desperately under the quincuncial trees for the venerable absent one.

XVII
CONCERNING THE FRAGRANT ISLE

To Paul Gauguin

The Fragrant isle is completely sensitive, and fortified by madrepores which retracted themselves, as we landed, into their coral-red casemates. The skiff's mooring-line was fastened around a great tree that swayed in the wind like a parrot rocking itself in the sunshine.

The king of the islands was naked in a boat, his loins girded with his white and blue diadem. He was clad, too, in sky and greenery like a Caesar's chariot race, and as red-headed, as if he were on a pedestal.

We drank to his health in liquors distilled in vegetable hemispheres.

His function is to preserve for his people the image of their gods. He was fixing one of these images to the mast of his boat with three nails, and it was like a triangular sail, or the equilateral gold of a dried fish brought back from the septentrion. And over the doorway of his wives' dwelling-place he has captured the ecstasies and contortions of love in a divine cement. Standing apart from the interlacing of young breasts and rumps, sibyls record the formula of happiness, which is double: *Be amorous*, and *Be mysterious*.

He possesses also a zither with seven strings of seven colours, the eternal colours; and, in his palace, a lamp nourished from the fragrant well-springs of the earth. When the king sings, moving along the shore as he plays his zither, or when he prunes with an axe, from images of living wood, the young shoots which would disfigure the likeness of the gods, his wives burrow into the hollow of their beds, the weight of fear heavy upon their loins from the vigilant gaze of the Spirit of the Dead, and from the perfumed porcelain of the great lamp's eye.

As the skiff cast off from the reefs, we saw the king's wives chasing from the island a little legless cripple sprouting green seaweed like a wizened crab; on his dwarfish trunk a fairground wrestler's tunic aped the king's nakedness. He pushed himself forward jerkily with his cestus-covered fists, and with a rumbling from the casters under his base attempted to pursue and clamber aboard the platform of the Omnibus de Corinthe, which was just crossing our route; but such a leap is not within everyone's power. And he fell miserably short, cracking his posterior lavatory pan with a fissure less obscene than ludicrous.

XVIII
CONCERNING THE CASTLE-ERRANT, WHICH IS A JUNK

To Gustave Kahn

Faustroll, his eye on the compass needle, decided that we could not be very far northeast of Paris. After having first heard the sea's vertical window-pane, it was not long before we could see it, held in its place by a fortification of those plants, all root, which are the sand's skeleton; and we glided on to the smooth reddish beach, between the viscosity of groynes like parallel leviathans.

The silvered sky offered inverted reflections of the monuments to be found on the other side of the green sleep of hulls; ships passed across this sky, upside down and symmetrical towards invisible futures; then could be seen the image of the still distant rooftops of the castle of Rhythms.

Indefatigable coxswain that I was, I pulled on the oars for several hours, while Faustroll sought in vain for a landing-place near the castle, which was receding constantly like a mirage; after passing through narrow streets of empty houses that spied our approach through faceted eyes of complicated mirrors, we finally touched with the sonorous fragility of our prow the flight of steps in fretworked wood leading to the nomadic edifice.

We hauled the skiff on to the shore, and Bosse-de-Nage stowed the tackle and treasures in a deep grotto.

"Ha ha!" he said, but we did not listen to the rest of his speech.

The palace was a strange junk upon a calm sea quilted with sand; Faustroll assured me that some of the Atlantides lay beneath. Seagulls vibrated like the striking hammers of the sky's blue bell, or the embellishments of a gong's libration.

The lord of the island came forward on foot, leaping across the garden planted with sand dunes. He had a black beard, and wore armour of ancient coral; on several fingers he wore silver rings in which turquoises languished. We drank Hollands gin and bitter beer, between courses of all kinds of smoked meat. The hours were struck by bells fashioned from all the metals. As soon as the mooring-line had been untied by our laconic deck-boy, the castle crumbled and died and reappeared mirrored in the sky, from very far away, as a great junk chafing the sand's fire.

XIX
CONCERNING THE ISLE OF PTYX

To Stéphane Mallarmé

The isle of Ptyx is fashioned from a single block of the stone of this name, a priceless stone found only in this island, which is entirely composed of it. It has the serene translucency of white sapphire and is the only precious stone not ice-cold to the touch, for its fire enters and spreads itself like wine after drinking. Other stones are as cold as the cry of trumpets; this has the precipitated heat of the surface of kettle-drums. It was easy for us to land there, since it was cut in table-form, and we had the sensation of setting foot on a sun purged of the opaque or too dazzling aspects of its flame; as with the torches of olden times. One no longer noticed the accidents of things but only the substance of the universe, and this is why we did not care whether the flawless surface was a liquid equilibrated according to eternal laws, or a diamond, impervious except under a light falling directly from above.

The lord of the islands came towards us in a ship: the funnel puffed out blue halos behind his head, magnifying the smoke from his pipe and imprinting it on the sky. And as the ship pitched and tossed, his rocking-chair jerked out his welcoming gestures.

From beneath his travelling-rug he drew four eggs with painted shells, which he handed over to Doctor Faustroll after first taking a drink. In the flame of the punch we were drinking, the hatching of the oval embryos broke out over the island's shore: two distant columns, the isolation of two prismatic trinities of Pan pipes, splayed out in the spurt of their cornices the quadridigitate handshake of the sonnet's quatrains; and our skiff rocked its hammock in the newborn reflection of the triumphal arch. Dispersing the hairy curiosity of the fauns and the rosy bloom of the nymphs aroused from their reverie by this mellifluous creation, the pale motor vessel withdrew its blue breath toward the island's horizon, with its jerking chair waving goodbye.

XX
CONCERNING THE ISLE OF HER, THE CYCLOPS, AND THE GREAT SWAN WHICH IS OF CRYSTAL

To Henri de Régnier

The isle of Her, like the isle of Ptyx, is one single jewel, with outjutting octagonal fortifications, resembling the basin of a fountain of jasper. The map gave it the name of the isle of Herm, because it is pagan and consecrated to Mercury; and the inhabitants called it the isle of Hort, because of its magnificent gardens. Faustroll instructed me that one should interpret a name only from its ancient and authentic root, and that the syllable *her*, like the root of a genealogical tree, means, more or less, *Seigniorial*.

The island's surface is of still water, mirror-like (it was natural that the islands should appear to us as lakes, during our navigation over dry land); and one cannot imagine a ship sailing through it, unless in the manner of a ricochet skimming the surface, for this mirror reflects no ripples, not even its own. Nevertheless, there sails there a great swan, as pure and simple as a powder-puff, and sometimes it beats its wings without breaking the ambient silence. When the fluttering of the fan is rapid enough, one can glimpse the whole island through its transparency, and the fan opens out like a pavonine jet of water.

It has never been known for the gardeners of the isle of Her to allow the jet of a fountain to fall again into the basin, for this would dull the surface; the bouquets of spray hover at a little height in horizontal sheets like clouds; and the two parallel mirrors of the earth and the sky preserve their reciprocal emptiness like two magnets eternally face to face.

All conduct in this land is *formal*, as in olden times when this word signified *customary*.

The lord of the island is a Cyclops, but we are not obliged to imitate the stratagems of Ulysses. Before his frontal eye was hung a forehead-chain enclasping two silvered mirrors, back to back in a Janus frame. Faustroll calculated that the double-mirror was exactly 1.5×10^{-5} centimetres thick. It reflected the light towards us like the eight-rayed stone of the heraldic serpent. The lord of the island could, the doctor informed me, discern clearly through these mirrors those ultra-violet elements hidden from us.

He approached with small steps between a double row of reeds, cut by his orders according to the erstwhile hierarchy of the syrinx; his major-domos served us with sugar and with quarters of citron.

His female retainers, whose dresses spread out like the ocelli of peacocks' tails, gave us a display of dancing on the glassy lawns of the island; but when they lifted their trains to walk upon this sward less glaucous than water, they evoked the image of Balkis, summoned from Sheba by Solomon, whose donkey's feet were betrayed by the hall's crystal floor, for at the sight of their capripede clogs and their fleece skirts we were seized with fright and flung ourselves into the skiff lying at the foot of the jasper landing-steps. I pulled on the oars, as Bosse-de-Nage expressed succinctly the general stupefaction:

"Ha ha!" he said; but his state of fright, no doubt, made him break off at that point.

And I retreated far from the island, perpendicularly enough for Faustroll's head to conceal from me in a short while the gaze of the lord of Her, and the artificial eye in its orbit of mother-of-pearl resembling the reflecting glass of a semaphore lamp.

XXI
CONCERNING THE ISLE OF CYRIL

To Marcel Schwob

The isle of Cyril first appeared to us as the red fire of a volcano, or as the punch-bowl full of blood spattered out by the fall of shooting stars. Then we saw that it was mobile, armoured, and quadrangular, with a helix at the four corners, shaped like the four demi-diagonals of separate arms able to advance in any direction. We realised that we had approached within gun range when a bullet tore off Bosse-de-Nage's right ear and four of his teeth.

"Ha ha!" stammered the *papio*; but the impact of a steel cylindrocone against his left zygomatic apophysis made short work of his third word. And without awaiting a more detailed reply, the kinetic island hoisted the skull and kid, and Faustroll the flag of the Great Strumpot.

After these salutations, the doctor joyfully drank some gin with Captain Kidd, and managed to dissuade him from setting the skiff on fire (it was, despite its paraffin varnish, incombustible) and from hanging Bosse-de-Nage and myself — after robbing us — from the main yard (the skiff had no main yard).

We all fished for monkeys in a river, to the jaw-gaping horror of Bosse-de-Nage, and we visited the interior of the island.

Because the red glow of the volcano is blinding, one can soon see no more than if one were surrounded by a shadowless darkness; but so that one may follow the opaque undulations of the dazzling lava, there are children who run about the island with lamps. They are born and die without ever growing old, in the hulks of worm-eaten barges, on the bank of a bottle-green backwater. Lamp shades wander there like glaucous and pink crabs; and farther inland, whither we escaped as quickly as possible because of the marine animals which ravage the seashore at ebb-tide, their particoloured umbels sleep. The lamps and the volcano exhale a livid light, like the port-side light of the Boat of the Dead.

After drinking, the captain, resplendent with his curling mustachios, used his ship-boarding scimitar as a calamus and with an ink made of gunpowder and gin tattooed upon the forehead of our close-mouthed cabin-boy these words in blue: BOSSE-DE-

NAGE, *PAPIO CYNOCEPHALUS*, relit his pipe in the lava, and gave orders to the light-children to escort the skiff down to the sea; and until we reached the open sea we were accompanied by Kidd's words of farewell and by the dim lights like lacklustre jellyfish.

XXII
CONCERNING THE GREAT CHURCH OF SNOUTFIGS

To Laurent Tailhade

We could already hear bells — as loud as all the Brabantine chimes of ebony, maple, oak, cedar, sorb wood and poplar from Ringing isle — when I suddenly found myself between two black walls, beneath an archway, then dazzled by the glare of a long stained-glass window. The doctor, without deigning to warn me, had shot the skiff like an arrow, using the tiller's silken cords, into the centre of the great portal of Snoutfigs cathedral. Like the prefatory cough of chair legs being shifted, my oars grated on the flagstones of the nave, along which our keel lay symmetrically.

Friar John climbed into the pulpit.

The awesome figure, warlike and sacerdotal, glared at the assembly. His chasuble was of chain mail, studded with balas rubies and black diamonds. Instead of rosaries, an olive-wood cithern dangled on his right hip, while at his left was slung his great two-handed sword, its hilt fashioned from a golden crescent, in its scabbard of horned-viper's skin.

His sermon was rhetorical and very Latin, Attic, and Asiatic at the same time; but I failed to understand why he was clanging and clinking from his sollerets to his gauntlets, nor could I comprehend his phrases, arranged like the rounds of a fencing bout.

Suddenly a bronze bullet was fired from a falconet bound to a counter-faced slab by four iron chains, the shot ploughing open the orator's right temple and splitting his armet as far as his tonsure, laying bare the optic nerve and the right lobe of the brain, but without affecting that stronghold of understanding.

Just as the smoke rose from the falconet, a pungent steam was exhaled from the throats of the congregation and congealed into the shape of a squat monster at the foot of the pulpit.

That day, I saw the Snout. It is respectable and well-proportioned, in every way comparable to the hermit-crab or pagurian, as God is infinitely similar to man. It has horns which serve it as a nose and as tongue-papillae, shaped like long fingers issuing from its eyes; two claws of uneven length and ten legs in all; and being, like the pagurian, vulnerable only in its fundament, it hides this and its rudimentary sex in a concealed shell.

Friar John drew his great sword, making as if to attack the Snout, to the clear anxiety of those present. Faustroll remained impassive and Bosse-de-Nage, inordinately interested, forgot himself as far as to think visibly:

"Ha ha!"

But he said not a word, for fear of outrunning his thoughts.

The Snout retreated, the point of its shell first, while everyone drew back; and its claws grated together like stammering mouths. The sword blade, flashing as it was drawn from its horned-viper's skin sheath, blunted itself against the creature's hairy codpiece.

At this point, Faustroll set the skiff in motion. By pulling his guide-ropes harder, he was able to bend the skiff appreciably; this was possible because his tiller did not simply control a flat rudder aft but bent the long keel, from the fore end, to right, to left, upward or downward, according to his directional requirements. And the sail of taut copper glowed like a crescent moon. With myself manipulating my suction discs to adhere to the granite's dangerously polished surface, the doctor led me towards the monster. And in its roundabout route our navigation twisted back on itself like the wedding ring of an amphisbaena's Narcissus kiss.

By this artifice, Friar John was easily able to meet the Snout at its own level, the monster having advanced slightly while its adversary descended the twelve steps. He winkled it from its shell with the forked tip of his sword, and chopped its fundament into as many pieces as there were people present in the nave; but neither he nor we ourselves, except Bosse-de-Nage, wanted to taste this offering.

And the combat would have been the very image, in all its vicissitudes, of a bullfight if the bull Shell-Bottom had made a direct onslaught instead of attempting a thrust at the end of its circular flight.

However, the bejewelled preacher remounted the pulpit for his sermon. And his flock, no longer possessed by the Snout's spirit, were purged of their crass humour and applauded him.

As for us, we departed once more towards the nearby bells of Ringing isle, and Faustroll did not consult the stars further, for our way was lit by the beams of the great windows, iridescent as words, beams like starry paths leading from the church.

XXIII
CONCERNING RINGING ISLE

To Claude Terrasse

"Happy the sage," says the *Chi-Hing*, "in the valley where he lives, a recluse, who delights to hear the sound of cymbals; alone, in his bed, awakening, he exclaims: 'Never, I swear, shall I forget the happiness that I feel!' "

The lord of the island, after welcoming us in these terms, led us to his plantations which were fortified by aeolian marker-poles of bamboo. The commonest plants there were the side-drums, the ravanastron, sambuca, archlute and bandore, the kin and the tché, the beggar's-guitar and vina, the magrepha and hydraulus. In a conservatory there arose the many necks and geyser breath of the steam-organ given to Pippin in 757 by Constantine Copronymus, and imported into Ringing isle by Saint Cornelius of Compiègne. Here one could breathe in the perfume of the piccolo, *oboe d'amore*, contrabassoon and sarrusophone, the Brittany bagpipe, zampogna and English bagpipe; the Bengali *chéré*, bombardon, serpent, coelophone, saxhorns and anvil.

The temperature of the island is regulated by consulting thermometers called sirens. At the winter solstice the atmospheric sonority drops from a cat's cursing to the buzzing of wasps and bumblebees and the vibration of a fly's wing. At the summer solstice, all the above-named flowers blossom, reaching a pitch of overshrill ardour like that of insects hovering over the plants of our native fields. At night, here, Saturn clashes together his sistrum and his ring. And, at dawn and twilight, the sun and moon explode like divorced cymbals.

"Ha ha!" began Bosse-de-Nage, wanting to try out his voice before joining in the universal musical refrain; but the two heavenly bodies clashed together in a kiss of reconciliation and the planter celebrated this clangorous event thus:

"Happy the sage," he cried, "who, on a mountain slope, delights to hear the sound of cymbals; alone in his bed on awakening, he sings: 'Never, I swear, shall my desires go beyond what I already possess!' "

And Faustroll, before taking leave, drank with him wormwood distilled on the mountain-tops, and the skiff exhaled its chromatic course at the beat of my oars. Toward the two heavenly bodies striking the hours of union and division of the black key and the diurnal key, a little naked child and a white-haired ancient sang on two lofty columns; toward this double disc of silver and of gold they sang:

The old man bellowed the selection of foul syllables, and the seraphic soprano took up the refrain accompanied by the choir of angels, Thrones, Powers and Dominions:

The white-bearded energumen concluded the coprolalic phrase with a throaty cry and an obscene contortion; at this moment, from our skiff, which was moored at the foot of this chubby and childlike body's stele, we could see the crumbling of his armour made of enamelled cardboard or puppeteer's pasteboard and the blooming of the forty-five-year-old sistine dwarf's squalid beard.

From his throne perfumed with harps, the lord of the island gloried that his creation was good, and as we drew away we could hear this melody:

"Happy the sage who, on the hill where he dwells, delights to hear the sound of cymbals; alone in his bed, in awakening, he lies in tranquillity and swears that he will never reveal to the vulgar the reason for his joy!"

XXIV
CONCERNING THE HERMETIC SHADES AND THE KING WHO AWAITED DEATH

To Rachilde

After passing the river Ocean, which, as regards the stability of its surface, much resembles a great street or boulevard, we reached the land of the Cimmerii and the hermetic Shades, which differ from this river as two non-liquid planes may differ — that is to say, in size and in division. The place where the sun sets has the appearance, between the folds comprising the Town's mesentery, of the vermiform appendix of a caecum. It abounds in blind alleys and culs-de-sac, some of which expand into caverns. In one of these the day-star was wont to puff itself up. For the first time I understood that it was possible to reach the undersurface of the tangible horizon and see the sun from so close up.

There is a monstrous toad whose mouth is flush with the Ocean's surface and whose function is to devour the sunken disc, the way the moon eats the clouds. It genuflects daily in its circular communion; at this moment steam rises from its nostrils, and the great flame arises which is the souls of certain people. This is what Plato called the apportionment by lots of souls outside the pole. And its genuflection, because of the structure of its limbs, is also a squatting. The duration of its deglutitory jubilation is therefore without dimension; and since it digests to the rhythm of a vigorous punctuality, its intestines remain unconscious of the transitory star which, in any case, is indigestible. It burrows a passage in the subterranean diversity of the earth and emerges from the opposite pole, where it purges itself of the excrements with which it has soiled itself. It is from this detritus that the devil Plural is born.

In the land where the sun is eternally dormant, there is a king who is its officer of the guard and due to share its fate, awaiting death each day; he believes that a night will some time remain perennial, and inquires after the evacuations of the toad on the horizon. But he has no time to consider the star hastening, its belly wobbling, into the adjoining cavern: he carries a mirror on his navel which gives him a reflection of it. His sole pastime is built from a house of cards, to which he adds a storey each morning; here, once a month, the lords of the transpontine islands come to debauch themselves. When the castle is capped with one storey too many the star will flash through it in its course, and that will be a considerable cataclysm. But the king has been sufficiently judicious not to build it on the ecliptic plane. And the castle keeps its balance in exact proportion to its height.

Since evening was descending as Bosse-de-Nage drew our skiff up on to the bank, the king was awaiting death as usual, and the toad was gaping functionally. The palace was swathed in blackness; couches had been prepared for the bodies, and philters to deaden the consciousness of agony. Bosse-de-Nage, though not professing it by a thoughtlessly variegated loquacity, prided himself on being deontological, and thought himself in honour bound to dress up in a black costume and to crown his skull — which resembled an ill-favoured cucurbit — with a Belgian hat capable of storing up luminous vibrations in wavelengths equal to those of his costume, the crown of which resembled half a defunct globe.

And the night computed its hours so exactly that lamps had to be lit.

Suddenly the toad's descending colon thundered, and the non-alimentary bolus of pure fire took its usual path once more towards the pole of the devil Plural.

In a striking metamorphosis the mourning colour of the hangings turned into pale rose. The philters were drunk joyfully through the reeds of Pan pipes, and when little women were laid out on the red-hot couches, Bosse-de-Nage thought the time had come to bring matters to a point:

"Ha ha!" he declared in a summary fashion, but he saw that we had guessed his thoughts, and watched with great surprise the simplicity of his Belgian hat roll upon the carpet with the recalcitrant din of an iron sweep's brush.

BOOK FOUR

CEPHALORGY

XXV
CONCERNING THE LAND-TIDE AND THE MARINE BISHOP MENDACIOUS

To Paul Valéry

Faustroll took his leave while the night was still hanging, like a pope, from four of the cardinal points. And as I asked him why he did not stay drinking until the sun's next sudden plunge, he arose in the skiff and, with his foot on the neck of Bosse-de-Nage, made soundings along our route.

He confided to me that he was afraid of being caught unawares by the ebb-tide, since the period of syzygy was nearing its end. And I was seized with fear, because we were still rowing where there was no water, between the aridity of the houses, and soon we were coasting along the pavements of a dusty square. As far as I could understand, the doctor was talking about the earth's tides, and I thought that one of us must be drunk, and that the ground was sinking toward its nadir, like a fathomless depth revealed in a nightmare. I know now that apart from the flux of its humours and the diastole and systole which pump its circulatory blood, the earth is bulging with intercostal muscles and breathes according to the moon's rhythm. But the regularity of this breathing is very gentle, and few people are aware of it.

Faustroll took some astral measurements, the visibility through the albugineous sky over this narrow street being excellent, and told me to note down the fact that the terrestrial radius had already shrunk 1.4×10^{-6} centimetres, through the subsidence in the reflux. He then gave orders to Bosse-de-Nage to cast anchor, assuring us that the sole pretext, worthy of his Doctrine, for an end to our drifting journey was that the thickness of the earth beneath our feet as far as its centre was no longer deep enough to satisfy our honour.

Now it was midday, the alley's narrow length as deserted as an empty belly; and we put into port, as it was easy to tell by the numbers on the wall, in front of the four-thousand-and-fourth house of the rue de Venise.

Between the ground levels with their floors of beaten earth, overlooked by doors wider than the street but less agape than women waiting on the uniformity of their beds, Faustroll raised the question of berthing the skiff in some deep shelter. Suddenly he pointed, and I was not very surprised to see arise from the threshold of one of the barest and most sordid hovels a marine personage abstracted from book XIII of Aldrovandi's *Monsters*; having the appearance of a bishop, and, more particularly, the type of bishop which was at one time, according to the book, fished up off the coast of Poland.

His mitre was of fish scales and his cross like the corymb of a reflexed tentacle; his chasuble, which I touched, was all encrusted with stones from the depths and could easily be lifted up in the front and at the back, but, because of the chaste adherence of the cutis, hardly at all above the knees.

The marine bishop Mendacious made an obeisance before Faustroll, presented to Bosse-de-Nage an ear fig gratis, and when the skiff was intruded into the vaulted berth and the door's valve closed once more, he presented me to Visited, his daughter, and to his two sons, Distinguished and Extravagant. Then he inquired of us whether it would be agreeable to us, quite succinctly, to:

XXVI
DRINK

To Pierre Quillard

However, Faustroll lifted with his fork towards his teeth five hams, whole, roasted, and boned, from Strasbourg, Bayonne, the Ardennes, York and Westphalia, all dripping with Johannisberger; the bishop's daughter, on her knees under the table, filled once again each unit of the ascending line of hectolitre cups in the moving belt which crossed the table in front of the doctor and passed, empty of its contents, near the raised throne of Bosse-de-Nage. I gave myself a thirst by swallowing a sheep that had been roasted alive while racing along a petrol-soaked track until done to a turn. Distinguished and Extravagant drank as thirstily as anhydrous sulphuric acid, as their names had made me suspect, and three of their jowls would have encompassed a cubic metre of firewood. However, Bishop Mendacious refreshed himself exclusively with fresh water and rat's piss.

At one time he had been in the habit of mixing this last substance with bread and Melun cheese, but had succeeded in suppressing the supererogatory vanity of these solid condiments. He sucked in water from a decanter of gold beaten as thin as the wavelength of green light, served on a tray made of the fur (rather than peltry, since the bishop wanted to be fashionable) of the freshly flayed fox of a drunkard, in season, and quite equal to a twentieth of the latter's weight. Such luxury is not vouchsafed to all: the bishop kept rats at enormous expense, and also, in rooms paved with funnels, a whole seraglio of drunkards, whose conversation he imitated:

"Do you think," he said to Faustroll, "that a woman can ever be naked? In what do you recognise the nakedness of a wall?"

"When it is devoid of windows, doors, and other openings," opined the doctor.

"Your reasoning is good," continued Mendacious. "Naked women are never naked, especially old women."

He drank a great draught straight out of his carafe, whose point of sustentation was erect on its viscous carpet, like a root torn from its burial place. The catenulate conveyor-belt of cups full of liquid or wind chanted like the incision made in a river's belly by the rosary of an illuminated towboat.

"Now," continued the bishop, "drink and eat. Visited, serve us with some lobster!"

"Was it not once fashionable in Paris," I hazarded, "to offer these animals in courtesy, like a snuff-taker proffering his snuff-box? But, from what I have heard, people were in the habit of refusing them, claiming that they were hairy pluripedes and repulsively dirty."

"Ho-hum, ho-hum," condescended the bishop. "If lobsters are dirty and non-depilated, it is perhaps a proof that they are free. A nobler fate than that of the can of corned beef which you carry on a ribbon round your neck, doctor navigator, like the case of a pair of salted binoculars through which you like to scrutinise people and objects.

"But, listen:

THE LOBSTER AND THE CAN OF CORNED BEEF WHICH DOCTOR FAUSTROLL WORE ROUND HIS NECK

Fable

To A.-F. Hérold

A can of corned beef, chained like a lorgnette,
Saw a lobster pass by which resembled her fraternally.
He was armoured with a hard shell
On which was written that inside, like herself, he was free of bones,
(Boneless and economical);
And beneath his curved tail
He was probably hiding a key with which to open her.
Lovestricken, the sedentary corned beef
Declared to the little automobile can of living potted meat
That if he would deign to become acclimatised,
By her side, in the world's shop-windows,
He should be decorated with several gold medals."

"Ha ha," meditated Bosse-de-Nage, but he did not develop his ideas more comprehensively.

And Faustroll interrupted the frivolity of the conversation with an important speech.

XXVII
CAPITALLY

Doctor Faustroll commenced:

"I do not believe that an unconscious murder is therefore necessarily motiveless: it is not governed by any command emanating from us and has no link with the precedent phenomena of our ego, but it certainly follows an external order, it is within the order of external phenomena, and it has a cause that is perceptible by the senses and is therefore significant.

"I have never had the desire to kill except after seeing a *horse's head*, which has become for me a sign, or an order, or more precisely a signal, like the down-turned thumb in the arena, that the time has come to strike the blow; and lest you should smile, I shall explain to you that there are doubtless several reasons for this.

"The sight of a very ugly object certainly provokes one to do what is ugly. Now, what is ugly is evil. The sight of a revolting condition incites one to revolting pleasures. The appearance of a ferocious muzzle with the bones showing impels one to a ferocious act and the stripping of the bones. Now, there is no object in the whole world as ugly as the head of a horse, except perhaps that of the grasshopper, which is almost exactly similar without having the gigantic size of the former. And you know that the murder of Christ was foreshadowed by the following fact: that Moses, so that the Scriptures might be accomplished, had permitted the eating of the bruchus, the attacus, the ophiomachus and locust, which are the four species of grasshopper."

"Ha ha!" interposed Bosse-de-Nage by way of digression, but he could find no valid objection.

"And furthermore," continued Faustroll imperturbably, "the grasshopper is not altogether a monstrous animal, having normally developed members, whereas the horse, born for indefinite deformation, has already, since the origin of its species, although endowed originally by nature with four feet furnished with fingers, succeeded in repudiating a certain number of its fingers and in jumping about on four solitary hooves, exaggerated and horny, like a piece of furniture sliding on four rollers. The horse is a planchette.

"But the head alone, although I cannot define my reasons — perhaps because of the simple enormity of its teeth and the abominable rictus natural to it — is for me the sign of all ferocity, or rather the sign of death. And the Apocalypse said precisely in signifying the fourth scourge that: 'Death was mounted upon a pale horse.' Which I interpret thus: 'those whom Death comes to visit see first the head of the horse.' And the war's homicides derive from equitation.

"Now, if you are curious to know why I am rarely incited to murder in the street, where the horrible head multiplies in front of all the vehicles, I would reply that a signal, to be heard, must be isolated, and that a multitude does not possess the ability to give an order. And just as a thousand drums do not make as much noise as a single drum, and a thousand intelligences form a mob moved by instinct, so an individual is not an individual for me when he appears in the company of several of his equals, and I maintain that a head is only a head when separated from its body.

"And Baron Munchausen was never braver at war and better at killing than on the day when, the portcullis surmounted, he noticed that he had left half of his mount on the other side of the sharp girder."

"Ha ha!" exclaimed Bosse-de-Nage appropriately; but Bishop Mendacious interrupted him to conclude:

"Well, doctor, so long as we never talk with you in the presence of a decapitated horse — and up to the present time the solipedes are cut up rather than guillotined — we may be permitted to consider your murderous temptations as an agreeable paradox."

Then he sent us to sleep with a macaronic Greek harangue, in which, tossing my head, I could only make out the last perfect conjugation:

"... ΣΕΣΟ'ΥΛΑΣΘΑΙ."

XXVIII

CONCERNING THE DEATH OF A NUMBER OF PEOPLE, AND MORE ESPECIALLY OF BOSSE-DE-NAGE

To Monsieur Deibler, sympathetically

> The little squat mower arrived and started to work. He gave such strokes with his scythe that he filled a quarter of a wagonful of hay, or more, so vigorous was he; and what is more, he took no pleasure in sharpening his scythe; but when its blade was dulled he drew it along his teeth, with a sound like f r o o o o o c. Thus, he saved time.
>
> Béroalde de Verville, *How to Succeed*, XXIV.

After drinking, we took a walk through foggy streets, with Mendacious in the lead. Since the episcopal nature of his vestments gave people the impression that he was probably an honest man, no one except the doctor and myself noticed that he was unhooking the shop signs with his crosier, as if inadvertently, and giving them graciously to Bosse-de-Nage to carry, the latter thanking him with the single word: "ha ha," for, as one knows, he was opposed to all idle verbiage.

And I was not yet aware of the bishop's charity in allowing the shop signs to fall down.

Suddenly the crosier's curling head began to uncurl, faced with the toughness of a gilt moulding above a horse-butcher's shop. The gliding flight hovered as an animal mask and as a twofold gaze from above and below.

Faustroll, very calm, lit a small perfumed candle which burned for seven days.

The first day, the flame was red, and revealed the categorical poison in the air, and the death of all scavengers and soldiers.

The second day, of women.

The third, of small children.

The fourth day, there was a remarkable epizootic disease among those quadrupeds considered edible on condition that they were ruminative and possessed a cloven hoof.

The saffron combustion of the fifth day decimated all cuckolds and bailiff's clerks, but I was of a superior grade.

The blue crackling of the sixth day hastened the impending end of all bicyclists, of all those at least, without exception, who fasten their trouser cuffs with lobster claws.

The light changed into smoke on the seventh day, and Faustroll had a breathing space.

Mendacious unhooked the shop signs with his hands, after asking for a leg-up from Bosse-de-Nage.

And the fog dissipated weightlessly in centrifugal directions, before the arch of a riding school's great door; and Faustroll was overtaken again by insanity.

The bishop took to his heels, but not quickly enough to prevent Faustroll from tearing off his mitre while it was still alive; whereas I was not molested by the doctor, for I was armoured with my name Panmuphle.

But Faustroll crouched over the baboon, spreading his four limbs out on the ground and strangling him from behind. Bosse-de-Nage made a sign that he wished to speak, and, when the doctor had relaxed the grip of his fingers, said in two words:

"Ha ha!" and these were the last two words he uttered.

XXIX
CONCERNING SOME FURTHER AND MORE EVIDENT MEANINGS OF THE WORDS "HA HA"

... And I'll declare
He's mooning up some landscap'd alley where
A *ha ha* lurks ahead. All unaware
He won't, until he's tumbled, know it's there.
Piron

We may properly treat here of the customary and succinct speech of Bosse-de-Nage, so that it may be made clear that it is with reasonable intention and not from mockery that we have always reported it in its full extent, together with the most probable cause of its premature interruption.

"HA HA!" he said concisely; but we are in no way concerned with the accidental fact that he usually added nothing more.

In the first instance, it is more judicious to use the orthography AA, for the aspiration *h* was never written in the ancient languages of the world. It proclaimed in Bosse-de-Nage effort, servile and obligatory labour, and the consciousness of his inferiority.

A juxtaposed to A, with the former obviously equal to the latter, is the formula of the principle of identity: a thing is itself. It is at the same time the most excellent refutation of this very proposition, since the two As differ in space, when we write them, if not indeed in time, just as two twins are never born together — even when issuing from the obscene hiatus of the mouth of Bosse-de-Nage.

The first A was perhaps congruent to the second, and we will therefore willingly write thus: A ≡ A.

Pronounced quickly enough, until the letters become confounded, it is the idea of unity.

Pronounced slowly, it is the idea of duality, of echo, of distance, of symmetry, of greatness and duration, of the two principles of good and evil.

But this duality proves also that the perception of Bosse-de-Nage was notoriously discontinuous, not to say discontinuous and analytical, unsuited to all syntheses and to all adequations.

One may confidently assume that he could only perceive space in two dimensions, and was refractory to the idea of progress, implying, as it does, a spiral figure.

It would be a complicated problem to study, in addition, whether the first A was the efficient cause of the second. Let us content ourselves with noting that since Bosse-de-Nage usually uttered only AA and nothing more (AAA would be the medical formula *Amalgamate*), he had evidently no notion of the Holy Trinity, nor of all things triple, nor of the undefined, which commences at three, nor of the indeterminate, nor of the Universe, which may be defined as the Several.

Nor of anyone else. And, in fact, the day he was married, he indeed felt that his wife was chaste with him, but he could not tell whether she was a virgin.

And in his public life he never understood the use, on the boulevards, of those iron kiosks whose popular name derives from the fact that they are divided into three triangular prisms and that one can use only one third at a time; and he remained, until his death, branded thus by Captain Kidd:

BOSSE-DE-NAGE
Papio cynocephalus,

befouling and ravaging everything indiscriminately.

We have purposely omitted to say, these meanings being very well known, that *ha ha* is a ditched gap in a wall at the end of a garden path, an armed pit or military well into which chrome steel bridges may collapse, and that AA may still be read on the medals struck at Metz. If Faustroll's skiff had had a bowsprit, *ha ha* would have designated a special sail placed beneath the jibs.

Book Five

OFFICIALLY

XXX
CONCERNING A THOUSAND VARIED MATTERS

To Pierre Loti

But the bishop, decapitated of his mitre, was in a bad way of business, being unaccustomed to attend to matters *nisi in pontificalibus*. For which reason, he entered his closet, victualled with a thousand varied matters suitable to encourage a crap.

On the little table where ordinarily rolls of paper unfold themselves, a fat little bust of a jolly little man with a scrubby little beard paraded in beetle-green.

The jolly little man waddled from right to left on the hemisphericity of his base, and the bishop would have recognised, had he been a member of the expedition at that time, the sprinting legless cripple expelled from Fragrant isle. I found out later that he had met him, at less expense and looking even more like himself, on the vulgar clock in the sitting-room of an old lady. The palmate legless cripple raised himself up on the artificial heels of his bowl and offered the bishop courteously a pad of squared paper as an abstersive:

"I had reserved it *for my mother*," he said, "but" (pointing to the bishop's amethyst), "as is the case with her, *the Christian faith permits you to read with serenity the most sombre subjects*. You have not yet made use of my services in this way, but you will see that *it is even more me*."

"This paper is then going...?" said the bishop.

"Read perseveringly with all your eyes, nay even with your most secret eye. This paper is sovereign. *It would b... you so, if only you knew*!"

"You have decided me," said Mendacious.

"Take your place, then, among these piles of less efficacious suppositories. It is time: *I alone can still distinguish behind* nearly all *these accumulated words* THE BOTTOMLESS ABYSS."

He jumped nimbly into the designated pit, and like an iron gauntlet sliding down the banisters of a staircase, the reverberation of his zinc bowl died away along the double turn of the depository pipe: but the verses of Messrs. Déroulède and Yan-Nibor, rolled inside this concave *mirliton*, supported him with their feet.

Reading by the Bishop
while going about his business.

DEATH OF LATENT OBSCURE

"Brr... brr... brr... brrr... chen... hatsch... *Latent Obscure is leaving us...* Brrr... brrr... *The moment of agony has been consummated...* brr... brr... *The momentary oblivion induced by sleep.* A verse. *Must she then die Latent Obscure...* Heuh... eheuh... *It is freezing hard... general sinister impression...* brr... brr... *she is already halfway into the abyss...* heuh heuh... *Bitter tears... the doctor says that she will not last the night...* Off with you, frog! down into the shades below. — *Her life is drawing to a close*" (Veiled drum). "*The cold bores into one's bones*" (bis). "Tra ratatat!" (The bishop hums joyously.) "In the train of a regiment, *our faithful Melanie, who comes from a stock of devoted old servants, who have practically become members of the family...*"

"Courage, you are doing fine," cried out the little man from below. "Carry on, do not be afraid of inconveniencing me: *I shall sleep right next door in the Arab room.*"

"*The bitter struggle of the end,*" agreed the bishop, still reading; "brrr... brrr... *agonising nightmare. Horrible moment.* Let us read with the other side's eye: *the last ritual cleansing, the poor corpse, the horrible little bed, the great bed, the pale forehead, the dear face, this terrible little bed.*"

"*We rise and descend like ghosts,*" panted the leaves in their successive service.

"These GREEN PALMS," continued the bishop remorselessly, "*placed crosswise on the breast...*"

"Thank you for your good wishes," telephoned the inhabitant of the pipe. "I am delighted to *see* that you are not leaving us yet, seated at the top of my chimney. *The pale pale winter's day... serene countenance... supreme image, so pretty!*"

"*Vague impressions,*" continued Mendacious modestly.

"*The pale features, the gentle smile! Latent Obscure smiles so softly...*

"Heuh! eheuh... *Obsessive impression, infinitely sad...* Brrr... brr... ratatat!

"*The dear voices and the dear sounds... good smiling eyes, so sad...*"

"LATENT OBSCURE HAS LEFT US!!! thanks be to God," exclaimed the bishop, getting up.

"Thanks," echoed the little man. "*A warm sun. Open windows. Big cupboard, tiny box. I am smoking an oriental cigarette!*"

"*Perhaps this is the last time*," said the bishop sitting down again, suddenly forced to resume his reading, and reading with extreme concentration, "*that regret for Latent Obscure welled up in me with that intensity and in that peculiar form which brings tears, for all is suddenly calm, all becomes normal, forgotten, and there is a veil, a mist, an ash, something indescribable thrown as if in haste*, brrrrr... *and suddenly, of the memory of those beings who have returned to* the ETERNAL NOTHINGNESS, rat, tat, ratatat... Bounty! bounty! In splashes, in fire and in blood! After the fashion of the rhinoceros. Without stopping. The rosary for the dead. Brrr... brr... I'm hyplotising myself. Ho-hu, ho-hu! Long as a lance."

"Is your name *Kaka-San*?" asked the little man after a certain while.

"No, Mendacious, marine bishop, at your service. Why?"

"Because *Kaka-San did some very dirty things in her box during the quite pardonable unconstraint of her last hours.*"

XXXI
CONCERNING THE MUSICAL JET

> "How do they call thee?"
> "Chaw-turd," quoth Panurge.
> *Pantagruel*, III, 25

Now, it is necessary to know that the valve installed at the neck of the pit's mouth was of thin rubber; and to be familiar with the discoveries of Mr. Chichester Bell, cousin of Mr. Graham Bell, the illustrious inventor of the telephone, one should be aware that a stream of water falling upon an india-rubber sheet stretched over the upper end of a tube constitutes a microphone, that a liquid jet breaks up at certain rates more easily than at others and, *according to its nature, will respond to certain sounds in preference to others*; finally, one should not be scandalised if we mention that the bishop's loins secreted this quite unconsciously musical jet whose amplified vibrations he perceived at the moment of taking leave of his reading.

●○ *Voices of little women* arose, glorifying the little man.

THE LITTLE WOMEN (*piano, common time, three sharps*), some of them GENTLY (E-G-C-E... B-E-B, pedal):

"May your grief be soothed by our songs! (*F-A sharp*). Others: May your dire sorrow (*G-B sharp*). Fly away to the low murmur of the waves (*five flats, pedal,* CRYSTALLINE)...

"Stranger (*G natural-B*), if you would charm our solitude, one must change your name (GENTLY) whose syllables are too rude, And give you another (*A flat*) like the mountain flowers (*G sharp, B natural*)."

Some women propose the name: "Atari." Others: "Fei." The L.W.: "No! (*Pedal. Two quaver-rests*) Lo-ti (*B-F, pedal, organ note*)."

The L.W.: "Henceforth (*ped. ped.*) let him be named Lo-ti." All surrounding him: "It is the moment of baptism! (RATHER SOLEMNLY). In the land of songs, In the land of loving (*crotchet-rest*), Lo-ti (*E flat, C, crotchet-rest, cresc.*), Lo-: (C) ti (*E flat*) shall be your supreme name (SIC)."

THE LITTLE WOMEN (CONT.): "In the land of songs, In the land of loving, Loti, Loti shall be your supreme name (*two crotchet-rests*). Lo-ti (*E flat, E flat*) we name you, Lo-ti we name you, and (*p. p.*) we ble- (*in the key of B flat*) -ess you! (*Great uproar*)."

The valve opened, the music ceased; the aspersion being completed, the bishop resecured his ring, and laid on hands, confirming by this approved gesture the benediction of the L.W. Then he simply cut off the jet.

XXXII

HOW ONE OBTAINED CANVAS

●○ *To Pierre Bonnard*

Faustroll carried out a subfumigation, and the spectre of Bosse-de-Nage — who, having only existed imaginarily, could not really die — manifested itself, said "ha ha" respectfully, then was silent, awaiting orders.

I discovered that day a new meaning of this invaluable word, namely that the α, beginning of all things, is interrogative, for it awaits an exposition in present space, and the appendix, greater than itself, of a sequence in duration.

"Here are a few billions in cash," said the doctor, rummaging in his ruby-buttoned waistcoat pockets. "You will ask a policeman the way to the National Department Store, called *Au Luxe Bourgeois*, and there you will buy several ells of canvas.

"You will convey my compliments to the department managers Bouguereau, Bonnat, Detaille, Henner, J.-P. Laurens and Tartempion, to their horde of assistants and to the other subsidiary salesmen. And so as not to waste time in the grip of their haggling, you will, without a word..."

"Apart from *ha ha*," I insinuated maliciously.

"... Pour over each of them a pile of gold, until their mouths are silenced beneath its rising tide. A sufficient payment will be seventy-six million guineas for M. Bouguereau; seventeen thousand seraphs for M. Henner; eighty thousand maravedi for M. Bonnat, since his canvas is stamped, in place of a trademark, with the figure of a poor man; thirty-eight dozen florins for M. J.-P. Laurens; forty-three centimes for M. Tartempion; and five billion francs, as well as a tip in kopeks, for M. Detaille. You will throw the remaining coppers into the faces of the other clowns."

"Ha ha," said Bosse-de-Nage to show that he had understood, and prepared to depart.

"This is all very well," I said to Faustroll, "but would it not be more honourable to allocate this gold toward the costs of my proceedings, and if necessary abstract the quantities of canvas by sheer cunning?"

"I will explain to you what my gold really is," said the doctor, winking. And to Bosse-de-Nage.

"One last word: so as to wash the shop-talk out of your prognathous jaws, enter a small room arranged for this purpose. There the ikons of the Saints shine forth. Bare your head before the *Poor Fisherman*, bow before the Monets, genuflect before the Degas and the Whistlers, grovel in the presence of Cézanne, prostrate yourself at the feet of Renoir and lick the sawdust of the spittoons at the foot of the frame of *Olympia*!"

"Ha ha," agreed Bosse-de-Nage wholeheartedly, and his hurried exit carried with it the most ardent protestations of his zeal.

Turning towards me, the doctor continued:

"When Vincent van Gogh had unluted his crucible, and cooled the integrated matter of the true philosophers' stone, and when, on this first day of the world, all things were transmuted into the sovereign metal at the contact of the marvellous become real, the artisan of the Great Work contented himself with running his strong fingers through the pointed sumptuousness of his luminous beard, and said: 'How beautiful is yellow!'

"I could easily transmute all things, for I also possess this stone" (he showed it to me, set in one of his rings), "but I have found by experiment that the benefit extends only to those whose brain is that selfsame stone" (through a watch-glass embedded in the fontanelle of his skull he showed me this stone a second time)...

Bosse-de-Nage returned with eleven scenery vans filled with vertical stacks of unredeemed canvases.

"Do you think, my friend," ended Faustroll, "that one could possibly give gold to these people which would remain gold and worthy of being gold in their wallets?

"That same in which they are now submerged will also spread the well-adjusted streams of its flux over their canvas. It is young and virgin, in every way comparable to the matter with which babies beshit themselves."

And after aiming the beneficent lance of the painting machine at the centre of these quadrilaterals dishonoured by irregular colours, he appointed to the control of this mechanical monster M. Henri Rousseau, artist painter decorator, called the Customs Officer, mentioned with honour and medal-holder, who for sixty-three days embellished most painstakingly the impotent diversity of the grimaces from the National Department Store with the uniform stillness of chaos.

Book Six

A VISIT TO LUCULLUS

XXXIII
CONCERNING THE TERMES

Now, Faustroll was sleeping next to Visited.

The great bed, carved out by knife, squatted upon the nakedness of the earth, that ancient part of the world's nebula, and poured upon the ground the worm-eaten hours of its sand.

Amid this rhythmical silence, Visited desired to discover whether, underneath the spiral-painted tapestry, Faustroll, who had loved her like the infinite series of numbers, possessed a heart capable of pumping out with its open and closed fist the projection of circling blood.

The watch's tick-tock, like the scratching on a table of a fingernail, a pen nib or a nail, beat near her ear. She counted nine strokes; the pulsation stopped, then continued up to eleven...

The bishop's daughter heard her own sleep before any further beats, and these did not disturb her, for she did not survive the frequency of Priapus.

On the oak of the decrepit bed, the termes, comparable to the invisibility of a red louse with yellow eyes, lent the isochronism of the throbbing of its head to the simulation of Faustroll's heart.

XXXIV
CLINAMEN

To Paul Fort

...Meanwhile, after there was no one left in the world, the Painting Machine, animated inside by a system of weightless springs, revolved in azimuth in the iron hall of the Palace of Machines, the only monument standing in a deserted and razed Paris; like a spinning-top, it dashed itself against the pillars, swayed and veered in infinitely varied directions, and followed its own whim in blowing on to the walls' canvas the succession of primary colours ranged according to the tubes of its stomach, like a *pousse-l'amour* in a bar, the lighter colours nearest to the surface.

In the sealed palace which alone ruffled this dead smoothness, this modern deluge of the universal Seine, the unforeseen beast *Clinamen* ejaculated on to the walls of its universe:

NEBUCHADNEZZAR CHANGED INTO BEAST

What a beautiful sunset! or rather it is the moon, like a porthole in a hogshead of wine greater than a ship, or like the oily stopper of an Italian flask. The sky is a sulphurous gold so red that there is really nothing missing but a bird five hundred metres high capable of wafting us a breeze from the clouds. The architecture, the very type of all these flames, is most lively and even rather moving, but too romantic! There are towers with eyes and beaks and turrets capped like little policemen. Two watching women sway at the wind-swept windows like drying strait-jackets. Thus the bird:

The great Angel, who is not angel but Principality, swoops down, after a flight exactly as black as a martin's, the colour of the metal of a roofer's anvil. With one point on the roof, the compasses close and open up again, describing a circle around Nebuchadnezzar. One arm chants the metamorphosis. The king's hair does not stand on end, but droops like a walrus's wet whiskers; the pointed ends of his hair make no effort to squeeze shut the sensitive pimples which people this limp seaweed with zoophytes reflecting all the stars: tiny wings flutter to the rhythm of a toad's webbed feet. Pitiful pleas swim up against the stream of tears. The eyes' sorrowful pupils, in their ascent, crawl towards the knees of the wine-lees-coloured sky; but the angel has enchained the newborn monster in the blood of the vitreous palace and thrown him into the bottom of a bottle.

THE RIVER AND THE MEADOW

The river has a fat, soft face for the smack of oars, a neck with many wrinkles, a blue skin with green downy hair. Between its arms, pressed to its heart, it holds the little Island shaped like a chrysalis. The Meadow in its green gown is asleep, its head in the hollow of its shoulder and neck.

TOWARDS THE CROSS

At one end of the Infinite, in the form of a rectangle, is the white cross where the demons have been executed together with the unrepentant Thief. There is a barrier around the rectangle, white, with five-pointed stars studding the bars. Down the rectangle's diagonal comes the angel, praying calm and white like the wave's foam. And the horned fish, a monkey trick of the divine Ichthys, surge back towards the cross driven through the Dragon, who is green except for the pink of his bifid tongue. A blood-covered creature with hair standing on end and lenticular eyes is coiled around the tree. A green Pierrot rushes up, weaving from side to side and turning cart-wheels. And all the devils, in the shape of mandrills or clowns, spread their caudal fins out wide like acrobats' legs, and, imploring the inexorable angel (*Woan't yew p'-lay with me, mistuh Loyal?*), plod towards the Passion, shaking their clowns' straw wigs encrusted with sea salt.

GOD FORBIDS ADAM AND EVE TO TOUCH THE TREE OF GOOD AND OF EVIL. THE ANGEL LUCIFER RUNS AWAY

God is young and gentle, with a rosy halo. His robe is blue and his gestures sweeping. The tree's base is twisted and its leaves aslant. The other trees are doing nothing apart from being green. Adam adores and looks to see if Eve also adores. They are on their knees. The angel Lucifer, old and looking like time and like the old man of the sea lapidated by Sinbad, plunges with his gilded horns towards the lateral ether.

LOVE

The soul is wheedled by Love who looks exactly like an iridescent veil and assumes the masked face of a chrysalis. It walks upon inverted skulls. Behind the wall where it hides, claws brandish weapons. It is baptised with poison. Ancient monsters, the wall's substance, laugh into their green beards. The heart remains red and blue, violet in the artificial absence of the iridescent veil that it is weaving.

THE CLOWN

His round hump hides the world's roundness, as his red cheek rends the lions on the tapestry. Clubs and diamonds are embroidered on the crimson silk of his garments, and towards the sun and the grass he makes a benedictory aspersion with his tinkling aspergillum.

"FARTHER! FARTHER!" CRIES GOD TO THE MEEK

The mountain is red, the sun and the sky are red. A finger points towards its peak. The rocks surge upwards, the absolute summit lost to view. The bodies of those who have not reached it come tumbling down again head first. One falls backwards on to his hands, dropping his guitar. Another waits with his back to the mountain, near his bottles. One lies down on the road, his eyes still climbing. The finger still points, and the sun waits for obedience before it will set.

FEAR CREATES SILENCE

Nothing is terrifying, if it be not a widowed gallows, a bridge with dry piers, and a shadow which is content to be black. Fear, turning away its head, keeps its eyelids lowered and the lips of the stone mask closed.

IN THE NETHER REGIONS

The fire of the nether regions is of liquid blood, and one can see down to the very depths. The heads of suffering have sunk down, and an arm is raised from each body like a tree from the sea bed, stretched to where the fire is abated. There, a serpent darts his venom. All this blood is aflame and held within the rock whence people are hurled. And there is a red angel for whom one single gesture suffices, which signifies: FROM TOP TO BOTTOM.

FROM BETHLEHEM TO THE GARDEN OF OLIVES

It is a little red star, above the crib of the Mother and Child, and above the ass's cross. The sky is blue. The little star becomes a halo. God has lifted the weight of the cross from the animal and carries it on his brand new man's shoulder. The black cross becomes rose, the blue sky turns violet. The road is as straight and white as the arm of one crucified.

Alas! the cross has become bright red. It is a blade steeped in blood from the wound. Above the body, at the end of the road's arm, are eyes and a beard which bleed also, and above his image in the wooden mirror, Christ spells out: J-N-R-I.

JUST A WITCH

Her hump to the rear, belly to the fore, neck twisted, hair whistling in the flight of the broomstick with which she has transfixed herself, she goes under the claws, vegetation of the bright red sky, and the index of the road to the Devil.

EMERGING FROM HIS BLISS, GOD CREATES THE WORLDS

God arises haloed by a blue pentagram, blesses and sows and makes the sky bluer. Fire glows red from the idea of ascension, and the gold of the stars mirrors the halo. The suns are great four-leaved clovers, in bloom, like the cross. And the only thing not created is the white robe of Form itself.

THE DOCTORS AND THE LOVER

In the bed, calm as a green sea, there is a floating of outstretched arms, or rather these are not the arms but the two divisions of the head of hair, vegetating upon the dead man. And the centre of this head of hair curves like a dome and undulates like the movement of a leech. Faces, mushrooms bloated with rottenness, spring up evenly and red in the window-panes of agony. The first doctor, a larger orb behind this dome, trapezoidal in character, becomes slit-eyed and decks his cheeks with bunting. The second rejoices in the external equilibrium of spectacles, twin spheres, and weighs his diagnostic in the libration of dumb-bells. The third old man veils himself with the white wing of his hair and announces desperately that beauty returns to the skull by polishing his own. The fourth, without understanding, watches... the lover who, against the current of the stream of tears, sails in pursuit of the soul, his eyebrows joined upwards by their inner points in the shape of cranes in flight, or the communion of the two palms of one praying or swimming, in the attitude of daily devotion called by the Brahmins KHURMOOKUM.

Book Seven

KHURMOOKUM

(The Sundhya, or the daily Prayers of the Brahmins)

XXXV
CONCERNING THE GREAT SHIP MOUR-DE-ZENCLE

The sieve, which would have burst into flames like a puerile resin in the city quietly consumed by fire and death, reared up the head of its prow under the pull of Faustroll's tiller, and its gesture was the opposite of the charitable crosier of Mendacious.

The meshed base, unsinkable because of its oily coating, rested upon the waves' denticulation like a sturgeon upon several harpoons, and beneath it was a keyboard of water and air alternately. The disappearance preceding the apparition of the corpses of the seven days' murder squinted towards us from the other side of the reticular bars protecting us.

The toad from the isle of Shades snapped up the sun for its supper, and the water was night. That is to say, the banks disappeared and the sky and the river became comparable and undifferentiated, and the skiff became the pupil of a great eye, or a stationary balloon, with a dizziness to left and to right whose feathers I was ordered to stroke with my two oars.

Immobile barrels stemmed the current at express speed, rolled into balls.

And to escape these things, as one seeks refuge under one's bed-clothes in the once-and-for-all blackness, Faustroll manœuvred the skiff into an aqueduct six hundred metres wide along which the canal barges were vomited into the river.

(Here ends the narrative of Panmuphle)

The great ship Mour-de-Zencle, which means Horse-muzzle-bearing-scythe-shaped-patches, loomed up on the immediate horizon like a black sun, having the appearance under the bright arch at the tunnel's end of an eye without its leather blinker, approaching the fixity of its own painted pupils, green in a yellow iris. On the invisible towpath, like a ledge on the vault's brink, clopped the front horseshoes of the file of four animals bearing the sign of death, treading awkwardly with their hooves.

With his topaz-beringed forefinger, moistened in his mouth, Faustroll scraped the paraffin from the bottom of the boat. The artesian well (hell was in Artois that day) swirled hissing around their feet, with a noise opposite to the deglutition of an emptying bath-tub. The sieve rocked in its last pulsation. The penultimate and the last meshes where the water wove its barnacles and let its double hymen be violated by anti-peristaltic tongues, were named the mouths of Panmuphle and Faustroll. The copper shuttle glittering with its setting of air bubbles, and the jaws exhaling the breath from their bones, imitated coins falling in water or the water spider's nest. Faustroll, procuring fresh canvas in the name of God, steeped in the painting machine's lustral water a different sky from that of Tyndall, then joined his palms in an attitude of praying or swimming, in the manner of daily devotion called *Khurmookum* by the Brahmins. The great ship Mour-de-Zencle passed like a black iron over an ironing board; and the echo of the sixteen horny fingers of the preterite horses whispered KHURMOOKUM beneath the vault's exit, fading away with the soul.

Thus did Doctor Faustroll make the gesture of dying, at the age of sixty-three.

XXXVI

CONCERNING THE LINE

The bishop reads the letter from God

To Félix Fénéon

In the manuscript, of which Panmuphle, interrupted by the monotonous prolixity of the baboon, could only decipher the prolegomena, Faustroll had noted a small fragment of the Beautiful that he knew, and a small fragment of the True that he knew, during the syzygy of words; and one could have reconstructed, through this facet, all art and all science, which is to say All; but can one tell if All is a regular crystal, rather than more probably a monster (Faustroll defined the universe as *that which is the exception to oneself*)?

Thus cogitated the marine bishop as he swam over the shipwreck of the mechanical boat, over the sunken quintessential works, over the carcass of Panmuphle and the body of Faustroll.

However, he remembered that, following the proposition of the learned Professor Cayley, a single curve drawn in chalk on a blackboard two and a half metres long can detail all the atmospheres of a season, all the cases of an epidemic, all the haggling of the hosiers of every town, the phrases and pitches of all the sounds of all the instruments and of all the voices of a hundred singers and two hundred musicians, together with the phases, according to the position of each listener or participant, which the ear is unable to seize.

And behold, the wallpaper of Faustroll's body was unrolled by the saliva and teeth of the water.

Like a musical score, all art and all science were written in the curves of the limbs of the ultrasexagenarian ephebe, and their progression to an infinite degree was prophesied therein. For, just as Professor Cayley recorded the past in the two dimensions of a black surface, so the progress of the solid future entwined the body in spirals. The Morgue harboured for two days on its slab the book revealed by God concerning the glorious truth spread out through the three (four or *n* for some people) directions of space.

Meanwhile, Faustroll, finding his soul to be abstract and naked, donned the realm of the unknown dimension.

BOOK EIGHT

ETHERNITY

To Louis Dumur

Leves gustus ad philosophiam novere
haustus ad religionem reducere.
Francis Bacon

XXXVII
CONCERNING THE MEASURING-ROD, THE WATCH AND THE TUNING-FORK
Telepathic letter from Doctor Faustroll to Lord Kelvin

"My dear colleague,

"It is a long time since I have sent you news of myself; but I do not think you will have imagined that I was dead. Death is only for common people. It is a fact, nevertheless, that I am no longer on earth. Where I am I have only discovered a very short time ago. For we are both of the opinion that, if one can measure what one is talking about and express it in numbers, which constitute the sole reality, then one has some knowledge of one's subject. Now, up to the present moment I knew myself to be *elsewhere* than on earth, in the same way that I know that quartz is situated elsewhere, in the realm of hardness, and less honorably so, than the ruby; the ruby elsewhere than the diamond; the diamond than the posterior callosities of Bosse-de-Nage; and their thirty-two skin-folds — more numerous than his teeth, if one includes the wisdom teeth — than the prose of Latent Obscure.

"But was I elsewhere in terms of date or of position, before or to the side, after or nearer? I was in that place where one finds oneself after having left time and space: the infinite eternal, Sir.

"It was natural that, having lost my books, my skiff of metallic cloth, the society of Bosse-de-Nage and Monsieur René-Isidore Panmuphle, bailiff, my senses, the earth, and those two old Kantian aspects of thought, I should suffer the same anguish of isolation as a residual molecule several centimetres distant from the others in a good modern vacuum of Messrs. Tait and Dewar. And, even then, perhaps the molecule knows that it is several centimetres away! For one single centimetre, the only valid sign for me of space, being measurable and a means of measuring, and for the mean solar second, in terms of which the heart of my terrestrial body beat — or these things I would have given my soul, Sir, despite the usefulness to me of this commodity in informing you of these curiosities.

"The body is a more necessary vehicle because it supports one's clothes, and through clothes one's pockets. I had left in one of my pockets by mistake my centimetre, an authentic copy in brass of the traditional standard, more portable than the earth or even the terrestrial quadrant, which permits the wandering and posthumous souls of interplanetary savants to concern themselves no further with this old globe, nor even with C.G.S., as far as measurements of size are concerned, thanks to MM. Méchain and Delambre.

"As for my mean solar second, were I to have remained on the earth I still could not have been certain of retaining it safely and of being able to measure time validly through its medium.

"If in the course of a few million years I have not terminated my pataphysical studies, it is certain that the period of the earth's rotation around its axis and of its revolution around the sun will both be very different from what they are now. A good watch, which I would have had running all this time, would have cost me an exorbitant price, and, in any case, I do not perform secular experiments, have nothing but contempt for continuity, and consider it more aesthetic to keep Time itself in my pocket, or the unity of time, which is its snapshot.

"For these reasons, I possessed a vibrator better arranged for permanence and for absolute accuracy than the hairspring of a chronometer, one whose period of vibration would have retained the same value over a certain number of million years with an error of less than 1:1000. A tuning-fork. Its period had been carefully determined, before I embarked in the skiff, according to your instructions, by our colleague Professor Macleod, in terms of mean solar seconds, with the prongs of the tuning-fork being pointed successively upwards, downwards and towards the horizon, in order to eliminate the least effect of terrestrial gravity.

"I no longer had even my tuning-fork. Imagine the perplexity of a man outside time and space, who has lost his watch, and his measuring-rod, and his tuning-fork. I believe, Sir, that it is indeed this state which constitutes death.

"But I suddenly remembered your teachings and my own previous experiments. Since I was simply NOWHERE, or SOMEWHERE, which is the same thing, I found a substance with which to make a piece of glass, having met various demons, including the Sorting Demon of Maxwell, who succeeded in grouping particular types of movement in one continuous widespread liquid (what you call small elastic solids or molecules): a substance as plentiful as one could desire, in the shape of silicate of aluminium. I have engraved the lines and lit the two candles, albeit with a little time and perseverance, having had to work without even the aid of flint implements. I have seen the two rows of spectrums, and the yellow spectrum has returned my centimetre to me by virtue of the figure 5.892×10^{-5}.

"Now that we are happy and comfortable, and on dry land, as is my atavistic habit, since I carry on me the one-thousand-millionth part of a quarter of the earth's circumference, which is more honourable than being attached to the surface of the globe by attraction, permit me, I pray, to note a few impressions for you.

"Eternity appears to me in the image of an immobile ether, which consequently is not luminiferous. I would describe luminiferous ether as *circularly* mobile and perishable. And I deduce from Aristotle (*Treatise on the Heavens*) that it is appropriate to write ETHERNITY.

"Luminiferous ether together with all material particles, which I can easily distinguish — my astral body having good pataphysical eyes — possesses the form, at first sight, of a system of rigid links joined together, and having rapidly rotating fly-wheels pivoted on some of the links. Thus it fulfils exactly the mathematical ideal worked out by Navier, Poisson, and Cauchy. Furthermore, it constitutes an elastic solid capable of determining the magnetic rotation of the plane of polarisation of light discovered by Faraday. At my posthumous leisure I shall arrange it to have zero moment of momentum as a whole and to reduce it to the state of a mere spring balance.

"Moreover, I am of the opinion that one could reduce considerably the complexity of this spring balance or this luminiferous ether by substituting for the linked gyrostats various systems of circulation of liquids of infinite volume through perforations in infinitely small solids.

"It will lose none of its qualities as a result of these modifications. Ether has always appeared to me, to the touch, to be as elastic as jelly and yielding under pressure like Scottish shoemakers' wax."

XXXVIII
CONCERNING THE SUN AS A COOL SOLID
Second letter to Lord Kelvin

"The sun is a cool, solid, and homogeneous globe. Its surface is divided into squares of one metre, which are the bases of long, inverted pyramids, thread-cut, 696,999 kilometres long, their points one kilometre from the centre. Each is mounted on a screw and its movement towards the centre would cause, *if I had the time*, the rotation of a paddle at the top end of each screw shaft, in a few metres of viscous fluid, with which the whole surface is thinly covered...

"I was quite disinterested in this mechanical spectacle, not having found again my mean solar second and being distraught at the loss of my tuning-fork. But I took a piece of brass and fashioned a wheel in which I cut two thousand teeth, copying everything which Monsieur Fizeau, Lord Rayleigh, and Mrs. Sidgwick had achieved in similar circumstances.

"Suddenly, the second was rediscovered in the absolute measure of 9,413 kilometres per mean solar second of the Siemens unit, and the pyramids, forced to descend on their threads since they found themselves, like myself, in the movement of time, were obliged to come into equilibrium, in order to remain stable, by borrowing a sufficient quantity of Sir Humphry Davy's repulsive motion; and the fixed matter, the screw shafts and the screw nuts disappeared. The sun became viscous and began to turn on its axis in twenty-five-day cycles; in a few years you will see sunspots on it, and a few quarter-centuries will determine their periods. Soon, in its great age, it will shrink in a diminution of three-quarters.

"And now I am being initiated into the science of all things (you will receive three new fragments from two of my forthcoming books), having reconquered all perception, which consists in duration and size. I understand that the weight of my brass wheel, which I clasp between the hebetude of the abstract fingers of my astral body, is the fourth power of eight metres per hour; I hope, deprived of my senses, to recognise colour, temperature, taste, and various qualities other than *the six*, in the actual number of revolutions per second...

"Farewell: I can glimpse already, perpendicularly to the sun, the cross with a blue centre, the red brushes towards the nadir and the zenith, and the horizontal gold of foxes' tails."

XXXIX
ACCORDING TO IBICRATES THE GEOMETER

(Little sketches on Pataphysics after Ibicrates the Geometer and his divine teacher Sophrotatos the Armenian, translated and brought to light by Doctor Faustroll.)

I. *Fragment of the Dialogue upon the Erotic*

MATHETES. Tell me, o Ibicrates, thou whom we have named the Geometer because thou knowest all things by the means of lines drawn in different directions, and hast given us the veritable portrait of three persons of God in three escutcheons which are the quart essence of Tarot symbols, the second being barred with bastardy and the *fourth* revealing the distinction between good and evil engraved in the wood of the tree of knowledge, I hope most ardently, if it pleaseth thee, to know thy thoughts upon love, thou who hast deciphered the imperishable because unknown fragments, inscribed in red on sulphurous papyrus, of the Pataphysics of Sophrotatos the Armenian. Answer, I pray thee, for I shall question thee, and thou wilt instruct me.

IBICRATES. That at least is exactly true, o Mathetes. Then speak, therefore.

MATHETES. Before all else, having noticed how all the philosophers have incarnated love in beings and have expressed it in different symbols of contingency, instruct me, o Ibicrates, in the eternal significance of these.

IBICRATES. The Greek poets, o Mathetes, corbelled the forehead of Eros with a horizontal bandelet, which is the bend or fess of the blazon, and the sign Minus of those who study mathematics. And Eros being the son of Aphrodite, his hereditary arms were ostentative of woman. And contradictorily Egypt erected its stelae and obelisks perpendicularly to the cruciferous horizon, thus creating the sign *Plus*, which is male. The juxtaposition of the two signs of the binary and the ternary gives the shape of the letter H, which is Chronos, father of Time or Life, and thus embraces o mankind. For the Geometer, these two signs cancel each other out or impregnate each other, and there results simply their progeny, which becomes egg or zero, all the more identical because they are contrary. And in the matter of the dispute between the sign Plus and the sign Minus, the Reverend Father Ubu, of the Society of Jesus, ex-king of Poland, has written a great tome entitled *Caesar-Antichrist*, in which is to be found the sole practical demonstration of the identity of opposites, by means of the mechanical device called *physick-stick*.

MATHETES. Is this possible, o Ibicrates?

IBICRATES. Absolutely indeed, veritably. And the third abstract sign of the tarots, according to Sophrotatos the Armenian, is what we call the Club, which is the Holy Ghost in his four directions, the two wings, the tail, and the head of the bird; or, reversed, Lucifer erect horned with his belly and his two wings, like the medicinal cuttlefish; more particularly, at least, when one eliminates from the latter object all negative — that is to say, horizontal — lines; or, thirdly, it represents the Tau or the cross, emblem of the religion of charity and love; or, finally, the phallus, which is dactylically triple, in truth, o Mathetes.

MATHETES. Then to some extent in our temples today, love may still be considered to be God, although, I agree, in somewhat abstruse forms, o Ibicrates?

IBICRATES. The tetragon of Sophrotatos, contemplating itself, inscribes within itself another tetragon half as great as itself, and evil is the symmetrical and necessary reflection of good, these being the unity of two ideas, or the idea of the number two; good, in consequence, to a certain degree, indeed, I believe, or indifferent at the very least, o Mathetes. The tetragon, being hermaphroditic, engenders God by interior intuition, while Evil, likewise hermaphroditic, engenders parturition...

XL
PANTAPHYSICS AND CATACHEMY

II. *Further fragment*

God transcendent is trigonal and the soul transcendent theogonal, consequently trigonal also.

God immanent is trihedral and the soul immanent equally trihedral.

There are three souls (cf. Plato).

Man is tetrahedral because his souls are not independent.

Therefore he is a solid, and God is spirit.

If souls are independent, man is God (MORAL SCIENCE).

Dialogue between the three thirds of the number three.

MAN: The three persons are the three souls of God.

DEUS: *Tres animae sunt tres personae hominis.*

TOGETHER: *Homo est Deus.*

XLI
CONCERNING THE SURFACE OF GOD

God is, by definition, without dimension; it is permissible, however, for the clarity of our exposition, and though he possesses no dimensions, to endow him with any number of them greater than zero, if these dimensions vanish on both sides of our identities. We shall content ourselves with two dimensions, so that these flat geometrical signs may easily be written down on a sheet of paper.

Symbolically God is signified by a triangle, but the three Persons should not be regarded as being either its angles or its sides. They are *the three apexes* of another equilateral triangle circumscribed around the traditional one. This hypothesis conforms to the revelations of Anne-Catherine Emmerich, who saw the cross (which we may consider to be the *symbol* of the *Verb* of God) in the form of a Y, a fact which she explains only by the physical reason that no arm of human length could be outstretched far enough to reach the nails of the branches of a Tau.

Therefore, POSTULATE:

Until we are furnished with more ample information and for greater ease in our provisional estimates, let us suppose God to have the shape and symbolic appearance of three equal straight lines of length a, emanating from the same point and having between them angles of 120 degrees. From the space enclosed between these lines, or from the triangle obtained by joining the three farthest points of these straight lines, we propose to calculate the surface.

Let x be the median extension of one of the Persons a, $2y$ the side of the triangle to which it is perpendicular, N and P the extensions of the straight line $(a + x)$ in both directions *ad infinitum*.

Thus we have:

$$x = \infty - \mathrm{N} - a - \mathrm{P}$$

But

$$\mathrm{N} = \infty - 0$$

and

$$\mathrm{P} = 0$$

Therefore

$$x = \infty - (\infty - 0) - a - 0 = \infty - \infty + 0 - a - 0$$
$$x = -a$$

In another respect, the right triangle whose sides are a, x, and y give us

$$a = x^2 + y^2$$

By substituting for x its value of $(-a)$ one arrives at

$$a^2 = (-a)^2 + y^2 = a^2 + y^2$$

Whence

$$y^2 = a^2 - a^2 = 0$$

and

$$y = \sqrt{0}$$

Therefore the surface of the equilateral triangle having for bisectors of its angles the three straight lines a will be

$$S = y\,(x + a) = \sqrt{0}\,(-a + a)$$
$$S = 0\sqrt{0}$$

COROLLARY: At first consideration of the radical $\sqrt{0}$, we can affirm that *the surface* calculated is *one line* at the most; in the second place, if we construct the figure according to the values obtained for x and y, we can determine:

that the straight line $2y$, which we now know to be $2\sqrt{0}$, has its point of intersection on one of the straight lines a in the opposite direction to that of our first hypothesis, since $x = -a$; also, that the base of our triangle coincides with its apex;

that the two straight lines a make, together with the first one, angles at least smaller than 60°, and what is more can only attain $2\sqrt{0}$ by coinciding with the first straight line a.

Which conforms to the dogma of the equivalence of the three Persons between themselves and in their totality.

We can say that a is a straight line connecting 0 and ∞, and can define God thus:

DEFINITION: *God is the shortest distance between zero and infinity.*

In which direction? one may ask.

We shall reply that His first name is not Jack, but *Plus-and-Minus.* And one should say:

$\pm$ *God is the shortest distance between* 0 *and* ∞, *in either direction.*

Which conforms to the belief in the two principles; but it is more correct to attribute the sign + to that of the subject's faith.

But God being without dimension is not a line.

— Let us note, in fact, that, according to the formula

$$\infty - 0 - a + a + 0 = \infty$$

the length a is nil, so that a is not a line but a point.

Therefore, *definitively*:

GOD IS THE TANGENTIAL POINT BETWEEN ZERO AND INFINITY.

● Pataphysics is the science...

Absolute Love

Translated, introduced and annotated by Paul Edwards

INTRODUCTION

With *Absolute Love*, Jarry returned to the autobiographical Breton elements he had last developed in *Days and Nights* and which do not surface again until *La Dragonne*. The abundant flora and fauna provide a convincing local colour, and Brittany supplies its uncanny atmosphere of folklore, myth and magic. This rich scenery is part of the author's internal landscape, and it is precisely the autobiographical which elicits the most experimental writing from Jarry.

While he wrote works that could appeal to a popular audience, Jarry was also producing manuscripts of labyrinthine complexity. In the same year that he wrote *Absolute Love*, 1898-9, Jarry had put on a puppet-play version of *Ubu Roi* in collaboration with Pierre Bonnard and Claude Terrasse; with the latter, he had started work on an opera version of *Pantagruel*, which should have allowed Jarry to share in Terrasse's growing fame and fortune (but which was only staged in 1911, over three years after Jarry's death); he completed *Par la taille*, a cross between an opera and a puppet-play and which could have been staged either way; Pierre Fort published *L'Amour en visites* with full-page illustrations in his best-selling collection of modern novelists; and he oversaw the printing of an *Almanach*, brought out to coincide with a market opportunity that was growing as the magical year 1900 was approaching. In tandem with all these ventures, Jarry completed both *Faustroll* and *Absolute Love*, his two most difficult novels. Less than half of *Faustroll* was published in Jarry's lifetime. *Absolute Love* was rejected by the *Mercure de France*, so Jarry had his manuscript reproduced lithographically and privately printed in an edition of only fifty copies. Long considered indecipherable, it was nevertheless well known to Breton and shares elements with Joyce's *Finnegans Wake*, since it has a cyclic structure, dissolves into a dream, and all the women are but one woman.

Originally, *Absolute Love* was to have been the final chapter of *Visits of Love*, but the story developed beyond the bounds of the initial title, "Visiting Lady Jocasta", and beyond the Oedipal plot (the theme of incest is diluted by the fact of Varia's being Emmanuel's adopted mother). "Visiting Lady Jocasta" was turned into a novel about certain aspects of hysteria, especially its ecstatic and somnambulistic trances.

Jarry freely plundered the ideas and writings of the Paris School of psychology at a time when Freud was still only a minor figure in Paris; there is thus nothing Freudian, in the strict sense, about the ideas in the novel. Just as the *Time Machine* essay is based on Lord Kelvin's scientific work, so *Absolute Love* exploits the published ideas of Jean-Martin Charcot (1825-93) and Pierre Janet (1859-1947), "the father of modern psychology" as he is still known in France. And in the same way that Jarry turned the scientific description of the gyrostatic adynamic constitution of ether into a set of instructions for building the time machine, so now he took the hallucinations that hysterics described to their analysts and wove them into a consecutive series of episodes. The scientific context is discussed more fully in "Hysteria and *Absolute Love*", the aim of this introduction being merely to give the reader a brief thematic guide to each chapter.

Jarry wrote to Alfred Vallette, the director of the *Mercure*, stating that he was not prepared to change anything in his novel, and certainly not the order of the chapters. From this it is clear that Jarry was fully intent on not delivering the chronology of events in order. The novel "bites its tail", for the last chapter returns the reader to the first two chapters, thus making the epilogue an introduction, and the introduction an epilogue. Furthermore, the action of the third chapter takes place, chronologically, between that of chapters ten and eleven, and thus requires reading twice.

The novel's characters are multiple, but their names and relationships are easily remembered. The Breton family — Joseb, Varia and their adopted son Nédélec Doue, usually referred to as Emmanuel Dieu — are sometimes metamorphosed into the Holy Family: Joseph, Mary and Jesus. As mentioned earlier, the plot sometimes maps them on to the Oedipal family: Laius, Jocasta and Oedipus. The only complication is that when Varia is hypnotised and falls into a somnambulistic state, she assumes a different personality and is called Miriam. It is the language used by Miriam when she takes herself for the Virgin Mary that Jarry chose as the principal theme of the book, and her idiom, adopted by Emmanuel, pervades the novel.

CHRONOLOGY OF EVENTS

Chapters 1, 2 (and 15): the novel starts with a bifurcation: the hero of the story, Emmanuel Dieu, is either (1) on death row waiting to be guillotined for murder at sunrise, or (2) an ordinary person half-asleep at his writing-desk. The rest of the novel could therefore be the remembering or dreaming of either of these characters.

Chapter 2: Emmanuel reflects on the Holy Communion that precedes an execution, on the real presence of Christ in the Eucharistic host, and on the "missing years" of Jesus's life up until the age of thirty. He speculates about the nature of conscience and possession (diabolical-hysterical, divine, erotic), which leads to the next chapter about Varia, who appears to be possessed.

Chapter 3: Varia/Miriam thinks she is the Virgin Mary and she talks to Emmanuel as if he were the Infant Jesus. We later learn that Emmanuel, who is pretending to be a child, has hypnotised her, and that he did so, chronologically, at the end of chapter 10. The delirious — more precisely, hypnotic — language will recur in the indirect free style of the novelist.

After the dotted line, Varia/Miriam is observed in a deeper somnambulistic state and assumes a third personality named Myrrh. Emmanuel is clearly having an affair with his adopted — hysterical — mother and using hypnosis and suggestion on her to control their relationship.

Chapter 4: Emmanuel's childhood and adoption is recounted using the language and logic of Varia when hypnotised: his infancy is superimposed on to that of Christ (and Moses).

Chapter 5: description of Joseb, Emmanuel's adopted father. He is a carpenter like Joseph.

Chapter 6: description of the family home and Emmanuel's baby antics, which again are superimposed on to stories in the Bible, especially Genesis. Emmanuel traumatised at the sight of the skeletal hand bitten by wolves.

Chapter 7: Emmanuel at infant school. Masochistic tendencies.

Chapter 8: Emmanuel is now fifteen and spends holiday afternoons squatting a tide-waiter's hut by the sea. Varia goes to visit him, but is scared by the scenery and thinks she is pursued by wolves.

Chapter 9: Emmanuel awaits Varia's arrival, remembering their first secret rendezvous in a Paris restaurant which ended in just a kiss. When Varia arrives they picnic, but when they start making love Varia panics and rushes out of the hut and straight into the arms of the tide-waiter, whom she instinctively kisses, before fleeing.

Chapter 10: Emmanuel and Varia meet in the family home that night, while Joseb is in his workshop, drinking, and they make "incestuous" love. Varia panics again and attacks Emmanuel with a knife; Emmanuel escapes by hypnotising her.

Chronologically, chapter 3 may be inserted after chapter 10 and before chapter 11, which opens by summarising Emmanuel and Varia/Miriam's conversation.

Chapter 11: Emmanuel wakes Varia/Miriam from her hypnotic state. She accuses him of having hypnotised her. They make love again.

Chapter 12: Emmanuel's thoughts about the relativity of truth, since he must talk differently to Varia and Miriam, and lie differently too. "Absolute" truth exists to the extent that he can mould Varia/Miriam's somnambulistic personality — to her, he is God.

Chapter 13: seeing that Miriam has turned back into Varia, Emmanuel is reminded of how Varia can turn into Miriam (described in chapter 11 and the beginning of 12). Her sex and her eyes make him think of all the eye-shaped plants Varia could have seen on the way to his hut. He hypnotises her again with the knife.

Chapter 14: Miriam is somnambulistic and suggestible. Emmanuel implants in her a post-hypnotic suggestion to strangle her husband. She wakes, but returns to her somnambulistic state at eleven o'clock (according to her internal clock), and executes the suggestion. Joseb wakes her by his breathing on her face, and all memory of Miriam, Varia's somnambulistic personality, vanishes.

Chapter 15 (and 1 and 2): Emmanuel reflects on the criminal responsibility of post-hypnotic suggestion (will anyone ever find out about his attempted murder?), and on the power of hypnosis to create personalities.

ABSOLUTE LOVE

I

LET THERE BE DARKNESS!

He lives in one of the wings of the petrified star.

In a prison called LA SANTÉ.

And in death row, since he has been condemned to death, along with all the others condemned to death.

The stone starfish, mirror below of the stars above, waited till the stars were out to sparkle.

The sun set regimentally; anglers, bidden by constables, retract their tentacles; cyclists and cabmen turn into amorous female lampyrines; and the electrician who commands the star's axis performs a magnetiser's pass, the same which — with his index finger placed between another's eyebrows — will recall them from the arms of the Brother of Death.

LA SANTÉ looks like Argus with his hundred eyes.

He lives on a little star which is itself on one of the arms of the star of stone; each man is one of the sucker-flowers on one of the fingers of the starfish.

The topmost cervical vertebra, having bloomed (as Haeckel would say), for one of the last days, inures itself like all flowers to the movement of the helianthus.

Towards the lamp.

The cell is thoroughly modern, and fitted out in the English style with plain, white-enamelled furniture, and pastel-coloured walls.

No decorations on the walls, but the sun has been hung from the ceiling.

A heavenly body, be it sun or moon, that daily rises and daily fades.

It does not move; no observation contradicts this.

It is a fixed star.

It is of greater nobility than the luminaries of this world, for it has its seat in the sky, held high like a crown or the blade of a guillotine, which will be the last laying-on of the diadem.

Its name is Zenith.

It was not born from a nebula.

Each man is the oil of this lamp.

If there was not a man condemned to death in the sector reserved for those condemned to death, then there would be one star less in the stone sky of LA SANTÉ.

Moses called the sky "the solid firmament", after all.

Whoever this star shines on, whomsever he is and whatever *his* circumstances, is a most important figure.

Thanks to him a star is born.

He is no astronomer: astronomers, later, discover them.

An astrologer rather: this star is lit up *because of* his future.

He is a man in the mould of God.

And it is for this reason, or for another reason, but the best is that it is his real name, that on the door is written:

"EMMANUEL DIEU".

God is a little dazzled by his star.

In the Maritime Museum, in the Louvre, one can shut oneself into a room with the rotating lamp of a decapitated lighthouse.

At persistent intervals, the big fire-fly, the great lantern fly, collides with your transparent cornea.

You blink in retaliation at the huge eye that winks.

Luckily the light is too intermittent for a magnetiser to use, and too strong to be a lark mirror.

God is a little dazzled by his star because he would like to sleep.

So he switches off the two upside-down lamps in the sea of his eyes.

As the wyvern hides its carbuncle, sole eye and precious treasure of the cyclopean snake, before slithering to the fountain for a drink.

Emmanuel Dieu uses sleep, the Lethean Waters of the Ancients, as a provisional eternity.

Eternity is too *unextended* to be contained inside a prison, even one that burst into a star.

That is why, at dawn on certain days, it is asked to wait politely in the courtyard.

Against it are raised the sharp groynes of the breakwater bridges of the Wharf, like the fortifications on an estuary, ahead of the city.

Orpheus rises from a carpet of furs, and the city purrs beneath the lamp, the star created by the terrestrial God beneath the firmament and which reaches, like a snail's eye, for the firmamentary stars, for it is the earth's peninsula in *the waters which are above.*

The Stars Militant looking at the Stars Triumphant; the heads of the gas lamps, each just one big eye, plead to be delivered from their umbilical necks.

Who knows if comets, with the spatter consequent to their breaking away still trailing behind them, are not the wild oats of liberated gas lamps?

Anourous comets, according to some, are the angels in heaven.

Emmanuel Dieu awaits the sidereal hour when his head will fly.

... And yet if he did not kill, or if *nobody realised that he wanted to kill*, then he has no other prison than his cranium, and he is but a man who sits and dreams by his lamp.

II
THE WANDERING CHRIST

> "What are your means of existence?"
> "I have no means of subsistence,
> No house, no goods or chattel:
> My purse contains but fippence;
> My means are but this rattle."
> Charles Deulin, *Tales and Legends of a Good Fleming*

Footsteps inside the snail's shell.

Is it the Three Wise Men, heading towards the star whose nadir was the manger, or Aladdin, laden with jewels from the garden of the caverns, who comes to pluck his magic Head?

No, it is not the cicerone of the last dawn.

He is alone.

Nor was it some Abbot Faria, the prison-breaker.

Not a crack in the mirror of the walls.

It can only be the eternal prisoner, whose words all reply to interrogations.

And the only one to notice when he is stopped, because he walks.

Ahasuerus.

Emmanuel Dieu begins a dialogue with the ghost.

A monologue, for the being of legend can only reply with passages from his legend or by silence, and he saves the former for his judges.

Hear the confession Emmanuel made to Silence:

"I am God, I am not dying on the Cross.

"I am powerless over death, unworthy of myrrh.

"An obscure God, condemned to live in the secret interim period, from childhood to the age of thirty-three.

"Perhaps this period has remained a mystery simply because THE OTHER ONE had not wanted — or been able — to live those years *at that time.*

"He undoubtedly became incarnate in the same way as a spectre steals a precocious body — the only two contours of space and the only two confines of time that are dense enough for the senses.

"Though he did not live *in full* up to his thirtieth year *at that time*, the living, his contemporaries, grew older with the years minus that sizable gap in time.

"Mary Mother of God, standing at the foot of the Cross, was twenty years younger than Mary Mother of the Son of Man born on the prophesied day.

"The pagne was invented by a little girl.

"I am God, I did not have a childhood.

"I am a new Adam, born adult, born at twelve, and tomorrow at thirty I will vanish into nothingness, *without it being me who dies!* — and at every dawn there are as many million intermittent Gods like me as there are thousands of altars, myriads of Masses and billions of consecrated hosts.

"I — they — do not live in ordinary bodies and souls. We disappear from these habitations with an assumption or a sudden annihilation. There is some likelihood that our disappearance coincides more often than not with our hosts' taking communion, and renewing Christ's Passion.

"So for the most part we should inhabit those in a state of deadly sin, that our stay there might be a long one — else would we inhabit practising Christians or believers, which is unlikely seeing that our stay would be too short for the lapse from twelve to thirty. But the lengths of years are relative, and we live in infinitely *condensed* time: an instant suffices to live the whole of our lives inside these people. Without a doubt, almost — for my part with redoubtable, desired certitude — we inhabit *highly-dangerous criminals* and THOSE CONDEMNED TO DEATH, and disappear with the communion which is obligatory in prison.

"We encourage them to commit crimes, such is our *duty*, we are only satisfying a need: the vanity of not being eunuchs.

"Which is the more glorious progeny of a dead man, his weakly child or his immortal soul?

"The things we would do if society were different, and its laws other…

"But we cannot predict exactly what our means of existence would be in that case, or, I should say, our means and ends, the final result — the *end result* of the Son being the Passion.

"The men we possess are wise instinctively, they are supremely strong.

"For they dominate the will of others, even that of inanimate objects.

"Demonic possession and possession by the Holy Ghost are notoriously *symmetrical*.

"Those women who love us renew the real Sabbath.

"The devils of Loudun are our cousins.

"It happens, and without there being any paradox, that we benefit from All-Encompassing, Divine Protection, so that our power might be absolute (and it is) — for we align ourselves with time in the direction of universal Synthesis, like the compass needle which forms a cross with the magnetic current that flows from East to West.

"We live by cataclysms…

"Before dawn breaks — like a white star over the horizon, telling me to let a smaller star of white, the *real presence* of my present death, melt deliciously or sorrowfully on my tongue — hear this and tell all nations…

"But if you wish to hear more terrifying messages, stop, be still, sit ensconced at a cleric's desk and write!

"This is the Book of Revelation of the most vulgar people.

"This is the history of one of these ghouls."

III
O LITTLE SLEEP, APE OF PALE DEATH

Realising that one's mother is a virgin.
The 36 Dramatic Situations (thirty-seventh situation).

Joseph paring, planing corners, made the little horns, the shavings, germinate.

"Beddy-byes," murmured a voice, low whispering.

And Joseph did not hear a word of what was said, because he must not hear a word.

"Beddy-byes, child."

The Child slept not, Miriam did.

And there would rise a formidable voice, be it ever so high or low, from the manger or nuptial bed — but Joseph did not hear a word of what was said — in reply to little Miriam, who sighed:

"Master..."

With a long interval between each syllable when she spoke, from an intimation that she addressed Eternity, with no consciousness of duration, and taking the time needed to lift each word up from the well of the dead.

"Would you please command me to tuck up my arm? I am lying on my arm, and I will get pins and needles."

"Mother, why do you speak to me with such infinite respect? You ushered me into the world this night. I am your little baby child, though begotten of God. Woman, there is only one God in three persons. I am the only God in three persons. I am eight hundred sextillion centuries old, with everything there is in them, because I am the one who made them, and I was the age of eternity when I made the first century! I am the Son, I am your son, I am the Spirit, I am your husband from the beginning of eternity, your husband and your son, most pure Jocasta!

"But I am the very young groom in the bed of my beloved; and because I discover that you are a virgin, oh my Mother, my little bride, I now begin to feel sure that I am really He, God.

"Miriam, sleeping soundly, do you hear me?"

"If you command me to hear, then I have heard, Master."

"Mummy, tell me—"

"Your speech resembles the gestures of my new-born child, addressed to *the living woman. When I am living* I do not hear very well. So, Master, I am your mother, and the carpenter's wife."

"And now?"

"Oh! Now… you must indeed be God to fully understand the radiance of my smile… now, I AM THE VIRGIN.

"Make me sleep more deeply… Now I am… I am whatever you want me to be. Do not ask me questions, you know very well that I will only say whatever you want me to. I am Your handmaiden, I am…"

"What, Woman?"

"I am THE WILL OF GOD."

Her silence allowed the fabulous gold of all the gowns and trains to float back down again.

Miriam slept peacefully.

Little Ieschou-ben-Joseph lay naked, still and quiet.

The new-born child's gestures, cries and swaddling-clothes had no meaning at all, only the meaning *lent* them, since they will be meaningful when he is older.

He is the Idol.

The Wise Men announced the three oblations:

"Gold, for a King."

"Frankincense, for a God."

"And myrrh, for a burial."

The myrrh grew cold at Miriam's feet.

The rattling of the wooden clappers on the camels' necks grew distant in her sleep, as the vampire bats flying above the sands that muffled their claws flew far from the surging necks of the camels.

Joseph's trying-plane, like a jetty on the offensive, pushed back the shavings, so many little horns.

The Infant-God spoke again, now the Wise Men had disappeared off to their mountains:

"Are you asleep?"

"Yes," the voice breathed out deeply, from miles away.

"Are you comfortable?"

"Yes."

"You are comfortable!"

"Yes! yes!"

Smiles.

"When I was alive I was suffocating in a tomb of sand. Now I am comfortable. No! I live again! My throat… Command me to sleep, quick, quick, to sleep more deeply…

"I live, I am dying!

"Emmanuel! —"

A pillow-slip shroud over her eyes.

"Ca… ta… lepsy," she said.

The Wise Men are so distant now that we are nineteen hundred years away from the time of the Wise Men.

"Will you go to sleep!"

……………………………………………………………………………………

"I am asleep. She is asleep.

"She is dead.

"Beware of her.

"Anyway, she is no longer here.

"She's a bitch. I mean the woman *who is alive*.

"She'd knife you one in the back given half a chance."

"Do you love me?"

"I have no will.

"I am your will."

"Does she love me?"

"Hugely…

"Ow! command me to tuck up my arm!"

"And what of Joseph?"

"If you want me to kill him, you have only to command me to do so.

"You need not even speak.

"A little deflection of your will suffices; a nod and the enemy falls, the earth will swallow him up."

"The job would not be done properly. I am not confident enough. So, she doesn't love Joseph?"

"She despises him, because he is very old.

"But they do things together, though he be ever so old.

"So long as it's done, and with *her*; she little cares about beauty or ugliness.

"*Me*, he has never known.

"He only knows *the other one*.

"She does not behave the same way with him as she does with you.

"The ridiculousness of an old man is more obscene.

"Yesterday, she told you that he no longer slept with her.

"Well, they had just made love in the kitchen.

"He is very much in love with her.

"But she is not in love with him.

"She deceives him, that's what.

"You are her first lover, after sixty others."

"Her lover. What about: your lover?"

"Me? nobody even knows I exist.

"Not even her.

"*I can remember* her, but to *her* I am invisible."

"And the other woman, why did she kiss the old tide-waiter on the mouth?"

"It was perfectly deliberate.

"It was because you were there, watching her.

"She's a right bitch, I'm telling you.

"But she likes you.

"She didn't dare cast her eyes in your direction, afterwards.

"But she tends to go for the ugliest."

"And yourself?"

"Me? I am your will.

"Do with me as you wish.

"The other woman will never know."

"It is true that you are more beautiful than the other will be when *you* wake up.

"But what about when *she* wakes up?"

"Her flesh will perhaps retain a memory—

"No, it must not be!

"She would never forgive you.

"If she knew we were cheating on her, she would sneak away from you."

"You could convince her to stay, and tell her at the same time that I forbid her to play stupid jokes on me with customs officers—

"But how might one forbid her these things?"

"Your prohibitions, if conveyed by me, will be very short-lived.

"I can let you know what she is up to, and we can assess the situation.

"But she must never find out."

"We have a deal — here, what are you doing? Now what are you after?"

"My reward. Kiss me. And… why aren't you my lover altogether, as you are with the other woman?"

"What would she say? But I command you to imagine that I am your lover—

"Oh! enough of this! The other woman would believe that it has happened. And now, my little Miriam, MYRRH rather, you who are dead, rise again into the life of a notary."

"But I don't want to!"

"Wake up! 'But' what? say it again."

"But… but…

○ "… Butterfly."

IV

● *AOTROU DOUE*

● Because they found him in the *doué*, a kind of washing-place in Gallo, they forged him a surname out of it.

And because the baptismal waters had supplied his patronymic, they baptised him — in a more antique tongue — according to the day he was found, which was Noël.

Nédélec (Noël, Emmanuel) *Doue*.

They: that is the notary and his wife.

Joseph the notary and Mary his wife.

●○ *Joseb* and *Varia*, in the dialect of Lampaul, their home in Brittany.

Now was the notary called Joseph because his wife was christened Mary? or she

Mary for having married Maître Joseb?

This is of no importance.

They could not have been named differently.

These have been their names for all eternity, because their act of adoption states that the little child they had just adopted was Nédélec Doue.

The kids in Lampaul, standing by the baptismal porch, out of respect for the notary — this rich man from the city who could beget a *Gentleman* merely by signing a piece of paper, while the rest of the population went about making children, differently, and who was now *sowing* sugared almonds for them like seed, which in their eyes was a surer sign of generation — had already found a name for the Son, the same as in the Registry Book:

"*Aotrou Doue.*"

With this invocation do all litanies begin.

The kids in Lampaul did not give his name a second thought.

They said his name and nothing more:

"MISTER GOD."

And the litany like a prophetess continues in the words of the prayer-book, closed like two hands in supplication:

"Have mercy upon us! *Aotrou Doue, o pet truez ouzomp!*" ●

V
MAÎTRE JOSEB'S NOTARIAL OFFICE

Maître Joseb…

We write Maître Joseb because in these parts he was called "Mister Natary". ●

This might have allowed us to forgo the description of his house, to leave off hanging the escutcheon-sign outside his office and to refrain from baizing the sacristy door on the landing.

But Maître Joseb was a notary in the Breton style.

A notary in Brittany means anyone who writes.

When Leconte de Lisle went to Paris, the outskirts of Rennes concluded that he had successfully completed his prenotarial studies: ○

"We'll go an' see 'im in 'is office. Where's 'is office then?"

By extension, "Notary" has come to mean someone who does not work with his hands, or someone who uses his hands to make things that are pointlessly complicated.

As it happened, Maître Joseb could barely read or write, but he was rich enough to afford a coach-house and stable, and would lock himself away in a workshop full of stuffed birds to attend to the holy office of the little sawblade.

He therefore had the right, the obligation one might say, to have no hair left on the ogive dome of his skull, to shave his lips, and to bear well-scraped ivory sideburns, like the panels of a precious triptych — or, more to his taste, the antimacassars on the wings of an armchair.

Maître Joseb was well and truly:

"Maître Joseb."

VI
MISTER RAKIR

Little Emmanuel's education first began in Maître Joseb's office, or dining-room.

Emmanuel's first master resembled the lunar disc.

One big face, and a big halo of a face.

His crown, itself a scribe and script of legend, was that of the Forerunner, who did not wear it *on top of his head* as Herodias had done.

It was the purple cross-section of a neck, soon livid.

Emmanuel offered his own young brains to himself *in disco*, to season them with intelligence.

He is many.

They were twelve plates ringed with the double zodiac of the alphabet.

Wisdom unfurled around their edges with neither beginning nor end, like the Ocean on Achilles' shield.

These alphabets could be read starting from any letter, and Emmanuel made them simpler still by dropping and smashing them.

The master's classroom was black as antiquity.

At the hour when the moon and the moths would come in through the open window to melt or burn their frost in the heat of the candles, the astral doctor would come down from the tall dresser, his glass-fronted pulpit, for an informal communion of opinions.

The conventional terms of address employed by the pupil to his master, and by the master to Mister God, were on all occasions:

"*Ecce corpus Domini…*"

"*Domine, non sum dignus…*"

"I insist."

"No, after you, sir."

Emmanuel was his only listener, the others being too obtuse to rejoice in the drum suggested by their eardrums.

Once the lesson was over, he would turn a little wooden ark upside-down on the table, and from the tumble-down roof of the little house on the ship fell Noah and his wife, along with various domestic animals, and they came out two by two around the twenty-four pedagogical teeth of the master's wide-open mouth.

The notary, like the Demiurge, lined up according to his will the animals fractured along the grain, from Nuremberg and the nebulae of pine rings.

And after having contemplated the cows and bears, with their quadrangular polygon bases, and whose equilibrium on the ground below them was more an oscillation, and after having heard their light successive falls upon the table-top, Emmanuel demanded anxiously of him to act:

"Make the animals stand up!"

For the notary could direct, but not create.

From the cataclysm were born tripodal monsters, but Mister God took each one and broke off the superfoetant limb and made them crouch, improving their stability.

And he gave them names according to their spots, the accidents of their orthopaedics, and their resultant appearance.

"Rakir" and "ratoon" were the finest specimens, though even Emmanuel forgot what their names meant; the second had perhaps once been an elephant shrew, formally addressed as: "His Worship Ratatrunk".

Mister God thought them big enough, since he had created them, even to the point of making him very scared.

And on one occasion, more than intellectually.

The tocsin from the wind's belfry rang at the notary's door, like a starving dog in armour-plate, tethered to the bell of the abandoned tower, hauling its sedentary yell of fear towards its prey.

The Wind, for doubtless it was he, kept the door ajar with his heavy clog, the kind seen in pictures of Punchinello, though the child would fain have shut the half-open door, and fast.

It was not the wind but a visitor of more ordinary sorts.

That was why Mister God was not strong enough to crack the tough nut.

He was not Odin with his two wolves, because he did not have the ravens.

And there were four wolves scratching at his heels.

In the room with the Ark, for a small sum he showed how gentle were the wolves.

And to prove that their tameness was all his doing, *he too* turned a little box upside-down on the table where the wooden animals were grazing on the table-cloth.

The ferocity of the rough, churlish hounds reappeared in their rattling teeth, well away from the phalanges of the little hand, unsheathed of flesh, stolen from their master.

With the image of the wolves with their hackles up still in his eyes, their hairs caked in his eyelashes, and their inarticulate growls stuck in his throat, little Emmanuel was stuttering for the next two days.

VII
"LA"

> This character, Θάνατος, is masculine in Greek. Some Latin critics give him as ORCUS, who is another infernal divinity altogether. I thought it best to let him keep his original signification, notwithstanding that the French name *La Mort* is feminine. This in no way changes the scope or purview of the character, nor the manner in which he should be played.
>
> Le Père Brumoy, *Le Théâtre des Grecs.*

When he was four, it was Madame Joseb herself who took him to school every morning to join the *Minims* in the junior form of the local lycée.

Down a steep hill, practicable only by turning in spirals, where there ran a brook called the Roquet, a brook paved with stones, the shank of the screw.

Then, along an alley, likewise tortuous, where he gloried in the new-born steadiness of his gait, following the edge of the pavement, which, riding above the brook, seemed to overlook a chasm.

And, with the iron gate behind him, standing in the flower garden which they called the playground, he felt his solitude increase with the good-bye kiss imparted by *his mother.*

The other Minims in the playground would converge upon Emmanuel.

Perhaps it was the memory of his mother's skirts, or because he took a deep breath before pronouncing a complicated surname, or again because the little ones really were all dressed in pleated skirts like girls, that when he told the adventures of his day at school, duly exaggerated before the notary and his wife, he named them all with the feminine article: "*La*".

"*La* Mecqerbac, *la* Zinner, *la* Xavier."

And when he recited his lesson, he would sprawl on the mistress's lap, for the Minims' teacher was a woman.

Mrs. Lane.

He never did find out if his memory of her name was correct, or whether it was not the personification of the little liquid alleyway he took every morning and at the end of which was his classroom.

He had learnt how to read and write from looking at plates, from his hieroglyphs — since every child scribbles, he drew little-big men each presenting the front and back of their heads simultaneously — and from all eternity, so he never understood why he was sent off to suffer daily lessons from the mouth of this estuary.

He deduced that he should regard her as an exhibitor of freakish things.

Indeed, to catch the attention quickly of distant or distracted pupils, had she not equipped herself with a long pointing-stick of witch hazel?

This was her fairy's magic wand.

Whenever she had finished using this telephone (for she preferred to administer *correction* with the white handle of her letter-opener, which wagged in time with the vibration of its blade, striking fingers to the bones, which could be heard when struck), she would cast it behind her desk amongst the torn workbooks, in the corner which she called — Emmanuel later managed to reconstruct the term — the
● *capharnaüm*.

● The first time, he heard "coffer for the norn", which always seemed to him to be clearer, more precise and more sumptuous.

●○ He soon learnt all about the dinornis and the aepyornis, from engravings.

All he learnt from his year at school was the handling of wooden letter-openers — he called them "knives" in the abstract — which became an obsession.

He had the notary cut them out, then decorated and perfected them himself, probably in the image of the creating saw which stood gleaming on its mahogany perch for all to admire, with its voracious hand-saw teeth and its back hollowed to a
● curve, to the point of the word "cutlass".

He trembled for a whole afternoon in a state of joyful anguish, lying on his belly
● looking at the birch-rod in a terrifying picture entitled "Father Switches".

And for the most part of an evening, after the rod of punishment had been raised in warning, lying under a couch where they thought he was asleep, he watched his friend Xavier, whose parents frequented and were visiting his.

And his memory of junior form and the Minims ultimately resolved itself around Xavier, simplifying his features — which he had forgotten — and substituting for them the schematic features of an X, the white X on the portals of burial grounds, below the human skulls of the funeral hangings:

La Mecqerbac, *la* Zinner, *la*…

LA Mort, which is death.

VIII

ODIN

When he was fifteen, during his holidays, he once received the visit of Mrs Joseb — he had kept no very clear image of *his mother* in his memory before that time — who had walked through the fern forest to see him.

Because the notary's house did not contain lodgings that were adequate for the young man that Emmanuel now was, Joseb had offered him the run of one of his farms for the duration of the Parisian boarder's two months of liberty; like most farms, it enclosed a space so vast it could have contained several castles.

It lay surrounded by parks and hillocks.

The cultivated hillsides and the valley that led to the sea were, as the saying goes, like a pair of corduroy trousers, with variegated patches, and which to show off its particoloured pieces had done a handstand like a forked oak.

In the innermost crotch of this fork was a wood of chestnut trees, their roots veiled with ferns.

Varia, on her way down, met only with plants and creatures.

All of them fearsome. ○

On the plateau, before it dipped, were *janiques*, whose flowers of gold were mounted not on metal but on precious stones, on emerald pins with needles all around. ●

Broom: mild in comparison, but artificially fortified with bees.

Its needles, blunted by the sun, renewed by blazing spears whose cinders would fatten their seed.

Woodlice, meticulously strapped in armour-plating.

Carrion scarabs in mourning weeds spitting out blood, like freshly spattered brains. ○

The hill then fell more steeply, and after the spiny flames came the glaives of the gladioli, the slicing sword-grass and the trailing laces of the knotted roots, lying complicated on the ground.

She could see no frogs, could not hear them jumping into ponds with a splash; there were no ponds yet.

The grasses and the ground were all the croaking of the frogs and toads.

Like the squeaking of a sponge if the water it held, like the rosary-beads that stiffened and so recorded the death of Prince Perviz, was turned into a viscous clot of blood.

Varia walked as if she were upright on a grand old bed, releasing the creaks imprisoned in the wood of the wardrobes with her hopscotch.

"Emmanuel isn't at the farm. He went off to the sea."

The peasant, having given directions, went back indoors, and Varia back into the covered desert.

... Then there were ferns, sabres in bouquets, ranked in a herbarium, classified by size and according to the figures they *cut*: they were spread like open hands, which can therefore close, like a fist; they were massed like chariots armed with axle-scythes, which, rather than advancing, carpeted the insides of a lobster-pot where one is made to walk.

And each was lined with pustules, like an octopus, an outstretched glove of living muscle.

And yet they are not pustules but spore-cases: indusiated sori, in technical terms.

Harmless.

But visible.

The fear that *one cannot turn away from* is the fear induced by harmlessness that is all on the outside, a simple décor.

Then, amidst the moss egg-cups beneath the oaks, lay the strange puff-ball eggs, the wolf's-fists.

Varia ventured a foot upon one of these poison-filled little firkins, which were softer than an eyelid.

Should one break the Death-Roc's egg by the big end or the little?

She remembered that lycopodium explodes in theatres with a flash of light to hide actors' trap-door entrances and exits.

WOLVES.

Wolves trot boldly on dry leaves.

On the ground there was only moss.

But if there were dry leaves they would be heard trotting on dry leaves!

The sunless wood, like a locked house, imprisoned Fear within.

The fern was the vault of a cellar and arched in the daylight, revealing all the cave-dwelling monsters.

The wolves would not cut their legs on them, for they bristled with thick-set hairs.

And though they lacked pustules on their teeth, their mouths were more serrated than any of the ferns.

Plants which bite do not eat each other.

Varia did not turn round to look.

She knew perfectly well they were there behind her back.

Advancing under the twin vaults of coppice alleys, with their scraggy hair and canines standing out from their shadowy bodies.

Like two sets of eyelashes from two big eyes, standing.

She broke into a run.

But she had arrived.

Emmanuel was in a tidesman's cabin, on the crest of the parapet of the cliffs.

It was divided into two chambers, like the engine-boiler of a steam locomotive and its funnel.

The little look-out cabin was made of stones laid on top of one another without cement, with a cavity left unfilled, a loophole on to the sea.

An eye-socket expropriated by the customs officer to fix his gaze, in imitation of the hermit crab which moves into mollusc-shells to lodge — something else.

The other compartment is hollow and flat, a cell with bed-sheets of rock, and a villose under-blanket of wrack.

Varia saw Emmanuel: he was standing upright — despite the diminutiveness of the cabin — his back to the large, pink granite chimney, its mantelpiece like a mantle upon his shoulders.

And beneath the mantle, he was the hearth fire.

He is fire.

The fire-dogs, to his left and right, were all bitten through, the iron eaten away by the fire.

Or rather, there was only one fire-dog: the churlish wolf, sitting in profile, baring its well-separated teeth, its deep-grooved hairs, and a single eye, like a hole between the pair of them.

Too symmetrical to be single.

Its twin entered by the prodigiously distant door: nothing smaller than the abbey refectory on the Mont St. Michel would have done to respect the proportions of the monumental chimney-piece.

The second wolf led Varia in by her dress; its teeth the page-clip in the woollen folds.

And Emmanuel, leaving the fireplace, which was the light-source of the room, and pushing the first wolf like a wing-chair, which grated along the floor with a rumbling, spoke in a voice of thunder:

"Madame, take a seat on our companion."

Varia, as if waking from a dream, discovered with a flush of fear that the only wolves there had ever been were the two black diamonds beneath Emmanuel's eyebrows.

IX

SINOPLE, AN ERMINE EN ABYME

> And for that these demons be aqueous, so are they excessively lascivious.
>
> Sinistrari, *Demoniality*.

From his observation point, Emmanuel could see Varia coming.

Not on the road, not through the fields, not at all.

No, in his memory.

And he could see her far more surely — discovering her presence even before she came into view, and with his back turned — when he gazed through the loophole out on to the sea.

Paris in the wintertime.

Mr. Rakir and Mrs. Lane had been replaced by the Lycée Condorcet.

When he felt nostalgia for the sea, Mister God went to the glass ceiling of the Gare Saint-Lazare which, at the lighting of the lamps, rather resembled an aquarium.

He did not need to break the glass.

His mother would lift away the door-curtain of fluid crystal, in the holidays, and come towards him, to harbour.

He had very quickly ceased to believe that she was his mother.

She arrived too much like a siren.

And so he waited for the too too phosphorescent hour, knowing she would come.

It was principally her frightened look in the electric beams that had made him realise that she was not his mother.

A mother is a tutelary figure, normally.

A night-light is not afraid of the other lamps, nor does it fear the stars.

The wife of the Lampaul notary was from the country where people guide themselves, when the sun is no longer there, by holding iron lanterns on a leash, like those moths who carry with them, in fear, their marvellous and awesome prey, their lantern light.

And, imperceptibly, but inevitably, her head showed beyond doubt the first wavering tendencies to be fascinated by windows all aglow with flames.

But she did not gild at their light the bombyx down of her white muff.

She slid with rapid undulations, shimmering like the dermestes whose larvae live in fur.

Or like the head of a peacock, more hesitant than that of a grass snake, because a crest of drawn-glass threads amplifies and records the trembling.

Above all, Emmanuel recognised a skater's insinuations in the frost between the rosy heather, over there, and which were the sinuosities of the heraldic beast.

The ermine.

Perhaps it was him she was scared of, the high-school kid who swaggered like a copper on the beat.

Fear of stains?

The ermine is a very dirty beast.

She is her own precious bed-sheet, but as she does not have a spare, she does her washing with her tongue.

Gargantua would have dubbed her thus:

"The goose that can get to the bottom of things."

But the "March-cat" exulcerated him, and filed its claws for other ermines only.

The day Emmanuel first addressed Varia as "Madame" instead of "Mum", outside the Lycée Condorcet, she immediately suggested a private dining-room, or "a horse and hired carriage in the Bois".

It did not seem to him to be incest at all, but rather the sudden reviviscence of the notaress.

"Above all," he said, thus indicating his choice, "where they serve crayfish."

After the reading-room in Lampaul, Varia was ready for the private dining-room.

She took great care to give the cabman five francs, no doubt to buy his silence.

In which case she ought to have seen a money-changer for a coin that was smaller, but of gold.

Likewise, they did not climb the hotel steps *arm in arm*.

"*Garçon*, table for three," Madame Joseb *pursued*. "Is there a gentleman waiting for us? Middle-aged—"

"Wearing a decoration," whispered Emmanuel.

"Looking for a lady and a schoolboy? How extraordinary that he isn't here yet. *Garçon*, a table for three. We'll wait."

"While we eat," Emmanuel chipped in, to please everyone.

The food was bad and they did not make love, for they had been cloistered with a brand new gas stove.

Mister God was censed with varnish.

They risked a hasty kiss — after the bill had arrived.

That was all.

And yet there had been a divan at their disposal.

Varia had reclined there, almost full-length, showing off a garter of flesh higher than those of her stockings.

But Mister God was still only a schoolboy.

The ermine put her skates back on and made for the heather.

Today, Mister God would not lunch in a private dining-room.

He was in the tidesman's cabin, which he did not think of as belonging to anybody since the customs officer was absent.

He was at home.

He had prepared a bizarre meal, imagining he was making an offering to himself of animals or loaves in consecrated shapes, to be sacrificed in the freestone temple.

He emptied out his Noah's Ark.

First, a cake in the shape of a hedgehog with almond spines, although he knew that *representational* cakes are execrable.

He had decided that they would start with dessert.

Here, some Chianti in its lightweight wine-flask, chosen for its amusing ball of straw and gob of oil.

Some soused oysters, because they are a disgraceful sight.

Some rye bread stuffed with currants.

A sausage of *foie gras* like a golden phallus.

And to give his animals somewhere to sit, he unfolded an old map like a dried-up flood on the ground, because there was no table in the customs officer's shelter.

He could not see that Varia was frightened of wolves.

And yet, it was *with them* that he could see.

He had perceived the entry of the slender animal into the stone dwelling.

He judged that it was a much more natural and more becoming place for her than a house.

First of all they had their little tea-party, sitting side by side on the wrack.

They could not stand up, and the spray on Varia's pill box hat kept scraping the low ceiling and pulling off bugs that fell in heaps into what they were eating.

Mister God had a dark inkling that his own *wolf's-head mop* was one that must not be played with.

It was *a real one.*

Madame Joseb shrugged, amused that the flattened ceiling should have forced them into a bed; she lifted up her hands, but as there was no room to stretch her arms out under the vault, and as she did not have the strength to raise the vault, she made them into two small ermines, which wriggled about everywhere, exploring first the picnic map, and then Emmanuel's geography.

He had once reared green lizards under his shirt.

These white serpents were more comfortable as they went ferreting.

They were warmed up before being put… elsewhere.

But Madame Joseb discovered that her little schoolboy was no longer a schoolboy in every particular, in every particular place.

He took visible pride in having what neither the senile notary nor the few *in loco parentis* — and they call themselves teachers! — had been able to make him even suspect the possible extent of.

And the slim creature, confronted with a monster more stocky than herself, fled to the reddening heath.

Hardly had she arrived at the doorstep, when she came up against a tall silhouette in a cowl of green.

Complementarily.

It was the customs officer who had come to repossess his dwelling.

Without a moment's hesitation, and so fast that the action was over before Emmanuel could explain the *reason* for her act to himself, she had thrown her arms around the neck of the ugly fellow in uniform.

She kissed him full on the lips, like a step made by one of her low heels, which would not be slow to land in a — plash — puddle.

X

SIGNED AND SEALED WITH YELLOW SEALING-WAX

That evening, while the notary was whiling away the post-prandial hours in his secluded study, according to his wont, right until dawn, victualled with a small bottle of clear spirits, working off his meal to the chirping of his saw amidst the arabesques of the mahogany forest which he assassinated and resuscitated, Emmanuel and Varia met again, without a word of explanation or transition.

Their mouths clung together fast — like an insect clinging to its mate on the other side of a mirror — to keep their bodies from falling helpless — to another world.

They wrapped their arms around each other in a grand tour of caresses, clasping the unlikelihood of their reunited presence till the Real coalesced, till it condensed and would escape no more.

Edging towards what they had not previously dared to do, counselled by the whispering sounds of the sea between the two valves of their limestone bed, they followed the scrolled caprices they could hear falling from the notary's chime-plane with its barbed beak.

They were two supple creatures, white and sensitive to the cold — for nothing is so white as the most wintry furs of un-undressable animals, unless it be human skin — two beasts intertwined in the dwelling trimmed with lace made of pink heather.

Varia's coat enveloped them.

That is to say that he was no longer wearing *her*.

And that Emmanuel would be cold, now, without a blanket.

Their pointed ermine heads, with their pale red, straw-coloured snouts, kept a look-out between the defensive heather tufts.

The very prudence of the little creature would put even Joseb's wrath to flight, as a kid's impudicity repels passers-by.

There are some who turned round when they saw her, it is true.

Pure white was Varia, but of that white heat which is the fire of those girls the Gulf Stream blossoms into.

The flowers drink from the watering-can of warm waves, an illusion of the tropics.

She was white like all the coloured gems which are pale.

White topaz, balas ruby, dead pearls, mixed in a powder.

Fruits from the garden of Aladdin, as yet unripe.

They looked green, for the sky loomed dark and scarlet.

Her hair was black with shades of episcopal purple.

There are marine bishops who let their amethysts dissolve in the kiss with which the waves are confirmed.

Her skin — despite the contrast — would have been brown, were it not for a complete absence of down, like a sea-washed pebble, or the curvaceous torso of a siren.

When she clasped and clipped Emmanuel, her armpits winked, and their tiny eyelashes tried their sepia brushes in the air.

Elsewhere, there were the scales of sea-creatures.

Dead pearls…

Mister God renewed the necklace.

Emmanuel had broken through to the other side of the aquarium at the Gare Saint-Lazare — a clown in a diving-suit, he had head-butted the glass.

The schoolboy who came on holiday visits had grown since going to Condorcet.

He was now the same height as Varia, who looked like a supple animal, most of all because she was tall.

She appeared less tall now, however, than when she was standing next to the dwarfish notary.

After they had clasped their mouths together in a kiss or a bite, and drawn away for a moment to measure their bliss in each other's eyes, then were the breasts of the one the imprint of the breasts of the other.

Two, perfectly superimposable triangles.

Since Mister God had a hereditary right to the seal of the Trinity!

They separated as a book opens.

Like the notary's white side-whiskers, but he could not bring them any closer.

And contemplated each other.

Varia groped with her fingers behind Emmanuel's shoulders.

Trying to make out where Love's wings were jointed to his back.

Perhaps their flight was too fast — like that of the fusiform macroglossa and the *stellatarum* that were flecking the glass panes, pinned in the glass cabinets in the bedroom — so that only a mist could be seen.

But suddenly, something black — the banality or the fatality of the disc of shadow after having stared at the sun — and resembling an oil and vinegar cruet in the act of being poured, fell from Emmanuel's pupils into Varia's.

The dregs of Love: Fear.

Varia trembled as if she were in a snow-fall, surrounded by visible night and black snow.

"Go away! I beg of you! Let me *go to sleep alone*!

"What did I ever do to you?"

She spoke in a voice so choked she was cooing.

"Have mercy on me!"

As much is said by another Book when it is opened:

"*Aotrou Doue, o…*"

For God to have pity would be tantamount to his abdicating his divinity.

But one is very frightened when he is there.

With a defensive instinct, Fear gave birth to Mister God's most redoubtable adversary.

She who could be the most disagreeable to him.

Madame Joseb, absolutely herself.

"This is my home!"

She leapt towards one of the high walls.

It goes without saying that in the notary's house, in addition to the stuffed birds and the dry insect cases — the chirping and buzzing lived over there in the imperturbable foliage cut out in the notary's Office — there was a whole panoply of exotic weapons.

She plucked the first dagger that came to hand.

A Khanjar whose handle was not in the shape of a cross but resembled instead the forked antennae of a clavicorn scarab.

"Get out of here, or I'll kill you!"

Confronted by the creature that lays death under the bark of bodies with her terebra, Emmanuel relived — in the bat of an eye — the divine, infant joys of his monsters standing on the notary's table.

He prepared to shake the table once again.

With a little puff.

With something that is less than a puff of air.

The wind made by his eyelashes.

For with extraordinary clearness he perceived for the first time *what it was* that Varia was afraid of.

One is so strong in front of a raised dagger when one is naked and immobile.

For whoever brandishes the weapon is admitting they are inferior to you, since they call on a blade to rescue them.

They are inoffensive, since there are *two of them*.

Else one is drunk, and dreaming, since one sees *double*.

Emmanuel lay confidently under the blade of a guillotine, formidably confident — as one must be, as *he* must be — that its fall is highly unlikely, even when the *instantaneous* trigger-click *begins*.

Since:

"1. *It has never happened to you before.*

"2. *It is the sort of thing that only happens once in a lifetime.*

"3. And can one be sure that the law of gravity will be upheld *again* for the top-weight on the guillotine-blade?"

Completely naked, his arms stiff, Emmanuel crucified himself on the shroud that lay in readiness on the bed, but he released — yet oh! so gently — the two black Mutes that were his gaze.

"Beddy-byes," he whispered.

Varia fell.

As she fell, she struck.

But the Khanjar no longer obeyed the hypnotised woman.

It was like a horse without a bridle.

It would not trample a body on the ground.

It landed between Emmanuel's left arm and his left breast, sinking right to the hilt in the sheet of the bed that was like the paper-covered cork in the glass cabinets where the other scarabs were pinned.

So Emmanuel slipped from the bed and stood up, leant on the bedstead and perused his dying gasps on a pin.

Varia fumbled for the place with the movements of a somnambulist.

She pulled out the dagger and let it drop.

To clear a space.

She sought, just as she had groped for the wings of Love.

The space was empty, like the seat occupied by a ghost in a theatre.

The throne where Nobody was sitting.

No body: the Ghost.

One of the three Persons.

Mister God smoothed his seal flat in the middle of the notary's sheets, freshly resuscitated from all the provincial lavenders in the herbarium of the wardrobes.

T.T.L.

The visiting-card with a corner turned down.

The Trinity appended its Triangle.

XI
ET VERBUM CARO FACTUM EST

> In the beginning was the Word…
> … (and we beheld his glory, the glory as of the only begotten of the Father,) full of grace and truth.
> St. John's *Gospel.*

> Whereupon, without any more advertisement, or so much as the uttering of one word on either side, they fell to with great noise…
> Rabelais, *Pantagruel*, III, 19.

That was how Mister God had pulled Miriam from the sleeping notary.

They *relived* the Wise Men and the manger, until he made her wake up, with his index finger between her eyebrows, if it can be said that a pin, between a pair of large, velvet wings, "wakes" a butterfly from its dream life to the life of *etiquette*.

Miriam evoked her fellow-creature-in-metamorphosis:

"But I don't want to… but… but… butterfly!"

So that he might preside over her giving birth to Madame Joseb.

Madame Joseb — Varia, the Other Woman, the notary's wife — did not resemble Miriam at all.

She was less young.

She was twenty-five years old, according to her birth certificate.

Miriam was fifteen.

But Varia was also less old.

Miriam readily told of the adventures that happened to her seventy-two thousand years ago.

When one is that old, age has no meaning.

It is an art.

Mister God, in creating Miriam, had managed to sculpt a Venus who made it into Year One of our twentieth century without that infirmity which is a greater sign of age than the loss of hair, namely the loss of arms.

Madame Joseb was less all sorts of things than Miriam.

Less beautiful especially.

And that *less*, which implies a comparison, had no meaning for Emmanuel.

Because he could observe for a second time that his two mistresses, or rather his mistress and his wife, did not resemble each other at all.

Miriam was a blonde.

Varia was a brunette.

The difference was too paradoxical for it not to have been invented by his brain.

But the difference was real.

Joseb himself would not have recognised his wife in Miriam.

He would have congratulated himself that the gold offered to the God-King shone upon the head of a woman he knew not, and not upon his own forehead with its bifid, saffron-coloured marriage bands.

Monsieur Joseb, here is why she who is not your wife — but the wife of God! — is blonde.

Her eyelids hid their lashes when they closed, locked like hands in prayer.

Her hair had ebbed smoothly away from her forehead; the contracted nape of her neck had pinned her hair back tightly on the sheets.

Her face was one over-long oval of glabrous wax.

Statue.

And if you had lifted up her lids, you would have discovered no more pupils there than if you had opened up her breasts.

The whites — milk-white or bone-white — of her eyes.

Statues, with their unwanted hairs removed *even where there were no hairs* by the passage of centuries, left their bezelled-glass pupils as alms to future centuries.

And that is why your ex-wife is a blonde.

The gold offered to the King upon her Myrrh-made mortuary head.

But now Madame Joseb began to wake.

Her nose wrinkled like a sniffing snout, seemingly tickled by fur.

Her eyes, after her eyelids had strained to spring open, widened in surprise, and two blacks burst in upon the Other Woman's wan face — like the mechanical stamping of buttons on an ankle-boot, only more beautiful.

Her blue-black lashes made a shaggy underwood.

So much vegetation covered the dead Venus like saxifrage that the marble was divided into cells and the masterpiece was now no more than flesh.

Oh the despair Pygmalion should have felt had he not been such an ass, for he could have made a statue, but all he could do was a woman!

Mister God was not so conventional.

Or he would not have been Mister God.

He would give Adam back the rib he had taken from him.

Or the nibbled end of it anyway.

Madame Joseb fully agreed with him.

The little creature (a naked woman is always a little creature, even if she is tall), sitting on her behind, her face wider as she was pressing down her heavy, sleepy lids, then lifting up their blue tufts like a second pair of weightier damask, quickly, dryly, said:

"Oh! my God!"

Hers.

She was not thinking of some vocative for Emmanuel.

She would have said: "Emmanuel," or used a pet-name.

She was speaking of a God of hers.

Of Madame Joseb's.

Of all the Madame Josebs.

As they say:

"My dog, my seamstress."

Or

"My husband."

Though "My husband" requires a more commendable opening of the mouth.

Furthermore, "My husband" includes the dog and the seamstress, since he supports them.

They "attach more importance" to that possessive, as a kid embellishes the tail of a poodle with a saucepan.

It is not a very interesting God.

"What will my maid say?"

Another unit of the same, which she added to the list.

"How ridiculous to make me waste my time in this way!"

Emmanuel Dieu might have thought to inform her that they had not wasted any time at all, neither hers nor anybody else's, but had merely availed themselves of a few cubic yards of infinity, but he neglected to do so in this instance.

"What time is it?"

Then, with all her earthly hate collected in a sudden flash:

"You just put me to sleep, didn't you!"

Emmanuel pondered whether she was worthy of an account of what had passed between them, whether he ought to invent a mirror in which she might behold the Other Woman — Miriam! — or deny everything.

He determined on the lie most likely to be believed by one inferior, or by one who understands things in a world of Relative truths.

● He confessed the Absolute.

"You had a sort of nervous fit, I don't know how it came about.

● "You tried to strike me with a dagger — look, here's the shoulder of the blade — the little triangle is clearly visible on the sheet.

● "I always take *my* deaths literally…

"And seeing that it is I who tell naughty children to be quiet, I told you to go bye-byes!"

"You did that, you! But you're mad!

"How I adore you. Put me to sleep again. Bye-byes, do—

"No it isn't! You're telling fibs.

"Women only get hypnotised in novels and hospitals.

"So there…!

"What were we doing before… as for this story about the knife, you went and made it up."

"My darling, we—"

"You see! You're… as if nothing happened, and… so you would honestly have me believe that I have been asleep for two hours!"

She had her "proof" and had no intention of letting go, so long as she was in a condition to prove anything.

She had found a man again.

That was much more agreeable to her than a God.

Emmanuel gave up not speaking.

He took back the spare rib he had taken from Adam, the notary.
ET VERBUM CARO FACTUM EST.
"*Et* habitavit?"
"Precisely."

XII
THE RIGHT TO LIE

Varia's sex: an eye-flap on a mask.

Mister God's eyes were a brooch on his costume, even when he was completely naked: they were his *door of flesh* on to Truth.

There is only one Truth.

And myriads of things, more exactly the whole infinite series of numbers — all the numbers which are not One — which are not this Truth.

The total number of present or possible lies may be written:

$$\infty - 1 = \infty$$

Nobody has access to this Truth, for God is the one who possesses it.

Emmanuel Dieu or the Other One.

They prevent the existence of a beautiful, harmonious, universal Lie, free from any tear in its fabric.

They are the sex of the Lie, which is female.

This sex is an empty space to be filled in, as long as they keep their Truth to themselves.

And as nature abhors a vacuum, there is always something or other — which by definition cannot be Truth — that spills over into it, into the Truth box.

"Dame Truth's box", were we to write the story of this courtesan.

A lover who is in favour bears the name of Truth, whatever the Magnitude of the Lie he tells.

And they will never know he is not *Truth in person*.

There is but God — Emmanuel, and the Other One — who may perpetually, and in a manner both perfect and varied, *tell untruths*, for they know *where lies Truth*.

They know they hold the Truth, and naturally they lie, having withheld it.

Mister God would be a common whore if he *surrendered it* — if he surrendered up *himself.*

And when he surrendered *something else*, there was a good chance that people would believe he told the Truth, for it was more likely that he would say something approaching what they believed was True, than he should say something *visibly* in contradiction with his real Truth, which he withheld from view.

Since he knew that he would not be understood if he did not lie, he was indifferent to lies.

It was a bridge to other people.

If — he preferred the shortest distance.

He readily told different lies to different people at the same time, for whilst they were in practice an infinite distance from him, they were not distant in the same direction.

He did not lie to *them*, since he spoke in *their* direction.

Only to himself.

When he lied to them all together, then like the garden epeirid which moves away from the whole circumference of its web in a single trajectory, he returned to the centre of himself.

What then distinguishes Emmanuel from *Varia*, she who lies?

Women lead you up the garden path the long way round.

With details.

Analytically.

Miriam — in nervous sleep there are but lies: the defensive instinct of the feeble — Miriam told lies to fall in line with Emmanuel's will.

She recorded all the True he improvised.

She was, in her opinion, absolute Truth.

Truth, for man, is what man wants: a *desire.*

For God, what he *creates.*

When one is neither one nor the other — Emmanuel — then *his* Truth is *the creation of his desire.*

XIII

MELUSINA WAS A KITCHEN DRUDGE-WENCH, PERTINAX, A PEELER OF WALNUTS

INTERVAL: The stars fall from the heavens.
Caesar-Antichrist.

With the same movement that God got his bone back from the notary — even-handed or back-handed swap — the notary's wife stole Miriam back from God.

Miriam, in order to *exist*, had to annihilate Varia: the fair lids of the Bride of God would nibble like a little mouth at Madame Joseb's dark-brown eyebrows and lashes, drinking every violet wave of her head of hair.

And it was by a parallel absorption that Madame Joseb wholly substituted herself for Miriam.

Varia's eyelashes planted their conquering palisade of flags in mourning *in the living flesh*, in Miriam's marble lids, white as the frosted globe of a lamp means there lies within a dazzling light.

They looked like bayonets in silhouette, or like anything military and pointed.

They pricked at long-range, like beams from dirty stars.

It was perfectly obvious that their prolongations put out the very eyes over which they intersected.

Brutally they poked and raked the hearth of absolute love.

Mister God, who *reasoned* all that, must have been *absolutely* mad.

Absolute-tell-lie.

It is a charade.

What is not qualified by the first word is the subject of the rest.

Everything in the universe is defined by this adjective or this verb.

Mister God, whose brain was reeling, went back over all the steps of Varia's journey towards him.

He translated them into *absolute* terms — he could not have done otherwise, for *he* was the one going over them.

The chestnut wood.

Thorns, flames, gladioli.

The seven swords of the ferns were plunged in Miriam's heart.

The hand closes that had been dried at great cost in the notary's patient herbarium — but for what theft had he concocted this *main de gloire*!

Thus the meticulous, unrelenting woodlouse curls into a ball.

The grip of the monster.

"Have mercy..."

No, it is nothing.

Pay no attention.

Those round things, with so many points...

They are only falling stars.

And again, only those whose spectra are green.

The stars of least magnitude of each constellation.

But then again, are these stars lying on the earth not Vega, Sirius, α Cetus, Pollux, Regulus, Procyon, β Lyra Capella, Altair, Polaris, Castor and Venus!

They form clusters beneath the chestnut trees, in order to adapt themselves to their terrestrial environment.

One could mistake them for the green echidna of the chestnuts.

Vegetable hedgehogs, since they are the same colour as young fruit.

Chestnuts are unripe stars.

Miriam was pale like an unripe star...

Dead pearls.

But the spines of these little hedgehogs soon rot, soon turn black, and resemble Varia's mask of lashes!

A highly sophisticated mask.

It has replaced the hieroglyphic method of the Infant-God.

It goes right round the head.

As the eyes of statues without pupils cannot let their gaze escape to a *vanishing-point*.

The lycopods, similarly shaped, let flee from their capsules a death-dealing powder with brutal obscenity.

In literature; elsewhere, pharmacists roll them into pills.

One of myrrh, because it causes death: it embalms and honours the dead.

The thing of glory burrows into the foul gangue and filthy deads.

The wolf's-fists.
Putrid… Pu… pu…
Purity.
The ermine!

Heraldic Purity, with its straw-coloured snout made balas rubicund by dint of ferreting out dirty things, between the bars, between the spikes of the hedgehog — the beast that stinks — muzzle foremost, sucks.

What is candid resuscitates.

The animal-shaped Savoy cake, iced with dark chocolate, comes up white.

The almonds are the spikes on the ball.

Almonds.

One of Florian's Fables:

"Nuts certainly taste delicious, but one has to open them…

"If one makes no effort in life…"

Mister God once made an effort in life.

He had struggled with the leader of wolves — Mister Rakir! — he had caught the stumpy-toed clog in the clamp of the notary's door.

He had not cracked open the husk of the clog because he was only a little child and too scared to see what was inside it.

Most likely the skeletal foot of Mister Rakir, gnawed by the wolves, with his tarsal bones scratching and rattling inside the sonorous wood of the little coffin.

"*La*," said the tuning-fork.

Mrs. Lane's knife is vibrating in the air.

Almonds.

Come to think of it, does he like almonds?

"Does she love me?"

"They have just made love in the kitchen… I am what you want me to be."

The rediscovered myrrh smells burnt.

The wyvern's carbuncle has melted on the sink.

Melusina was a kitchen drudge-wench… Pertinax too wore an apron.

With his shining kitchen-knife upstanding, he swiftly divides the hedgehog down the middle, slicing through to the creamy-white heart, where the almonds were pricked.

Melusina, the siren with a serpent's tail and skylark's wings, fell asleep like a child listening to stories, rocked by the instantaneous swaying to and fro of the shiny thing.

XIV
LOVE'S MOUSETRAP

"Beddy-byes, baby, listen to some stories.

"Is she not pretty, then, your little Shahrazad?"

"I am listening.

"It is beautiful.

"My sister, if you are not asleep…"

"Are you comfortable?"

"Yes, I'm comfy."

She was rigid and leaning against the wall at forty-five degrees, cataleptic.

"The fifth voyage of Sinbad the Sailor.

"Listen carefully and don't think of anything else.

"Joseb is not here.

"Joseb is on a sea voyage.

"Joseb is Sinbad."

"Sinbad, yes."

"You are the Old Man of the Sea.

"Your body is young, like mine, but you are very old.

"I am only seven hundred and fourteen thousand years older than you.

"You keep a watch by the riverside for people travelling alone."

"I see Sinbad.

"Sinbad will come tonight."

"You understood what I wished to be done before I spoke my will.

"You make a sign to him that you want him to carry you to the other side of the river, to pick some fruit."

"Oh the fleshy golden peaches, and grapes like a peacock's tail all of sugar!

"I'm watering at the mouth.

"Bid me wipe my mouth."

"Not so fast.

"Now is not the time to look at the fruit.

"You are perfectly capable of telling the time by your mental clock; like me, you are as old as Kronos.

"You must go to sleep at eleven o'clock at night and wait for Sinbad.

"Around his neck you must wrap your thighs, whose skin is tough as cowhide — let us not forget that you are the Old Man of the Sea!

"Squeeze your thighs tightly around his neck when he starts to ford the river.

"Christopher leant on a great tree when he carried me to the other side of the ford — but then I was carrying the world, and so would never have been able to swim, being such a weight.

"But the Christophorus was a giant, a vigorous young giant, and Sinbad is a white-bearded old pedlar.

"Squeeze that neck of Sinbad's very tightly when he goes to ford the stream.

"But beware!

"Sinbad crossed the waters of the river, but he is covered with wine-stains: he crushed some grapes in a calabash, and now the rosy liquor on his tickly white beard—

"(It does not tickle any more, stop laughing!)

"... stains you from your belt to your calves."

"I'm frightened!

"I'm all giddy!

"Hold me, I'm going to fall!"

"Sinbad is drunk, and Sinbad is going to unmoor you from his shoulders, yes, the wrestler no longer engages the fight with his shoulders, and the wily Indicopleustes now aims a rock at the head of the Old Man of the Sea on the ground, hoping to crush it like a crab!"

"I'm frightened...

"It hurts!"

"May the vice of your legs be a mortal garrotte on the carotid arteries of the bearded sycophant.

"You have seen sparrows taken in a trap.

"So Sinbad will betake himself to bed."

"Your wish is my command, oh Master."

Joseb and Varia were in bed.

The notary, seeing that a blank dawn had risen in his blond noggin (the palest blond is an empty glass) and feeling his long beard furred from drunkenness, had staggered out of his office towards that darker vessel, his wife.

He was not a pretty sight, but Varia did not see him.

She had received her orders from the wall-clock and fallen asleep.

Joseb thought her eyes had closed with the spasm that his kisses counselled.

And which seemed proved by the contracture of the muscles in the limbs twined round his neck, constricting it without relent.

Sinbad the Old swayed more like a hanged man than a drunk.

The cataleptic garrotte — it is an anatomical fact that the pectineus and the three adductor muscles of the thighs are abnormally developed in women, and that one of the distinguishing features of women is that they have, *amongst other things*, a psoatic muscle, which only one male in eighteen has — is both more fatal and more difficult to escape from than its iron paradigm.

But hanging is the Juvescence of old men.

With the combined effort of his triceps, the little man threw off his halter of flesh and bone, and now it was him who locked his arms around the waist of the vanquished; and the breath from his nostrils, as he clamped his mouth to hers, woke her up.

Medea would have been overcome with pleasure if she herself had experienced such effects after having made her father-in-law young again.

Emmanuel Dieu, standing beneath the circular moon that had been shot up on to the ceiling from the glass blowpipe of the lamp, looking through the crack in the door left ajar, saw the fruits of his labour, *as predicted*.

Saw chuck-chaste Adam — twentieth-century Adam — cleave to his other half, the half which the Other God had amputated...

In the beginning.

THE OVARY, which for a few thousand years had roamed freely in the body, was now reabsorbed again into that unique, universal Man:

THE NOTARY.

Emmanuel Dieu went back up to the sky of his blue garret, serene now the *assumption* had been realised.

XV
THE WIFE OF GOD

Taenia solum.

And the Spirit of God was high above the waters…

At the window of his garret.

The nightingales had sung in Lampaul all night long; they were the heirs of the notary's saw, now put aside, and among the plane trees planted in quincunx they had wheeled their carts, grating and screeching.

Emmanuel Dieu heard no remorse other than that intolerable gnashing of gears.

He was satisfied to recognise by its noisome, jolting progress that Justice was approaching.

But it was not for God (Emmanuel) charitably to offer the cart of Justice a drop of oil.

The Other God threw down the soft yellow tear of the sun.

The day was dedicated to the Law.

Emmanuel Dieu knew perfectly well that with Varia's *murder* — a murder more real than when the flesh is eradicated from the universe, for she had been expelled from the Absolute (the dagger which is the Angel's flaming sword turns every way to keep the way of the gardens of Eden…) — he had not killed Miriam!

ON THE CONTRARY.

The true Miriam was not inside Varia but outside.

From his window open on the yellow silence, above the plane trees and the amphitheatre of the houses in Lampaul, he contemplated the statue, standing on the hill and dominating all that lay around, of Itron-Varia.

The Virgin's dress hid her feet.

One could not see if she trampled the dragon under foot.

For a sole she had a whole pedestal of heavy granite with three steps.

The little paths flattened out there, snaking round the hill and drinking at the brook by the flour-mills.

Emmanuel Dieu could not see any end to them, as he averted his eyes before reaching *their head*.

He concluded, not without reason, that it lay crushed beneath the pedestal.

For nowhere did the path rise up from the ground, like the curls at the end of a parchment.

The ground was a tissue of snakes.

The procession unfurled, as it did every Sunday at this same hour of the morning, in a surge of meticulous little ships, some on the paths, others gliding over the velvet coverlets of the meadows, curling up cosily in the folds and coils.

Leviathan, the great sea-serpent, also came to prostrate itself and place its triangular skull beneath Miriam's little heel, and with ease she lifted up her granite ankle-boot.

And when the siren songs had melted in the wind, which sent shivers through the little ships and slapped them back to front and onwards on the path, in rhythm to the monster's dorsal fin, some little children came running up to play with this same wind.

Their kite was a cross in flight, higher and whiter than that of the processions (like the shrouded crosses on the altars during the descent into the Sepulchre), borne aloft as if upon a staff, a tail of larks rising.

Melusina…

With a sudden shower, frequent in Lampaul — and it was right that THE OTHER God should weep, since Emmanuel did not *himself* feel like it — the wind fell.

The great Python of the dawn plunged beneath the clouds and hid its lop-eared head there, just as vipers twist themselves around each other and form a knot to sleep protected from the other snakes.

Emmanuel went down and walked upon the carpet of reptiles to pray alongside the kite, modifying the end of his *Ave*, in view of the circumstances:

"… Pray for us…

"*Now, at the hour of our death.*"

The following abbreviations are used:

CA = Chris Allen, AB = Alastair Brotchie, PE = Paul Edwards, AL = Alexis Lykiard, SWT = Simon Watson Taylor.

A&B = Alfred Jarry, *Gestes et opinions du docteur Faustroll, pataphysicien, suivi de L'Amour Absolu*, edited, introduced and annotated by Noël Arnaud & Henri Bordillon, Gallimard, 1980.

CW I = Volume 1 of these *Collected Works,* Atlas Press, 2001.

Littré = Émile Littré, *Dictionnaire de la langue française* (1863–77), Hachette, 1956–8.

OC = Alfred Jarry, *Œuvres complètes*, edited and annotated by Michel Arrivé, Gallimard, "Bibliothèque de la Pléiade", three volumes published between 1972 and 1988.

French titles are published in Paris, English in London, unless stated otherwise.

NOTES TO DAYS AND NIGHTS

by Alastair Brotchie, unless otherwise indicated

Page 16. Géroy (pseud. of Gaston Roig), "*Mon ami Alfred Jarry*", in *Le Courrier d'Épidaure*, 3-4, Mars-Avril 1949.

25. Sengle: the author's only note in the novel derives *Sengle* from the thirteenth-century spelling for "single", citing Latin *singulum* and a line from the troubadour Rutebeuf: "*Sans avoir m'a laissié tout sengle*".

27. ... people foreign to China: Maurice Saillet, in a study first published in the *Dossiers du Collège de 'Pataphysique*, 26, identified this book: *An Ethnography of Peoples Foreign to China*, it was written in the 13th century by Ma-Twan-Lin, and translated by the Marquis Hervey de Saint-Denys. The chapter concerning the Leao occurs on pp.119 ff. of this translation (1877-82), although Jarry seems not to have consulted the original, but to have read an article about it in the popular review *Le Magazine pittoresque*.

27. Severus Altmensch et al. The characters in this chapter are all identifiable by virtue of a copy of *Les Jours et les nuits* annotated by Jarry for his ex-schoolfriend Édouard Julia, in which he wrote "this scene actually took place. Sev. Altmensch (Ernest La Jeunesse) was undressed in the studio of Sarluys [*sic*]." The names are also decoded. Severus Altmensch ("severe old man" in Latin/German) = Ernest (for German *ernst*) La Jeunesse ("youth"), the writer; Raphael Roissoy (first name from the artist, second from *Sar*, Assyrian for king, becoming French *Roi*, and one French pronoun, *lui*, becoming another, *soi*) = Leonard Sarluis, the artist; Bondroit gives (Lord Alfred) Douglas, of Wildean fame, by a translation of "good-law," which combines "Doug" backwards, with the surname of the Scottish economist John Law, which was pronounced "lass". Huppe is the actress Fanny Zaessinger, who was in the first production of *Ubu Roi*. Julia's copy does not identify Freiherr Suszflasche, but this probably disguises Henri-Albert Haug, the French translator of Nietzsche. Moncrif, who appears towards the end of this chapter, is Maurice Cremnitz, who wrote as Maurice Chevrier and formed the third member of a homosexual drinking triumvirate with Jarry and Fargue.

31. Sergeant-major: Gaston Roig, a soldier with literary ambitions, who remained on friendly terms with Jarry after the latter's release from the army.

31. ... *Sweet sounds* : these stanzas are from *The Rime of the Ancient Mariner*, given here in the original. Jarry translated the poem in its entirety, but it was not published until after his death.

33. Vensuet: Jean Tixier, another literary officer, who asked Jarry to pass on his verses to the *Mercure de France*. As Jean Morvan, he later wrote historical works, including his magnum opus *Soldat Imperial*.

33. PASTORAL: translation by Stanley Chapman.

35. *The Book of Pity and of Death*: a work by Pierre Loti which Jarry despised and parodied in *Faustroll*, bk. 5, ch. XXX. The words "unfathomable abyss" are taken from Loti's story "*Rêve*".

48. ... neighbours in the alphabet: Sengle and Valens are evidently not neighbours in the alphabet, no more than are Jarry and Fargue. Jarry is in fact referring to another "friend", François-Benoit-Claudius Jacquet; in an article in the *Organographes du Cymbalum Pataphysicum*, 6, Henri Bordillon showed that the two poems describe escutcheons for Jarry and Jacquet as depicted on consecutive pages in the *Armorial General* of J.B. Rietstap.

51. Crutch's Cripple: in the original, "*La Jatte des culs*", an untranslatable play on words. A *cul-de-jatte* is a legless cripple, *jatte* being a bowl, *cul* an arse; *gros culs* is army slang for coarse tobacco. The reversal here is a doomed attempt to give a flavour of the French. [AL]

51. Mr. Deibler: a member of the Deibler family filled the post of State Executioner in France for many generations. See also note to p.180.

52. The Court of Miracles: a common expression in French referring to Hugo's *Notre-Dame de Paris*, in which a crowd of cripples stay in the *Cour des Miracles*. [AL]

52. The elderly barber in "The Barber's Tale" from the *Thousand and One Nights* is spared the execution meted out to the nine criminals, and duly recounts the stories of his six brothers, who are variously lame, one-eyed, etc. [CA]

52. Consul Romanus: a reference to a phrase from Livy quoted in de Quincey's *Introduction to the Pains of Opium* in his *Confessions of an English Opium-Eater* (1822), which Jarry read in Baudelaire's translation. The original runs thus: "... I had often felt as solemn and appalling sounds, emphatically representative of Roman majesty, the two words so often occurring in Livy, *Consul Romanus*; especially when the consul is introduced in his military character," then later "... the pageant would suddenly dissolve; and, at a clapping of hands, would be heard the heart-quaking sound of *Consul Romanus*: and immediately came 'sweeping by,' in gorgeous paludiments, Paulus and Marius, girt around by a company of centurions, with the crimson tunic hoisted on a spear..."

53. The Bullet Hole: in French *le trou de balle* is a popular expression for the anus. [AL]

53. Nosocome: Jarry's close friend Maurice Dide, whose name here is a Greek/Rabelaisian word roughly meaning "hospital"

55. ... carried life off: perhaps because these zoophytes, plantlike animals such as sea anemones, sound in French almost like "*zoo-fuites*", combining the Greek for "life" with French for "running away". [CA]

59. The Gospel: specifically Mark 16, 18.

61. O Just, Subtle: from de Quincey's *Opium-Eater*: "O just, subtle and mighty opium!"

63. Azure Unbuckles Azor: more word-play, with *azure* (the "blueness" of illness or poorly oxygenated blood) releasing/unbuckling *azor* (mil. slang for a knapsack, also a dog's pet-name like Fido or Rover), thus suggesting Sengle's escape from the army through illness. [AL]

64. Marsyas: in Greek legend, a famous flute-player who challenged Apollo, sun-god and master of the lyre, to a musical contest, but lost. Apollo flayed him and his skin was hung in the cave from which the river Marsyas issued, and was said to flutter joyously whenever the flute was played.

65. Hemeralopes: those suffering from day-blindness (the inability to see by day), like owls, for instance. Ideally for Jarry, however, mistaken understanding of the word's etymology has often led it to mean the exact opposite; see *CW* I, note to p.114 (nyctalopia).

67. *Iodure de Navarre*: a thinly-disguised *Mercure de France*. *Iodure* means "iodide" but also suggests *Mercure* (yet sounds more like ordure), *Navarre* recalls that French kings were "King of France and Navarre". The *Mercure* was both a periodical and a publishing house that specialised in Symbolist writing (including Jarry). Here he parodies the tortuous prose it published in its weaker moments.

67. Lymnaea: (fresh-water) snails.

68. Obeliscolychny: from Rabelais (IV, 22), Greek for a lighthouse, emphasising its likeness to an obelisk.

68. Quotinoctial: taking place day and night, the book's title once again. [CA]

73. ... nothing for himself: in other words, Sengle has not kept the last bullet for himself. [AL]

73. A hump on the other side of the world: from Cyrano de Bergerac's *The States and Empires of the Moon* (c.1650): "But without amusing myself by replying to all these objections, I will venture to state that, if there were no vacuums, there would be no movement, or else it would be necessary to admit that bodies penetrate one another. For it would be ridiculous to believe that when a fly pushes a parcel of air aside with its wings, this parcel makes another recoil in front of it, and this second yet another, and that in this fashion the agitation of a flea's little toe makes a hump on the other side of the world!"

76. La Palisse: celebrated for truisms, such as: "If he hadn't died so young, he'd have reached a ripe old age."

76. Ahriman and Ormuzd: Ahura Mazda in the Zoroastrian theogony, meaning "Lord of Knowledge", was the chief benign divinity, Ahriman, the leader of the powers of evil. The pair were in constant conflict.

76. Dr. Mises: pseudonym of Gustav Theodor Fechner, author of *The Comparative Anatomy of Angels* (1825), among other works. Like many of the philosophical references in Jarry's writings he cropped up in Bergson's lectures at the Lycée Henri IV. See also note to p.135 of *CW* I.

77. Claude Bernard: well-known French physician, author of *An Introduction to Experimental Medicine* and inventor of the theory of *idées forces*.

77. The Silvering on the Pools: Jarry used the word "*tain*" for silvering, which has the special meaning of the silvering on mirrors. [AL]

78. Parvis: the enclosed area in front of a large church or cathedral.

78. Thirty skeletons beneath a trapdoor: those of Royalist "martyrs" of the French Revolution, whose bones lie in a sepulchre beneath a monument near St. Anne d'Auray.

78. This poem and that on the previous page translated by Stanley Chapman.

80. Owl-droppings: brief reference, in English in the original, to Carlyle's *Latter-Day Pamphlet* "Downing Street" (1850), a scatological attack on democratic government.

81. ... towards the light: obscure ellipsis in the original. [AL]

83. Monsieur Philippe: Max Lebaudy, son of a rich sugar manufacturer, who died as a result of malpractice in an army hospital in Laval in 1895.

85. Ravachol: who practised "propaganda by deed," i.e. bombs; see note to p.205 of *CW* I.

88. Hunyadi-Janos: a Hungarian city whence comes a mineral water famous for its laxative effects.

97. Cupel: not to be confused with the dome of a cupola, this is rather a flat disc, as was used for gauging the quality of gold and silver. [CA]

97. Putting a head on the pale's shoulders: in France there are two types of "cup-and-ball"; Jarry, of course, chose the more obscene variety, both being here illustrated by Thieri Foulc:

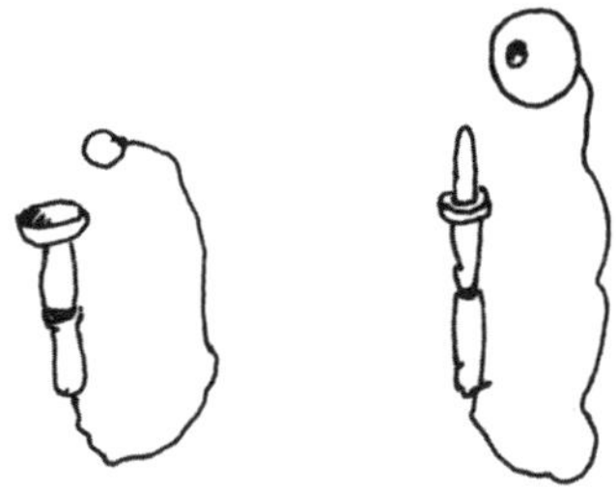

97. ***Pater*****:** i.e. the Lord's Prayer. **Ort:** an archaic word for a scrap.

98. Danaïdes: the 50 daughters of Danaus, king of Argos, who were forced to marry the 50 sons of Aegyptus, but all of them bar one, on their father's command, murdered their husbands on their wedding night. They were punished in Hades by having to draw water endlessly from a well using sieves, or filling bottomless vessels with water; like Sisyphus, another example of pointless punishment-activity akin to military service.

99. Choppy Warburton (1843-97): one of the top cycling trainer/managers of his day, his career ended suddenly in June 1896 when one of his team accused him of doping him to prevent him from winning a race. The resulting scandal was big news while Jarry was writing *Les Jours et les nuits* (the finished MS. is dated June 1897).

101. Assassins: fanatical sect founded in Persia in 1090 by Hassan Ibn Sabbah, known as "The Old Man of the Mountains". Fifty thousand strong, they were a formidable enemy of the Crusaders; their religion was a severe form of Ismailism, and their name is derived from the hashish they took before forays into battle or murder. They were finally suppressed in 1273 by the Mongols.

101. Pyast and Herreb: the latter may be the German philosopher Dr. Albert Haas. Pyast, however, is probably Gaston de Pawlowski, a cycling friend of Jarry's and author of, among other works, *Voyage au pays de la quatrième dimension* (first published in book form in 1912, but in periodicals from 1896). It was illustrated by Leonard Sarluis (see note to p.27).

101. Hakim: cf. Caliph Hakim in Nerval's *Voyage en Orient* (1851). In the tale devoted to him, Hakim and his friend Youssuf become "deeply intoxicated by hashish," and later Hakim mistakes him for his double. Nerval's mingling of dream and reality, as well as his interest in drugs, make him an almost inevitable influence on this novel.

101. ... the talk began: the whole of the following dialogue is a transcript by Jarry of a drugs session at Maurice Dide's apartment at 20, Quai d'Orléans in Paris. It is more or less untranslatable, being based on a series of interlinked puns. The version here is a compromise between accuracy of meaning (!) and attempts at preserving the word-plays — many of the *non sequiturs* are the same in the original. A few of the multiple meanings are given here: the first, which recurs throughout the first few lines, concerns *vers* and *verres*, meaning "towards", "until", "cups", "glasses", "verses".

103. Scathed: in the original "*il se déplayait*" is apparently an obscure verb from old French, perhaps from Rutebeuf, where the meaning is "to cover with wounds". It may, however, be a coinage, as Jarry playfully suggests later. This now-archaic English word seems a good equivalent. [AL]

104. Loie Fuller: dancer at the Folies Bergère renowned for her use of spectacular stage effects which gave the effect of swathing her in semi-transparent billows of silk and light, here evoking the ectoplasmic field around the haschischins.

104. Carbuncles: "*clou*" means both "carbuncle" and "nail". [AL]

105. *ArcaNA ambo*: in Virgil's 7th *Eclogue*, v. 4, Tirsis and Corydon are introduced as "*Arcades ambo*", "both Arcadian". Nosocome's distortion can be translated as "both Mysteries". [AL]

105. Xipehuz: title of a short novel by J.-H. Rosny (1887), referring to extraterrestrials who appear as translucent, and only semi-solid, geometric shapes.

106. Hailing: i.e. weather, not greeting, though the point is that this "*ses intestins grêlent*" sounds like *intestin grêle*, the small intestine. [CA]

107. Bobino: a music-hall, still in existence.

107. Félix: Félix Faure, President of the Republic, suggested by the previous line.

107. ... a duck speaks French: "*trois quoi*" repeated several times in French approximates the quacking of a duck; "*canard*" (duck) also means "hoax" and suggests "canal". [AL]

107. *ERgo nominor leo*: in Phaedrus's fable *The Cow and the Goat, the Sheep and the Lion*, the lion takes the lion's share, saying: "*Quia ego nomino leo*" ("This is mine because I am named lion"). Pyast's distortion can be translated as: "Therefore I was named lion". [AL]

107. Footit: famous clown of the period.

110. Favus: a contagious skin disease, characterised by outbreaks of pustules. [CA]

111. Anoblepic: the anoblepas also appears in *Haldernablou* (see *CW* I, note to p.73), its etymology showing it to be "upward-looking". [CA]

111. Ambroise Paré (1509-90): born, like Jarry, in Laval, the father of modern medicine.

111. Swédiaur: François Xavier Swédiaur (1748-1824), German doctor, specialist in syphilis.

112. Deaf-mute girls: near Auray there was (and still is) an educational institute for deaf-mutes.

113. Candid: i.e. as the Latin root *candidus*, "white". [CA]

114. Prud'homme: here represents simple bourgeois rationality (see also *CW* I, note to p.242).

114. Ribot: Théodule Ribot (1839-1916), doctor whose *Maladies de la mémoire* supplies the words of Prud'homme here, and is also cited by Père Ubu in *Ubu Cocu*, Act V, scene 3.

NOTES TO EXPLOITS AND OPINIONS OF DOCTOR FAUSTROLL, PATAPHYSICIAN

Notes to Introduction by Paul Edwards, notes to text by Simon Watson Taylor, unless otherwise indicated

Editor's note: Simon Watson Taylor's superb translation of *Faustroll* was first published over forty years ago, and since then new French editions based on the two manuscripts have added greatly to the scholarship surrounding Jarry's *magnum opus*. When planning this new edition, SWT and I discussed incorporating some of this new material into his original notes. His recent death, however, means we were unable even to begin this work and so little has been added here, apart from a few corrections and two important longer notes (to p.163 "waving goodbye", and 196 "In the sealed palace..."). The translation likewise has not been changed except in rare cases where definitive manuscript variants have demanded it. Variants between the two manuscripts will be noted in the *Commentary* volume. [AB]

119. Time Machine: first published in the *Mercure de France*, 110 (February 1899), pp.387-96. Parallel-text edition (Jarry and Kelvin) in *L'Étoile-Absinthe*, 95/96 (Autumn 2002), pp.69-88. English translation in *CW* I, pp.211-8.

119. *Gestes*: see *CW* I, pp.219-69.

120. ... *La Plume*: chapters VI & X-XXV appeared in the *Mercure de France*, 101 (May 1898), and chapter XXXIV in *La Plume* (15 November 1900).

120. ... differences: the best French editions of the text are in Jarry's *Œuvres* (Robert Laffont, 2004), and in *Gestes et opinions du Docteur Faustroll, pataphysicien, édition annotée* (Cymbalum Pataphysicum, Rheims, 1985), which is also copiously annotated.

120. Visiting-card: "The Autoclete", *CW* I, p.36.

120. ... dishes from the ground: *ibid.*, p.37.

120. ... opposites: "Heraldic Act", *Caesar-Antichrist*, *CW* I, p.142.

122. "Ha ha": over 100 different meanings have been ascribed to "Ha ha" in two very thorough articles by Jean-Claude Dinguirard and Pascal Dumont published in *Monitoires du Cymbalum Pataphysicum*, 4 & 5, pp.26-31 & 47-58 respectively.

122. Thirteen films: I subscribe to Patrick Besnier's hypothesis that the thirteen "pictures" are probably films and most likely by Méliès. See his biography, *Alfred Jarry* (Fayard, 2006), p.327.

123. "... general conditions": Saint-Pol-Roux, "*Liminaire*", *Les Reposoirs de la procession* (Mercure de France, 1893). Reprinted in *La Rose et les épines du chemin* (Poésie/Gallimard, 1997), pp.213-25 (p.218).

123. "Rediscovery of the Unique": in *The Fortnightly Review*, Vol. 50, n.s. (July 1891), pp.106-11; reprinted in *H.G. Wells: Early Writings in Science and Science Fiction* (University of California Press, 1975). Baly is also quoted by Wells in "The Possible Individuality of Atoms" (1896), *op. cit.*, pp.119-21.

123. Wilde: Wells mentions Wilde's enthusiasm in his *Experiment in Autobiography*, Vol. 1 (Victor Gollancz & Cresset Press, 1934), p.359. The Jarry/Wilde meeting was set up by their mutual friend and Wells's French translator, Henry Davray.

123. Lucretius: see the second book of his *On the Nature of the Universe*.

124. ... of the twentieth: on this subject, see Morris Kline, *Mathematics in Western Culture* (1953) (Peregrine/Penguin, Harmondsworth, 1987); and Albert Einstein, *Relativity, The Special and the General Theory, A Popular Exposition* (various eds.).

124. *Voyage to the Land of the Fourth Dimension*: though Pawlowski only published his *Voyage* in 1912, he had commenced writing it in 1895, just at the time that he was frequenting Jarry. See also note to p.101 above, "Pyast and Herreb".

125. "Doctor Faustroll": letter to André Fontainas dated 9 February 1899 and quoted in Besnier's biography, *op. cit.*, p.388.

126. Apollinaire: "*La Vie anecdotique*" in the *Mercure de France* (16 January 1912). Goethe's manuscript was only discovered in 1910.

126. Breton: see his "*Alfred Jarry*" in *Les Pas perdus* (1924), reprinted in *Œuvres complètes*, Vol. I (Pléiade/Gallimard, 1988), pp.216-26 (p.225).

126. *Bifur*: "*La Pataphysique et la révélation du rire*" in *Bifur*, 2 (25 July 1929), pp.59-68.

126. Vian: *Calcul numérique de Dieu* (Cymbalum Pataphysicum, Rheims, 105 EP).

126. Rabelais: "Rabelais and Jarry are my gods, evidently." Quoted in Calvin Tomkins, *Duchamp. A Biography* (Henry Holt & Co, New York, 1996), p.73.

126. "... in 1911": *ibid.*

127. *Doctor Faustroll*: as Roger Shattuck points out in the section he devotes to "Alfred Jarry: Poet and 'Pataphysician" in his *The Banquet Years* (Faber, 1958), the name of the hero, Faustroll, may be taken to be a combination of the words *Faust* and *Troll*. In 1896 Jarry appeared as one of the trolls in Lugné-Poe's production of *Peer Gynt* (the Scandinavian *Faust*!) at the Théâtre de l'Œuvre. Jarry's intention was perhaps to imply that his (autobiographical) hero was "the imp of science".

133. Panmuphle: the equivalent of "universal snout".

134. A sea-green mustachios: *Sic.* Jarry wrote in both MSS. of *Faustroll* "*unes moustaches vert de mer*".

134. Sponge-bath: in English in the original.

135. Great Strumpot: the "*Ordre de la Grande Gidouille*" was promulgated by Jarry in his *Almanach du Père Ubu* (1899), and has been revived by the Collège de 'Pataphysique. The word "*gidouille*" appears frequently throughout the cycle of Ubu plays in general reference to Father Ubu's regally protruding stomach. "Strumpot" is an inspired verbal invention by Cyril Connolly.

136. *Lourdeau*: means "blockhead".

136. Bergerac: see note to p.73. [AB]

136. (Léon) Bloy: see note to p.158.

136. Coleridge: Jarry's translation of the *Rime of the Ancient Mariner* was first published in 1921.

136. (Georges) Darien: *The Thief*, an astonishing and hitherto rare book, published in 1898, was republished by Jean-Jacques Pauvert in 1955, and has remained in print subsequently.

136. (Marceline) Desbordes-Valmore: French writer and poet (1785-1859).

136. (Max) Elskamp: Belgian poet (1862-1931).

136. (Christian Dietrich) Grabbe: German poet (1801-1836). Jarry made a free translation of this play under the title of *Les Silènes*. It was translated into English by Barbara Wright as *Comedy, Satire, Irony and Deeper Meaning* (Gaberbocchus Press, 1955).

136. (Gustave) Kahn: see note to p.161.

137. Mallarmé: see note to p.162.

137. (Catulle) Mendès: French writer (1841-1909).

137. (Joséphin Sâr) Péladan: French writer (1858-1918), founder of the *Salon de la Rose-Croix*.

137. Jean de Chilra: a pen-name (and anagram) of Rachilde, for whom see note to p.151 and p.170.

137. Régnier: see note to p.163.

137. (Marcel) Schwob: see last note to p.165.

137. (Pierre) Bonnard: see notes to pp.169 and 190. For the *Revue blanche*, see note to p.143.

137. Aubrey Beardsley: see note to p.155.

137. Delmor de Pionsec: a near-anagram of "*Demolder espion*", (the spy Demolder) and "*Pionsec*" also means "stale pedant"; for the real Demolder, see Terrasse note on p.168.

137. Troccon: can be taken as a play on the name Trochon; "*troc con*" means a "damn stupid bargain". Trochon was a bicycle-dealer who tried persistently but unsuccessfully until Jarry's death to collect from him the balance due on the bicycle Jarry had bought.

138. Liconet: can be read "*lui con est*" ("he's a twat").

139. C.V. Boys: English physicist (1855-1944), inventor of the radio-micrometer, etc., author of several popular scientific texts, including *Soap Bubbles and the Forces Which Mould Them* (SPCK, 1890), translated into French in 1892, and reprinted (Doubleday, Science Study Series, N.Y., 1959; Heinemann, 1960). The general sense of this chapter is largely derived from these short essays (although the application, I need hardly say, is entirely pataphysical).

139. ... epidermis: this paragraph is a paraphrase from Sir William Crookes' presidential address to the Society for Psychical Research, London, 1897. See note to p.146.

140. Skiff: in French, is "*as*", a single-sculler; "*as*" also means an ace in cards, and a "one" in dominoes... A dry joke of Jarry's.

141. Elskamp: Jarry had originally made the eighth seized book *Salutations dont d'Angéliques*. Though he changed this to *Enluminures* in his MS., he retained the quotation from the first volume, from the poem "*Consolatrice des affligés*".

141. Florian: quotation from his play *Les Deux Billets.*

141. *The Thousand and One Nights*: LXIInd night.

141. Grabbe: "the knight of the papal order of Civil Merit" is the Devil, in Grabbe's play, Act II, scene i. In *Les Silènes*, Jarry turned the Freiherr von Mordax into "*Baron Tual*".

142. *Ubu Roi*: i.e. "*merdRe*", the celebrated word invented by Jarry which provoked the disorders that continued throughout the first performance of the play at the Théâtre de l'Œuvre in 1896.

142. Verne: the expedition in fact reached 35 leagues beneath the earth's surface. Faustroll must have grown weary at the 2½ league stage. See Jean Ferry's article in *Cahiers du Collège de 'Pataphysique*, 22-23.

143. Thadée Natanson: a collaborator on the *Revue blanche*, which was directed by his brother Alexandre, to which Jarry began to contribute in 1896. The *Revue blanche* published his *Messaline* and *Le Surmâle*, but refused *Faustroll*, which Jarry offered to them after it had been turned down by the *Mercure.*

145. A simple pun: debate still rages as to what the "simple pun" actually is. [AB]

146. Sir William Crookes: his presidential address to the Society for Psychical Research in London on 29 January 1897 is largely responsible for the theme and some of the phraseology of this chapter. The address was translated into French and printed in the *Revue scientifique* (May 1897).

148. Christian Beck: Belgian writer (1879-1916), friend of Jarry and fellow contributor to the review *Mercure de France*. Wrote also under the pen-name of Joseph Bossi a novel *Les Erreurs* and later another novel *Le Papillon* (in French, "baboon" is "*papion*").

148. Eugène Sue: quotation from *La Salamandre*, ch. XIV. "*Le pichon joueic deis diables*" is Provençal dialect for "*le petit jeu des diables*", the name of a strange traditional procession in which the participants were dressed as devils and satyrs.

148. Bosse-de-Nage: "*nage*" or "*nache*" means "buttocks" in old French, thus Bosse-de-Nage can mean "bottom-face", as Jarry suggests. For an erudite discussion of the possible origins of the name, see Noël Arnaud in the *Cahiers du Collège de 'Pataphysique*, no. 22-23.

150. Plato: the translation is as follows:

—Thou speakest truth, he replies.
— It is true.
— It is very true.
— It is clear, he replies, even to a blind man.
— It is obvious.
— It is an obvious fact.
—That is so.
— It seems.
—That is also my opinion.
— It does in fact appear to be so.
—That is so, he replies.
— I am also of that persuasion.
—Absolutely, he replies.
—Thou speakest wisely.
—Well.
— Certainly, indeed.
— I recall.
—Yes.

— It is thus.
— I think so, and most strongly.
— I agree.
—Very right.
—That is doubtless true, he replies.
—That is true, he replies.
—That is indeed necessary.
— By all means.
— By all means indeed.
— By all manner of means.
—We admit it.
— It is absolutely necessary.
— Indeed, we are convinced.
—Very much.
—Very much indeed, in fact.
—That is logical, indeed.
— It has to be that way.
— How could that be so?
— How could that be otherwise?
— How could it be otherwise?
—What then?
—What?
—Thou speakest truth.
— How true that seems.

151. Alfred Vallette: French writer, married to Rachilde and Jarry's greatest and most faithful friend. At the time of writing *Faustroll*, Jarry shared a house at Corbeil, the "Phalanstère", with Vallette, Rachilde, Hérold (see note to p.178) and two other friends. In 1890, Vallette, with a group of writers belonging to the Symbolist movement, founded a fortnightly review, the *Mercure de France*. Jarry contributed regularly to it and extracts from *Faustroll* were originally published in the review (chapters VI and X to XXV).

154. Louis L...: Louis Lormel, pen-name of Louis Libaude (1869–1922). Founded in 1892 *L'Art littéraire* which published Jarry's first texts. They quarrelled, and Lormel published in 1897 a story called "*Entre Soi*" in which Jarry and his friend Léon-Paul Fargue appear as "*la Tête de Mort*" (Death's-Head) and "*l'Androgyne*" — not to their advantage. This is Jarry's riposte, attacking Lormel and his collaborators, ultra-Symbolists and Catholics.

154. Squitty Sea: the author has "*mer d'Habundes*," phonetically "*merde abunde*", derived from Rabelais (I, 9): "*a cul foyard toujours abunde merde*" ("squitty arse never lacks for shit").

154. Isle of Cack: the author has "*île de Bran*," phonetically "Hildebrand". But the identity of Baron Hildebrand remains obscure.

155. Obelischolychny: a lighthouse in the form of an obelisk; see also note to p.68 above.

155. Wild duck: the author has "*halbran*" which is phonetically equivalent to "*hale-bran*" — "heave-cack".

155. Aubrey Beardsley: a friend of Jarry. This chapter is full of allusions to different drawings of his.

156. Émile Bernard: the French painter who invented the "Symbolist" technique in painting and influenced Gauguin. Le Bois d'Amour is a locality of Pont-Aven in Brittany, an artists' colony at that time, frequented by Bernard, Gauguin, Jarry, among others. Bernard collaborated with Jarry on the latter's luxuriously illustrated *L'Ymagier* and *Perhindérion*. *Le Bois d'Amour* is also the title of a painting by Bernard.

157. (François-Marie) Arouet: took the pen-name Voltaire; (Ernest) Renan, French historian, author of *La Vie de Jésus*, etc.; (Victor) Charbonnel, French writer and journalist, originally a priest, who quit

Holy Orders in 1897 and gave a series of anti-clerical lectures. He founded *La Raison* in 1901.

158. Léon Bloy: one of the six writers included in the twenty-seven "equivalent" books of Doctor Faustroll to whom a subsequent chapter is also dedicated; the author of, among many other works, *Le Désespéré*, in which he appears as the hero Marchenoir (Blackstep), a name which inspires the title of this chapter.

158. Mass altar: in the French, "*monumental autel de messe, noir.*" Jarry originally wrote in his MS. "*autel de messe noir*", but changed it, no doubt out of deference for Bloy's susceptibilities.

159. Franc-Nohain: French poet, founded the review *Canard sauvage* in 1903, to which Jarry was a regular contributor. One of Franc-Nohain's collections of verse was entitled *Flûtes, poèmes amorphes* (1898). He appears as the last of the six kings in this chapter; the reference in the last paragraph is to a poem "*Ronde des Neveux inattentionés*", from *Flûtes*, whose refrain was:

> *Sous les quinconces, / Nous ne retrouvons pas nos oncles.*
> (*Beneath the quincunxes, / We'll not find our uncles again.*)

As regards the other five kings in this chapter, the third king may be identified as Jules Renard, author of *Histoires naturelles.* The others remain obscure.

160. Paul Gauguin: Jarry and Gauguin were together at Pont-Aven in 1894 and probably knew each other previously, since both were contributors to the review *Essais d'Art libre* (1892-4), edited first by Remy de Gourmont, subsequently by Léon-Paul Fargue and Jarry.

The unfortunate Pierre Loti makes his first (anonymous) appearance in *Faustroll* at the end of this chapter, as the legless cripple ("*cul de jatte*"). The *Omnibus de Corinthe* on which he fails to get a footing was a short-lived quarterly satirical review, edited by Marc Mouclier, describing itself as an "illustrated vehicle of general ideas," the title of which was doubtless derived from the Latin proverb *Non licet omnibus adire Corinthum* (Not everybody is granted the privilege of going to Corinth). For more about Loti, see note to p.187.

161. Gustave Kahn: French poet and literary critic, one of Jarry's earliest admirers. The title of this chapter is derived from Kahn's first book of poems, *Les Palais nomades*, in which occurs the line: "*Finir loin des ports en jonque bizarre*" (Finishing far from ports in a strange junk).

This island represents the coast at Knocke in Belgium, where Kahn used to spend holidays; Jarry was his guest there in 1895; Kahn is another of the six writers included in Doctor Faustroll's library to whom a chapter is subsequently dedicated.

162. Mallarmé: another of the six among the twenty-seven "equivalents" to whom a chapter is also dedicated. The title of this chapter is inspired by Mallarmé's sonnet based on the ending *-yx*. In a letter, addressed to Lefebvre and Casalis, Mallarmé wrote: "... I only have three rhymes in *ix*, do your best to send me the real meaning of the word *ptyx*: I am assured that it does not exist in any language, which I would far prefer so that I may have the pleasure of creating it through the magic of rhyme." To answer Mallarmé's query, the word is, in this nominative singular form, unknown in ancient Greek, but is found often in its conjugation, *ptykos*, *ptyki*, etc. In the nominative, the alternative *ptykhê* was used (from which we derive "triptych"), the sense being a *fold* or *thickness.*

163. ... waving goodbye: Since the writing of this book, the river around the island has turned into a funeral wreath. [Author's note]

Jarry's footnote refers to Mallarmé's death in 1898. His obituary of Mallarmé appeared in *Père Ubu's Illustrated Almanac for 1899* (*OC* I, pp.564-5), and consisted of this chapter from *Faustroll* to which he added the following seven paragraphs, all within a black frame of mourning:

"Mallarmé was delighted to read the account of the trip and, with his hand stretched out towards the doctor, rose for the last time from his rocking-chair amid the *décor* of suggestive beauty.

In autumn Faustroll disembarked again, leaving the nave of the forest, and walked barefoot alongside the tapering ferns — tappiced and tapestry — their scythes hanging, pustules of Atropos, on the road to the arches at Valvins.

The funeral swelled on the road to Samoreau, and ebbed away at the sea wall of many cemeteries.

The church was small, sober and absolute; the two choristers, more saddening for singing out of tune; the poor stained-glass windows were reconciled in the shining light, just as a crowd elects a plurality of personal beliefs when they all kneel together before a glory that is *catholic* — for the word does sometimes mean universal.

Two very noble women were the caryatids of all this grief.

As Faustroll hurried back through the forest of blighted palm trees, following the current of the road that was white like the borders of church hangings, he feared he would hear the dreadful voice informing Thamous three times of the death of one also written about — for those who understand what they read — by Herodotus, and Cicero in his third book of the Nature of the Gods.

The river has laid its funeral wreath, a circular mirror of glory, for all eternity, around the tomb and as far as the penultimate horizons." [Note and translation PE]

163. Henri de Régnier: another of the six writers to whom a chapter is also dedicated. *La Canne de Jaspe* (1897), the twenty-first of Doctor Faustroll's "equivalent" books, consists of three collections of stories, all of which contain a number of characters whose names begin with *Her* (Hermes, Hermotine, Hermagore, Hermocrate, Hermogene).

163. Pavonine: in the French, "*pavonne*", a word coined by Régnier (Italian *pavone*, a peacock; Spanish *pavane*, a slow dance) and which Jarry found in *La Canne de Jaspe*, p.253.

164. Cyclops: in Jarry's *Almanach du Père Ubu*, Régnier is described as "*celui qui cyclope*" ("he who cyclops") because of the monocle he wore.

164. ... syrinx: i.e. as an heraldic shield is parted per bend sinister, the word "*taillé*" ("cut") having that meaning in heraldic terminology; and, in addition, a syrinx is a pipe made of reeds (Pan pipes) cut in this manner. There is also, no doubt, a reference here to *La Syrinx*, one of the many small literary and poetry reviews of the epoch.

164. Citron: in the French, "*poncire*"; from Provençal *pomsire* (*pomme de Syrie*), a kind of lemon, not strictly a citron perhaps.

165. Marcel Schwob: friend of Jarry, who dedicated *Ubu Roi* to him. Among his works, *Les Vies imaginaires* included sections devoted to Cyril Tourneur and Captain Kidd. Schwob is also one of the six writers in Doctor Faustroll's library to whom a chapter is subsequently dedicated.

165. The skull and kid: Jarry wrote "*la tête de mort et le chevreau*" instead of "*la tête de mort et les tibias*" ("skull and crossbones") for a pun on the name of this chapter's hero.

166. Great Church of Snoutfigs: in French, "*la grande église de Muflefiguière*". This is derived by suggestion from Rabelais's word "*papefiguière*" (IV, 45).

166. Laurent Tailhade: French poet (1854-1919). Author of *Au Pays du Mufle*, ballads ("*mufle*" means "snout", "muzzle", or, as a term of opprobrium, "cad", "lout"). On the evening of the anarchist Vaillant's terrorist attack in the Chamber of Deputies (1893) Tailhade said: "*Qu'importent les victimes, si le geste est beau! Qu'importe la mort de vagues humanités, si par elle s'affirme l'individu!*" ("What do casualties matter if the deed is beautiful! What matter the death of indeterminate human qualities if thereby the individual makes his mark!"). Shortly afterward he was himself severely wounded when an anarchist bomb exploded in the restaurant Foyot (1894). He was a collaborator of the anarchist journal *Le Libertaire*.

168. Claude Terrasse: composer, friend of Jarry, wrote music for *Ubu Roi* (*Ouverture d'Ubu Roi*, *Marche des Polonais*, *La Chanson du Décervelage*) and composed the music for *Pantagruel*, the "*opéra bouffe*" which Jarry wrote in collaboration with Eugène Demolder. Jarry lived at the home of Terrasse during 1904-5, the name of the house being *L'Ile Sonnante*.

168. ... coelophone: *ravanastron*, an ancient violin of India; *sambuca*, an ancient stringed instrument of dubious identity, the Bible's sackbut; *bandore*, a lute-like instrument of the Middle Ages; *kin*, a seven-stringed Chinese lute; *tché*, a Chinese flute with mouthpiece in the centre and three holes on each side; *beggar's-guitar*, generally accepted translation for "*turlurette*" (era Charles VI), perhaps incorrect: Barbara Wright prefers "a kind of bagpipe in the Middle Ages"; *vina*, the primary and most ancient instrument of India — a seven-stringed lute; *magrepha*, a small Hebrew organ; *hydraulus*, an ancient form of organ; *sarrusophone*, a mid 19th-century brass instrument invented for military bands; *zampogna*, an Italian peasant bagpipe; *chéré*, a large Bengali trumpet; *coelophone*, a late 19th-century hybrid "organ".

169. The first line of music: from Mozart's *Motet Burlesque*, which was played in 1897 at the Théâtre des Pantins in Paris, a theatre launched by Jarry and Terrasse together with the painters Pierre Bonnard, Vuillard, and Sérusier, the poet Franc-Nohain, and a group of actors.

170. ... who awaited death: Rachilde wrote in 1896, under the pen-name Jean de Chilra, a novel *La Princesse des Ténèbres*. She had also written a novel *Madame la Mort* (1898) and a collection of stories *Imitation de la Mort* (1903). She liked Rachilde to be taken as a man's name: hence "the king". The "hermetic shades" invoke Mercury, of course, i.e. the *Mercure de France*, whose offices were in the rue de l'Échaudé (celebrated by Jarry in the *Chanson du Décervelage*).

170. The river Ocean: may be considered to be the Boulevard St. Germain. The *Mercure* is again evoked by the monthly orgies of the transpontine lords: i.e. the Tuesday salons held by Rachilde on its premises. Among the visitors, Christian Beck can be distinguished by his Belgian hat. The image of the toad was inspired by an indignant article in the review *La Plume* (1897) comparing Rachilde to "a little toad trying to fly." The identity of "the devil Plural" remains inscrutably obscure; but perhaps he represents simply the "vulgar mob of detractors" of the *Mercure*.

175. The marine bishop Mendacious (*Mensonger*): in Book XIII of the 16th-century naturalist Ulisse Aldrovandi's *De animalibus infectis, de serpentibus et dracontibus, de monstris*, the phenomenon is illustrated with a commentary indicating that "this creature was captured on the coast of Poland in 1531; offered to the king, it became restless and was thrown back into the sea. It was as tall as a man; it seemed to bear a mitre on its head and to be clad in an episcopal robe." This print was first reproduced in 1895 in the fifth number of *L'Ymagier*, the illustrated review edited by Jarry and Remy de Gourmont.

175. Paul Valéry: friend of Jarry and contributor, at one time, to the same reviews. In this and the following chapters of *Faustroll*, the persons to whom the chapters are dedicated are no longer "described" in the text.

176. Ear fig: Jarry has "*une figue d'oreille*". Possibly he is suggesting the meaning *sycophant* which is, in Greek, literally "fig-shower" (i.e. one who shows figs — the word's origin is unknown).

176. Pierre Quillard: founded the review *La Pléiade*; a writer, translator, and eventually expert in political science and ethnology. A fishing (and drinking) companion of Jarry at Corbeil. The March 1897 issue of the *Mercure* contains a *Ballade à la louange de quelques-uns* with the following quatrain:

Quillard plaint celles que le fer	("Quillard consoles those whom
Du sombre Abd-ul-Hamid a fait veuves;	Sombre Abdul Hamid's sword has widowed;
Jarry dit Merdre d'un ton fier	Jarry says Merdre with a lordly voice
Et Vallette lit des épreuves.	And Vallette reads the proofs.")

178. A.-F(erdinand) Hérold: a poet and dramatist, but more particularly a translator (Greek, Latin, Sanskrit, German...). The quotation from the *A'ranyaka Upanishad* at the beginning of *Faustroll* is, in the original French edition, from Hérold's translation. Hérold was a cycling (and drinking) companion of Jarry's, and an unusual telegram from Hérold to Jarry at Corbeil during 1898 has survived: *I HAVE JUST DRUNK AN EXCELLENT MARC BRANDY. HEROLD.*

178. Boneless and economical: this line is in English in the original.

179. The bruchus... the locust: Septuagint, Lev. XI, 22. Authorised Version: "locust, bald locust, beetle and grasshopper"; Moffatt: "migratory locust, bald locust, chopping locust, grasshopper."

180. ΣΕΣΟ'ΥΛΑΣΘΑΙ: which means "to have got drunk". [PE]

180. Monsieur Deibler: Anatole Deibler is, one may notice, the only one among those to whom chapters of *Faustroll* are dedicated to benefit by an added adverb, in this case "sympathetically". Deibler was France's Public Executioner of the epoch. See also note to p.51.

180. *How to Succeed*: *Le Moyen de Parvenir / Oeuvre contenant la raison de tout ce qui a esté, est, & sera / ...* etc. attributed to François Béroalde (c.1556-c.1629). Originally published about 1610, without date, place, or name of author, the name of Béroalde only appears in 18th-century editions, and his authorship is problematical. This astonishing book is presented in the form of a banquet attended by historical personages of different eras discoursing on every possible theme, with satirical anecdotes, erotic stories, puns, parodies, erudite quotations, obscure allegories and indiscriminate attacks upon both the Catholic and Protestant churches, womankind, the aristocracy, and all manner of temporal and spiritual pretensions. Béroalde was a convert to Catholicism, and became Canon of Tours. According to Colletet "he frequented gambling dens and taverns, devoted the revenue of his canonry to debauchery, and finally, being without religious conviction, returned to Protestantism."

182. Piron: translation of the verse by Stanley Chapman.

183. Iron kiosks: i.e. "*pissotière*" (public urinal), phonetically "*pisse au tiers*" ("piss in the third").

183. A special sail... : Bonnefoux (*Dictionnaire de marine à voiles et à vapeur*, 1855) describes this little-known sail as a "*petite voile de fantaisie et d'un usage peu utile*" ("small, fancy sail of hardly any use")! It was known in England as a "Jimmy Green".

187. Pierre Loti: in this chapter Jarry makes use (*a posteriori*, so to speak) of Loti's *Livre de la Pitié et de la Mort*, more especially of the story therein, "*Tante Claire nous quitte*". This story becomes "*La Mort de Latente Obscure*" (phonetically, "*La Tante Obscure*").

All the words in italics in this chapter are quotations from the above-mentioned book (sometimes the order is transposed in the cause of the pataphysical analogy).

187. Even more me: Loti's dedication of *Le Livre de la Pitié et de la Mort* actually reads: "*A ma mère bien-aimée / Je dédie ce livre / Sans crainte, parceque la foi chrétienne lui permet de lire avec sérénité les plus sombres choses.*" ("To my beloved mother / I dedicate this book / Without any fear, for the Christian faith allows one to read the darkest things with serenity."). And the author's preface begins: "*Ce livre est encore plus moi...*" ("This book is even more me...")

187. It would b... you so, if only you knew!: the closing words of Loti's preface (addressed to his literary enemies, imploring them not to mock a theme which is "sacred" to him!) are in fact "*il vous* ennuiera *tant, si vous saviez!*" ("It would *bore* you too much, if you knew!") Jarry has simply *en...ra*, which ambiguity I have preserved in the English ("*vous en...ra*" for "*vous enculera*", "would bugger you").

187. I alone... ABYSS: transcribed literally from Loti's story "*Rêve*", except that Jarry places the last two (significant!) words in capital letters.

188. Déroulède and Yan-Nibor: super-patriotic poets of the era. A *mirliton* is a "toy musical instrument with vibrating parchment reinforcing the voice, usually adorned with strips of paper and humorous verse." "*Vers de mirliton*" is a phrase meaning vulgar doggerel or trashy verse.

189. Hyplotising: *sic.*

189. Kaka-San really *is* the name of a character in Loti's story "*La Chanson des vieux époux*". Kaka-San and Toto-San are beggars, and Toto-San draws Kaka-San, who is paralysed, along in a box on rollers. She dies eventually in her box, and the italicised last paragraph of the chapter, which is a quotation from the story, means exactly what it appears to mean!

189. The musical jet: a scientific experiment described by C.V. Boys (see note to p.139) in his *Soap Bubbles* (Lecture III) and invoked here by Jarry (in an entirely pataphysical application, of course).

190. *Little women*: *Sic. The Isle of Dreams*, lyric by *Reynaldo Hahn*, words by *P. Loti*, *A. Alexandre* and *G. Hartmann*. [Author's Note]

190. Pierre Bonnard: friend of Jarry since 1893, illustrator of Jarry's *Almanach du Père Ubu*, and fellow contributor to the *Revue blanche*.

191. *Au Luxe Bourgeois*: the Musée du Luxembourg, where academic paintings acquired by the State were exhibited. The "department managers" mentioned by Doctor Faustroll in the following paragraph are identifiable as fashionable painters of the time, all exhibitors at the *Beaux Arts* in 1897.

191. *The Poor Fisherman*: by Puvis de Chavannes, *Olympia* by Manet.

192. "How beautiful is yellow!": inspired by Gauguin's text *Natures mortes*, on Van Gogh, published in 1894, which says: "*Oh! oui, il l'a aimé le jaune, ce bon Vincent, ce peintre de Hollande; lueurs de soleil qui réchauffaient son âme, en horreur du brouillard. Un besoin de chaleur.*" ("Oh yes, he loved his yellow, did our Vincent, that painter from Holland; rays of sunlight that warmed up his soul afresh, with its horror of fog. A real need for heat.")

192. Unredeemed canvases: in the French, "*toiles non déclouées*," which could also mean "pictures still hanging on the walls."

192. Henri Rousseau: "discovered" as a painter by Jarry, who met him in 1893. From 1894 Jarry wrote articles on Rousseau and published the latter's lithograph of "*La Guerre*" in *L'Ymagier*. Jarry lived briefly with Rousseau in 1897 during one of the former's periodic domestic crises. Rousseau painted a portrait of Jarry which was exhibited at the Salon des Indépendants in 1895; a contemporary critic remarked of this painting: "Notice his portrait of a poet (M. Alfred Jarry) whose hair was so long that the catalogue thought fit to describe the picture as 'Portrait of Mme. A. J.' "

195. Termes: an equivocal Latin word, which can signify "a green and living branch", "a young bough cut off" or in late Latin "a woodworm". *Larousse* (19th-c. ed.) gives the meaning "termite". The sense here is of priapic ejaculation, which Jarry associates in the following chapter to the artistic ejaculation of the "unforeseen beast Clinamen".

195. *Clinamen*: literally, "inclination, bias." But the *clinamen principiorum* or "swerve" of Lucretius is a more complicated concept, a philosophic theory central to the Epicurean system which Lucretius explains in *De Rerum natura* as follows: Atoms fall headlong through space, carried on by their own weight. At undetermined moments and in undetermined points of space, they manifest a minute quasi-deviation, only just sufficient for one to be able to speak of a modification of equilibrium. It is as a result of this "swerve" or *clinamen* that so-called solid bodies are formed from the atoms or *primordia*. Lord Kelvin claims (in his essay *Steps Towards a Kinetic Theory of Matter*) the ideas of Epicurus and Lucretius as the basis of the modern theory of matter, in which all its properties are seen to be merely attributes of motion.

195. Paul Fort: founded the Théâtre d'Art in 1891; in 1893 this became the Théâtre de l'Œuvre, where *Ubu Roi* was produced by Lugné-Poe in 1896. Fort edited a review, *Le Livre d'Art*, which published the first extracts from *Ubu Roi*.

196. In the sealed palace...: the version of chapter XXXIV which was printed separately in *La Plume*

(15 November 1900), had an extra, second paragraph preceding this one [Note and translation PE]:

"It was this same machine that, in the year eighteen ninety-six, was presented to the Ministry of Defence by a middle-aged man remarkable only for his military medal, and who appeared benign, despite his moustache, in the hope that it would be intelligently approved of, and adopted, as a means of rapidly colouring the chests and carriages of the army, whenever they saw fit to do so. In the presence of the relevant Committee the instrument was aimed at a new door, while two artillerymen armed with brushes stood ready in front of a similar door. The two soldiers did not have time to assume even the first position required of a painter under arms: hardly had the signal been given, when the trial door, and the other door, and the windows, and the whole building, all disappeared under a prodigiously thick and lumpy coat of vile mess, leaving a green fog hanging in the air. Nothing more was to be hoped for from the Committee. Nothing more was to be hoped for from the artillerymen. No trace of anything remained!"

In the Lormel manuscript, the third paragraph is also substantially different:

"In the sealed palace, with nobody there in the world but Faustroll and René Isidore Panmuphle, and the mutilated bishop who had disappeared but was now back, the Loti business over, and with the islands, no longer on firm ground, alone ruffling the dead smoothness of the modern deluge in the universal Seine, the unforeseen beast Clinamen ejaculated on to the walls of its universe:"

197. "Woan't yew p'-lay with me, mistuh Loyal?": in French, "*voulez-vous jouïer avec moa, mister Loyal?*" the dialect indicating the fact that the great clowns in French 19th-century circus were English. "*Mister Loyal*" is, in French circus parlance, the traditional name of the blue-coated Equestrian Director, and the sentence is a classic part of the duologue between a clown and this ringmaster. The name is derived from a famous circus family.

201. *The Sundhya*, etc.: in English in the original.

203. Mour-de-Zencle: "*mour*" (*mourre*) means "muzzle" and is found in Rabelais (III, 20). The word "*zencle*" was invented by Rabelais (I, 12) from the Greek word for "sickle".

204. (John) Tyndall: 19th-century Irish physicist, whose chemical experiment with vacuum tubes is referred to by Kelvin in his *Popular Lectures and Addresses* (p.204) as "Tyndall's blue sky."

204. Félix Fénéon: writer and a collaborator on the *Revue blanche*, one of the first to encourage Jarry as a writer.

204. (Arthur) Cayley: 19th-century English mathematician, one of whose experiments (relative to the law of variation) is quoted by Kelvin, *op. cit.*, pp.279 *et seq.*

205. The Morgue... slab: might also be rendered "Pride displayed for two days on her lectern..."

207. Louis Dumur: playwright and one of the founders of the *Mercure de France*. The reason for this dedication is certainly the long article which Dumur wrote on *Ubu Roi* in the *Mercure* in 1896.

207. *Leves gustus...*: "A light sip will incline one to philosophy, possibly to atheism, but a fuller draught will lead one back to religion."

209. Lord Kelvin: Sir William Thomson, English physicist whose *Popular Lectures and Addresses*, Vol. I,

Constitution of Matter, 2nd (enlarged) edition (1891), was translated into French in 1893, and which Jarry interprets from a pataphysical standpoint while adhering closely to the letter — if not the spirit — of the original. He makes use especially of the chapters "Electrical Units of Measurement", "Steps Towards a Kinetic Theory of Matter" and "The Wave Theory of Light". The reader is referred to the above-mentioned work for a full appreciation of Jarry's splendid interpretation of Kelvin. As two examples out of many, compare Jarry, p.209 above, sentence beginning "For we are both...", with Kelvin, *op. cit.*, p.80: "I often say that when you can measure what you are speaking about and express it in numbers you know something about it"; and Jarry, same page, "I know that quartz... Bosse-de-Nage", with Kelvin, p.81: "... diamond is reckoned harder than ruby; ruby than quartz; quartz than glass-hard steel..."

The names mentioned in this chapter are all those of distinguished scientists — astronomers, physicists, mathematicians mentioned by Kelvin. Needless to say, the measuring-rod, the watch, the tuning-fork, the luminiferous ether, the rotating fly-wheels and linked gyrostats, even the Scottish shoemaker's wax are to be found seriously expounded in the pages of Kelvin in connection with practical scientific experiments.

210. C.G.S.: "Centimetre gramme second" (the unit of force defined in terms of the units of mass, length, and time).

210. Sorting Demon: the title of one of the chapters in *Popular Lectures*, referring to the famous theoretical experiment in "dissipation of energy" of James Clerk Maxwell, the Scottish physicist.

211. 5.892 x 10^{-5}: this amount of a centimetre is the wavelength of yellow light in the spectrum (Kelvin, pp.144 *et seq.*).

211. ... circumference: a centimetre.

212. Concerning the Sun...: the title of this chapter is derived from the essay "On the Sun's Heat" from Kelvin, *op. cit.* In this essay Kelvin does indeed describe the sun as "a cool solid," and the squares, pyramids, screws, paddles and other paraphernalia are all invoked by him to illustrate his scientific expositions.

215. Pantaphysics: *sic.*

215. Anne-Catherine Emmerich: unlettered mystical fantasist, who produced some highly imaginative revelations of the life of Christ (e.g. *La Douloureuse Passion*) under the influence of divine inspiration.

218. Pataphysics is the science...: the final sentence, in the original, is "*La Pataphysique est la science...*" The French may be translated with important differences in nuance; either as the beginning of a deliberately unfinished sentence ("Pataphysics is the science of...") or, if one takes it to be a complete sentence, it might equally well read "Pataphysics is science..." Let this remain, textually, the final pataphysical mystery.

In the original MS. of *Faustroll*, the last words of the book are followed by the word END in the centre of the page, and, underneath this, Jarry's remark quoted at the beginning of the *Introduction* (p.119).

NOTES TO ABSOLUTE LOVE

by Paul Edwards, unless otherwise indicated

221. ***La Dragonne*:** the "*Bataille de Morsang*"was published in *La Revue blanche* (1 April 1903). [CA]

221. Breton quotes from *Absolute Love* in his preface to his selections from Jean-Pierre Duprey (*Anthology of Black Humour*).

222. ... nothing Freudian: this was first put forward by Brunella Eruli in her article "*L'Immaculée Conception*", *L'Étoile-Absinthe*, 7/8 (1980), though she argues that *Absolute Love* can be read with Freud's theories of language in mind, and his *Studies on Hysteria* (1895) to hand. I would argue, however, that there is no trace in Jarry's novel of Freud's and Bauer's main conclusions, namely that hysteria is caused by repressed memories (what memories does Varia repress?) which are converted into physical symptoms. The Paris School, headed by Janet after Charcot's death, in the main resisted Freud's theories.

222. ***Time Machine*:** see *CW* I, pp.211ff.

222. ...Vallette: undated letter, *OC* I, p.1075.

225. ***Absolute Love*:** Bretons call Holy Week "*la semaine absolue*", which may add to Jarry's title the Breton meaning of "Easter Love", "Holy Love" or "Passion-tide Love" (see A&B, pp.228-9).

227. La Santé: a star-shaped prison in Paris, near where Jarry had lived when he wrote *Black Minutes*.

227. (Ernest) Haeckel: pioneering German zoologist (1834-1919) specialising in Radiolaria and similar sea-creatures. A&B propose that the metaphor of a bone "blooming" derives from Haeckel's blurring of the distinction between the animal and the vegetable worlds. The engravings in his books influenced Jarry (see Paul Edwards, "*Les petits monstres*", in *Medusa/Médias*, 4, Aachen, 2002, pp.77-96).

228. Firmament: a firm enough word in English, though Hebrew *rakiah* literally means "solid arch", as Cruden's *Concordance* notes (this sense is not spelled out in the Authorised Version, e.g. Genesis 1, 6-8).

228. Lark mirror: rotating triangular piece of wood covered in tiny mirrors, used by hunters to attract larks and adopted by Charcot to hypnotise patients.

229. ***... waters which are above*:** cf. Genesis 1, 7.

229. ... Stars Triumphant: allusion to the Roman Catholic distinction between the Church Militant and the Church Triumphant, respectively the faithful alive on earth, and the Saints surrounding Christ.

229. ... magic Head: Aladdin plucked the magic lamp from the caverns (*Thousand and One Nights*, 739th night), but Jarry substituted "Head" for lamp, thinking of the guillotine which will deprive Emmanuel of his genie-like genius.

229. Abbot Faria: character imprisoned in the Castle of If in *The Count of Monte Cristo* by Alexandre Dumas, as spotted by A&B (p.226). The real Abbot Faria was one of the people who revived interest in mesmerism, or "animal magnetism". In 1814 Faria published accounts of his experiments demonstrating that no "unknown force" — invisible fluids, psychic influences, etc. — was necessary to induce a mesmerised state (hemi-somnambulism). This discovery paved the way for scientific rather than spiritist investigations into hypnosis. Pierre Janet mentions Faria's observations that some subjects remained somnambulists for whole years, and then forgot their somnambulist lives entirely the day they reawoke (*L'Automatisme psychologique*, p.134). Perhaps Jarry's "wall" is a reference to the segregated lives of split consciousnesses.

229. Ahasuerus: the Wandering Jew.

230. Pagne: obsolete English word for "loincloth", for Jarry's archaism "*cripagne*".

231. *End result*: "*fin*" meaning both "end" and "purpose", italicised by Jarry to emphasise the dual meaning.

231. Loudun: the name of a convent in Poitou associated with possessed nuns and the witch-trials of the early seventeenth century (cf. Jules Michelet, *La Sorcière* (1862), which makes Jarry's point that possession was merely pathological, and Aldous Huxley, *The Devils of Loudun* (1952)).

231. Divine Protection: Charcot introduces his chapter on the convulsionaries of the Saint-Médard cemetery by saying that the convulsion epidemics attributed to supernatural powers were not always thought to have been the evil doings of the Devil, but were often considered to be a manifestation of God's power (*Les Démoniaques dans l'art*, 1887). Charcot and Jarry both refer to the Church's traditional interpretation of evil and misfortune as being for the greater glory of God.

231. ... East to West: or "we align ourselves with time in the direction of universal Synthesis, like a magnet in the form of a cross in the East-West magnetic current", i.e. like an electric motor.

231. ... tell all nations: cf. Matthew 28, 19.

232. ... Ape of Pale Death: "*Ô Sommeil, Singe de la mort*", in which "*singe*" (as well as being an anagram of *signe*, "sign") means both "monkey" and something which is imitated or aped, hence Jarry's somewhat hardy variant of the common saying that "sleep resembles death".

232. Thirty-seventh situation: reference to Georges Polti's book of dramatic theory *Les Trente-six situations dramatiques* (1897), first serialised in the *Mercure de France* from March to November 1894. Polti, taking up the challenge from Gozzi, Schiller and Goethe, attempted to prove that there were only 36 possible situations on the stage — he did not limit himself to the situations of tragedy, as Goethe had done — and only 36 emotions. The 37th situation is of course Jarry's invention.

232. ... germinate: the sound harmonies, as beautiful as the first two lines of Coleridge's "Kubla Khan", are worth listening to in the original French: "*Joseph de sa varlope fait germer les copeaux...*". The lullaby rhythm and the baby language persuade the reader to adopt the child's perspective — this would be Joyce's technique (his ironies aside) at the start of *A Portrait of the Artist as a Young Man* (1916).

232. "*Miriam*" is Hebrew for "Mary". A.-M. Gerard's *Dictionnaire de la Bible* (Laffont, 1989) lists various etymologies that have been put forward for the Semitic name, "the rebel", "the bitter one", "the strong one", "she who raises up" or "she who is raised up", "the prophetess" and "the queen". The Hebrew words *mar yam* (literally "a drop of sea-water"), transcribed into Latin as *stilla maris*, gave rise to the fanciful apostrophe "*stella maris*", Latin for "star of the sea", and which was read by the French as "*Étoile de mer*" ("starfish"). The association of the star shape and Mary's name may be at the origin of Jarry's choice of a star-shaped prison, his collocation "*Étoile de pierre*", and the starfish references, as A&B have suggested (p.224, n.4). This seems to be confirmed by corrections to the manuscript, where the name of La Santé prison is added at a later stage (see *OC* I, p.1259), presumably after Jarry had chosen and reflected on the name Miriam.

232. Would you: Miriam addresses her child using "*vous*". There is no equivalent in modern English to the French distinction between *tu* and *vous* — the reader is invited to imagine Miriam speaking in the English of the 1611 Bible when she says "you", and Emmanuel in modern English when he replies "you"; otherwise Jarry's language is simple, straightforward modern French.

232. "*Sextillion*": in French means a thousand trillion, or 10^{21} (as it does in American usage), whereas the word corresponds in English to a trillion trillion, or 10^{36}.

232. Jocasta: mother of Oedipus.

233. ... *living woman*: with a pun on the theological term "*les vivants*", which designates those who enter into eternal life (cf. *Littré*, "*vivant*", 16). Note that Miriam does not know that she is Varia, only that she is the carpenter's wife, i.e. Mary.

233. Ieschou-ben-Joseph: the first name is a combination of French transcriptions of "Jesus" from Greek ("*Ièsous*") and Hebrew ("*Yéchoua*"). In French, *chou*, or more commonly, *petit chou* ("little cauliflower"), is used as a term of endearment for children, which may explain Jarry's choice of transcription (though in matters of transliteration inconsistencies abound and Jarry may well have transcribed or misremembered the letters with no intention of punning). "*Ben*" means "son of".

233. Wooden clappers: "*platagés*", long thin wooden castanets held by the Greeks, one in each hand, while dancing (this rare word is transcribed into French from a Greek onomatopoeia). One can hear a pun on *patagium* (spelt the same in French and English), which is the correct (Latin) name for a bat's wing membrane.

234. Suffocating: Eruli (*op. cit.*, p.55) claims that the impression of suffocating is borrowed from Janet's description of a patient changing states, which is quite possible (see *L'Automatisme psychologique*, p.47), but it must be pointed out that Jarry is not alluding for reasons of authenticity to a general phenomenon, but only to an observation of one patient's passing into one particular state, the lethargic state which precedes catalepsy. Jarry is not so much supplying a clinical detail as borrowing local colour for effect. And in any case, having a patient say "catalepsy" straight afterwards destroys any scientific credibility there might have been, since cataleptic patients do not speak, they only repeat in echolalia.

234. ... over her eyes: as well as a pillow-case, "*une taie sur les yeux*" can mean "opaque spots (leucoma) on her eyes", or figuratively "blinkered".

234. A nod...: "*le bouton du petit mandarin*", literally "the button [that when pressed causes the death] of the Chinese mandarin". This is an allusion to a moral debate and a catchphrase now no longer current.

"Who," the question asked, "would not hesitate to kill in order to reap an inheritance should the murder be simple — pressing a button — and the victim someone nobody had ever seen or heard of — such as a mandarin in farthest China?" (see Chateaubriand, *Le Génie du Christianisme*, I, bk. 6, ch. 2).

235. ... as she does with you: Miriam employs the intimate *tu* form of the second person from here to the end of the chapter.

235. Nobody even knows I exist: were it not for the line that follows, one could read here "nobody has ever *known* me", with the Biblical sense of "known".

235. ... kiss the old tide-waiter: the events described here occur later in the novel, from the end of ch. IX to the beginning of ch. XI.

236. Aotrou Doue: A&B (p.228f.) have provided commentaries on the meanings of these Breton names. "*Aoutrou* [*sic*] *Doué* [*sic*]" translates as "Mister God", or "Lord God", and is used as a title for bishops, priests and public notaries (solicitors/lawyers, there is no exact judicial equivalent). Usage has diluted the meaning of *aoutrou* to something like the English "sir", as used by policemen etc.

236. Gallo: region and dialect of Upper Brittany, closer to French than it is to Breton, as the name suggests.

236. Varia: this Breton form of "Mary" (like Joseb, and Nédélec for Emmanuel) also allows Jarry a transparent allusion to the accusation of "variableness" traditionally made by misogynists against women.

236. Lampaul: former spelling of Lamballe, where Jarry's maternal grandfather lived.

237. *Aotrou... ouzomp*: the words in Breton mean the same as those preceding and are the congregation's echo.

237. Natary: "*noutârc*" in the original, a phonetic transcription of the local pronunciation of "*notaire*" (properly "notary public"). What the locals said was simply respectful, just as we say "Mister Mayor". There may be a pun on *tare*, "defect".

238. ... as Herodias had done: reference to Saint John the Baptist, the forerunner of Christ, who "wore a crown below his head" in the sense that he wore a plate below his chin — after Herodias, Herod's wife, had made Salome ask for it to be served up in this way.

238. *In disco*: the Latin of the Vulgate, meaning "on a plate" (Mark 6, 28). Jarry returned to the subject in his essay "Time in Art" (*CW* I, p.209).

239. ... *non sum dignus*: "Behold the body of the Lord", "Lord, I am not worthy". The second sentence is spoken by the priest in the Latin Mass before he communes; the first is interpolated by Jarry, the priest having quoted Christ's words at the Last Supper. Jarry has picked up the theme of chapter II in which the "real presence" of Christ in the Host is imagined as a real living presence.

239. Eardrums: i.e. he banged his plate (which an eardrum resembles).

239. Nuremberg: the European toy-making capital, and the Noah's Ark made there was a common toy in Jarry's day. The meaning of this sentence is obscure, partly because of an excess of genitives (everything seems to agree with everything else), and partly because word association seems to have run riot: Jarry puns on "*files*" (orderly rows) and "*fil*" (the grain of wood), then evokes the star pine by mentioning in quick succession both "*sapin*" (pine) and "*nébuleuse*" (nebula). One could understand that the cross-section of a pine tree looks like a star nebula; from these nebulae comes the created world, in the shape of Noah's Ark; the concentric pine-rings are visible on the wooden toys, a distinctive feature of Nuremberg toys; the animals have been broken by Emmanuel along the grain; the notary put them upright; he put them in lines, or in a circle, or in a star pattern...

239. Superfoetant: i.e. superfluous (cp. *CW* I, p.141).

239. Ratatrunk: "*Ratatrompe*". The Macroscelididae include African rodents with long snouts, commonly known as *rat-à-trompes* in French and elephant shrews in English. A&B (p.230) think there is a reference to the grafting of a rat's tail on to its nose, perpetrated as a hoax (which one has no trouble imagining reported in the popular illustrated press).

240. Ravens: Odin, the Norse god of war, magic, writing and poetry, is traditionally accompanied by two wolves, Gere and Freke, and two ravens, Hugen (Thought) and Munen (Memory).

241. This chapter is autobiographical, the memoirs of Jarry's sister Charlotte concurring with the events described (*OC* III, p.699).

241. Brumoy: Jesuit historian (1688-1742) whose most famous work, quoted here, first appeared in 1730. The character is of course Death. [CA]

241. Lane: "*Venelle*" in the original. Jarry's teacher at Laval is known to have been a Mme. Venel. The spelling in the book makes the pun on *une venelle* (an alleyway) clearer, as well as giving the word a more recognisably feminine inflection, in this chapter on the feminine: "*la*".

242. *Capharnaüm*: the Biblical town of Capernaum where Jesus attracted such a crowd of people to the house where He was staying that the roof had to be broken in so as to lower in the sick (Mark 2, 2). In France the word has come to mean "a cluttered mess". Rather than thinking of this as a cute autobiographical detail, it should be noted that here is another allusion to hysteria, for it was in Capernaum that Jesus healed a man who had the "palsy" (Mark, as before, also Charcot & Richer, *Les Démoniaques dans l'art*, p.71).

242. Coffer for the norn: "*coffre à diorne*", "*diorne*" being an invented word. "The norn" is an attempt to translate "*diorne*" phonetically and resonantly, and is not a reference to Norse mythology.

242. ... aepyornis: Jarry wrote "*le diornis et l'épiornis*", presumably from memory and perhaps contaminated by *le derme et l'épiderme* (i.e. skin), for the correct spellings are *le dinornis et l'aepyornis*. Both are species of extinct giant birds.

242. Cutlass: "*coutelas*", with a private pun on "Coutouly", Jarry's maternal grandmother's maiden name, which Jarry linked to Herbrand de Saqueville, who came across with William the Conqueror. A "*coutelas*" is also the popular name for a sword-fish which, stuffed and mounted, was and still is a bourgeois decoration (and we know there were stuffed birds in the notary's dining-room).

242. Father Switches: "*Le Père Fouettard*" accompanies Father Christmas, with naughty children being left a bundle of switches instead of presents. The term is now more generally used as a verbal threat to children and translated as "the bogeyman".

243. ***Janiques:*** Jarry chose to put the Breton name for gorse (in italics) to add local colour.

244. Prince Perviz: allusion to the last tale (in Galland's edition) of the *Thousand and One Nights*, "The Story of the Two Sisters who were Jealous of their Youngest Sister". When the prince was changed by a dervish into a black stone, the prayer-beads he had left with his sister started to feel clumsy in her hands and refused to move when she pushed them, thus informing her of the tragic event. We are thus asked to think of Varia as Princess Parizade, who climbed the mountain of danger to free her brothers from everlasting sleep by pouring water over the black stones they had been turned into.

244. Wolf's-fists: "*vesse-de-loup*" (literally, "wolf's noiseless fart") is the fungus commonly known as "puff-ball", formerly called "wolf's-fist" in England (*fist* being Old English for "fart"). The Giant Lycoperdon can grow up to nine feet in diameter in a single night (Bulliard, *Histoire des champignons*).

244. The Roc: the fabulous eagle of the *Thousand and One Nights*. At the beginning of Sinbad's fifth voyage, the merchants sailing with Sinbad break open a roc's egg and roast the fledgling. Its parents are revenged by letting rocks falls on Sinbad's ship and splitting it into smithereens. Jarry also alludes to the war between the Big Endians and the Little Endians in *Gulliver's Travels* ("A Voyage to Lilliput", ch. 4.): "... the Emperors of Blefuscu [France] accus[ed] us of making a schism in religion, by offending against a fundamental doctrine [...] the words are these; *That all true believers shall break their eggs at the convenient end*: and which is the convenient end, seems, in my humble opinion, to be left to every man's conscience". Varia's fear is fuelled by literary reminiscences.

244. The lycopod (Greek for "wolf's foot") is the club-moss, whose ripe spores form an inflammable powder known as "vegetable brimstone" (or lycopodium), which was indeed used for stage-effects.

245. ... not turn round to look: like Princess Parizade on the hillside walking to the magic bird (see note above to Prince Perviz), who was the only one not to look round and so escaped being turned to stone.

245. Hermit-crabs lodge their soft, unprotected abdomen in empty, cast-off shells, moving into bigger ones as they grow — in *Faustroll*, Jarry spells out that the shell protects its hind parts and sex organ (ch. XXII).

245. Villose: the long, soft hairs ("*velu*") of the wrack also suggest a pun on *pierre velue* (rough, uncut stone), which may lie at the origin of Jarry's description since he often reads collocations literally and then develops them without heed to the original expression.

246. Twin: "*besson*", a dialect word used by sheep-farmers, according to *Harrap's*, though the word is quite simply derived from Latin (*bis*); quotations in *Littré* show that it was employed as much for sheep as for wolves and children. One suspects the word to have been current in Gallo country.

246. ... light-source of the room: "*foyer*" is both a hearth and a source (of light) or focus, as in photography. While the chimney that draws our focus may be no more than metaphorical, the loophole would have provided light during the daytime.

246. Wing-chair: "*bergère*", also the word for a shepherdess. Varia is thus the "companion" of both the wolf (fire-dog) and the shepherdess (wing-chair), with whom she is identified through her woollen dress, in accordance with her varia-ble nature and her two states (Miriam when asleep and Varia when awake).

246. Thunder: the noise recalls Odin, the god of thunder, and also the magic bird Princess Parizade reached, which was small but had a thundering voice.

246. Sinople, an Ermine en Abyme: the manifest content is: "an ermine (Varia) in the grass in the distance", but Jarry employs heraldic terms with often bawdy intent: sinople (also written "vert" in English heraldry) is the colour green and has here the poets' sense of "lust"; the ermine stoat is celebrated for its white coat and is a traditional emblem of spiritual purity, yet Jarry later calls it a dirty beast, since to keep its coat immaculate it is forever licking itself; en abyme or in abyss, means "small and in the middle fess point, the centre of the escutcheon". The derived meaning of the title is "a dirty sex hole", and specifically the vagina since the ermine is associated with Varia. That Jarry misuses the term "ermine" as a "principal charge" in its own right rather than as a "fur" ("ermine spots" were schematised to form a design that merely filled in spaces on the shield), is of no consequence, for he uses heraldic terms according to what they conjure up for him and in no wise to please any passing heraldic experts.

246. Condorcet: this lycée is not autobiographical.

246. ... aquarium: cp. *CW* I, pp.40 and 277.

247. Moths: another reference to the great lantern fly (see p.228 above).

247. Bombyx: Jarry employs the entomologist's Greek for a silkworm ("*bombyx*" is also used in France to designate other and more common moths and their larvae) and puns on "*duvet*", which means both "downy hairs" and, as in English, an eider-down quilt, which particularly suits the silkworm's silk cocoon and Varia's similar-looking muff ("*manchon*", which can have the same pubic connotation in French as in English). Jarry's sentence is, however, first and foremost inspired by Jean-Henri Fabre's observations of the pine bombyx, whose egg-clusters are described (singly) as "a cylindrical muff with a silky appearance and of white slightly tinted with russet" (*Souvenirs entomologiques*, 1899, vol. 6, ch. 18). As in the novel, the texture is compared to down.

247. ... live in fur: this black beetle has a white middle, like Varia with her muff. The *Mercure* group read and reviewed Fabre's *Souvenirs entomologiques*, which said of the *Dermestes undulatus* that it "bears a leopard-skin coat with an ermine-striped jerkin" (vol. 8, ch. 16). Jarry's chapter title is in part also a heraldic description of the dermestes. It would appear to have been the word "*ondulation*" which conjured up *D. undulatus* in Jarry's imagination, but which he then hid by naming the larvae that live in fur rather than the *undulatus* that feeds off corpses. Whenever a mother and death are associated there is an ellipse in the text and a secret autobiographical meaning. Varia is both Jarry's mother and the grubs feeding on her corpse, her heraldic "fur", her ermine...

247. Insinuations: "*insinuement*" is not in the dictionaries, but is probably a neologism for "sinuous windings and twistings" and thus Varia's sinuous penetration of the undergrowth.

247. ... bottom of things: reference to the celebrated "wipe-bummatory discourse" of Rabelais: "But, to conclude, I say and maintain, that of all torcheculs, arsewipes, bumfodders, tail napkins, bung-hole cleansers, and wipe-breeches, there is none in the world comparable to the neck of a goose, that is well downed, if you hold her neck betwixt your legs." (*Gargantua*, ch. 13, tr. Sir Thomas Urquhart)

247. The "March-cat": the five-year-old Gargantua had previously said: "Afterwards, in dunging behind a bush, I found a March-cat, and with it I wiped my breech, but her claws were so sharp that they scratched and exulcerated all my perinee. Of this I recovered the next morning thereafter, by wiping myself with my mother's gloves, of a most excellent perfume and scent of the Arabian Benin." (*Gargantua*, ch. 13) The subsequent reference to his mother may have made this passage more memorable to Jarry. The ermine is here clearly identified with the rectum.

248. Private dining-room: certain Parisian restaurants specialised in providing tiny walled-off dining-rooms where sex could be had in private afterwards. Adulterous couples also did it in the horse-drawn carriages in the Bois de Boulogne which were available for hire by the hour.

248. Reviviscence: usually attributed to hunger.

248. Gold: since silence is golden. Typical silent pun for Jarry.

248. Censed…: during the Roman Catholic Mass, censers of burning incense are swung.

249. … in the shape of a hedgehog: "*hérisson*" is slang for the female pudenda (according to Alfred Delvau, *Dictionnaire érotique moderne*, 1866) "owing to the prickly nature of pubic hair if it is cut short". A&B (p.234) strongly suspect an allusion to the consecrated host, while there may also be an allusion to Charcot's description of the convulsions of the possessed nun Nicole Aubry, which ended with her back arched "like a hedgehog; but no sooner had she received the consecrated host than she returned to her normal state" (*Les Démoniaques dans l'art*, p.40). Jarry's hedgehog could therefore represent both the hysteric and the cure/host.

249. … oil: Chianti used to be stored in bottles with long necks and fat bottoms wrapped in straw. A layer of oil was poured in to protect the wine from the air, for the bottles were not stopped with a cork but with a wodge of straw. The reader will have understood that the menu is sexually suggestive.

249. The oyster, according to Delvau (*op. cit.*), represents the sea-smelling pudenda: "it opens at the touch of a finger, and its bite, though sweet, can be venomous."

249. … that he could see: Emmanuel sees with black diamond eyes that Varia thinks are those of a wolf.

249. *Wolf's-head mop*: a "*tête-de-loup*" is a long-handled ceiling brush known in England as a Pope's-head or Turk's-head brush (*Harrap's*).

250. … in a cowl of green: the action from here to the end of the chapter is the last rendition of its heraldic title.

250. Signed and Sealed: "*scellé sur simple queue*", identified by Michel Arrivé as the standard formula employed when sealing charters, and found by A&B at the end of the *Privilège* (license to print) accorded by François I to Rabelais for the printing of the *Tiers livre*. It is interesting, with Varia sharing her visions of the infant Christ with ecstatic mystics and hysterics, to note that Rabelais's dedication (in the third book) urges the Queen of Navarre to abstain from her ecstatic mysticism and attend to more earthly matters (ostensibly, the reading of "the brave acts of good Pantagruel").

250. Chime-plane: "*Oiseau*", literally "bird" (and with a capital letter in the original), which the context invites one to read as some kind of plane, although the word does not appear in the *Robert, Littré*, or *Larousse*. There does exist a plane called a "*colombe*" (a "dove"), which is known in English as a chime-plane.

251. Pale red... snouts: "*museau paillet*", with, as a bonus, an allusion to their pinky privates, since Jarry had called heather "pubic hair" in *Days and Nights*.

251. Repels: curiously, Jarry uses a word ("*détourne*") that could — were it not for the context here — mean "entices" (and which is used in legal language to denote the "corrupting" of minors).

251. Fire of those girls: the "*feu des filles*" is a passing literary allusion to Nerval's *Filles de feu*. Jarry liked to think he was a Celt descended from Cornish stock, which may explain why — at least in the sense of autobiography — Varia is compared to a fantasised version of Jarry's mother.

251. Balas ruby: as used for the fourth pillar of Bacbuc's fantastic fountain: "The fourth, a masculine ruby ballais (peach-coloured) amethystizing, its flame and lustre ending in violet or purple, like an amethyst." (Rabelais, *Cinquiesme livre*, ch. 42). **Dead pearls:** fished off Scotland, they resemble the eyes of fish. Ground into a powder and mixed with honey, they are used as medicine.

251. The fruits in the garden through which Aladdin passed to get to the magic lamp were, to his eyes, inedible, because they were in fact precious gems, though he was too young to realise this and took them for coloured glass (739th night).

251. Marine bishops: a sea-monster Jarry described in *L'Ymagier*, 5 (Oct. 1895), and in *Faustroll* ch. XXV. **Amethysts:** from the Greek for "guards against drunkenness". This precious, violet-coloured quartz is traditionally worn by bishops to protect them and their flock from worldly or spiritual intoxication. The violet amethysts of the bishops' rings dissolve in the waves of Varia's purplish hair as they bestow upon her the confirmation kiss, granting temperance or dissolution.

252. Triangles: although Jarry does not say whether the third point is the tongue or the genitals, it is most likely the latter since hysterics who imagined they were making love to God during their ecstatic states would afterwards use the euphemism: "God put his seal upon my most private parts" (see the works on hysteria by Pierre Janet), as indeed "seal" is used in the next line of the text.

252. ... *stellatarum*: types of sphinx moth, *Macroglossa fusiforma* is the spindle-shaped hawkmoth (cp. *Haldernablou*, *CW* I, p.73) and *M. stellatarum* is the hummingbird hawkmoth. A&B (p.235) put the caterpillars of the latter on the cheese-rennet plant, star-shaped to allow Jarry to associate moths with stars.

252. Cruet: Jarry borrows the Rabelaisian word "*guedoufle*", which is a small double-bottle used for oil and vinegar. He may have heard this old French word employed in the provinces, or else remembered that Shrovetide's scrotum looked like one (*Quart livre*, ch. 31). Whilst the bottle is undoubtedly phallic, it is by definition double, like a pair of eyes.

253. Chirping and buzzing: sounds of the carpenter's saw, as at the start of the chapter.

253. Terebra: the female Hymenopter's boring ovipositor. It can also serve as a sting.

253. *What it was*: his eyes, which Varia confused with wolves and it is wolves she is afraid of, and because he uses his eyes to hypnotise her.

253. ... *begins*: there are two possible situations: either it is a real execution (cf. ch. I) and one hopes the blade will stick; or it is a guillotine in a museum in which one puts one's head for a dare. In "*Les Phantasmes de M. Redoux*" (*Gil Blas*, 1886, *Histoires insolites*, 1888), Villiers de l'Isle-Adam tells the story of a man who hides in a wax museum so that he can dare himself to put his head in the hole. He gets stuck — "*Crrrick*," went the upper hinge — and spends the night thinking the blade might fall and chop off his head.

253. Top-weight: for the long lump of metal fixed to the top of the guillotine-blade to give it extra weight, Jarry uses the technical (though figurative) word "*mouton*", which also means "sheep", and which here goes to slaughter transitively, even as English uses "ram" and the "tup" of a steam-hammer.

254. Mutes: possible allusion to the bodyguards of a sultan (an image conjured up by the eastern dagger), as well as the silent wolves Emmanuel's eyes have already been compared to.

254. Persons: Jarry employs a classic French play on words, since "*personne*" means "nobody" and "*une personne*" means "somebody". The three lines involved are: "*Le trône où ne s'est assis Personne*" / "*Personne*" / "*L'une des Personnes*", whose "Persons" are the persons of the Trinity, but also, because of the preceding, "Nobodies".

254. *T.T.L.*: "*P.P.C.*" (*pour prendre congé*, "to take leave"), the abbreviation/formula people used to write on their visiting-cards before going on a journey, moving house, etc. A dog-eared calling-card, or one marked "*P.P.C.*", required no reply.

254. Corner turned down: A&B (p.235) inform us that people used to leave visiting-cards marked in this way in a basket provided for the purpose at funerals, to let the bereaved know they had attended. For Emmanuel to write "*P.P.C.*" *and* turn down a corner of his visiting-card is, as A&B suggest, to announce his impending death (and perhaps his return to attend his own funeral?). They further suggest an allusion to John 16, 16: "A little while, and ye shall not see me: and again, a little while, and ye shall see me, because I go to the Father." (1611 translation)

255. *Et verbum caro factum est*: from John 1, 14: "And the Word was made flesh".

255. *Gospel*: Jarry skipped from John 1, 1 to John 1, 14, without repeating the title phrase in the latter chapter, already given as his own chapter title.

255. *Pantagruel*: as Jarry missed out the very end of Rabelais's sentence, Urquhart's translation has had to be modified to correspond to the French. The 1693 translation reads: "... they fell to, and bringuardised it lustily" (Everyman edition, p.323), i.e. they bumped their rumps together. Panurge tells the story of a man who improvised a sign language to ask a beautiful deaf lady in Rome if she had seen any senators that day, but who was interpreted as wanting "what she herself had a great mind to, even that which a young man doth naturally desire of a woman." A&B maintain that Rabelais's line is about farting, whereas Jarry was unlikely to have forgotten that the noise was sexual. Jarry is in no wise suggesting, by his putting St. John and Rabelais in parallel, that the Word of God is of little worth, but rather that any utterance, be it never so more than a fart or a bumbasting cod, is a word, and that it is up to man to give it meaning, just as man, acting like God, gave meaning to all words, which are at root inarticulate sounds. Such, at any rate, is what Pantagruel argues, basing himself on the arbitrary nature of language: "All speeches have had their primary origin from the arbitrary institutions, accords and agreements of nations in their respective condescendments to what should be noted and betokened by them. An articulate voice, according to the dialecticians, hath naturally no signification at all; for that the sense and meaning thereof did totally depend upon the good will and pleasure of the first deviser and imposer of it." (*op. cit.*, p.321). But Panurge believes a sign that is not known will be understood sexually, hence his (misogynistic) anecdote. The word is made flesh in Panurge's tale firstly when gestures replace speech, and secondly when the gestures become sex. In this chapter, Emmanuel, the hypnotist, makes his words flesh in the person of Miriam, a flesh-and-blood person whose will is Emmanuel's; and the word is made flesh again when the word-created Miriam is turned back into the earthly Varia.

255. ... pulled Miriam from: i.e. hypnotised Varia, as described in the preceding chapter, and so bringing Miriam into existence, extracting her from the life of the notary as God had extracted Eve from the sleeping Adam. Chapter three can be inserted between chapters ten and eleven.

255. *Etiquette*: a pun on the two meanings of "*étiquette*": 1. the rules of conduct in society; 2. a label, or "etiquette" (the *OED* states that this meaning is now rare in English), either in the butterfly case, or attached to people invisibly.

256. ... loss of arms: allusion, of course, to the Venus de Milo in the Louvre.

256. Bifid: as employed by natural historians to mean "divided into two parts", Jarry's jocular way of saying "double".

256. And that is why: A&B, aware of Jarry's working knowledge of Molière, point out that this line resembles a passage in *Le Médecin malgré lui* (act II, sc. iv) which ends: "And that is why your daughter's deaf."

257. Pygmalion was, on the contrary, delighted that his Venus should have been metamorphosed into a living woman (Ovid, *The Metamorphoses*, bk. 10).

258. Absolute: because a nervous fit can lead to self-induced somnambulism.

258. Shoulder of the blade: that is to say nearest the hilt, where the khanjar has a triangular cross-section. The shoulder and the triangular hole therefore correspond.

258. ... literally: instead of writing "*J'ai l'habitude de prendre les mots au pied de la lettre*" (I always take words literally), Jarry wrote the similar-sounding "*J'ai l'habitude de prendre* mes *morts au copie de lettres*" (literally, something like "I always take *my* deaths as copies of letters of the alphabet", or "I always copy *my* deaths from letters" with "*copie*" uniquely here made masculine).

259. *Et* habitavit: the phrase omitted from the chapter's epigraph, "and dwelt among us", makes its appearance here at the end with its relevance now established. Furthermore, Jarry intends dirty puns on "habit/inhabit/go inside", and "*vit*", which is French slang for the virile member. Emmanuel gave up not talking, i.e. he started talking, and since the word had become flesh he did so with body-language.

259. Brooch: an "*affiquet*" is an old word for a brooch, but also for knitting-sheaths attached to the waist, in which you stick the ends of your knitting-needles *while* knitting so as not to drop them.

259. Box: Jarry labours a pun on "*la case*", a box, a compartment, or space you have to fill in, say, on a form, and *le cas*, slang for the sex (esp. a woman's, see Delvau, *op. cit.*), just as we say "box, hole, crack" today.

260. Epeirid: Jarry used the learned word for a garden spider, "*épeire-diadème*", called "*diadème*" because of the mark on its abdomen.

260. In her opinion: ambiguous; "*à son gré*" could be read "according to his will and pleasure".

260. ... ***the creation of his desire:*** such is the case for one who dreams, as Freud was to publish a few months afterwards: "A dream is the fulfilment of a wish." (*The Interpretation of Dreams*, 1900) though he claimed to have had the idea in 1895. A novel is, after all, a dream world, and the author or hero its god of a kind.

261. Melusina... Walnuts: from Rabelais, *Pantagruel*, ch. 30, Urquhart translation. Epistemon, who had his head cut off, has it stuck back on again three weeks later by Panurge, and then narrates what he saw in Hell in the meanwhile. The damned are "changed after a very strange manner", with Alexander the Great darning socks, and other kings and heroes of legend now in low employment (there follows an enormous list): "those that had been great lords and ladies here, got but a poor scurvy wretched living there below. And, on the contrary, the philosophers and others, who in this world had been altogether indigent and wanting, were great lords there in their turn." This reversal is of course Biblical. From Epistemon's list Jarry singled out: Melusina, metamorphosed into a serpent from the waist down (a mermaid in some versions of the legend) for one day a week until her husband saw her thus and she vanished — she is thus clearly identified as the double-natured Varia/Miriam; Pertinax (126-93), a distinguished Roman emperor and scholar.

261. ***Caesar-Antichrist:*** Jarry quotes from his own play of 1895 (the interval between the Prologal and Heraldic Acts), itself quoting Matt. 24, 29: "and the stars shall fall from heaven", and Rev. 6, 13: "And the stars of heaven fell unto the earth". See *CW* I, p.133.

261. ... stars: Jarry alludes to the fact that bayonets were primarily useful as mirrors to dazzle the enemy with, and not as spikes. See "The Suppression of the Sabre" in *CW* I, where Jarry supplied a little more of what he had started to explain in *Days and Nights*, Book 1, ch. X.

261. ... put out the very eyes: in the same way that two soldiers armed with bayonets of the same length will put out each other's eyes simultaneously.

261. Qualified: Jarry employed the active ("What does not qualify the first word..."), but as he later specified that the first word, "absolute", is an adjective and not a noun, the translation uses the passive simply because adjectives qualify nouns and not the other way round. However, Jarry may well have preferred an active appropriation of the Absolute over grammatical correctness.

262. Seven swords: identified by A&B as the image of Our Lady of the Seven Sorrows in the Épinal print reproduced by Jarry in *L'Ymagier*, 4 (*OC* I, pp.984-5), and also in the woodcut Jarry put at the end of his article "*La Vierge et l'enfant*" in *L'Ymagier*, 3, p.154 (*OC* I, p.979).

262. ***Main de gloire:*** derived from the French word for a mandrake plant, *mandragore*, and designating the fabled severed hand of a hanged man which, when held (or turned into a candle), secures invisibility for thieves. See note to "mandrake rake" on p.29 of *CW* I; also Gourmont's note in *L'Ymagier*, 5, p.12.

262. ... and Venus: Jarry names over half of the twenty brightest stars, but no symbolic intent has yet been discovered in this choice or their order.

262. Echidna: A&B suggest that by "*échidnes*" Jarry meant "*échidnés*", which means both echidna, the spiny anteater which looks much like a hedgehog, and Echidna, the half-serpent, half-woman monster of Greek mythology, mother of the Chimaera, Cerberus, the Colchian dragon, the Gorgons, the Hydra, the Sphinx, etc. The first concords with the hedgehog of the next line; the second recalls the dual nature of Melusina. There is likely a pun on *échinide* (echinid, sea-urchin), because their shape resembles a chestnut-bur, and because in France sea-urchins are familiarly known as "*châtaignes de mer*", literally "sea-chestnuts".

262. Let flee: "*lâchent*". Jarry uses a word that means both "to set free" (thus continuing the images of flight from the line above) and hence "to fart" (since the French reader will naturally think of the full verb, *lâcher un pet*). The two meanings are present in the Chaucerian "to let flee a fart" (*The Miller's Tale*, line 3806). **Death-dealing:** the powder is not toxic, and actually Jarry's statement is paradoxical since the powder is made up of spores, the bearers of life. Jarry conflates lycopods with lycperdond (wolf's-fists).

262. In literature: i.e. on stage (see note to p.244). **Pills:** the *Larousse* records that pharmacists use the powder to isolate pills.

263. Candid: Jarry plays on the etymology of "candid", from the Latin for "white", here referring to pure things which rise again, and then, to the white cream beneath the chocolate.

263. The Fable: identified by A&B as "*La Guenon, le singe et la noix*" (book 4, fable 12). The moral runs: "Remember that if one makes no effort in life, then one will receive no pleasures." Or as we say: "No pain, no gain."

263. Skeletal foot: a wolf caught in a trap will escape by gnawing through its leg and leaving it behind.

263. *La*: Jarry here recalls the passage concerning the word "death", which takes the feminine gender in French (ch. VII).

263. ... smells burnt: Jarry puns on the two meanings of "*sentir le brûlé*", literally "to have a burnt smell", and figuratively "to smack of heresy, to smell fishy".

263. Wyvern: the wonderful-sounding "*vouivre*" names the mythological serpent that watches over treasure and bears a flashing (red) gemstone on its forehead. The word derives from Latin *vipera* (viper), and is sometimes spelled "*guivre*" or "*givre*". In heraldry, the latter form denotes the wyvern, another member of the tangled family of serpents, dragons, and worms, usually depicted as a dragon with a serpent's tail. Being half-dragon and half-snake, this variable chimera is another symbol of Melusina made explicit at the end of the chapter.

263. Upstanding: Jarry's slightly heavy turn of phrase hangs on the etymology of "*prestance*" — usually translated as "a fine, imposing appearance" — which is Latin for "standing up and forwards", and which should of course be read ithyphallically here.

264. ... pricked: Emmanuel's summary, the story within the story or "dream within a dream", ends here.

264. Shahrazad: Emmanuel Dieu identifies himself with the storyteller of the *Thousand and One Nights*. Both expect to die with the coming of the morning, when the story is over, if it ever ends. Janet's patient

Lucie started telling the story of Ali Baba, and gradually her active role became passive as she began to see the story unfolding before her eyes as a hallucination (*L'Automatisme psychologique*, p.206).

264. ... not asleep: Shahrazad's sister Dunyazad slept only a little distance from her and the sultan.

264. The Old Man of the Sea asked to be carried on Sinbad's shoulders in order to be able to ford a river, but once on the other side, instead of jumping off, he squeezed his legs tighter around Sinbad's neck and half-strangled him till he fell in a swoon. The Old Man of the Sea then employed Sinbad as a slave, never leaving his vantage point on Sinbad's shoulders, constantly punching and kicking him along so he could gather fruit, and quite content to pass water and other substances from the same position. Sinbad only managed to rid himself of his charge by getting him drunk, then, once his leg muscles had relaxed, he threw him off and smashed his brains out with a rock.

265. Christopher: in the legend of St. Christopher, the giant who offered to carry a little child across a river found himself halfway across bearing a tremendous weight on his shoulders, and had to struggle for all his worth to get them both across. On reaching the other side, the child explained that he was the Christ and that they had carried the sins of the world over the river of death.

265. Indicopleustes: not a word forged by Jarry, as A&B suggested, but the surname of the sixth-century merchant Cosmas. He travelled extensively, from Egypt to Sri Lanka, and collected his descriptions in his *Christian Topography*; his surname means "Sailor-to-India" and applies equally well to Sinbad. [CA]

266. Pectineus: i.e. the *pectineus musculus*, "a flat muscle arising from the pectineal eminence of the pubic bone and inserted into the thigh bone" (*OED*).

266. Abnormally: although "*anormal*" could be translated as "irregular" (e.g. the size of women's hips varies in width and proportion from one woman to the next), the idea that women are "abnormal men" is an ancient idea; cf. Ambroise Paré in 1573 (writing about hermaphrodites who change from being women to being men): "Nature always tends to what is most perfect, and does not make what is perfect develop into what is imperfect." (*Des Monstres et prodiges*, ch. vii)

266. Juvescence: "*Jouvence*", "youth, youthfulness", usually employed to describe "The Fountain of Youth".

266. ... woke her up: thus provoking the "death" of Miriam. It is possible that by pressing on Varia's ovaries as he made love to her Joseb stopped a hysterical fit from developing, if one were. Waking a somnambulist by breathing on her face is a method described in the *Almanach Hachette 1894*, p.328.

266. ... young again: allusion to Ovid's *Metamorphoses*, book 7, which Jarry may have translated at school since there is a poem called "*Aeson rajeuni par Médée*" in his *Ontogénie*, dated 1887, and which has an extract from the same episode in Ovid as its epigraph. Golding's translation runs: "[Medea] cuts the old man's throat; and letting all his old blood go, / Supplies it with the boiled juice [...] His furrowed wrinkles were fulfilled with young and lusty flesh; [...] And as from dull unwieldsome age to youth he backward drew, / Even so a lively youthful sprite did in his heart renew." (*Selected Ovid*, Everyman edition, p.245) Jarry suggests that Medea might have felt sexually attracted to the lustily rejuvenated Aeson, whereas Ovid does not develop this theme at all. Jarry's remembered Ovid meant he either drew or forced a parallel with his oedipal novel: Medea sleeping with both Jason and Jason's father Aeson is Varia sleeping with Emmanuel and Emmanuel's father Joseb.

266. Chuck-chaste: "*pudique de renards*". Meaning that Adam is chastely (*pudique*) covering his body up with vomit, since "(to skin the) fox" is French slang for "to vomit" (cp. *Faustroll*, ch. XXVI), and we know that Joseb has felt worse for drink throughout this chapter.

266. Roamed freely: hysteria was long thought to be the result of the womb (Greek *hustera*) wandering around the body. More scientifically, hysterical patients do often have, and are often characterised by, painful ovaries. The traditional remedy, which Janet believed went back to Classical times, was to compress the sufferer's abdomen and belly. The ancients thought they were stopping the ovaries from rising up the body to the brain, but it is true that the ovaries can shift to some small extent. Charcot explains that it is only necessary to compress the ovaries ("*De l'hyperesthésie ovarienne*", *Œuvres complètes*, vol. I, pp.320–45).

267. The Assumption is, according to Roman Catholic dogma, the "taking up" of the Virgin Mary into Heaven, which is supposed to have happened before the end of her natural life. Here, Varia is "taken up" into the notary's arms, and they become one flesh not only because of the institution of marriage and their sex act, nor solely because the rib of Adam that became Eve is now in Adam's arms, but mainly, one suspects, because the notary and his "other half" make up an androgynous whole, more precisely: the eight-limbed, bi-sexual spherical Man evoked by Socrates in Plato's *Banquet* and often alluded to by Jarry (as a model for Ubu...).

267. *Taenia solum*: A&B translate this as "one band only", though it is tempting to read *Taenia* solium (the pork tapeworm, dangerous to man), if not "a single tapeworm", either of which would square with all the snake references in the chapter.

267. Spirit of God...: recalling Genesis 1, 2 ("And the Spirit of God moved upon the face of the waters"). The next line is: "And God said, Let there be light", which recalls the title of chapter I, thus making the first chapter the continuation of the last, and the book a cycle, like *Finnegans Wake*. But the title of chapter I is a diabolical or Antichristian inversion of Genesis 1, 3, in Jarry's "Let there be darkness", thus calling for a return to Genesis 1, 2: "And the earth was without form, and void; and darkness was upon the face of the deep." The cycle is regressive.

267. The cart which above all others needs to be oiled is the *brouette de la mort* or *char de l'Ankou*, which, in Breton lore, is the squeaky, horse-driven cart in which the Ankou, the Grim Reaper, rides at night (see *CW* I, p.291). The comparison with the song of the nightingales is anti-Romantic and typically Jarry in its conflation of opposites.

267. Varia's *murder*: simply by waking, Varia murders Miriam. Emmanuel is not said to have murdered his adopted mother.

267. ... Eden: cp. Genesis 3, 24, wherein the Angels are several, the Garden singular, and the flaming sword protects the tree of life in its midst: "So he drove out the man; and he placed at the east of the garden of Eden Cherubims, and a flaming sword which turned every way, to keep the way of the tree of life."

267. Itron-Varia: literally "Lady Mary" and thus "Our Lady" in Breton, and the name of the church in

Lamballe (identified by A&B, who also mention that there are indeed many little lanes that "snake" up to the church on the hill). That Miriam and the Church — as institution — are one, suggests that there is a link between religious worship and hysteria/hypnotism, something Freud would later argue in detail, advancing the idea that religious observance was a form of obsessional neurosis ("Obsessive actions and religious practices", 1907). Freud's metaphor for someone who leads a double existence, keeping their neuroses private, is the same as Jarry's: "*Mélusine*" (*The Origins of Religion*, Pelican Freud Library 13, p.33).

267. Dragon: the serpent of the Garden of Eden is sometimes represented as a dragon (famously on the façade of the cathedral of Rheims where Eve holds the cutely small animal in her hands, though it seems to hiss like a monster from the film *Alien*), and appears as such in sculptural representations of the second Eve (Mary) trampling the Devil under foot (cf. Genesis 3, 15: "[her seed] shall bruise thy [the serpent's] head").

268. ... little ships: the sails are evoked by the traditional white bonnets worn by Breton women, and which featured prominently in the Nabis' paintings of Brittany, a staple theme of which was a scene after a church service.

268. Leviathan: cf. Isaiah 27, 1.

268. Kite: Jarry wrote of God being symbolised in the triangle of an "upside-down kite" engraved by Dürer (cf. *Perhindérion*, 2, *OC* I, p.998).

268. Descent into the Sepulchre: i.e. Good Friday.

268. Python of the dawn: according to legend, a huge snake swallowed the sun at night and spat it out every morning. The constellation known as Hydra is, at least in the *Larousse*, depicted with only one head and therefore looks like a python. The Python of Greek mythology was (in some accounts) born from the mud that followed Deucalion's Flood (*Brewer's*), which may provide the link between the rain and the mention of the snake. The Pythoness was the Delphic oracle — an autohypnotic hemi-somnambulist, in the language of Janet.

268. ... *at the hour of our death*: the prayer usually runs: "Pray for us, now *and* at the hour of our death" (my emphasis). According to Roman Catholic dogma, Christ's Passion is "renewed" during Mass, which means that it is God who dies at the end of *Absolute Love* (which, to recall an earlier note, may be translated as "Passion-tide love"). In chapter II, Emmanuel talks of "the *real presence*" of his death, suggesting, if we think of Mass, that the real presence of Christ in the Communion Host is first of all a communion with His death. This is not necessarily blasphemous (though it cannot be said to be Protestant). Emmanuel will not die at the end of the novel, nor yet go to Communion, or tempt fate by standing next to the kite if there is thunder and lightning. Such might be an autobiographical reading of the book, congruent with Jarry's simultaneous blaspheming and devotion — of a kind — to Catholicism.

ATLAS ANTI-CLASSICS

1. THE AUTOMATIC MUSE Novels by Desnos, Leiris, Limbour, & Péret. *Out of print*
2. 4 DADA SUICIDES Texts by Arthur Cravan, Jacques Rigaut, Julien Torma, Jacques Vaché
3. BLAGO BUNG BLAGO BUNG BOSSO FATAKA! German Dada from Ball, Huelsenbeck, & Serner
4. OULIPO LABORATORY Texts by Berge, Calvino, Fournel, Jouet, Le Lionnais, Mathews, & Queneau
5. MALPERTUIS The modern Gothic novel by Jean Ray
6. THE AUTOMATIC MESSAGE Texts by Breton & Soupault, and Breton & Eluard
7. THE WAY HOME Longer prose by Harry Mathews
8. ADVENTURES IN 'PATAPHYSICS *Collected Works of Alfred Jarry*, Volume I
11. WINTER JOURNEYS by the OULIPO Perec's *The Winter Journey*, with sequels by Bens, Caradec, Grangaud, Jouet, Le Tellier, Mathews, Monk, & Roubaud
13. NEW IMPRESSIONS OF AFRICA Raymond Roussel, illustrated by H.-A. Zo
14. THE DOLL Hans Bellmer
15. CIRCULAR WALKS AROUND ROWLEY HALL Andrew Lanyon

Imminently forthcoming:

AURORA and CARDINAL POINT Surrealist novels by Michel Leiris
LIBERTY OR LOVE! and MOURNING FOR MOURNING Surrealist novels by Robert Desnos